The Ragtime Fool

Books by Larry Karp

First, Do No Harm

The Music Box Mysteries
The Music Box Murders
Scamming the Birdman
The Midnight Special

The Ragtime Mysteries
The Ragtime Kid
The King of Ragtime
The Ragtime Fool

The Ragtime Fool

Larry Karp

Poisoned Pen Press

Library of Congress Catalog Card Number: 2009931419
ISBN: 9781590587003   Large Print

Poisoned Pen Press
6962 E. First Ave. Ste. 103
Scottsdale, AZ 85251
www.poisonedpenpress.com
info@poisonedpenpress.com
Printed in the United States of America

Dedicated with thanks to

Mark Forster & Betty Singer
Genius Genealogist   The Sage of Sedalia

*who gave me more help throughout the
writing of all three books in this trilogy than any
ink-slinger could ever reasonably hope for.*

*"As far as doing the right thing,
go by what your heart dictates,
and I believe you will always be right."*
—Brun Campbell,
from a letter to pianist Jerry Heermans,
c. 1949

Acknowledgments

Betty Singer and Mark Forster graciously answered endless questions while I wrote *The Ragtime Kid, The King of Ragtime,* and *The Ragtime Fool.* Specifically for *The Ragtime Fool,* Mark combed the Internet for new information on the life of Brun Campbell. Betty did extensive research into the social, cultural, and political climates of Sedalia in 1951. She provided me specifics about Ku Klux Klan activities in and around Sedalia; information on the Pacific Café, the MoPac railway station, and other local landmarks of fifty years ago; and biographical material on Tom Ireland, the Curd family, Abe and Fannye Rosenthal, Lillian Fox, and Blanche Ross.

Special thanks to ragtime pianist-historian Richard Egan, who sent me several helpful articles by and about Brun Campbell, then blew me away with a surprise package containing copies of the extensive correspondence between Brun and pianist Jerry Heermans. (As a bonus, the material also included letters to Brun from Tom Ireland and Lottie Joplin). Being able to read more than fifty letters in Brun's hand was invaluable in reconstructing his speech, attitudes, and behavior during the last years of his life. Rich requested that I mention he'd received the material some years earlier from Trebor Tichenor, and I'm glad to do that.

Ragtime historians were, as always, generous with their help. A tip of the hat to Adam Swanson (at age 17, already a first-line ragtime performer and historian) and Max Morath for providing me a copy of the handwritten Blesh-Janis notes for *They All Played Ragtime*, and a second nod to Max for passing along his extensive first-hand information about Rudi Blesh. David Reffkin also sent me biographical information on Blesh. Edward A. Berlin fielded my questions with his customary timeliness and tact.

Brad Kay, ragtime musician and longtime Venice resident, contributed general information about his city, and suggested where Brun might have played piano in 1951 and whose band might have been the main attraction. Betsy Goldman and Big Jim Dawson helped orient me to the history and geography of Venice.

Firefighters Julie Wolfe and Robert Caropino, of Fire Station 63 in Venice, gave me a detailed street map, so I had the city literally at my fingertips as I wrote.

I referred often to Becky Imhauser's books *All Along Ohio Street* and *Sedalia.*

Thanks to Fran Fuller, Lillian Watson, and Ralph Turner for their tutorials on the use, abuse, and dangers of dynamite. Rosamond Haupt also educated me on the subject of explosives. Craig Harvey, Chief Coroner Investigator and Chief of Operations, County of Los Angeles, provided me information about the state of toxicology studies in Los Angeles in 1950, and clarified some police department terminology.

Dan Brown had ready answers to my questions about pianos and entertainment figures of the time. Dale Lorang patiently enlightened me about matters of religion. Peter Greyy found the perfect solution to a dilemma involving the name of a character.

I'll always be grateful to the many ragtime historians, performers, composers, and administrators who have gone out of their way to make me feel welcome in their world. I'm looking forward to the continued pleasure of their company.

Big hug for Peg Kehret, author and dear friend, for helpful editorial consultation, and countless insightful and wise suggestions about writing books and promoting them.

And another big hug for my love, Myra, mender of loose threads, dialect coach, and tolerant and indulgent hostess to the people I pluck from history or thin air, and bring to live with us for extended periods.

Chapter One

Sedalia, Missouri

Sunday, April 1, 1951
Late evening

An unshaded bulb in a ceiling fixture sent gro-
tesque shadows dancing around the six men in
the basement of Otto Klein's small house on East
Fifth Street. The mood in the room was ugly as
the weather. One man, a squat, balding farmer in
striped overalls, muttered a curse as a gust of wind
slapped rain against a window. He rubbed his hands
together, stamped his feet. "Christ a'mighty, Otto,
it's cold as my wife's heart down here. Why the hell
can't we sit upstairs and talk?"

Below his sloped forehead and receding crew-
cut hair, Klein's dark eyes smoldered. "God A'mighty,
Rafe, sometimes I think you ain't got sense enough
to pound sand down a rat hole. We can't have *my*

wife or my daughter hearing any of this, okay? You know how women do. One gabby word at the beauty shop, and next minute, it's all over town. If it's too goddamn cold for you, go on back home, sit in front of your fire, and toast a marshmallow."

A couple of men laughed. Rafe bit his lip.

Klein looked toward a rangy man with bright blue eyes and a haystack spilling over his forehead. "Think anybody else's coming, Jerry?"

Jerry Barton plucked a toothpick from his mouth. "Not as I know. Whyn't we get started?"

Klein nodded. "Yeah, I guess. Time was, we had a meeting, we could count on ten times what we got here."

"Times change," said Barton. "And it ain't just here. Klan membership's down everyplace. It ain't enough that niggers got their freedom, now people just stand around and pick their nose while the government gives the whole stinkin' country to the colored." He coughed. "God damn Franklin Delano Rosenfeld. When the son of a bitch died, I figured we were gonna be okay again, Harry being a good old Missoura boy and all that."

Derisive laughter filled the room. "Wouldn't be surprised if Harry goes on Saturdays and sits in Rosenfeld's pew in the Jew-church," drawled Johnny Farnsworth, a short, rawboned man with two days' worth of stubble on his face.

"I knew we was in trouble when he integrated the Army," said Rafe Anderson. "Next thing you know, it's gonna be okay for a colored man to marry a white woman, and before you can say Jackie Robinson, we'll be a country of half-breeds, don't care about nothin' but gettin' laid and stealin' chickens. Might as well just hand over the White House keys to the Russkies and be done with it."

Klein held up a hand. "Okay, then. But that's exactly why me and Jerry got you boys here tonight. Somebody's got to take a stand, and I say why not us? Show this country that decent white men ain't gonna let America go to hell in a black handbasket." He waggled a finger in the direction of a small, bald man still in his Sunday-go-to-church suit and tie, sitting on a stained, battered couch, rubbing his hands together. "Luther, what happened at the meeting today? This ceremony really is gonna go down, is it?"

"'Fraid so," came in Luther Cartwright's prissy countertenor. "I told them they ought to give a whole lot of thought about what just might happen if things get outa hand. Said I wasn't real happy about the idea of my drugstore getting damaged, say, in a riot or a fire. But Charlie Bancroft called me a lily-liver. He thinks the publicity'll be good for the town, and besides, accordin' to him, 'It's the right thing to do.'"

"Charlie always did like his chocolate," Barton said. "If that hoity-toity wife of his don't have at least a couple drops outa of the tar bucket, I'll eat my hat." The laughter in the room encouraged him on. "People don't get a sun tan at Christmas like she's got. Well, don't worry none about your drugstore, Luther. Push comes to shove, it's far enough away from Charlie's grocery, you'll be okay."

"Wait a minute now," Klein shouted. "Just hold on one minute. There ain't gonna be any fire, and no riot neither. Luther, you didn't let on about nothin', did you?"

Cartwright humphed. "Come on, Otto. How dumb you think I am?"

"Dumb enough to say you were even thinking about a fire or a riot."

Cartwright got halfway to his feet, but Barton pushed him back onto the couch. "Relax, Luther. You too, Otto. Last thing we need is for us to get on each other. Luther, you were supposed to go to the meeting and just listen, not talk. Best if everybody in this town stays nice and calm, nobody thinking about riots, fires, or anything else. If we're gonna blow up a high school, we don't need the whole damn town pointing fingers in our direction. Now, what about Herb Studer? What's the mayor thinking?"

Cartwright's face darkened. "He told that kike who's the head of the Mens' Choral Club—"

"Abe Rosenthal?"

"Yeah. Fancy-pants little Jew. Herb told him he'd be glad to give a speech at the ceremony. He thinks it'd be good to show people how Sedalia's moving ahead with good race relations."

A sound like swarming bees swirled through the little group. "Oh, he did, huh?" Otto Klein was furious. "Don't that just top all. Guess he wants to see niggers eatin' in restaurants, right at the next table to him, and sittin' with him in the movie theaters. What the hell's the matter with Studer? Them colored breed like rabbits, and one fine day they're gonna be tellin' *us* what we can do and what we can't. I wouldn't never have believed in a million years I'd live to hear the mayor of Sedalia say it's just fine and dandy to have white and colored go up on a stage together. An' in the colored high school to boot."

"Well, that's the way I heard it," said Cartwright. "But there's even more. Some old white guy's coming in from California, wants to play piana at the ceremony. He says he was here fifty year ago, and took piana lessons from Scott Joplin."

"He comes here and does that, he's gonna be a dead white piana player." That from Clay Clayton, an angular man with an uncombed thatch of gray hair cut short above his ears. "They're gonna find pieces of him, come down to earth as far away as Kans' City."

Rafe Anderson, the man who'd complained of the cold, patted Clayton on the shoulder. "Damn right, Clay."

Klein turned to Farnsworth. "Johnny, you're sure you can handle this, huh? Once we get started, be hard to back out."

The little man rubbed at his bristly chin, then grinned. "Work with dynamite, y' don't get to be near as old as me if y'ain't good and goddamn sure what you can handle. Don't you worry none, Otto. If a pussy mayor don't have it in him to tell them people what their place is, I do."

"Good." Barton raised a clenched fist. "Guess we're ready to give them Hubbard-High pickaninnies something else to think about besides their ABCs. *And* send a message to Mr. Mayor Herb Studer."

The bee-swarm sound told Barton he had a unanimous vote of confidence. "Okay, then," he said. "Ever'body up."

The six men formed a circle under the unshaded light bulb, each extending a hand toward the center to grasp the hands of the others. They lowered their heads. "Oh, Lord who set the black man on earth to serve the white," Barton intoned. "We ask your blessing on us as we set out upon our holy mission, to make manifest your design for your children, through the ministry of your beloved son, Jesus Christ. May all evildoers perish, and those who truly honor you thrive. Amen."

A chorus of amens, then the petitioners raised their heads. "Man alive, Jerry." Clay Clayton grinned. "You pray as good as any preacher I ever heard."

Barton coughed. "My old man *was* a preacher. Grow up with him, you learn to pray in a hurry. When I was a kid, I used to pray the whole day long he didn't catch me smoking back of the barn, or just get himself in a bad enough mood he'd give me a licking for the hell of it and tell me it was payment in advance."

Klein broke the heavy silence. "Well, okay, that's it. Ceremony's on the seventeenth, so we got two and a half weeks. Let's do some thinking, and then get together next Sunday night, see where we are."

"What say we meet by Jerry's place," said Rafe Anderson. "Ain't nobody else lives out there to hear us, so it'll be all that much more private. Besides, we could sit in his upstairs, and not freeze our ass off."

Everybody laughed.

"Fine with me," Barton said. "I'll get us a keg."

"I ain't gonna argue with that," said Klein. "See y'all in a week, then. If Herb Studer or anybody else thinks white people who got any self-respect are gonna just sit back while they put on some kinda fancy ceremony for an old-time nigger whorehouse piana player, they got another think coming."

Chapter Two

Venice, California

Monday, April 2
Early afternoon

The old man banged the final notes of "Maple Leaf Rag" out of the piano, then jumped to his feet and spun around as he heard applause from a single pair of hands. The hands belonged to a young man with shining black eyes, ears off a loving cup, and a grin all over his face. "Jesus H. Christ, Cal, you scared the living crap outa me. I never even heard you comin' in."

Cal laughed. "Well, how *would* you hear me, the way you were beating the life out of that poor old piano? Who the hell keeps a piano in a barber shop, anyway?"

"A man whose wife don't approve of ragtime

and won't let him play it in his own house," Brun muttered.

Cal tried to hide his embarrassment for the old barber. "Come on, Brun. You wouldn't have heard me if I'd set off a grenade. I said hello twice, but Scott Joplin had your ears, didn't he? Bet he was telling you not to play his music too fast, that it's never right to play ragtime fast. Right?"

Brun glanced at the sepiatone photograph on the wall above the piano, a dark-skinned Negro man and a white boy, side by side on a piano bench, looking over their shoulders at the photographer. "Don't mock, Cal."

The young man struggled to hear the whispered words, then walked across the room, and plopped into the barber chair. "Hey, Brun, I'd be pretty dumb to mock you right before you pick up your razor and scissors. Come on, let's get it over with."

Brun sighed. They never quit joshing him about how bad a barber he was, and he had to admit, there was something to what they said. He'd never wanted to be a barber, but a guy had to make a living, and forty years ago, he'd let his pop talk him into giving it a shot. Campbell and Son, Barbers. Just temporary, Brun had told himself, but as things worked out, it became temporary in the same way a man's life is temporary. He shook his head, then reached to the shelf behind the chair, pulled a strip of tissue from the box, wrapped it around Cal's neck, snapped the striped apron clean, and fastened it over the tissue.

Cal gave him a theatrical fish eye. "Still that same old clipper, huh? Jeez, Brun, go down and sell it to Molly Stearns in the antique store. It's so damn old, I'll bet you'd get more for it than you'd pay for a new one."

Brun pushed the button, ran the clipper up the back of Cal's neck. "Shut up, kid," he growled. "I got a fondness for antiques. I'm one myself."

"Ow-*ow*!" Cal jerked forward, grabbed at his neck. "Would you two antiques mind leaving just a little skin on me."

Brun swallowed whatever he was going to say. For a couple of minutes, the only sound in the room was the whir of the clipper and the snipping of scissors, but Brun Campbell never could manage long periods of silence. "Betcha don't know what yesterday was."

Cal started to turn, thought better of it. "Sunday."

"I don't mean what day of the week. I mean what's important about yesterday?"

Cal narrowed his eyes. "Today's April second… okay. If you're gonna tell me they gave you the Barber of the Year Award yesterday, I'll tell you yesterday was April Fool's Day—ow, my *ear*. Jesus Christ, Brun! You cut my ear."

"Sorry," the old man mumbled. "You got me all worked up. Yeah, yesterday was April Fool's, all right, but it was also the day Scott Joplin died. April first, 1917. Thirty-four years ago. Died in that New York crazy house where he ended up after nobody would publish his opera. *Treemonisha*."

What he died of was syphilis, Cal thought, but the young man wasn't about to argue the point, not while the barber was trimming furiously above his right eye.

"Nothing in any of the papers yesterday," Brun shouted. "Not a word on the radio. It's like Scott Joplin never lived. Greatest American composer ever. I was working on a book, gonna call it *When Ragtime Was Young*, and it'd have everything in it about Scott Joplin that people oughta know. But last year, this guy Rudi Blesh from outa New York, he went all around the country and talked to everybody, me included, then he took what the people said and made it up into a book. But it's all fulla mistakes. I tried telling him he shouldn't do it that way, you know, too many chickens spoil the broth, but he didn't want to listen. Now I don't know if *my* book is ever get published, and if it don't, when I'm gone, there ain't gonna be nobody to tell people about Scott Joplin and his music."

Cal's eyes bulged. He raised a hand under the apron. "Brun, put down that razor."

The barber glanced at his hand, then hunched his shoulders and stared at Cal. "What d'you mean, put down the razor? How the hell am I supposed to get the edges clean."

"Just use the scissors," said Cal. "You're waving that razor around like a sword."

Brun couldn't seem to decide what to do.

"Put it down." Cal spoke gently. "Before you say one more word about Scott Joplin."

Slowly, the old barber laid the razor on the shelf, picked up the scissors, and went back to work. "I'm trying everything," a dull monotone. "I show young kids how to play the music right. I write articles about Joplin, they get published in important music magazines. I make phonograph records. I get interviewed by music professors and experts. I'm workin' with Ethel Waters…you know who she is?"

"Yes, Brun. I know who Ethel Waters is. I've even heard her sing."

"Well, then." The wind picked up; Brun's sails refilled. "I got Miss Waters interested in making a movie about Joplin's life, but the people down there in Hollywood, they don't want to let a colored woman say nothing but Yassir and Yas'm in a film, so I'm afraid that ain't ever gonna happen. Christ, kid, I'm sixty-seven years old. How much longer do I—"

A howl from Cal broke off the barber's speech. The young man reached from under the apron to grab the side of his head. "Jeez, Brun, can't you sharpen those scissors once in a while? You're pulling my hair out by the goddamn roots."

The barber looked contrite. "Sorry. Sometimes I get myself carried away. But I ain't givin' up. People in Sedalia're puttin' on a big ceremony, couple of weeks from now. They're gonna present a big bronze plaque to hang up in the colored high school there, saying how it was in Sedalia that Scott Joplin signed the contract with Mr. John Stark to publish 'Maple Leaf Rag.' I'm working along with them, gonna go out and play at the ceremony, but also, I think maybe I can talk Louis Armstrong into giving a scroll to Mrs. Joplin in New York, right at the same time as they present the plaque in Sedalia. And I want the radio people to broadcast the whole shebang over their network."

Cal nodded, but didn't say anything.

Brun read his thoughts. "I know, a plaque in a high school ain't the same as a monument in front of the City Hall…or a museum, say. That's really what they ought have in Sedalia, a museum. While I'm out there, I'm gonna see if I can't get them cracking on setting one up for Mr. Joplin and ragtime. Hell, that town's been on the edge of the grave since the Depression. Just think about the tourists who'd come in to see a museum, and hear ragtime music."

A smile curved a corner of Cal's lips. "So you're going out to Missouri."

If I can figure out how to get food for the Greyhound, Brun thought, and sighed. "I gotta."

The old man pulled the apron away from Cal's neck, then shook it with a quick downward flip of his wrists. A sharp crack, then a cloud of dark hair fluttered to the floor. Brun tore the tissue from Cal's neck, held a mirror up to the back of the young man's head. Cal cringed.

"Guess it ain't one of my better jobs," Brun mumbled. "Figure it's on the house."

Cal pushed a dollar bill into the barber's hand. "It's not the worst you've done. If you could only talk about something beside Scott Joplin and ragtime, at least while you're cutting peoples' hair."

"Damn, boy, what in creation *should* I talk about? I ain't never had anything in my life come close to Scott Joplin and ragtime."

Cal considered the words in his mind, then spoke them. "Brun, not to offend you, but Joplin is dead, and so is his music. R.I.P. You've got to move on in life."

The barber cocked his head, narrowed his eyes. "How old're you, kid?"

"Twenty-eight."

"Hmmm." Brun seemed to think that settled the question. He started toward the cash register.

Cal wasn't finished. "Yeah, I know I'm still young. But I'm not going to end up like those old guys, sitting all day at the train station, jawing about how much better everything was fifty years ago. Yesterday's gone, Brun, tomorrow's coming. There's a reason I write science fiction, and when I'm seventy, or eighty, or however old I get to be, my eyes are still going to be on what's ahead, not what's already been."

Brun slipped the dollar into the register, then slowly looked Cal up and down. Cal thought if the old man had long, floppy ears, he'd be the spitting image of the little beagle that lived down his block. "How's your book doing?" Brun asked.

The mildness of the barber's voice took Cal aback. "Oh…good enough, I guess. Selling better than my first."

"What's it called?"

"*The Martian Hangover*. Tell you what. I'll bring you a copy, and I'll sign it for you."

Brun smiled weakly. "That'd be nice. Hey, you really do make enough to live off, writing those books?"

"Short stories, too. And articles, you know, for magazines. I just sold one to *Science Fiction Quarterly*. A thousand words, they paid me two hundred bucks."

"Twenty cents a word? No fooling?"

"God's truth."

"Well, I guess I'm in the wrong business. All them words I shoot out in the air, if I just put 'em on paper, I'd be a millionaire ten times over." Brun waved toward the door. "Better go on. You already lost ten bucks standing here, talking to me."

Cal chuckled, then started for the door, but halfway there, turned around. "Brun don't you ever take off that hat?"

The old man reached a hand to his gray fedora, as if to remind himself it was there. He loosed a hoarse laugh. "Hell, no. You think I want people to see what a lousy barber *I* go to?"

◇◇◇

A continent away, in the living room of a solidly middle-class house in Hobart, New Jersey, Alan Chandler sat at a Steinway baby grand, playing "Maple Leaf Rag." A week earlier, he'd pulled the piece from the Old Sheet Music rack at Mrs. Selvin's Music House, along with one called "Crazy Bone Rag," and another, "Magnetic Rag." He'd also bought a handful of 78s, all of whose titles ended with the word, "rag." Mrs. Selvin had looked surprised as she thumbed through the material on the counter. "Since when have you been interested in ragtime, Alan?" Her eyes glistened behind rimless glasses. "These were all so popular when I was a girl."

"I listen to Oscar Brand, you know, the folksinger," Alan said. "He's on WNYC Sunday mornings, and yesterday, he played a bunch of tunes he said had been recorded a few years ago by an old barber, who lives in California. Mrs. Selvin, I just couldn't keep my feet still! The man told Mr. Brand he was the only white pupil of a colored ragtime pianist named Scott Joplin. Did you ever hear of him?"

She nodded. "He was very famous for a while. He wrote the first big ragtime hit, the sheet you've got right here. 'Maple Leaf Rag.'"

Alan's eyes widened. He spread the sleeved 78s across the counter, then grabbed one and held it up to the shopkeeper. "See here? 'Maple Leaf Rag,' played by that barber, Brun Campbell. Oscar Brand played this same record on the radio, and I've never heard anything like it. I've got to learn it."

Mrs. Selvin smiled. "It's not an easy piece. For most people, I'd suggest one of the simplified folio arrangements, but I imagine you can handle the original. It will take some practice, though."

"That doesn't bother me. I don't waste my time on simplified folios. Do you have anything else you think I'd like?"

The boy's cheeks glowed. His chest heaved. Mrs. Selvin embarrassed herself with the thought that if she were seventeen again, she'd lock the door, take him in the back, and give him something he'd really like. She reached back into the window display, brought out a book. "You might enjoy this, dear. It was just published last year, and it will tell you all about ragtime music and Scott Joplin. In fact…let me see…yes, here. It's even got a few pages about your barber."

Alan took the book from her with a move that could have been considered rude, if his enthusiasm were not taken into account. *"They All Played Ragtime."* He ran a finger down the table of contents, then laid the book on top of the pile of sheet music. "Great, Mrs. Selvin, thanks. I can't wait to read it."

But first things first. He was home in record time, into the living room, onto the piano bench. In one motion, he threw the sheet music for "Maple Leaf Rag" up on the rack, drew a huge breath, and hit the keys.

It took only a couple of minutes for him to decide Mrs. Selvin had been right on the money. This was as tough a piece of music as he'd ever tried to play. His right hand kept tripping over his left. But the tune had him by the throat. He played "Maple Leaf Rag" all that afternoon, and every afternoon the rest of the week.

Now, after six days of practice, he'd gotten a decent handle on it. He stretched his arms, took it from the top. Through the A strain, into the B, back to the A, yeah. He ignored the sweat dripping from his forehead onto the keys as he swung into the C strain.

"Alan! For the love of God, can't you play anything but that silly tune? You're driving me crazy."

He muffed a G-chord, struggled to recover.

"Alan, I'm talking to you."

The boy let his hands flop to his lap, and stared up into his mother's face.

"Don't you give me that look."

"Damn it, Ma. I was finally getting it right, and you made me blow it."

"Out the window is where I'd *like* to blow it. And don't you swear at me or give me backtalk. You've spent a whole week playing that one tune, over and over again, until I could just scream. Mr. Bletter wasn't happy with your lesson last Friday, and I'm not surprised. I don't think you spent fifteen minutes the whole week long practicing real music."

"This *is* real music. Mr. Bletter couldn't even play it when I showed it to him. He looked like his fingers were all knotted up."

"Mr. Bletter wouldn't waste his time trying to play that. He's a classical pianist, the best teacher in Hobart. He says you have God-given talent, and if you'd only apply yourself…"

Her mouth kept moving, but her words had drifted into white noise. Alan turned back to the piano, set his fingers to the keys, played the first chord of the C strain. But then, a smack to his cheek nearly sent him to the floor. "Don't you dare ignore me when I'm talking to you. Just who do you think you are?"

He locked eyes with his mother, said nothing.

Her lips were bloodless. "Mister, you are getting too big for your britches. I don't suppose you've done your homework, have you?"

On the verge of telling her he didn't have any, an idea came to him. "I've just got to write a little history report."

Mrs. Chandler looked at her watch, then at her son. "It's past four o'clock. You are not going to play this garbage all afternoon, then stay up till all hours to practice your piano lesson and do your homework. One week of that monkey business was more than enough. Now, put away that sheet music, and get to work."

Alan snatched "Maple Leaf Rag" off the piano rack, then marched past his mother, out of the living room, and up the stairs. "Like talking to a wall," Mrs. Chandler shouted. "Seventeen years old, and he doesn't have the sense he was born with. Lord only knows what's going to become of him when I'm not—"

The slam of his bedroom door cut off the rest of the speech. Only five months to go, less than half a year. Then he'd be at Juilliard, out of this place, and she could talk to all the goddamn walls she pleased.

He flung the sheet music onto the foot of his bed, then sat at his desk, pulled a sheet of paper and two air-mail envelopes from cubbyholes, grabbed a pen, and began to write:

Dear Mr. Campbell,

I heard about you last Sunday on Oscar Brand's radio program on WNYC in New York. He played some of the tunes that a man named Spiller recorded of you at the piano, and I have never heard anything like that in my life. I play piano myself, mostly classical, but I went down to the music store last week, and got some sheet music and records of the old-time rags, and I've been trying to learn to play them. My mother hates it, but I don't care.

I read about you in THEY ALL PLAYED RAGTIME, by Rudi Blesh and Harriet Janis. Also, Oscar Brand played some comments by you. I think it's very impressive that you were just a little younger than me when you went to Sedalia to study with Scott Joplin, and you're the only white pupil Scott

Joplin ever had, and except for Scott Joplin, no one has ever played ragtime as well as you.

I can't figure out why some of the tunes that have Rag or Ragtime in the title, like DAT DRAGGY RAG, and THE RAGTIME VIOLIN, and YIDDLE ON YOUR FIDDLE PLAY SOME RAGTIME don't sound anything like what Scott Joplin wrote.

I've played your record of MAPLE LEAF RAG probably a hundred times, now, and I've learned a lot by listening to it. I'm hoping you can give me some advice about how to play ragtime right. Anything you can tell me, I will really appreciate. I'm enclosing a stamped, self-addressed envelope for your convenience.

Sincerely,
Alan Chandler

The boy read the page slowly, then reached to the floor to pull a record from the turntable of an old wooden phonograph. Copying from the yellow label at the center of the record, he addressed his piece of mail:

Mr. Brun Campbell
c/o Brun Recording Co.
711 Venice Blvd.
Venice, California

He wrote his own name and address on the second envelope, folded it into the letter, checked his watch. Twenty minutes to five, better hurry. He charged out of his room, down the stairs, through the front hall, to the back door. As he passed the kitchen, he called, "Gotta go to the library, Ma, and check out something for my history paper." Before she could reply, he was outside, to the garage, onto his bike and away, pedaling to the post office, where he bought two six-cent air-mail stamps, put one onto each envelope, then sealed the outer envelope and dropped it into the slot.

◇◇◇

About the time Alan wheeled his bike back into the garage, Elliot Radcliffe glanced out his office window. Through the early spring twilight, he could just barely make out the Hudson River. Most of the neighboring skyscrapers were dark, their occupants by now at home or in a nice, congenial bar, enjoying a stiff martini. The editor tried to sneak a peek at his wrist, but his visitor caught him. "Oh, come on, now, Ellie, I'm not going to make you all that late for dinner. Just give me a few minutes."

Radcliffe started to object, then took off his glasses and rubbed his eyes. When Rudi Blesh got into one of his fits of enthusiasm, he could drive a man nuts. With his retreating hairline, and that sly smile coming out of the precisely-trimmed Van Dyke beard, Blesh put Radcliffe in mind of his Uncle Lou, who always used to hold out his hands, fists closed, and tell little Ellie to pick the hand holding candy. And every time, every single goddamn time, Ellie would tap the wrong hand. The editor blinked. "Rudi, it's late, and I'm tired. Not everyone has your six-o'-clock fervor."

"That's all right. I have enough for both of us. Listen. I've been after Mrs. Joplin for almost two years, and she's finally agreed to let me consider Joplin's personal journal for publication." Blesh held up a professorial index finger; Radcliffe's gut cramped. "And then, there's the matter of that basement of hers, full of manuscripts she's been sitting on since Joplin died. Ellie, for God's sake, think about it. Hundreds of unpublished, unknown Joplin manuscripts. If she and we can get together on the journal, all that music might come next. I don't want to sound callous, but the woman's eighty years old, and not in the best of health. She's also gotten a little flighty. I'd hate to have her change her mind."

Radcliffe rested his elbows on his desk, then lowered his chin into his hands. "Rudi, slow down. Please? I know what this means to you, but try to see it from my point of view. Publishing that journal would be chancy at best. People aren't going to flock to read the memoirs of an unknown composer."

"They will if your publicity staff does its job. A first-hand retrospective account of the critical initial creative period of an American composing genius? I'll write a commentary to go with it, and that book will become a standard. A work for the ages."

Radcliffe's colon went back into spasm. Blesh's drive and determination were standards for the ages. The man was an expert on jazz, modern art, silent movies, interior design. He'd hosted a syndicated radio show, run a high-class record company. You don't get that kind of C.V. by being laid-back and patient. And what Rudi promised, he delivered. Some of the people at Knopf had frowned pretty hard at his proposal for what became *They All Played Ragtime*, but out he'd gone, he and Harriet Janis, all over the country, and in less than a year and a half had put together…what? A standard, a work for the ages.

The editor coughed politely. "All right, Rudi. As usual, you make a strong argument. But I simply can not give you a go-ahead right now." He ticked off points on his fingers. "Number One, Mr. Knopf *will* have some reservations about sales possibilities. Number Two, as for Joplin's hundreds of unpublished manuscripts—"

"Might be thousands."

Radcliffe blew. "Damn it to hell, Rudi, I don't care if it's millions. Knopf is not a music publishing house. Not to say we wouldn't consider something unusual, but I'd have to be insane to tell Mr. Knopf I gave you final approval on my own. And Number Three, you said it yourself. Mrs. Joplin is elderly and flighty. Before I'd ever agree to a project like this, I'd need to check with our legal department. By the way, have you even discussed the matter of money with Mrs. Joplin? What are her expectations?"

"There won't be any problem. She'd want five hundred up front, which you can take out of my advance. Then, she and I would split the royalties."

Radcliffe couldn't help smiling. "All right." He started to unroll his shirt sleeves. "I'll talk to the lawyers, and have everything together by the time Mr. Knopf is back."

"Which will be when?"

Radcliffe turned as stern an eye on Blesh as he could manage. "Probably the end of next week."

Now, Blesh exploded. "The end of…suffering catfish, Ellie! Where is he? Can't you call him?"

"He is in Europe, and no, I'm not going to call him there to present a proposal of this sort. He'd question my judgment damn seriously, and he'd be right. I'm sorry, but you'll just have to wait."

"I don't want to lose this chance," Blesh

snapped. "If you're not interested, I suspect Columbia University Press would snap it up."

"I'm sure you're right. But you'd better think
about what you and Mrs. Joplin would earn if
you go that route. Look. Tell her I'm definitely
interested, and her terms would be acceptable,
but I need to wait a week and a half to hear what
The Boss says." Radcliffe stood, pulled his jacket
off the back seat of his chair, slipped it on. "If she
can't understand that, I'm not sure it would be
reasonable to work with her. Now, that's it, Rudi.
I'm going home."

Radcliffe got to his feet with an "Oomph,"
grabbed his briefcase from the floor, and with the
other hand, took Blesh by the elbow and steered
him toward the door. They walked through the
outer office, past dark-skinned Mickey Thurman,
in his janitor's coverall, emptying the secretary's
wastebasket into a large sack. Thurman watched
them go out the doorway and disappear into the
hall. Like they couldn't see me, he thought. Like
they didn't even know I'm here. Like I don't have
ears. He smiled.

◇◇◇

The few late-afternoon customers in Ozzie's Bar,
a half-block off the Venice boardwalk, fell silent as
Brun shouted, "Okay, everybody. Roscoe Spanner

here's eighty today, an' we're gonna sing Happy
Birthday to him." There were a few giggles as
the barber stood, pulled a cupcake out of a white
cardboard bakery box, and set it in front of the old
colored man beside him at the table. Then he took
a small candle from his pocket, stuck it atop the
pastry, flicked a lighter into flame, and lit the candle.

"Oh, jeez, come on." Brun's companion covered his face.

The barber waved his hands in imitation of a
conductor, and started to sing. Most of the crowd
joined in. As they finished, to scattered applause,
Brun pointed at the candle. "Hey, Roscoe, you gotta
blow it out now. Else you ain't gonna get your wish."

The old man turned a wry face onto his friend.
"Shit, Brun. What the hell's an eighty-year-old man
supposed to wish for?"

"That he was twenty again. Come on, Roscoe.
Blow.

The old Negro's expression said he'd humor
the pest. He puffed out his cheeks, then blew out
the candle. Brun raised his whiskey glass, clinked
it against Roscoe's. As he sat, he noticed his friend's
eyes had filled.

"Way you treats me." The old man's voice was
husky. "You's the best friend a man could have."

"Well, hell. We *been* friends more'n fifty years."

"Fifty-one, to be exact. It was 1900, first time

you come inside Tom Turpin's. I was behind the bar."

"I remember. Not half an hour after I got there, some redneck called you nigger."

"An' *I* remembers. You hit him so damn hard, he didn't wake up for more'n ten minutes. I thought you killed him."

Brun started to laugh. "And then you got me upstairs with the best girl in the house. Free for nothin'."

Roscoe shrugged. "I don't like owin' people."

The two old men stared at each other, then burst into full laughter. "Lord, what we've been through together," Brun said. "St. Lou to Tulsa to California. We couldn't even begin to keep records on what we owe each other."

"Ain't never even had one argument."

Brun's laugh was laced with sarcasm. "Maybe I shoulda married *you*."

Roscoe's hands went up. "Don't even go thinkin' about that kinda thing."

"Hey, you know I'm kiddin'. Just sayin' how you were a whole lot smarter'n me, not ever gettin' married."

"Maybe just luckier." Roscoe looked up at the clock on the wall behind the bar. "You better start gettin' on home. Your old lady's gonna have some kinda fit."

Brun shook his head. "Won't be anything

new or different. Go on, now, eat up your cake. It's your favorite, all chocolate." Brun waved to the bartender. "Hey, Oz, two more Jack Daniels." He grinned at Roscoe. "Gotta have somethin' to wash it down with."

Chapter Three

Roscoe turned the knob on the barber-shop door, but it wouldn't open. Only then did he notice the CLOSED sign on the other side of the glass panel. He shaded his eyes. There was Brun at the piano, stomping his usual hell out of the beat with his left foot, banging notes as if the keyboard was some kind of mortal enemy. Three men, two white, one black, stood around the bench. Roscoe pounded at the door. "Brun…hey, Brun. Open up."

The black man on the near side of the piano bench turned.

Roscoe pointed toward Brun, then toward himself, then again toward Brun. "Open the door," he shouted.

The black man tapped Brun's shoulder. The barber looked around, startled, saw Roscoe, hustled off the piano bench to open the door.

Roscoe turned a hard eye on the barber. "Only three o'clock and you're closed?"

Brun laughed. "Yeah, you bet. Hey, Roscoe…" He gestured toward the three men at the piano. "These guys're from Chicago, terrific trio…what'd you say your name was again?"

"The Windy City Ragtimers," said one of the white men.

"That's it. Sorry, it just slipped outa my mind. They're in town to do a show this weekend, so they come by to learn how old Brun plays ragtime. Let's see how I can do with their names. Harry Willis, George Baldwin, Terry Singleton. That right?"

The three men looked at each and nodded exaggerated surprise.

"Boys, this here's Roscoe Spanner, him and me been friends longer than any of you've been on earth. He was one of Tom Turpin's guys in St. Lou, best damn bartender you ever did see. Now he lives out here, like me. Couple old guys getting away from the crappy weather."

Roscoe and the musicians shook hands.

"I'm showing them how Scott Joplin taught me," said Brun.

Roscoe nodded. "Somehow, that don't surprise me overly much. You're gonna be a while, then, I suspect."

"I guess. Why don't you hang around and

listen?" Brun pointed to the barber chair. "Go on, get a load off. I won't even sneak up on you with scissors."

Everyone chuckled. Roscoe shook his head. "I gotta go fix a loose step by old Mrs. Vollmer's before she breaks a leg on it. But I was goin' right past here, so I thought I'd stop a minute. Come by my place tonight after supper, okay?"

Brun shrugged. "Well, sure, I can do that. 'Bout seven, seven-thirty be all right?"

Roscoe nodded. I'll see you then. He waved toward the Windy City Ragtimers. "Nice meetin' you boys."

Three yeahs.

As Roscoe closed the door behind him, Willis, the black man, murmured, "Something's on that man's mind."

Brun sighed. "I hope he ain't gonna tell me some doctor just gave him bad news. Get to be my age, never mind his, you don't know who of your pals is still gonna be there when you wake up in the morning…*if* you wake up in the morning." He walked quickly to the upright piano, opened the lid, pulled out a bottle of Jack Daniels, unscrewed the cap, took a long swallow. Then, he wiped his mouth with the back of his hand, and passed the bottle to Harry Willis, who took a more moderate swig. Brun coughed his throat clear. "Well, we're all

of us still here today, so let's play us some ragtime."
He sat on the bench. "Here, now, I'm gonna show
you exactly how Scott Joplin did."

◇◇◇

Brun moved his napkin to his mouth to cover a
burp. His wife shot him a sour look. "If you'd get
home on time, and didn't keep supper waiting, it
would go down better."

Face on her like she spent all day at a funeral.
"Now, May, come on. I was only a few minutes late."

"Nearly an hour's not a few minutes. And
would it hurt you to come home a little *before*
dinner time? Some men come from work, sit in a
chair a bit, and tell their wives about what went on
at their job that day."

Some men's wives have a drink waiting when
their husbands come in through the door, Brun
thought. But no point throwing gas on a fire. "Well,
okay. I can try."

May's face said she'd believe it when she saw it.

"I had me a visit at the shop today, three boys
from Chicago, great musicians. Yes. They came in
special, just to see how I play rag…music the way
Scott Joplin taught me."

May set down her fork with a deliberateness
that set Brun's nerve endings tingling. "Wonder-
ful. You took off time from work to play that

filthy music you've wasted your whole life on. You promised you'd give up ragtime, and cigarettes and whiskey too, if I'd marry you. Your promises aren't worth listening to."

Brun slammed a fist on the table. Silverware danced. "When a girl asks a man for a promise at just the right time, he'll swear off breathing for her. I might've had a chance if you'd just stopped with the smokes and the hootch."

"Oh, it's my fault, is it? You made a promise and you broke it, so now it's my fault for asking you. Brun Campbell, your whole life has been one big broken promise."

Any appetite he had left vanished. Yeah, he'd wrecked his life over a broken promise, but not the one she was talking about. The promise that mattered was the one he'd made to Scott Joplin, who'd taken a fifteen-year-old white boy under his wing, and taught him how ragtime should be played. Then Brun had gone forth to spread the gospel according to Joplin, in hotels and restaurants, in tonks and pool halls, in theaters and on steamboats, and the looks on faces as he played told him the people understood Scott Joplin was High Lord of Ragtime, and Brun Campbell was his prophet. But on the first day of April, 1917, Scott Joplin died, and when they laid him to rest, they put ragtime in the ground with him. Jazz became the be-all and end-all, and joints that had welcomed Brun for years started looking the other way, at trumpets, clarinets, and saxophones. The High Lord was dead, and the prophet lost faith. Opened a barber shop, met pretty May Gibson, and yeah, she did seem to have a bit more enthusiasm for churches and preachers than Brun would have preferred, but her old man was a good joe, liked to tell stories and share a bottle with his daughter's suitor. It looked to be a good life. Trying to make up for the broken promise to his teacher, Brun made some new ones.

"I gather you have nothing to say."

Brun blinked back to the present. He looked around the little kitchen. What had that good life come down to? A wife and three daughters, all of them convinced that one fine day, while they were sitting around on nice white clouds, playing gold harps, their husband and father would be down you-know-where, choking on sulfur and brimstone while Old Scratch played "Maple Leaf Rag" on a battered, out-of-tune piano. Which, of course, grieved the four women no end.

"No," he murmured. "I don't suppose I do."

May's face softened. She pointed toward his plate. "Go ahead, eat up. I made your favorite, pork chops, the old Oklahoma way."

He nodded, forced a forkful in and down. "Good. Real good."

May put on the smile of a woman trying to convince her child that the cough medicine in the spoon was actually pretty tasty. "Your daughter had an interview for a new job today, and she thinks she's going to get it. Would you like to hear about it?"

"Sure. Shoot." Brun filled his mouth with pork.

◇◇◇

He washed, she dried. He squeezed out the dish-cloth, hung it on the edge of the drainer, looked up at the white plastic clock over the sink. Almost seven-thirty. Brun sighed; she wasn't going to like this. "I've got to go out," he ventured. "Roscoe came by the shop earlier, and he wanted to talk to me about something. Sounded like it might be important."

She surprised him. "I hope he's not sick."

"That's what I'm worrying about. He looked okay, but you never do know. Get to be eighty, you've already beaten a lot of the odds."

May sighed. "Well, I'll say a prayer. He's a good man, even if he is colored."

Brun bit on his tongue. If she knew what-all Roscoe did in St. Louis fifty years ago, serving up liquor and running traffic for the rooms upstairs, she'd be saying how it'd be God's punishment, never mind why it took the Almighty all that time to get around to it. He bent to kiss her cheek.

"You won't be late, will you?"

He shook his head, almost said, "Promise," but swallowed the word. Then he walked to the front door, picked up his fedora, planted it on his head, strode outside.

◇◇◇

The sun was setting as Brun walked to the corner. He took in a deep breath, blew it out very slowly. A puff of breeze came off the ocean; the hair on his arms stood up. Little chilly. Maybe he should go back and get a jacket? Nah, he'd be okay. Besides, he was already late.

He walked quickly down Crestmore to Oakwood, turned left onto Woodlawn, then continued all the way down to Roscoe's small white stucco house on Zeno, in a neighborhood a rank below Brun's middle-class surroundings. Some of the lazy bums who'd been living in the cheap rents around the canals had moved up here; they called themselves Beats, Brun guessed, because they were too beat from staying up all night writing poetry and smoking reefer to get an honest job. They didn't get on with the old-timers, and there had been some nasty scenes, cops coming in with sirens howling, heads getting bashed with billy clubs. Brun didn't like for Roscoe to be living there, but what choice was there for an old colored man who made his living doing odd jobs?

The barber walked up a narrow concrete strip from the street to the little stoop at the front door. Doggone place needed painting, probably also a roof, and at least a couple new windows. Roscoe never seemed to have time to take care of his own property. Like the shoemaker and his kids, Brun thought. He climbed the three rickety steps to the porch, and knocked at the door.

No answer. Brun looked at the grimy doorbell, but that hadn't worked in more years than he could remember. "Roscoe," he shouted. "Hey, Roscoe! Where the hell are you?"

The barber pulled the screen door open, then turned the knob on the front door. Roscoe never locked up. Whenever Brun suggested that might not be a good idea any more, his friend shrugged mildly, and said, "Anybody want to try and steal what I got in that house just be wastin' his time."

Brun called Roscoe's name again, still no answer. He trotted through the living room, the bedroom, the bathroom, then walked back into the living room. No luck. Maybe when Brun didn't show on time, Roscoe got impatient, and went on over to Brun's? Naw. They'd have had to cross somewhere along the way.

Then, Brun noticed the basement door was open. Well, sure. Roscoe was probably down at his workbench, fixing a chair or a little table that Mrs. Vollmer or one of the other old white ladies who kept him in pocket change had sent home with him. Down there, he wouldn't have heard anyone calling him.

The barber hustled to the door, started down the stairs, but stopped as he saw it was dark below. Shoot! Roscoe just plain wasn't here. Might as well go back home, try and catch up with him tomorrow. But as Brun turned to leave, he caught a familiar smell. Whiskey. There was rotgut down there, or his name wasn't Sanford Brunson Campbell.

He reached around the corner of the top stair, flipped the light switch, froze. "Roscoe," a moan. He whipped down the stairs.

His friend sprawled a couple of feet from the stairway. A thin line of blood ran from the lower corner of his mouth to form a small pool on the concrete floor. Two teeth lay just past the blood. The reason for the whiskey odor was obvious, a wide dark stain on the concrete next to Roscoe, with chunks, splinters, and flakes of glass scattered through the puddle and beyond. Roscoe's left hand lay across the capped bottle neck at the edge of the stain, as if his last thought had been to try to get just one more drink out of life. Brun squatted, felt at the wrist, then dropped the doughy hand and stood, clutching at his chest. Shaking fingers pulled a little metal pillbox from his shirt pocket; he extracted a small green tablet, slipped it under his tongue, then breathed slowly, deeply. Pain receded, another stay of execution. The old barber trudged up the stairs and outside, back along Woodlawn to Oakwood, then out to Venice Boulevard and into the Venice Police Station, a block down from his barber shop.

◇◇◇

Brun sat on the gray twill couch in Roscoe's living room, taking care to avoid the spring that poked through the fabric of the middle section. A uniformed cop stood beside him. At the far end of the couch, a detective in street clothes sat, taking notes as Brun told his story. The coroner had come and gone, attendants had removed the body, and the cops had been talking to Brun for nearly an hour. Finally, the detective, a slim man in his forties, with a sand-colored crew cut and a mouth like a gash, shut his notebook. "Thanks, Mr. Campbell. I appreciate your help."

"But you don't believe what I said."

The two cops looked a question at him.

"I mean about maybe it wasn't any accident. Roscoe liked a shot or two after work, but he never got himself falling-down drunk, 'least not that I ever saw, and I've known him pretty darned good for fifty years now. These no-good kids around here, them Beats, they ain't got a pot to piss in. Maybe they came in to rob him, and he wouldn't give them nothing. He was just telling me last week—"

The detective held up a hand. "We're going to get an autopsy, Mr. Campbell. You know, have doctors examine him. They'll look for anything suspicious, and check to see how much alcohol he had in his stomach and his blood. But there is something you ought to think about. If somebody really did give your friend a push down the stairs, who would be Suspect Number One?"

"Oh, sure. And then I walked right over to the station and reported it."

The younger cop shrugged. "You wouldn't be the first guy did that, figured it'd take the heat offa him."

"Tell you what, Mr. Campbell." The older officer's voice softened. "I'm sorry about your friend, and I know you're upset. Just give us a little time. Like I said, we're going to do the autopsy, check for fingerprints in the house and on the pieces of glass, look for anything out of the way. Maybe it'll turn out he had a seizure, say, or a stroke. When we're done, I'll give you a call and tell you what we found. How's that sound?"

Brun snorted. "Great, except I ain't got a phone."

"All right. Come by the station a week from now. Maybe we'd even have something by Friday." He took a business card from his pocket and gave it to Brun. "Detective Bob Magnus. Just ask for me, and they'll get me out to talk to you."

Brun nodded. "I appreciate that."

"No trouble. Can we give you a lift home?"

The old barber shook his head. "Thanks, I'll walk."

Chapter Four

Wednesday, April 4
Morning

Dr. Brooks Gervais slipped his stethoscope into the pocket of his white jacket, then sighed. "Brun…"

Looks like a man with bad hemorrhoids, sitting on a slab of cold concrete, Brun thought. "Time for the lecture, huh, Doc? What's the blood pressure this time?"

Gervais shook his head. "It's been worse. But one-seventy-two over a hundred's not good."

The barber made a face.

"I'm sorry, Brun. I've got you on medication, but you need to help yourself, too. If you'd only cut out the whiskey and cigarettes…you smell like an old ashtray. How many packs a day?"

"Two. Three, tops. But I went offa the Camels, I only smoke filtered now. Newports."

The doctor covered his eyes with a hand. "Brun, for crying out loud. Filters, no filters, it doesn't matter. And you play piano in those night-clubs till all hours. You're killing yourself."

Brun worked his tongue around inside his mouth. "How long you think I got?"

Dr. Gervais held out both hands, palms up. "There's no way to tell. You could drop in the street tomorrow, or you could go on a while and die slowly in your bed. But when it happens is partly up to you. Keep on the way you're going—"

"Doc, what the hell're you saying? I should quit smoking, quit drinking, quit playing piano? What am I supposed to do?" He paused, then went on in a softer voice. "Hey, Doc, I can't even…you know. I used to think that song was pretty funny, 'My Handyman Ain't Handy Any More.' But I ain't laughing now."

The doctor rested a hand on his patient's shoulder. "You're sixty-seven, Brun. A lot of men—"

"I ain't a lot of men, Doc, I'm just one. Ain't there anything I could take…" His voice faltered as he saw Gervais shake his head sadly.

"Brun, I'm sorry. There's nothing that works, and some of the stuff people try can do real harm. Is Mrs. Campbell…well, is she unhappy?"

The doctor winced at the bitterness in the old man's laugh. "Not as she says, anyway. It ain't something she'll talk about, but you ask me, she wouldn't have minded if I got this way twenty years ago."

Gervais looked at his shoes. How many times had he listened to this same story, practically word for word? The doctor wondered how he'd react when his time came. He raised his eyes. "Look at it this way, Brun. When a man is having relations, his blood pressure goes sky high. Yours would be off the charts. Impotence might be God's kindness to old men, a sort of protection, so they don't—"

The barber stamped a foot. "Hey, Doc, cut the crap, okay? If I wanted to hear that kinda stuff, I'd go to church with May on Sundays. If God's being so all-fired kind to me, he could at least stop me from *wantin'* to do it." The barber grabbed his shirt off the hook behind the door, threw it on, began buttoning. "Well, at least He ain't got around to makin' my fingers go limp, so I'm gonna keep playin' piano. And I'll have me a smoke or a shot of whiskey when I feel like it." He aimed a finger at the doctor. "If sittin' in a rocker and chewing gum is all I can do, then to hell with it."

"Fine, Brun. It's your..." On the point of saying 'funeral,' Gervais cut himself off, and said 'life' instead. He chuckled. "Maybe you've got a point." He put two prescription notes into the old man's hand. "At least take your medicine."

I been taking my medicine for a long time, Brun thought.

As he folded the prescriptions and slipped

them into his shirt pocket, he glanced at the calendar on the wall, a Christmas scene, ice skaters on a frozen lake. 'Wishing You Merry Christmas and a Happy 1951, from the Edgmar Dairy Company, Venice, California.' Brun inclined his head toward the skaters. "It's weird to think I might not ever see some of those days up there."

Dr. Gervais smiled. "Everyone on this planet can say that, Brun."

◇◇◇

At twelve o'clock, Brun locked up the shop, then started walking slowly up Venice Boulevard to Pisani Place. Sun had broken through morning fog, and the warmth seemed to loosen the old man's shoulders. At Amoroso Court, he turned right, went on half a block past Oakwood, up to a small white clapboard house, and knocked at the door.

It took a few minutes for Cal to answer. Brun leaned into his young friend's face. "You okay?"

"Yeah. Sure." Cal shook his head back and forth. "Just writing a story. When I'm writing, I go off into another world."

Brun chuckled, then his face turned serious. "Well, actually, that's why I'm here. I got something bothering me, and I thought what with you being a writer, you could help me figure it out."

Cal turned a hard eye on the old man. "You're for real?"

"I ain't whistlin' Dixie. Come on, let's go down by Bayless'. I'll stand you to lunch."

◇◇◇

They ordered tuna sandwiches, coffee for Brun, a chocolate shake for Cal. The writer listened carefully to Brun's account of finding Roscoe on the basement floor, then said, "I'm really sorry to hear that. Roscoe was a good guy."

"The best. Which is why it bothers me so much to think maybe it wasn't any accident. Now, suppose you're writing a story, and the detective finds a guy—"

Cal's eyes narrowed. "I write science fiction, Brun, not murder mysteries."

"Same difference. People die, people get killed. Say one of your Martians finds a guy from the moon laying at the foot of the stairs, dead, with a bottle of Jack Daniels in pieces all around him, and his hand on the neck of the bottle. Is that Martian just gonna decide it was an accident, and that's that?"

Cal considered saying that moon people don't drink, but decided not to crack wise. "Well, maybe it does sound a little questionable."

"A little? If you went down a flight of stairs, ass

over teakettle, would you be grabbing for the neck of a broken whiskey bottle after you hit?"

"No, of course not. But maybe that's just the way he fell. His arm could have flown out in front of him, and happened to land on the bottle neck. And if he was badly hurt, he wouldn't have been thinking awfully straight. Who knows what he might've thought that bottle neck was?"

The waitress set their food in front of them. Brun took a savage bite from his sandwich, then talked from the corner of his mouth. "Listen, Cal. What if I say the reason I went over there last night was because Roscoe came by the barber shop in the afternoon, said he had something he needed to talk to me about, and I should be sure and stop by his house later? Would you write that in a story, and then have the guy take an accidental ride down a staircase to a cement floor?"

Cal corrugated his forehead. "I guess not."

"Okay, then. Now, think about those Beatnik bums for a minute. They always got their eye out for dough they don't have to work for. Just last week, Roscoe was telling me how a couple of them hit him up for a handout on the street, and when he wouldn't come across, they got nasty with him. Told him old people're useless, they're holding society back and all that, they oughta just lay down and die. I tried telling that to the cops, but they weren't about to listen. Just gave me a bunch of crap about how I should shut up and wait for the autopsy and the tests."

Cal paused, then decided to say it. "Brun, if I'm going to be honest with you, I've got to say that's not unreasonable."

The barber slammed down his coffee cup. Brown liquid sloshed into the saucer. "Come on, Cal, gimme a break. You think I oughta just up and believe whatever the cops try and get past me? Out where I grew up, when a colored guy got killed, 'less the bozo who did it was standing right there in plain sight, the cops called it an accident. Less work for them. Nowadays, maybe they need to be a little more careful, but I'm betting they still cheat when they can. Who's gonna complain about some old colored guy, got pushed down a flight of stairs?"

Cal swallowed a mouthful of milk shake. "Outside of you."

Brun nodded. "That's it. Okay, then, Writer. What would that Martian do after he found the moon man?" Brun pointed at Cal's remaining half-sandwich. "There ain't no free lunches."

Cal laughed out loud. "Fair enough. I guess if my Martian thought the cops didn't care about moon men, he'd go around and talk to the moon man's neighbors. See if the moon man was having trouble with anyone. Or if a neighbor saw anything suspicious yesterday."

Brun clapped his hands. "Yes! I knew you could help me." He paused, then added, "Scott Joplin was my friend, just like Roscoe."

Cal was going to ask what that had to do with the price of fish, but the look on Brun's face persuaded him to keep his smart mouth shut except to finish his lunch.

◇◇◇

Forty endless minutes of math class stood between Alan Chandler and the afternoon dismissal bell. It had occurred to the boy to try shifting octaves in the third theme of "Maple Leaf Rag," and he couldn't wait to hear how it would sound. He also wanted to see what he could do with the three new pieces he'd bought from Mrs. Selvin during lunch hour. He moved his fingers over an imaginary keyboard on his desk. The teacher's voice became a soft drone at the farthest reach of his awareness.

The instant the bell rang, Alan was out of his seat, to his locker, and on his way home at a run. He charged through the back door, tossed his books onto the chair next to the telephone table in the hall, hustled into the living room, slid onto the piano bench, and began to play.

He hadn't gotten past the opening measures

when his mother flew into the room, hands plastered to her temples. "Alan, if I hear that tune one minute longer, I am going to scream."

Without looking up, he muttered, "Ma, I'm trying—"

She grabbed his wrists, pulled them away from the keys. He wrenched free, but before he could hit another note, she slammed down the fallboard, then sat on it and pointed toward the stairs. "Get up to your room...*now*. Get your homework done."

"Christ Almighty, Ma!" He grabbed at her shoulder, pulled with one hand, shoved with the other, but she gripped the edge of the piano, and held her position. "Take your hands off me," she spat. "How dare you lay a hand on your mother?"

"All right, I'm sorry. Ma, listen. I just need to try one thing, it'll take less than two minutes. Then, I'll—"

"You're not trying anything, not even for two seconds. I said get, now get. You'll talk to your father later."

Alan grabbed his music, leaped off the bench. "You mean, I'll listen to my father. He talks, everyone else listens." The boy stomped toward the doorway.

"You've got a wise mouth, Mister," his mother shouted after him. "It's going to get you into a lot of trouble."

◇◇◇

As quickly as Alan sat at the dinner table and reached for a fork, his father fixed a smoldering eye on him. "I hear you've been disrespectful to your mother."

Alan's throat tightened; he dropped the fork. "*She* was being disrespectful. All I wanted to do—"

"It doesn't matter what you wanted to do. When your mother tells you to do or not do something, you will obey her. You will not give her backtalk. Do you understand me?"

Alan ground his teeth. Dr. Ronald Chandler, Professor and Chairman of Physics at Hobart State Teachers College, was a man whose every opinion was truth, universal and self-evident, as far beyond dispute as the Second Law of Thermodynamics. The Professor drew himself full upright in his chair, and glared down his nose at his son. "I don't hear your answer."

Alan made a disgusted face. "Yes, I understand you fine. I just don't agree with you."

His father's face tightened. "There's another matter. How much money have you spent the past two weeks on sheet music and phonograph records?"

"Eighteen dollars and some change."

Dr. Chandler clapped a hand to his temple. "Eighteen dollars! Young man, there are people who work for seventy-five cents an hour. At eight hours a day, that's three days' wages you threw away on rubbish that doctors have proved to be damaging to the developing brain of a young person. Now, hear me and hear me well. From this moment on, you will not spend another penny on ragtime music, and you will not play ragtime music in this house, not ever again. Do I make myself clear?"

Alan tried to hold on, but went over the edge. "It's my money. I earned it mowing lawns and shoveling snow, and I'll spend it any way I damn please."

Dr. Chandler bounded to his feet, stood over his son. He reached toward his belt buckle. "This is not your house," he barked. "This is my house and your mother's, and if you're going to live here, you'll live by our rules. When you come of age, you can get your own place to live, and then if you want to throw away your money and your life, that will be your business. Do you understand *that?*"

"Yes, I understand. And I still don't agree."

His father drew back a fist. Across the table, Alan's mother said, "Ron!"

Dr. Chandler's hand seemed to lower against his will. His shoulders rose to obscure his neck; Alan thought he looked like a vulture, ready to descend on a chunk of spoiled meat. "Insolent puppy! You're going to find yourself trouble you'll wish you'd never encountered. Now, you will apologize to your mother."

"For *what?*" Alan slammed his napkin onto the table. "She's the one who was rude. Let *her* apologize to *me.*"

Blotchy maps spread over Dr. Chandler's cheeks. "Go to your room, right now," he roared. "I've seen the last of you for this day."

"Fine with me," Alan shouted at his father. "I've seen more than enough of you for the rest of my goddamn life."

He ran past his mother, into the hall, took the stairs three at a time, charged into his room, slammed the door, locked it. Fists clenched, he looked around for a moment, then launched a hay-maker at the closet door. The wood splintered. The boy pulled back his hand and extracted a fair-sized sliver from his middle knuckle. Gingerly, he flexed his fingers; no pain, and they all seemed to work fine. "Stupid!" a growl. "Should have kicked it."

He gathered his records and sheet music from the floor and the desk, carried them to his dresser, opened the bottom drawer, slid the music under a pile of sweaters. "He finds it there and takes it, I'll kill him," the boy muttered.

◇◇◇

Not a customer all afternoon. Brun sat at his piano, and played ragtime tunes and cakewalks, but for once, his heart wasn't in it. Finally, about four-thirty, he locked up the shop and walked off.

Ten minutes later, he stood in front of Roscoe's house. Next door, an old white man in an undershirt and gray work pants clipped unenthusiastically at some low shrubs. Brun tramped up to him.

The man lowered his clippers, rubbed his forearm over his face, then turned a pair of beady black eyes onto Brun. Lot of gray hair above the top of his undershirt, not much on his head. He plucked a cigarette from between thick lips, flicked it onto the sidewalk, studied his visitor. "I seen you yesterday," he said. "You a plainclothes dick or something? Here about what happened to the old spade?"

Brun thought about letting the man believe he was a detective, but decided against it. Venice was just too small a place. "No, I ain't any cop." He extended a hand. "Brun Campbell's the name, I run the barber shop over on Venice Boulevard. I'm a friend of Roscoe's."

The man shook Brun's hand. "Horace Randall. Yeah, now you mention it, I think I seen you here before. I didn't know your friend except we said hello when we saw each other. Seemed like an okay guy, but I ain't much on mixin' with colored. They got their place, I got mine, we get along fine, know what I mean? What happened to him, anyway?"

"Fell down the stairs to his cellar."

"Mmm." Randall stroked his bristly chin. "Hell of a way to go."

"There's worse. Cops think it was an accident, but myself, I ain't so sure."

Randall's eyes narrowed to slits. "Like you think somebody pushed him, or something?"

Brun nodded. "You didn't see anybody over there yesterday afternoon, did you? Between about three and seven?"

The man shrugged. "There's always people comin' and goin' in any house. Friends, Fuller Brush Man, the mailman, some Jew sellin' insurance. You know."

"Yeah, I know. But did you see anybody particular yesterday?"

Randall tried to wave away the question. "I don't want to get mixed up in nothin'. I mind my business, and I got good health. I'd just as soon have it stay that way."

He half-turned back to the shrub, but Brun caught him by the arm. Randall shifted his feet, and looked toward the house, as if he thought there might be help there. "Listen," Brun said. "Roscoe was my friend, and he was a hell of a better man than a lot of white people I've met in my time. Now, I want to know. Did you see somebody going in there yesterday?"

Randall pulled roughly away, then faced up to Brun. "I already told you once, I don't go messin' around where it ain't none of my business. Somebody blows out a nigger's lights, it ain't no never-mind to me. He had his booze and his skirts, just like all of us, and now he's dead, that's how it goes." Randall gestured with his chin toward Roscoe's house, then growled, "Place is a goddamn dump. I'm hopin' they'll tear it down and put in a decent-looking house." He snatched the clipper handles, and picked up where Brun had stopped him.

Brun stood, waited. After a minute or two, Randall stopped again, turned Brun's way, and shouted, "You can stand there till it snows, and I ain't gonna talk to you no more. Now, go on, get the hell outa here. Else I'm gonna call the cops myself." He gave the shrub a ferocious clip.

Chapter Five

Thursday, April 5
Noontime

When the bell rang at the end of English class, Alan gathered his books and started for the door, moving so fast he didn't notice the foot out in the aisle. As he went sprawling, books flying in every direction, he heard, "Hey, Chandler, know what? Maybe you shouldn't be in such a big goddamn hurry."

He looked up. Eddie Bernstein, that son of a bitch greaser with his slicked-back D. A. hair, was laughing like a donkey. Alan made a move toward him, but then turned away, swept his books into a pile, got up, and started to walk away.

"Hey, Alan," Eddie called after him. "Aren'tcha gonna at least say excuse me, you kicked me in the foot?"

Alan glanced around. "Yeah. Excuse me, Eddie, I was aiming for your balls. Next time, I won't miss."

A couple of girls giggled. Alan hustled out of the room, into the hall, and to his locker. He stopped just long enough to grab his brown lunch bag and the three new music sheets from Mrs. Selvin's, then ran down the hall to the music room, half a peanut-butter-and-jelly sandwich jammed into his cheek. He dropped two of the sheets onto the piano bench, put "The Entertainer," by Scott Joplin, onto the rack, and began to play.

Within twenty minutes, he thought he had a good feel for it, but then heard a sound behind him, a strange sort of honk, and lost his place. Bang, both hands down hard onto the keyboard. He swung around on the bench to face the intruder.

She was a girl about his age, blue eyes huge behind soda-bottle glasses. Her face was narrow as a pickle jar, and her carrot-colored hair looked as if she'd put it through a Mixmaster. The girl took a quick step back. "Oh, I'm sorry. I didn't mean to distract you."

Alan waved off her concern. "Don't worry. I can just start again. You don't have to cry about it."

"I'm not crying about that. I mean, I'm sorry I messed you up, but it's the music. I've never heard music like that. It makes me feel so happy."

"It makes you so happy, you're crying?"

"That's part of the happy feeling. Don't you ever feel like that?"

Girls! "Actually, no."

She snuffled, wiped at her eyes with a sleeve. "I guess it sounds dumb to you, then, but I can't help it. What kind of music is that?"

"It's called ragtime. I just found out about it myself a couple of weeks ago, on Oscar Brand's radio program. I thought it was great music, so I went down to Selvin's and bought some sheets and records of it, and a new book that tells all about the people who started it going. My parents won't let me play it at home, though, so I've got to play here, lunchtimes."

His face positively glowed. That's for the music, not me, the girl told herself, but still, she felt warm all over, a little light in the head. "Your parents don't let you play it at home? Why not?"

"They say it's trash, and I should only play classical."

"Well, *I* like it. In fact, I love it." She thrust a hand forward; Alan had to duck away so as not to get fingers in his eyes. "My name is Miriam Broaca. I'm not in any of your classes, but I've seen you around."

Alan didn't remember ever seeing her. He gripped her cold, damp hand, tried not to let his reaction show. "I'm Alan Chandler."

"I know." A giggle escaped. Damn it, she thought, he's going to think I'm silly.

"Were you walking by and heard me play?"

She nodded, but it wasn't true. She'd been stalking him for days, trying to get up the nerve to ask him to take her to the Sock Hop in the gym Saturday night, and time was running out. Today, before Social Studies, Linda Ralston had dared her to go up and ask him. "He never goes out," Linda had said. "He's probably shy with girls. And he *is* cute." So Miriam had hurried out of her classroom at the end of the hour to wait at the door of third-period English, but when that moron Eddie Bernstein tripped him, he'd looked so sore that Miriam lost her nerve. She followed him to his locker and into the music room, but couldn't bring herself to say boo. All the while he played, she tried to drag her invitation from her mind to her tongue, but all that came through was that big stupid honk.

The girl looked up at the big clock on the wall. She still had half an hour. "Do you care if I stay and listen to some more?"

"No, of course not." Alan picked up the two pieces of sheet music, then patted the bench next to him. "Sit here. Do you play?"

Miriam hoped her face wasn't anywhere near as red as it felt. She smoothed her skirt. "No… well, just a little bit. Not like you. I'm not awfully good at music."

Alan grinned. "What are you good at?"

The girl gripped the edge of the piano bench. "Well…math, I guess. I'm pretty good with numbers."

Alan seemed to be thinking. "Broaca," he muttered. "Broaca…"

"Yeah, you've got it," Miriam said. "I'm the one they call Stock Broaca. My father's been teaching me about investments since I was five years old. You want to know whether the Dow-Jones Average went up or down yesterday, and how much? You want the closing price of General Motors? IBM?"

Alan laughed. "I don't even know what IBM is."

"You're pulling my leg. International Business Machines? It's the hottest company on the market."

He shrugged. "I don't care much about business machines. It's music I'm interested in, which is why I'm here. I don't mind if you want to sit and listen, but—"

She intended to say okay, she'd shut up and listen, but what came out was, "WillyoutakemetotheSockHopSaturdaynight?"

Alan's face suggested the girl had just landed a solid punch, smack on his nose. She edged away from him. "I mean, you don't have to if you don't want…I just thought maybe…" She scuffed one penny loafer over the other.

An image came to Alan's mind, one of his mother's good china plates dropping from his hand and shattering past any hope of restoration. "I don't know any of the dances," he said. "But yeah, I guess I could take you, if you want."

He thought she was about to throw her arms around him. She was, but managed to hold back. "There's only twenty minutes till lunch is over," she said. "Play me some more of your ragtime, okay?"

"Sure," Alan said, and turned to the keyboard. "This is the one I've worked at the most so far." He played a few notes. "It's called 'Maple Leaf Rag.'"

What beautiful music, she thought. But she knew she'd be thinking the same thing if he were playing "Chopsticks."

◇◇◇

Brun did a double-take at the woman walking into his shop. Colored lady, probably in her forties, wearing a spiffy, tailored dark-blue suit over a cream-colored blouse, and a blue pillbox hat with a little veil. Face made up to the nines. She smiled at the barber. "Mr. Campbell?"

Brun lowered the comb and scissors from his customer's head. "Yes, ma'am, I'm Brun Campbell, all right. What can I do for you?"

"I want to talk with you." The woman pointed toward the customer. "I'll wait until you're finished."

Brun pointed with the scissors toward the piano bench. "I ain't got much in the way of chairs. Pretty small place."

She smiled. "That's fine, Mr. Campbell. I'm sure I'll be comfortable."

Talks like some kind of businesswoman, Brun thought, or maybe a schoolteacher. "Okay, then," the barber said. "I'm almost done. Be with you in just a few minutes."

"Don't you go hurryin', Brun," drawled the customer, a older man with purplish wattles that would have done a turkey proud. "I want to get out of here with all the blood I came in with."

◇◇◇

As the door closed behind the customer, the woman stood. "I hope you'll excuse me for coming to your place of business," she said. "I stopped at your home, and your wife told me it would be all right." She smiled an apology. "Mrs. Campbell said you're usually not terribly busy."

Brun nodded. "Sorry to say, but she's on the mark. We get by, that's about it."

The woman looked at the piano, then back to Brun. "I've never seen a barber shop with a piano in it."

"Me neither, except for mine. I play ragtime, been doin' it for more years than you've been on this earth, but my wife don't like it. So I do most of my playing here, in between customers."

The woman leaned over the piano to peer at the sepiatone on the wall. "That's me," Brun said. "Fifteen years old, in Sedalia, Missoura, 1899. Man with me is Scott Joplin, he wrote the greatest rag ever, 'Maple Leaf Rag.' He gave me piano lessons, and my nickname, too, The Ragtime Kid. I was Scott Joplin's only white pupil, and…"

Brun's monologue ground to a stop as he saw tears roll down the woman's cheek. "You all right, ma'am?" he asked. "Did I say something to get you upset?"

"No…not really." She blinked several times, then forced a little smile, pulled a lace-edged handkerchief from her purse, dabbed at her eyes. "I know about you, Mr. Campbell. I've read articles in the newspapers, and I've been to some of your performances in the clubs…oh, Mr. Campbell, I'm sorry, I should have introduced myself. My name is Bess Vinson."

"I'm pleased to meet you, ma'am."

"And Scott Joplin was my father."

It was a rare occasion to find Brun Campbell speechless, but all the old barber could do was stare at the woman.

"I never did know him, though. When I was born, my father and mother were living in St. Louis, and they were having their troubles. Unfortunately, I was sickly, which put even more of a strain on my mother. While my father was away, playing in Jefferson City, she gave me to a couple who couldn't have children of their own. Then, when my father came back, she told him I'd died and she'd had me cremated. And then she left town herself, went to Chicago, and died there a few years later. At least that's what my new parents told me when I was older. They gave me their last name, Vinson, but they wanted me to know my father was Scott Joplin. I wish I could have met him, but by the time I found out, he'd already died."

Brun shook his head slowly. "I don't know as I've ever been in more of a flat spin." He took off his glasses, wiped them on a shirt sleeve. "You really are Scott Joplin's daughter?"

"If what my second parents said was true. But I don't know why they'd have said it if it wasn't."

"I'll be! I heard Mr. Joplin and his wife had a baby, and it died." Brun shook his head. "Well, you just never know, huh? What is it I can do for you...is it *Miss* Vinson?"

"That's right. Actually, it's more what I might be able to do for you. I just found out my father kept a journal, starting from when he was composing 'Maple Leaf Rag' till almost the year he died.

It's in Mrs. Joplin's hands, in New York. You know of Rudi Blesh, don't you?"

Brun looked like someone who'd just downed a swallow from a glass of spoiled milk. "I don't just know *of* your Mr. Blesh, I know him, period, and I can't say I think a whole lot of him. I've been working for years now on a book about your father and ragtime. Yes. Well, Rudi Blesh was out here last year, interviewing me and other people for his own book, and I let him borrow my manuscript and pictures. Then, after he went back to New York, I wrote and asked him for twenty-five of his books and fifteen percent of the motion picture rights, for using my information. I thought that was a very generous offer. But since then, I can't hear a word from him."

Bess Vinson raised a finger. "Well, first of all, he's not *my* Mr. Blesh. I don't care for him, either. He tracked me down when he was doing his research, and he just set my teeth on edge, he was so pushy. I finally told him to go away, I wouldn't talk to him."

"I wish I'd been smart as you. Now, I don't know if I'm ever gonna get my own book published."

Bess smiled. "Sometimes we get a second chance. That's why I'm here." She opened her purse again, and this time pulled out a sheet of yellow-lined paper, which she unfolded and handed to Brun. "Go ahead. Read it."

Brun adjusted his spectacles, then read slowly, moving his lips as he mumbled the words. "I was working in the Maple Leaf Club with Otis Saunders today when a young white boy came in and begged me to give him piano lessons. He said he met Otis last fall in Oklahoma City, and played 'Maple Leaf Rag,' and he liked the music so much, he rode a baggage car to Sedalia to learn ragtime from me. He seemed quite serious, so I agreed to take him on." Brun turned the page over. "A white boy, my first white student. If my music is ever going to be looked upon as respectable, whites will have to think well of it. I might just be on my way."

Brun looked back to Bess Vinson. "This is—"

"Copied right out of my father's journal. That book in Mrs. Joplin's basement is filled with material just like what you've got in your hand. Mrs. Joplin wouldn't let Rudi Blesh see it while he was writing *They All Played Ragtime*, but now she seems to have changed her mind. Blesh wants to publish it with his commentary—"

"His commentary! Scott Joplin don't need some stuffed-shirt professor to help him tell people what he had to say. He could speak just fine for himself."

"Well, I certainly think so," said Bess. "And

if you really do want to make people know who he was, I can get you that book. You can publish it as it's written, or put it together with something you've written yourself. Maybe you and my father would both have something to say. After all, the two of you were there. Rudi Blesh wasn't."

Brun's heart whacked against his chest cage. He hoped he wouldn't need to pop a nitro under his tongue, then stand and wait for it to melt away the pain. He took in a deep breath, blew it out. "Okay, Miss Vinson, drop the other shoe. What do I got to do to get that journal?"

Bess crossed one foot over the other, rocked side to side on her heels. "That's the problem, Mr. Campbell. Blesh has got the inside track, and we've got to knock him out of it. Mrs. Joplin is supposed to get five hundred dollars—"

"Five hundred? For the inside story of Scott Joplin's life? That's highway robbery."

"They're also promising her royalties, telling her they'll amount to a small fortune over the years. But that's the catch. Mrs. Joplin is close to eighty, and has no children, no one to leave anything to. A pile of royalty income in five or ten years can't mean a lot to her. But some money right now would buy her a bit of comfort, maybe someone to look after her and make sure she gets the things she needs. I think five thousand would turn her head."

"Whew." Brun took off his hat, scratched his forehead, put the hat back on. "Look around this place, Miss Vinson. And you heard what my wife told you. You think I got five thousand dollars just sittin' around?"

"Maybe you could get it from different people. Get a group together, share the cost and share the profits."

"Well, then, how about you? You gonna put something toward it?"

She laughed lightly. "I wish. I mean, my first thought when I heard about it was that I'd like to see whether Howard or Fisk University Press would publish it. But there's no way I can do that. I run a little beauty shop in Santa Monica, and I've got a young daughter and no husband. The best I can hope to do is get somebody else interested, someone who doesn't want to let Rudi Blesh cash in on my father's work."

Brun walked slowly to the window, looked out for a moment, then turned and walked back to Bess. "Not that I want to be rude," he said. "But how is it you know about all this stuff going on in New York, being you're in Santa Monica with a little beauty shop?"

Bess didn't miss a beat. "My brother-in-law, my late sister's husband. He lives in New York, and…will you promise to keep this strictly to yourself? I don't want him to get in trouble."

Brun nodded. "Sure."

"All right, then. You're on your honor. He's a janitor at Knopf, the publisher's, and Monday afternoon, while he was cleaning up outside an editor's office, he heard Rudi Blesh pitching to the editor. They left the door open…you know how it is, Mr. Campbell." Sly smile. "A colored man's invisible. My brother-in-law heard every word. They have to wait for Mr. Knopf to come back from Europe, but the editor sounded pretty sure he'd okay the deal. My brother-in-law plays jazz cornet, so he'd read *They All Played Ragtime* when it first came out. That's how he knew about you, and why he thought you just might be interested in the journal. So when he got off work, he went over to see Mrs. Joplin, told her he'd heard about Blesh's offer, and said he could do a lot better for her. Then he got her to let him copy what I just gave you, and called me." She spread her palms and smiled. "And here I am."

"And this is all outa the goodness of his heart? Nothing's in it for him."

For the first time, Bess looked uncomfortable. "He says he'll take ten percent for his trouble. Five hundred dollars, that seems fair, doesn't it? Considering the risk he's taking?"

"And you, Miss Vinson? How about you?"

She shook her head. "I'd just like to see my father get the recognition he deserves...well, and I'd also love to give that Rudi Blesh a good screwing-over."

"I sure ain't about to argue with that. But I'm sorry, Miss Vinson, one thing does bother me. How do I know you're really who you say you are?"

"I thought you might ask." Again, Bess opened her purse, pulled out a folded piece of paper and gave it to Brun, who unfolded it. It was a worn document, crisp and yellowed, corners long gone. The barber moved his glasses into reading position. "Certificate of Birth," he mumbled. "State of Missoura. Louise Bess Joplin. Mother, Belle Jones. Father, Scott Joplin. Date of Birth, December 14, 1902. Hmmm." He refolded the paper, passed it to Bess; she slid it back into her pocketbook. "How come you never wrote anything about your father, or talked to people about him?"

"What could I say about a father I never knew? And why should I tarnish the reputations of the good man and woman who brought me up. Besides, the person who helped my mother and father get me adopted is still alive. She could go to jail."

Brun coughed. "You make a fair point. But I still don't even start to know how I'm ever gonna find five thousand dollars."

"I've got to leave that to you," said Bess. "But I do hope you can. We've got somewhere between one and two weeks." She pulled out a little pad and a pen from her pocketbook, scribbled on a page, then tore it out. "Here." She pressed the paper into Brun's hand. "My phone number. Well, actually, it's the drug store downstairs. I can't afford a phone, but they'll take a message for me. Why don't you give me your number?"

"Can't give you something I ain't got," said Brun. "I'll have to call you when I have something to say."

Bess smiled. "I'm so pleased to meet you, after all I've read about you. I do hope you'll be able to publish my father's journals."

Brun sighed. "Can't do more than try."

◇◇◇

Midway through dinner that evening, Brun worked up his nerve, then cleared his throat. May set down her fork and knife. When her husband broke a silence by hawking, he usually had something to say that he knew she wouldn't appreciate. "Something funny happened at the shop today," the barber said.

"Oh, really?" May tried to keep her voice level.

"Yes indeed. I had me an interesting visitor. The colored lady who came by here, looking for me."

While he told the story of Bess and her proposition, May drummed a finger on the table top. Then she said, "Well, I guess that is pretty funny, isn't it? Asking you for five thousand dollars? She might as well ask for the moon."

And for what she's got, I'd *give* her the moon, Brun thought. "May, listen. This ain't no lark. A whole journal written in Scott Joplin's own hand? I been thinking, it's nice they're going to put a plaque in the high school for him, but that ain't near good enough. If I had that journal, I bet when I could go out there for the ceremony, I could talk to the mayor and some of the big businessmen—"

"Brun Campbell, what ever are you saying? If I thought you were serious, I'd be calling Dr. Gervais."

Brun reached to his pocket, then stopped. No point even showing her the page copied from the journal. "Come on, now, May," a plea. "You got it all wrong. I just want to get Mr. Joplin the reputation he deserves to have. This Rudi Blesh is a johnny-come-lately, but now, all of a sudden he's the world's biggest expert on ragtime. He'd take Mr. Joplin's journal and mess it all up with his big-shot 'commentary.'"

"Oh, Brun, you try my patience! Playing that awful music in bars at night, writing articles for silly little newsletters, planning schemes, every one of them more foolish than the last. Scott Joplin,

Scott Joplin, Scott Joplin. And what's ever come of it? Only that you've got people convinced you're soft in the head. How do you even know this Bess woman really is who she said she was?"

"She showed me her birth certificate. 'Louise Bess Joplin'."

"People can get phony birth certificates these days."

"Well, it sure looked real to me. Old. And it had Scott Joplin down as father, and Belle Jones, that was his wife's name before she married him, as mother."

May sighed extravagantly. "Brun, I've given up trying to make you see the light and use a little common sense. If you want to spend the rest of your days hollering 'Scott Joplin' at deaf people, I guess you'll just have to go right ahead. But don't you even think of doing something like mortgaging our house to pay for this craziness."

How did she always know what was in his mind? "May, I'd never—"

"Yes, you would. And you'd better forget about it. I'm not going to ask you for a promise, because I know what your promises are worth. But if you put us in debt over this, I will walk out the door and never come back, and you'll have to figure your own way out of your mess. That's my final word on the subject."

"May, come on, you know I wouldn't do it. I owe a big debt to Mr. Joplin, but I wouldn't mortgage the house."

May sighed. He looked like a little boy, caught reaching for the cookie jar up on a high shelf. She pointed at his plate. "Eat your supper, Brun. Cold spaghetti's pretty bad."

◇◇◇

After dinner, Brun told May he was going for a walk. Once outside, he tapped a cigarette from its box, lit up, then walked to Venice Boulevard and into the Rexall drug store. He got the soda jerk to change a fin, took the coins into the phone booth at the front of the store, closed the door, pulled a little notebook from his shirt pocket, and began to dial.

When he came out of the booth, he had thirty-five cents in his pocket and a glum look on his face. After fourteen calls, the kindest reaction he'd gotten was, "I'd like to help, Brun, but I'm hurting right now, myself."

The old barber trudged out of the pharmacy into the warm spring evening, started to drag his feet homeward, but then stopped. "Yes!" he muttered, pumped a fist into the air, and took off at a codger's stiff-legged trot, up Amoroso Court to Cal's tiny cottage, where he banged on the door and called, "Hey, Cal, open on up. I got to talk to you."

◇◇◇

They sat on opposite sides of the tiny living room, each with a partially-drunk bottle of beer. For what seemed to Brun like forever, Cal just stared at him, didn't say a word. Finally, the young man gestured with his bottle. "Let me get this straight. A woman walks into your barber shop, tells you she's Scott Joplin's long-lost daughter, and offers you the opportunity of your life. For a mere five thousand dollars, you can own Scott Joplin's personal journal."

"You got it," Brun said. "And I need the dough in about a week."

"Okay. Now, the first question is, why the hell are you talking to *me*? You don't really think I've got five grand burning a hole in my pocket."

"No, 'course not. But I got to start someplace. Maybe you…" His voice wound down as he saw the look on Cal's face.

"I couldn't give you even *one* thousand, never mind five," Cal said. "And not to hurt your feelings, but if I did have anything like that kind of money, just about the last thing I'd do with it is give it to you to publish Scott Joplin's memoirs. If they really are Scott Joplin's memoirs. Jesus, Brun—"

Brun pulled the page from his pocket. "Here, wise guy. Take a look at this."

As the young man read, a twisted smile crept across his face. "Okay, now I get it. 'The Reminiscences of Scott Joplin…brought your way by the one…the only…ta-da! Brun Campbell.'"

"Jeez-all-Pete, kid. If you didn't talk so pretty, you could really piss me off." Brun snatched the paper from Cal's hand, slipped it back into his pocket. "So, what's wrong with that? A man lives for as long as I have, he gets to askin' himself, well, what did I *do*? Scott Joplin was a thing that comes along maybe once in a hundred years, and he put a ton of hope on me. And then I pissed my life away, cutting peoples' hair when I shoulda been talking up Mr. Joplin's music every place I could. Now, looky here, I ain't bughouse. I never thought you could bankroll me. Why I came over was to see if maybe you know some book publisher who'd want to publish Mr. Joplin's journal, and then the five K would be a…what do you call it again?"

Cal's face was smeared with doubt. "An advance?"

"Yeah, that's it. But it looks like you don't think too much of the idea."

"Brun, it's crazy. No, I don't know a publisher who'd do that. Mine sure wouldn't. And you say you've got only a week or two to beat out Blesh. Any way you cut it, a deal like that would take months. No publisher in his right mind is going to hand you a contract and five thousand dollars without seeing the journal and reading a sample from your book. I'm sorry, Brun, I really am. But there's no way that's going to work."

The barber got to his feet and stretched. "Okay, then. Thanks for listening. And thanks for the beer." He walked halfway to the door, then looked over his shoulder. "See you at Roscoe's funeral?"

"Sure," Cal said. "Friday, ten o'clock, right?"

Brun nodded. "First Baptist Church."

Chapter Six

Fri, April 6
Early afternoon

There was barely room in the little barber shop for the five men. Brun sat in one barber's chair, like a king on his throne, while Cal perched between two colored men on the piano bench. A third colored man lounged against the piano. "I say it's a cryin' shame," Brun growled. "A good man like Roscoe dies, and nobody shows up to see him off."

The man at the side of the piano, a round Negro with no visible neck, spoke in a high voice incongruous with his build. "Hey, Brun, I don't exactly think I'm nobody."

"Come on, Charley, you know what I mean," the barber said. "If Roscoe'd died forty years ago in St. Lou, there'd be more people than the church coulda held. But with everybody out here he did stuff for, all them old ladies, nobody except for the five of us could bother to show up."

"Most of them old ladies was white," Charley said. "They ain't gonna come down and sit in a colored church."

"Well, why the hell not?" Brun barked. "Sorry, it still don't seem right to me. Just like how he died don't seem right."

"You gonna go on about thinking he was killed?" That from the Negro to Cal's right on the piano bench. "Man takes a little too much to drink, slips and falls down the stairs onto a cee-ment floor, it sure sounds like an accident to me."

"I ain't never seen Roscoe fried," Brun said. "Sure, he'd have himself a shot or two, but that was it."

"Just because you ain't seen it don't mean it didn't happen," the dark man replied.

"Fred, now you cut that out," Charley piped. "You ain't supposed to talk bad about the dead."

"Hey, Charley," Brun shouted. "Don't get yourself all worked up, and bust your fat ass through my piano." The barber turned his attention to the trio on the bench. "Monday afternoon, when Roscoe come in here and said he had to talk to me, he didn't look like he just wanted to pass a little time. I wish to God I'd took a few minutes to hear him out right then and there."

"You didn't have any way to know," Cal murmured.

The day's mail slid through the slot in the door below the CLOSED FOR FUNERAL sign, and spread across the floor. Brun walked over, bent laboriously, picked up the envelopes. "Fraternal Order of Eagles, crap." He tossed the envelope onto the little counter next to the cash register. "Bill for light and power." That quickly joined the F.O.E. on the counter. The third white envelope sported a red, white, and blue border; the barber waved it at his friends. "Air-mail, from New Jersey. To 'Brun Recording Company.'"

Cal spoke. "Maybe you're getting famous, Brun. Could be a big record company wants to give you a contract."

The colored men snickered.

"Wiseass," Brun muttered, then took up his barber scissors, slit the top of the envelope, pulled out the letter, unfolded it. He read slowly, moving his lips and following a finger down the page. When he finished, he thrust the sheet of paper into Cal's hand. "What do you think of this, huh? From a kid all the way 'cross the country. He musta got my address offa one of my records. Says he heard about me on a New York radio station, and he wants me to tell him how to play ragtime right."

Cal looked up from the letter. "It's fan mail, Brun, nice. I get it, too. I write back and say thank

you, I'm really glad you liked my book, and that's
that. It's no big deal."

The colored man to Cal's right hauled himself
off the piano bench. "I better be gettin' to work.
Mr. Parsons gave me time off for the funeral, but
I stay here a lot longer, I ain't gonna have a job to
go back to. He started for the door; the others followed. "See you, Brun," a chorus.

The shop seemed unnaturally quiet. Brun
glanced at the letter in his hand, then walked to
the barber chair, sat, read the letter again. "Even if
my mother does hate it…" he mouthed. "…They
All Played Ragtime…Rudi Blesh…except for Scott
Joplin, no one ever played ragtime as well as you…
anything you can tell me, I will really appreciate."

Brun looked toward the door, as if his companions were still in sight. "'No big deal,' huh? Just
a kid writing a fan letter? Canal water!" The old
man jumped to his feet, dashed to the counter, took
a lined paper pad and a pencil from a drawer, then
went back to the barber chair and began to write:

> *Friend Alan Chandler:*
>   *I'm very glad to recieve your letter and*
> *find out that kids like you are interested in*
> *ragtime and want to know how to play it.*
> *Well, you come to the right place. It would*
> *suprise you to see the letters I get from all*

over the world, that is inquiries about the Old Rag Numbers. The reason why those tunes you asked about don't sound like ragtime is because they are not ragtime. When the mugs in Tin Pan Alley saw how popular Scott Joplin's music got to be, they all tried to copy him. Yes! But they didn't have the knowhow. They call their music ragtime, but I can see you have got the right kind of ear so you know better. Forget about all that Tin Pan Alley stuff because it is a waste of your time and money. You should look for music by Mr. Joplin and James Scott and Joseph F. Lamb, who lives in Brooklyn which is near by New Jersey, and Charles L. Johnson, and Tom Turpin (who wrote HARLEM RAG and also BOWERY BUCK and other fine compositions). You should practize your piano at every chance, for that's important. Practize is what makes you perfect, that is my advice. Yes! To be better than the other guy, you must practize more than he does. And do not play the music too fast, play them all as written. Mr. Joplin always give me the holiest hell when I played faster than he wrote it should be. And don't try to imitate anyone's style, stay with what you <u>feel</u> in your playing.

Brun stopped, chewed at the top of the pencil, then wrote on:

You know from that book by Rudi Blesh (who found out that I was going to write a book on ragtime, and jumped in and stole my thunder. But what will be will be) that Scott Joplin composed MAPLE LEAF RAG in 1899 in Sedalia, Missouri. Well, they are finely getting round to paying him some of the honor he ought to get. On April 17 this year, there will be a big ceremony in Sedalia where they're going to present a plaque to hang in the colored high school. It's too bad you live so far away from Sedalia because if you could be there you'd hear both from me and my old friend Tom Ireland (colored) all about how ragtime got started, and you'd also hear a lot of Mr. Joplin's music played like it should be, including by yours truly. I might give a speech, too, because in my opinion having a plaque on a high school wall ain't close to what kind of honor Scott Joplin ought to have. By rights there ought to be a statue of him on a big street corner, and the city should start a museum about him and ragtime, because it all came from Sedalia. Yes! In fact I'm right now in some tough negotiations, trying to get Scott Joplin's own personal journal from Mrs. Joplin, who lives in Harlem, New York. The reason why it's tough is that Rudi Blesh is hot to get his hands on it so he can publish it, but I don't trust him to do it right. He'd put in a whole bunch of his own comments and push Mr. Joplin right off the stage. Now if I can get that journal which tells all about Sedalia and announce at the ceremonies how I'm going to see it gets published, then I think people who make things happen in that city would understand, and get a statue and a museum built to honor Scott Joplin. I need to raise five thousand dollars this week, which I got no idea how I'm going to do it. But if I don't I figure to die trying, because I owe that to Scott Joplin. Well, Alan, like I said, I was very glad to hear from you, and make sure you practize your piano all you can and keep your nose clean and you will some day be a great ragtime player. Will say so long for now. With my best wishes.

Sincerly yours
Brun Campbell

The old barber dropped the pencil into his lap, then looked over what he'd written, all the while absently massaging the fingers of his right hand. Then he nodded sharp satisfaction, and folded the three sheets of paper into the return envelope with the air mail stamp.

◇◇◇

At five o'clock, Brun locked the shop, walked to the corner, and dropped his letter into the mailbox. Then he backtracked along Venice Boulevard to the police station, paused a moment outside the door, set his chin, and walked inside.

Across the lobby, the ruddy-faced desk sergeant looked up from a ledger. Brun walked over to the man. "Detective Bob Magnus in?"

"What's the problem?"

Brun pulled a business card from his shirt pocket, laid it on the desk in front of the sergeant. "He said I should come by today. About a murder."

"Okay. What'd you say was your name?"

"Brun Campbell."

The sergeant lifted himself out of his chair, and waddled off down a hall to the left. A couple of minutes later, he was back with the detective, who nodded hello to Brun. "What can I do for you, Mr. Campbell?"

"You said come by today and you might have some information about Roscoe Spanner."

Magnus motioned for Brun to follow him.

They walked silently along the hall to the detective's office, a small room with an institutionally-gray metal desk and chair, and two matching file cabinets. The walls were painted bile-green. On the detective's desk was a framed photo of a pretty, dark-haired woman with a little girl on her right, a boy on the left. The woman and the girl were smiling, but the boy's face said he wasn't giving anything away, smiles included. Brun glanced at Detective Magnus. Chip and block.

The detective gestured with his head toward the chairs across the desk. Brun lit a cigarette, then blew a cloud of smoke as he sat.

Magnus pushed an ashtray across the desk, and cleared his throat. "Not a lot I can tell you so far, Mr. Campbell. Your friend broke his neck, not to mention his shoulder and a leg, going down those stairs. He probably died instantly. Nothing anybody could have done for him."

"What about your tests for booze?" Brun asked. "In his blood and his stomach?"

Magnus shrugged. "They don't do those toxicology tests overnight. Probably be several more days."

Brun wondered whether the detective was feeding him a line, but couldn't think of any way to ask that wouldn't get him tossed out on his ear.

"But I do have one thing to tell you." Magnus

leaned across the desk. "We're trained to do our work, Mr. Campbell, and everything considered, I think we do a decent job. But it usually gets tougher when an amateur tries to give us some help. We got a complaint from a Mr. Horace Randall that you were snooping around there, asking questions. Bothering him."

"All I did was ask if he saw anybody—"

"That was no help. It might even turn out to be a hindrance. Suppose Randall did see someone. By now, that someone could have a warning. You need to stay out of our way and let us do our job. Police know how to ask questions so as to have the best chance of getting useful answers. Go on home, now, have yourself a drink, and I'll call you when I've got something to say. All right?"

"I already told you, I ain't got a phone."

The look on the old man's face kept Magnus' angry words in his throat. "That's right," the detective said. "Sorry. Why don't you just come back sometime the middle of next week. Just don't get your hopes up too high."

Brun got to his feet. "Mr. Detective, I'm sixty-seven years old, and I learned a long time ago not to have too much in the way of expectations. But damn, that hope is a bitch. I can't seem to get rid of it altogether."

Magnus couldn't keep from smiling.

Chapter Seven

From nearly a block away, Alan caught sight of his destination, and gulped. Miriam hadn't told him she lived in a palace. He looked down at the small tear on the sleeve of his sweater, then glanced at his shoes. He'd meant to put a shine on them. He thought of running back home and setting his appearance right, but there wasn't time. Better a little sloppy than a lot late.

He turned into the circular drive directly opposite the entrance to Eastside Park, and walked up to the marble mansion, all arched windows like in a medieval castle. The boy hesitated, then pushed the button. A loud Westminster chime sounded, and when the door opened, Alan found himself facing, or better, looking up at, a massive Negro in a dark suit, white shirt, and tie. The man was easily six and a half feet tall, and a good three hundred pounds; his shaved head reflected light from the crystal chandelier above him. The giant cracked a grin down at Alan. "You be Miriam's young man, right?"

Not quite the way Alan would have described himself. After their first meeting on Wednesday, Miriam had come to the music room Thursday and Friday to listen to Alan play and talk about ragtime and that barber in California he'd written to. Which, Alan thought, didn't quite make him her young man. But he was not about to argue the point. He grinned back at the huge Negro. "Guess so."

The man shut the door. "Well, come on in, and I'll let her know you be here."

He led Alan down a long hallway, paintings covering both walls. Alan wasn't much on art, but he had the feeling these works were not cheap. He craned his neck to get a close look at one canvas with odd lines going every which way, and saw PICASSO written in bold strokes near the right lower corner.

At the foot of a large circular stairway, the Negro told the boy to wait, then started up the stairs two at a time. Alan peered down the hall, to where it opened into a large room; he could see part of a massive wooden table surrounded by heavy chairs. At the far end of the room, a Negro woman in a white uniform and cap appeared briefly, then vanished.

At the rapid click-click-click of shoes on stone, the boy looked up to see Miriam descending much faster than he thought anyone should come down that stairway. The Negro was well behind her. She waved, then ran down the rest of the stairs and up to Alan. "Hi."

It seemed as if she wanted to say more, but couldn't get out the words. He smiled. "Hi. You look nice."

He'd never seen anyone blush that hard. The soda-bottle glasses didn't do much for her, but she'd brushed out her long red hair so it covered her ears. He thought the white skirt with its pink poodle was stupid, but a lot of girls were wearing them, who could figure?

The Negro came off the last stair and up to the couple. Alan saw him jab Miriam's shoulder with his elbow. "Now, Miriam, I wouldn't never've recognized this boy. From what you been tellin' us, I was thinkin' he was captain of the football team, got him muscles like that Charles Atlas guy. Never thought he'd be a skinny li'l thing like he is."

The sly smile on the man's face set Alan to laughing. Miriam rained punches on the man's chest and arms. "Slim, now you stop that."

'Slim'? Alan thought.

The man broke into uproarious laughter, then threw both arms around Miriam, pinning her hands to her sides. She wiggled furiously, but got nowhere. "Okay, now." Slim chuckled. "I'm just havin' me some fun, you knows that." He looked back to Alan. "But fact is, she ain't stopped talkin' about you since Wednesday. She say you plays jazz like nobody else in the world." The big man let up on Miriam, who pulled away, straightened her blouse, then gave him a withering look, but couldn't keep it up. They both laughed.

"Well, not jazz," Alan said. "Ragtime."

"Same thing, ain't it?"

Alan thought Slim might be pulling his leg. The man looked to be in his late thirties or early forties, and he was colored. How could he not have heard of ragtime? The boy shook his head. "Ragtime came before jazz. You've heard of Scott Joplin, haven't you?"

"Hmmm. Yeah. Old-time piana player, right?"

"And a composer. "'Maple Leaf Rag?'"

Slim looked like someone searching for an object hidden in a dark corner of a room. Finally, the Negro took the boy by the elbow, led him toward an open doorway down the hall. "You can play it for me, maybe I'll recognize it." Miriam started to object, but Slim silenced the girl by raising a huge hand. "On'y take a minute, now. Let the boy play me his music, then I'll drive you on

down to your dance." He held out his free hand.
"What be your name, boy?"

"Alan. Alan Chandler."

Alan watched his hand disappear, but the
big man's grip wasn't painful. "My real name be
Millard," he said. "But people calls me Slim." He
patted his huge paunch and grinned. "Ain't that a
laugh, now?"

◇◇◇

Eleven-thirty, night air warm and fragrant. Alan
and Miriam walked slowly up the steep Park
Avenue hill, toward Miriam's house. She slipped
her hand into his. "Thank you for taking me," she
said. "I really had a good time. And you're not such
a bad dancer at all."

"I'm not very good," Alan said. "But if you
don't mind, I guess I don't." A thought took him
by surprise: *he'd* had a good time. He paused, then
added. "We can do it again, if you want."

In the light of the street lamp, she looked as if
he'd just given her the moon and stars. "Oh, I'd love
to…and it's such a nice night, I'm glad we decided
to walk back. Better than having Slim pick us up."

"Yeah."

She looked concerned. "Is something the
matter?"

"No, no. I've just been wondering how it could

be that Slim didn't know anything about Scott Joplin. And didn't think he'd ever heard 'Maple Leaf Rag?'"

Back to ragtime. Miriam swallowed disappointment. "You mean because he's colored?"

"Well, yeah. Doesn't that seem weird to you?"

She shrugged. "I don't know. Slim and Sally—that's his wife, she's the cook—have worked for my parents for more than ten years, and I've never heard either one of them sing or play a song. Just because you're Negro doesn't mean you're interested in music."

As they turned in at the circular driveway, Alan pointed toward the marble mansion. "You never told me you lived in a place like this."

"Why should I have? What difference does it make?"

"Well, no difference. You just don't seem like a girl who lives in a place like this."

She stopped short. "What should a girl who lives in a place like this be like."

"I didn't mean…all right. I'd expect she'd be pretty snotty. Stuck on herself. Spend a lot of time looking in a mirror. Like that."

Miriam smiled. "Every Negro man doesn't care for music, and every girl who's got a rich father isn't stuck on herself. Some of them get stuck on somebody else."

Before Alan could react, she threw her arms around his neck and pressed her lips against his. He hesitated, then rested his hands on her shoulders. Her tongue moved into his mouth, and she tightened her hold on him. Finally, she pulled away, and flopped her head onto his chest. Her breath came in short gasps. "I like you, Alan," she said. "I like you a lot."

"I like you too," he said, which was true enough. But he wished he could like her in the same way she liked him.

◇◇◇

Inside the grand hall, Slim gave the young couple a cagey look. "I guess you both had yourselfs a nice time."

Sally, as slender as her husband was round, poked him in the ribs. "Don't go teasin' 'em now, Slim."

"It's okay," Alan said. "We did have a nice time."

Sally cleared her throat. "Your mother and father called and said they was gonna stay over in New York tonight."

Miriam nodded. "Thanks." She looked at Alan. "They're at a big charity function for the Metropolitan Opera. Sometimes on a weekend when it's late, they just stay in a hotel there. Then, they do something or other the next day, and don't come home till evening."

Something on her face and in her tone pulled at Alan's heart. "Well, then, how about we go downtown tomorrow and see a movie? *Sunset Boulevard's* at the Fabian, it just won the Oscar."

And it's set in Los Angeles, she thought. Right near Venice and the ragtime barber. But she didn't hesitate. "Oh, I'd love to. I was going to go see it with Ellen Ralston, but—" On the brink of embarrassment, she caught herself. "What time?"

"Show starts at one. I'll pick you up at twelve-thirty, okay?"

"I'll be ready."

Alan thought she might start jumping up and down. "Great." He took a step toward the door. "See you then."

"Hold on there, boy," Slim boomed. "I'll drive you on home."

"Oh, that's all right," Alan called over his shoulder. "I can walk."

"Well now, it's after midnight, and we don't want your mama and daddy gettin' worried over you, do we? I think I best drive you." Big grin. "Besides, then we can have us some man talk, y'know?"

Sally clucked. "Slim, you are such a big tease, shame on you."

◇◇◇

They rode in silence for a few blocks, then Slim

said, "Boy, before we gets to your house and your mama see you, you want to take out your handkerchief and wipe off you' mouth."

Alan grabbed at his pocket, did as he was told. The sight of Miriam's bright red lipstick on the cloth ignited his cheeks. His hand shook as he shoved the handkerchief back into his pocket.

Slim rumbled a laugh. "That be better. Don't want your mama seein' you like that, I bet."

"No, I guess not. Thanks."

"You ever get a blowjob, boy?"

Alan glanced sidewise at Slim, then looked the other way. The lock button on the door was up, good. If he had to, he'd open the door, wrap his arms around his head, and roll out. "No," he said, as casually as he could manage. "Have you?"

Slim's laugh shook his huge belly. "I been gettin' blowjobs since I was a whole lot younger'n you. They's places downtown I can take you, we can both of us get one."

"Both of us? Wouldn't Sally care?"

Slim laughed again. Why's she gonna care? If it wasn't for me gettin' blowjobs, I'd be every year puttin' her in a family way." The big man's smile vanished, and he shifted to look squarely at Alan. "One good thing about blowjobs is there ain't no babies ever come from it."

"But aren't there...can't you use—"

"A rubber? Sheeit! Fuckin' a woman through a rubber's like eatin' a good steak with the butcher paper still on it. B'sides, they's too many guys out there, like to punch a li'l hole in rubbers, just to be mean." Slim shook his head. "You remember that, an' don't you take no chances. Put a girl in a family way, you buys yourself a whole lifetime of the worst kinda trouble. I can get you a good blowjob any time you wants, just ask me. White girl or a colored, don't make no never-mind."

Alan swallowed hard. "Thanks, Slim."

"Don't you forget, now, boy. Don't you dare forget."

◇◇◇

The Saturday night crowd in the Aragon Ballroom whooped it up as the Lawrence Welk Orchestra finished "Twelfth Street Rag." People at the little tables clapped; a shrill whistle cut through the room. Couples on the dance floor mopped at their faces. Welk, a stocky man with a ruddy face, smiling like a man selling food dicers on late-night TV, reached around his accordion to grab the mike. "Sounds as if you liked that."

The crowd made it clear they did.

"Well, if it's ragtime you like, you'll love what's coming now. The band's going to take a little break, but you won't be bored, I promise you that. You're about to hear from a man who was there when rag-time started, back in Sedalia, Missouri, in 1899. Put your hands together, now, for the only white pupil of the great Scott Joplin. Mr. Brun Campbell."

The old man in the gray fedora set low on his forehead shambled out onto the stage. Applause was polite. A conversational buzz arose from the audience. Brun tipped his hat, then without a word, sat at the piano, turned a look onto the crowd that said, "Shut up and listen to this," and began to play.

There were a few snickers and murmurs, but the old man's playing quickly silenced them. He assaulted the keyboard, banging out a double-handed attack, all the while keeping time with an exaggerated stomp of his left foot. The sound was raucous, visceral, and when Brun pulled his hands back from the keys and swiveled on the stool to face the audience, there was a moment of silence, followed immediately by an explosion of cheering, clapping, whistling. Brun gave his listeners a moment to show their appreciation, then stood and stepped over to the microphone. "Thank you, ladies and gentleman," he rasped, as the applause faded. "That was a piece of my own, I call it the 'Barber Shop Rag.' Never did publish it, but that's how it used to be, back fifty, sixty years ago. Piano men those days didn't write down their music, they just listened to each other play a piece, and then went off and did it by their own style. But then along come Mr. Scott Joplin, and he was determined he was gonna make ragtime over into real classical music like they write in Europe, you know, where the piano man's supposed to play it just like the composer put it on the paper. Now, I bet everybody here's heard 'Maple Leaf Rag,' ain't that right?"

Mild applause and a few yeahs.

"Okay, then. But ain't none of you ever heard it played like what I'm gonna do for you now. This is exactly the way Scott Joplin taught it to me, back in the summer of eighteen and ninety-nine."

Brun repositioned himself on the stool, then began to play. His left foot still stomped hard enough to be heard at the back of the room, but the music, though lively and spirited, was considerably more measured than the previous piece, with none of that tune's hectic velocity. Aside from the music, there was no sound in the room. Even the clinking of glasses stopped. But when the old man finished, applause was tremendous. Like they're in a concert hall, Brun thought, and smiled to himself. He got to his feet and walked the few steps to the microphone. "Guess you can hear the difference, huh?"

More applause.

"Now, then. I'm gonna play you a few more tunes before I let Mr. Welk back on the stage, but first, there's something I got to tell you. There's a book, just been found, it's Scott Joplin's own journal, and it tells all about how he got ragtime going, single-handed. I want to buy that book and take it out to Sedalia, and show it to the mayor and all the important people in the city. Maybe then they'll see they oughta set up a ragtime museum in honor of the man who started ragtime right there in their own town. Yes!" Brun removed his hat, bent stiffly from the waist to set it upside-down at the edge of the stage. "Any of you want to help me get Scott Joplin the respect he shoulda got a long time ago, I'll be in your debt. Now I'm gonna shut up and go back to the piano."

Applause started slowly and hesitantly, but caught on, and by the time Brun began to play, he thought every pair of hands in the room was clapping.

◇◇◇

Two in the morning, customers gone, the Aragon Ballroom so quiet as to seem unnatural. A small man with a spine badly twisted to the left pushed a wet mop over the floor past the small table where Brun and Cal sat over partly-filled glasses. Cal glanced at his wrist. "Getting late, Brun." He knocked down the rest of the whiskey in his glass. "Your wife's going to have a fit."

Brun chuckled. "Naw, no trouble there. May's been sleeping probably four hours already, and when she gets up in the morning to go to church, I'll be asleep. By the time she gets back home, it'll be after noon and she'll be so full of Jesus, I won't hear a word the rest of the day. Saturday night's the best time for me to play."

"Saturdays, you get the best crowds, too." Cal pointed at Brun's hat, now back in its usual jaunty position on the old man's head. "How much did you take in?"

"Almost a hundred-twenty. Not too shabby, but I was hoping some guy with more in his bank-book than he could figure what to do with just might decide to bankroll me." Brun shook his head. "Lotta dough to have to come up with in just a week or so."

Cal blinked hard. "I wish I could help you."

Brun patted the young man's hand. "I appreciate the thought. At least I got enough from the crowd so I can take the train. Won't have to ride a goddamn Greyhound bus. Maybe I can find me a sugar daddy in Sedalia, wants to make his town proud." The old man drained his glass, poured himself a refill. "Damn, Cal, didn't I have them stomping tonight? Everybody likes my music. Everybody but my wife, that is."

Cal pushed back from the table. "Come on, Brun. I'll get you home."

"No hurry." Brun jabbed a finger toward the half-filled bottle. "No sense wasting good whiskey. Might as well get hung for a sheep as a lamb."

Chapter Eight

Sunday, April 8
Late evening

Gray fog filled Jerry Barton's basement. Clay Clayton, Rafe Anderson, and Barton chain-smoked cigarettes, lighting new ones from the butts of their last. Little Johnny Farnsworth puffed at a fat cigar. Otto Klein eyed him through the haze. "Christ a'mighty, Johnny, you look like you're eatin' a turd."

"Smells like it, too." Luther Cartwright snickered. The others laughed.

Farnsworth blew a mouthful of smoke in Klein's direction. "You don't like my ceegar, too goddamn bad," the little man snarled. "If it bothers y'all too much, I'll just pick up what I brung here, take it home, and do my smokin' there."

Barton scrambled to his feet. "Otto, Luther, shut the hell up. This's my house he's smokin' in, and what I say is, anybody brings around what

Johnny brung can smoke shit, eat shit, or toss shit, whatever he wants." Barton pointed toward three round sticks on the floor across the room. "How'd you get your hands on that, Johnny?"

Farnsworth laughed, a dismissive sound. "Just figure some people're more careless than they oughta be. A guy spends as many years as me workin' as a blaster, you can give him a week, and he won't have no trouble comin' back with enough dynamite to bring down any building you'd like. That's all you gotta know, and that's all you're gonna know…what the hell's the matter with *you*, Rafe? You look like you got a fart stuck in your ass."

Anderson shrugged. "I was just thinkin'. That's all it's gonna take? Just three sticks?"

Farnsworth's face said he was through suffering fools. "Yeah, Rafe, that's all it's gonna take. Usin' too much is as bad as not usin' enough. Set up them three sticks just right, and you'll have every person in that auditorium under six feet of plaster and stone."

"The newspaper boys'll take proper notice of *that*," Klein crowed. "A schoolhouse fulla white and colored, all sittin' together in the same room, gets blown to kingdom come? Bet it'll be in the papers coast to coast for a good long while. Make people think mighty hard before they ever try'n do anything else like that again."

"Be on all the news broadcasts too," Anderson

said. "Every station in Jew York's gonna be hollerin' about it."

"Sure," Cartwright said. "They sure'n hell will. And before we even got time to turn around, here comes the FBI."

Johnny Farnsworth's face said the concern was beneath consideration. "What the hell you sayin', Luther? That we oughta run scared? Let the FBI stop us? And maybe one day we'll see our grand-children workin' for the colored?"

"Wait a minute now, all of you. Just hold on."

When Jerry Barton spoke in that tone, people went quiet. Everyone in the room turned his way. Even Klein looked deferential.

"Let's not get too personal with Luther," Barton said. "He's got himself a fair point. Yeah, the feds'll be here in nothing flat, people in town're gonna talk, and that means we gotta be more than careful. We can't figure to just do the job, then run on home afterwards and wait for guys with badges to knock on our doors."

Klein looked around the room. Anderson and Clayton studied their feet; Cartwright shot glances at the cellar door. "Jerry's right," Klein said. "But shit, we got us more'n a week. Let's do somethin', then get back here next Sunday night and put the whole thing together, every detail, beginning to end. Make sure what we do gets in the history books, everything except our names."

Grunts of general approval. Then, Farnsworth pointed at the three reddish sticks on the floor. "Bet I won't even need an hour to poke around that school, and I'll know exactly how to bring it down."

Barton smirked. "Good. And speakin' of school, that's another thing. None of us can afford to go flappin' his lips out of school."

Anderson snickered.

"I ain't pilin' on the applesauce," said Barton, and again, the room went silent. "All it'd take is for one of us to tie on a few too many, and then go blabbing to the guy across the table." He glanced at Cartwright. "Or maybe to his wife. Or to have somebody get cold feet at the last minute, and run out and leave the rest of us high and dry. Time to shit or get off the pot. Who's in?"

Barton put up a hand. Klein followed suit, then Farnsworth, Anderson, and Clayton, and finally Cartwright. Barton nodded. "Okay, then. We're all in. Now. Do y'all swear that from this minute till after we're all done, nobody's gonna take a drop?" He looked at his glass of whiskey, stepped to the sink, poured it down the drain.

"Oh, that hurts," Farnsworth groaned. But the little man picked up his glass and sent his undrunk liquor after Barton's.

Barton grabbed an empty shot glass from the shelf next to the sink, blew dust off it, held it up. "Okay, everybody. Get out your knife."

The men pulled jackknives from their pockets, flipped the blades open. Then, they went to work on their fingers. Three stabbed with the tips of the blades; the others drew knives across finger tips. One by one, they held their fingers over the shot glass in Barton's hand, and pushed out drops of blood. Barton stirred the little pool with the tip of his knife, then applied the mixed blood to the wound on his finger. The other men did the same.

"Okay, then," Barton said to the sound of knives clicking shut. "That's a blood oath we just took, so now we're all blood brothers in this thing. We're gonna swear that this week, we'll keep on thinkin' about what-all we're up to, but we ain't gonna breathe one word about it to anybody else. Whoever breaks this oath, he's no brother anymore, and it's the responsibility of the rest of us to take a proper vengeance. I swear."

He pointed at Farnsworth. The little man pushed, "I swear" through tight lips.

Barton directed a bloody finger at each of the other men in turn; they all swore allegiance to the oath.

Barton nodded satisfaction. "That's it, then. Ten o'clock next Sunday night, back here. Anything comes up in the meanwhile, anybody hears anything, you call me, and I'll get the word out. Right?"

A one-word chorus cut through the smoke. "Right!"

Chapter Nine

Monday, April 9
Morning

A few minutes before ten, Brun turned the corner onto Venice Boulevard, walked up the block to his barber shop, and pulled out his key ring. Before he could unlock the door, though, he saw he had a visitor. The woman smiled. "Good morning, Mr. Campbell. I thought it was time we had a talk." She motioned with her eyes toward the barber shop.

"Well, yeah, Miss Vinson, sure." Brun opened the door, then followed the woman inside, leaving the CLOSED sign facing outward. He gestured toward the piano bench, but Bess remained on her feet, still smiling. "What can I do for you?" Brun asked.

"You must have some idea, Mr. Campbell."

"Well, I guess I do. But hey, Miss Vinson, give me a break, huh? Look around this place. He extended his arms, palms up. "You come by what, four days ago—"

"Five. Last Wednesday."

"Whatever. Where do you think I'm gonna come up with five thousand dollars? I never had that much money in my life."

"I don't know." Her voice was level, patient. "My brother-in-law's talked to Mrs. Joplin again, and that's what she says it would take to get the journal away from Mr. Blesh. Time's running out. Mr. Knopf will be back this coming weekend, and my brother-in-law says the editor and Mr. Blesh will be all over him the minute he gets a foot into the office. Then it will be too late. If we can't get the money to Mrs. Joplin this week, we'll have to forget the whole thing."

Brun tapped a rhythm on the counter next to the cash register. "Okay, listen a minute. It's too short of a time for me to send anybody a letter, and I already called everyone I know. Maybe we could make a deal with Mrs. Joplin. She wrote me some real nice letters a few years ago to say thank you for all I'm doing to get people to know about her husband, so how about if I give her a phone call? I could tell her if she lets me take the journal to Sedalia, I'll use it to pitch the crowd about a ragtime museum, and get ahold of the deep pockets there. Pitch *them* for her five K. How's that sound."

Bess seemed to be thinking the matter

through. "What if you don't get the money from the people at Sedalia?"

"Well…I'll think of something else."

Bess favored Brun with a long fish eye. "Mr. Campbell, have you seen Mrs. Joplin lately? Talked to her?"

"I haven't ever met her face to face. But like I said, she wrote me a bunch of nice letters—"

"She's almost eighty, her hearing's not so good, and she's…how should I say this? Her mind isn't all that it used to be. My brother-in-law heard Blesh tell the editor she's gotten pretty flighty. I'm afraid if you try to sell her that idea over the phone, she might get confused or upset, and just hang up on you."

Brun nodded, then raised a finger. "Hey, wait a minute. I been negotiating with some people in Hollywood to make a movie about Scott Joplin, Ethel Waters might be in it. Maybe they'd give us the money to read what's in his journal and use it in the movie."

Bess looked dubious. "You really think they'd give you five thousand dollars while they're still negotiating with you, and you don't even have the journal to show them? Besides, they'd probably just as soon make the story up, which they can do for free."

Brun sighed. "You're pretty good at shooting down a guy's ideas."

She smiled. "You're pretty good at making up

suits out of whole cloth. I'm sorry, Mr. Campbell, believe me, I am. We've got a chance here to make something happen, but it's going to take some cold, hard cash in Mrs. Joplin's hand." She moved toward the door. "You've got my phone number. I hope you can find a way to get the money."

"Not to be rude, Miss Vinson, but ain't there any chance at all you could help a little, yourself?"

She shook her head. "I wish. I've got a beauty shop that's no bigger than your place, a ten-year-old daughter, and no husband. You think *you're* strapped every month?"

"Well, it was worth a try."

She waved crossed fingers at him. "Good luck. I'll talk to you later."

Chapter Ten

Wednesday, April 11
Afternoon

Alan ran into the kitchen, dropped his books on the chair at the end of the white formica table, then froze as he noticed the air-mail envelope addressed to him in his own handwriting. He snatched it up, started to tear it open—and saw someone had been there before him. The boy took a couple of heavy steps toward the living room, but curiosity trumped anger. He pulled out the letter, sank into a chair, started to read.

The old-time writing style with its classic Ws and Ms took Alan back to second grade, a room full of kids moving their pencils up, then down, to the rhythm of Miss Baxter's chant of "Push-pull-Palmer, push-pull-Palmer." The letter filled three pages, and by the time Alan mouthed, "Sincerely yours, Brun Campbell," his heart was pounding so hard, he could barely breathe. There it all was, what he should play, how he should play it, all straight from the man who'd learned from the master. If Brun Campbell lived in Hobart, or even New York, Alan would have run directly to the old man's home, and apprenticed himself without another thought. But California?

With desire ruled out by geography, anger reasserted itself. The boy stormed into the living room, where he found his mother on the green tufted armchair, feet up on the matching footrest, nose buried in a novel. *All the King's Men*. She didn't notice him.

"Mother!" he shouted.

She looked up, reluctantly, he thought. "Well, hello, dear. I thought I might have heard you come in. Did you have a nice day at school?"

He brandished the envelope. "You opened my mail."

She seemed to find the reproach in his voice incomprehensible. "Why, yes. I couldn't imagine who might have sent you an airmail letter from California. Who *is* this Brun Campbell person, and where on earth did you ever turn him up? That letter reads as if a grade-school child might have written it, and not a very bright grade-school child, at that. 'Practice, p-r-a-c-t-i-z-e?'" She shook her head. "And 'r-e-c-i-e-v-e.' I before e, except after c—"

"Mother, shut up."

That got her attention. "Don't you dare speak to me—"

"Why did you open my mail?"

She set her book on the end table, a clear declaration of war. "Because you are not yet of age, and Lord help me, you are still my responsibility." Her voice was as severe as her face. "I'd be negligent if I didn't know with whom you associate, and I can't say I'm pleased, or that I approve. This phase you're going through with that ragtime music worries me."

"It's not a 'phase' and I'm not 'going through' it. Ragtime is good music. Not anybody can play it, at least not right."

"I'm sure they'll be impressed with you at Juilliard, playing ragtime!" She clucked disapproval. "Oh, Alan! One day I want to walk into Carnegie Hall, and as the usher seats me in the first row, I want to hear the people all around whispering, 'That's his mother.' Please don't spoil it for me." She pointed toward the piano. "Practice your lesson. I'll sit here and pretend I'm in Carnegie Hall, and—"

"Mother, you opened my mail. That's a federal offense."

Patronizing smile. "After you practice and do your homework, you can call the police and turn me in." She picked up her book.

Alan tore the novel from her hands, flung it across the room.

She drew herself poker-straight. "Mister, you will pick up that book and apologize for your behavior. Now."

"*You* apologize for opening my mail," Alan howled. "And then you can get your fat ass out of that chair and pick up the book yourself." He wheeled around, stormed out of the room, out of the house and down the sidewalk.

◇◇◇

Fifteen minutes later, he rang the doorbell at the stone and marble mansion on Park Avenue. Slim opened the door, looked the sweating boy up and down. "Horse gets in a lather like this, you put a blanket on him."

Alan gulped air. "I…ran…all the way…from my house."

"Must be important then." Slim pointed to a little wooden seat just inside the door, next to an umbrella rack. "Have yourself a sit-down, else you ain't gonna be able to tell Miriam nothing about it."

Alan nodded. "Thanks."

By the time Miriam hurried up the hall, the boy had pretty well recovered. Miriam tried to smile. "What's cooking?"

He waved the envelope. "Not exactly…" He

peered down the hall. "Tell you what. Let's go sit in the park."

She got it. "I'll tell Sally we're going out."

◇◇◇

Within three minutes, Miriam was back, a light pink sweater over her blouse, small leather purse swinging from one shoulder. Alan ushered her across Park Avenue, into the park, to a bench under a gigantic oak tree. The instant they sat, the boy started to talk. "Remember the barber I told you about in California? The one who took lessons from Scott Joplin?"

She had to laugh. "How could I not? You've told me about him at least once every day. Why?"

"He answered the letter I wrote to him." Alan slapped the envelope into her hand.

All the while Miriam read, the boy wiggled on the bench. Finally, she looked up, eyes shining behind thick lenses. "Alan…you ran all the way over here, just to show this to me?"

"My mother opened it."

Miriam looked him questions.

"I came home and found it on the kitchen table. She'd opened it and read it, because she wanted to know who was writing me airmail letters from California. She didn't approve of his grammar or his spelling."

Miriam laughed.

Anger rose, bitter, into Alan's throat. "I don't think it's so goddamn funny."

She reached for his hand, seemed to think twice, but grabbed it anyway. "No, no, that's not what I mean. It's not funny that she opened your letter. I was laughing because your mother's so worried about what you're doing, she has to spy on you, and *my* parents couldn't care less about what *I* do. But hey, what are we just sitting around for? Let's go down to Selvin's and get some of that music he's talking about. Then, we'll come back to my house, and you can play it for me."

◇◇◇

Alan ran a loving hand over the side of the lustrous piano in the Broaca parlor. Miriam felt a twinge. "You look absolutely moonstruck."

"Yeah, I guess. But when I played 'Maple Leaf' for Slim the other night, that was the first time I'd ever touched the keyboard of a nine-foot Steinway. It hurt to be finished."

"Well, you should hear my father." Miriam cleared her throat. "'That is a Steinway nine-foot concert grand. Style D. Mahogany, of course. I wouldn't have anything less for the artists I bring here to play for my people.'"

"I've only seen them in concert halls," Alan breathed. "Never in somebody's house."

Miriam gave him a little shove. "Go ahead. Play that ragtime we just bought. It'll be a nice new experience for the piano, too."

He worked his way through "Harlem Rag" and "Bowery Buck," and was trying "Eli Green's Cake Walk," when Sally marched up to the piano bench. "I hate interruptin' you," the cook said to Alan, then turned to Miriam. "But I'm gonna serve dinner in five minutes, and you knows how your daddy is when it's late."

Alan started to gather his music, but Miriam grabbed his arm. "Wait, don't go. I'll ask my mother if it's okay for you to stay for dinner. Then, afterward, you can play the rest."

"I don't know…"

The girl was halfway to the door. "Don't worry, she'll say yes. She won't care." Miriam pointed to the telephone on a little mahogany table beside a huge brass music stand. "Call your mother and tell her you're having dinner here." Then she was gone.

Sally looked at Alan, and guffawed. "I guess you' learnin' in a hurry, that girl don't never take no for an answer. Go on, now, call up your mama. Then, come on down the hall there, second door on your left, that's the dining room."

"I'll follow my nose," Alan said, and started toward the phone.

Sally laughed again. "You all right, boy."

As the cook walked away, Alan dialed his home number. When his mother answered, he said, "It's me, Ma. I'm at Broacas'. I'm going to stay here for dinner."

"No, you're not," Mrs. Chandler snapped. "What you're going to do is come right home and have a little talk with your father."

"Oh. Well, fine. Miriam and I are working on a project, it's due tomorrow—"

"What kind of 'project' are you working on?"

"History. The teacher assigned boy-girl pairs to look at different kinds of art in different civilizations, and we're doing music in early America. We went downtown to the library and got material, now we're putting it together. If we don't get it in on time, we both get automatic F's, and if that's what you want, I'll be right home."

He could have predicted the silence, waited just long enough, then said, "Look, Ma, they're sitting down to eat now. It'd be impolite to keep them waiting."

"All right." His mother's response was far short of full-hearted, but gained steam as she added, "Your father will be waiting for you."

Alan smiled as he followed his nose down the

hall. Maybe he should have felt ashamed of himself, lying like that, but he didn't. He thought he'd done pretty darned well, coming up with a story that good on the spur of the moment.

◇◇◇

Miriam's parents greeted Alan pleasantly enough, but with no apparent interest or enthusiasm. All through dinner, Dr. and Mrs. Broaca talked only to each other, as if Miriam and Alan weren't there. They discussed the father's trying day at his medical office, and the mother's afternoon at someone named Georgia's, where Mrs. Broaca and a bunch of women had played four hours-worth of mah jongg. Miriam's mother accompanied her story with movements of her bracelet-clad arms. The incessant clatter drove Alan to imagine driving forks through the woman's hands to pin them to the table.

Finally, over dessert, Dr. Broaca turned to Miriam. "What about General Motors today? Buy or sell?"

The girl coughed, grabbed her water glass, swallowed a mouthful. She wiped at her eyes with her napkin. "Dad…" She inclined her head toward Alan.

Dr. Broaca looked puzzled. "What?"

"I don't think Alan's interested in the stock market."

"If he's not, maybe he should be. Come on, Miriam. Buy or sell?"

"Neither one. It's down three-eighths, that's one and seven-eighths for the week. I think it's going lower, and if it drops another point, I might buy a hundred shares."

The doctor looked pleased. "Good thinking." He beamed a smug smile at Alan. "So money management doesn't interest you, eh?"

The boy shook his head. "Not really."

"Miriam tells me you're quite the little musician, you're going to Julliard. Do you think you'll be able to make a living as a musician?"

The pace of Alan's speech was like that of someone walking across a meadow he knew had been mined. "Some people do. But I haven't thought that much yet about making a living."

"Hmm." Dr. Broaca frowned; then his face relaxed. "Are your parents musical? There's a great deal to show that musical abilities run in families. Probably it's some kind of genetic trait."

Like I'm a freak, Alan thought. "No, I seem to be the only one. My father's a physics professor, and neither he or my mother plays an instrument."

"Really!" The doctor's eyebrows went up. "How on earth did you happen to discover your talent?"

Alan shrugged. "When I was little, I would

hear a song on the radio, then I'd go to the piano and pick it out."

"But you said your parents aren't musical. How did there happen to be a piano there?"

"It's my mother's. Her father bought it for her when she was a girl, but she never got very far with her lessons. She kept the piano, though, because it looks good in the living room when she has company."

Dr. Broaca took a moment to decide whether the boy was being deliberately impertinent. His jangle-armed wife filled the breach. "What kind of music was that I heard you playing in there before dinner?"

"Ragtime."

"Oh, yes." Mrs. Broaca simpered. "Irving Berlin, that sort of thing. I remember it from when I was younger than you." She began to sing, not nearly in tune, "Come on and hear, come on and hear, Alexander's Ragtime Band."

Alan took care not to look at Miriam.

"Come on and hear, da-da! Come on and hear, da-da! Alexander's Ragtime Band. Why on earth are you interested in that old stuff?"

"The same reason people are interested in old stuff by Beethoven and Mozart," said Alan. "Because it's great music."

Yes, Dr. Broaca, thought. He *is* being deliberately impertinent. "Now, wait just a minute," the doctor intoned. "Are you trying to tell me you think this ragtime is in the same class as work by Beethoven and Mozart? Why, I don't even know the names of the composers of that cheap stuff."

Alan winced as Miriam kicked him sharply under the table. "Well, sir, I think it's terrific," he said in a tone much milder than he had been about to use. "The most famous of the composers was Scott Joplin." Alan paused. It wouldn't do to tell this turkey that a small town in Missouri was going to honor Joplin by hanging a plaque in a high school. "In fact, there's going to be a big ceremony next week. They're going to unveil a statue in the main part of a city, and also start work on a museum in his honor."

The doctor's lips twisted into a sneer; he cocked his head and regarded Alan as if the boy were a half-wit who needed to be humored, lest he explode into a tantrum. "Well, that's very interesting. Just where is this big ceremony to be held?"

"Sedalia. Sedalia, Missouri. That's where Joplin was living when he wrote 'Maple Leaf Rag.'"

"Sedalia...Sedalia..." The doctor looked toward the ceiling, made a show of thinking hard. "Isn't that right down the road from Podunk?"

"Oh, I remember that song." Mrs. Broaca raised both hands. "You know it, Marty." She began to hum a melody, accompanying herself with her bracelets. To Alan's ear, it sounded nothing like "Maple Leaf Rag," nor, for that matter, like any tune he'd ever heard. Dr. Broaca's upper lip curled.

For once, Alan felt himself in sympathy with his host. "It's going to make musical history," the boy said. "One of Scott Joplin's pupils who lives in California now will be there, playing piano and giving a speech. I'd sure like to be able to go."

"Do you intend to be a ragtime piano player when you grow up?" Dr. Broaca, still humoring the half-wit.

"That sounds pretty good to me," Alan said.

The doctor ended the conversation with a dismissive laugh. "I suppose it would be all right, so long as you're not terribly fond of eating."

◇◇◇

After dinner, as Alan worked through the final passages of "Bohemia," by Joseph Lamb, Miriam sighed. "That's so beautiful. I'm sorry we don't have any more."

"We can stop at Selvin's on the way home from school tomorrow," Alan said. "I saw more pieces by Lamb in the rack."

Miriam clapped her hands. "Mr. Campbell said in his letter that Mr. Lamb lives in Brooklyn. Maybe you could get him to give you lessons. Maybe he could even teach you to write ragtime."

Alan nodded. "Yeah, I guess. But what I'd really like to do is what I said to your father. I wish I could go out to Sedalia next week, find Mr. Campbell, listen to him play, and get him to give me some tips. He learned from Scott Joplin, so if he gave *me* lessons, it'd be almost like learning straight from Joplin." The boy sighed. "If I could get that journal from Mrs. Joplin and give it to Mr. Campbell, I bet he'd give me all the lessons I want."

Miriam's forehead creased; her eyebrows moved closer together. "Alan, the way you talk sometimes. I mean, telling my father that they're going to put up a statue and start a museum? Isn't that only what Mr. Campbell said they ought to do?" She extended a hand. "Let me see the letter."

She pulled the folded paper from his shirt pocket, then while her eyes worked their way down the page, the boy said, "I didn't want him to make fun of Scott Joplin. Or me, either."

"He did anyway," Miriam mumbled. "'Sedalia, Sedalia, right down the road from Podunk.'" She lowered the letter. "Alan, you can't begin to put your hands on five thousand dollars, so why do you even think about getting that journal and taking it to Mr. Campbell? Are you going to go break into Mrs. Joplin's house and steal it?"

"No, of course not. But Miriam, don't you ever wish you could do something great? Even if you know you'll never really do it, just dreaming about it is better than putting it out of your head altogether."

Miriam thought he looked like one of those little boys in a Charles Dickens novel, standing ragged and starving outside a bakery window, nose to the glass. Without thinking, she threw her arms around him. For a moment, he sat quietly, then pulled back just far enough to look into her eyes. "I'm glad you came into the music room last week," he said. "I'm glad I met you. I like being able to talk to you about…things."

She started to cry.

Alan stiffened. "What's the matter? What did I say?"

She snuffled. "Nothing bad. I'm happy you feel like that."

He nodded as if he understood, then sighed. "I guess I better get on home, and face my old man's music. But I'll see you tomorrow, at lunch, won't I? In the piano room?"

She wiped a sleeve across her face. "Sure."

"And tell you what. After school, let's go get more music at Selvin's, then come back here and I'll play it for you."

"I'd love that."

She looked as if she'd never need another thing from life to be happy. Alan smiled, gathered up the sheet music, then walked out of the room and into the hall. Down to the left, he saw Slim walking noiselessly toward the kitchen, and wondered whether the big man had been eavesdropping. The boy shrugged. So what if he was?

Chapter Eleven

Thursday, April 12
Midafternoon

Brun, at his barber-shop piano, wound up "Ginger Snap Rag" with a flourish, then jumped as he heard applause.

"Didn't know you had an audience, eh?" someone said. "What's that tune called, anyway? I don't think I ever heard it."

The barber turned, and found himself facing a well-fed middle-aged Negro in a dark blue suit. The man's brown eyes blinked rapidly; a purse-string mouth smiled as if pleasantries had come under rationing. "I call it 'Ginger Snap Rag,'" Brun said. "Reason you ain't ever heard it is because I never did publish it. Just play it for my own enjoyment."

The little man permitted the smile to ratchet up a notch. "Nice piece of ragtime. You wrote it, did you? Sounds like a genuine colored rag."

Brun could scarcely contain himself. "Ain't

many people your age these days know ragtime from chicken fricassee. Nowadays, it's all jazz."

The Negro laughed. "Well, Mr. Campbell, when most of a man's clients are older colored folks, he gets to know some things he otherwise wouldn't." The man extended a hand. "I'm Sam Pepper."

Brun gripped the hand. "Somehow, I don't guess you're here for a haircut."

"You guess right." Pepper set a battered black-leather briefcase onto the counter, then took a business card from his pocket, and gave it to the barber. Brun squinted, read, "Samuel J. Pepper, Attorney-at-Law."

"I was Roscoe Spanner's lawyer," Pepper said. "I need to talk to you. I went to your house, but no one was there. And you don't have a telephone."

"I won't have one of those blasted things," said Brun. "Always ringing, ringing, breaking up your dinner or whatever you're doing, and never mind the expense. I've got along fine without one a lot of years now."

"People got along without inside plumbing, too," said Pepper. "But never mind. Here's the situation. Mr. Spanner named you his sole beneficiary."

Brun stared like an ox at the stubby lawyer.

"Apparently, he had no living relatives," Pepper added.

Brun's answer was a mumble. "Not so far as I know, and I've known him for a long while. Never got married, never had kids, no sisters or brothers I ever met."

"Well, what he's left you isn't exactly a fortune," Pepper said. "But it's not to be sneezed at either. Basically, it comes down to his house and the contents of a savings account. The house is valued at about thirty-eight hundred, and the savings account has just over twenty-six hundred in it. Nice little nest egg…Mr. Campbell?"

"What?"

"You feeling all right? Maybe you ought to sit down."

Brun waved off the man's concern. "Nah, I'm fine. Just thinking, is all. That comes out to what, about sixty-four hundred?"

"That's how I figure it, yes. You sound disappointed."

"No, no. You got that wrong. Like I said, I was thinking. Mr. Pepper, how soon can I get the money?"

Pepper's close-mouthed smile broadened even further. "I've heard that line once or twice, Mr. Campbell. It shouldn't take too long. We need to jump through the usual hoops, you know. Dot all i's, cross the t's. Shouldn't take more than a month—"

"A *month*? Damn!" Brun punched his right fist into his left palm. "I need…Mr. Pepper, is there some way I can get an advance on that dough?"

Pepper took Brun's measure. "You've got some sort of pressing need?"

"You could say that. Look, you know about ragtime, you must know who was Scott Joplin, right?"

"Of course I know who Scott Joplin was. Why?"

"Well, here's the thing. Next week, in Sedalia, that's in Missoura, they're having a ceremony in honor of Mr. Joplin." Brun tried to slow himself down, but his speech only accelerated. "I've got the chance to get his personal journal of how he first created ragtime, and I think if I can take it to Sedalia, I can get the people there to think for real about starting a Scott Joplin museum—"

"Where is this journal now?"

"His missus' got it. In New York."

Pepper nodded. "That does sound interesting. Maybe I can help. How much do you need?"

Brun braced himself. "Five K."

Pepper's jaw fell. The lawyer gaped at Brun. "Five *thousand*? Whew. I was thinking I might be able to lend you, say a few hundred. But five thousand?" He shook his head.

"Now, wait, wait just a minute." Brun's tongue went into overdrive. "I wasn't thinking about you giving me anything outa your own pocket, but looky here. You're saying I'm in line to collect something like sixty-four hundred inside of a month, right?"

Pepper held up a hand. "There's never a one hundred percent guarantee, Mr. Campbell. But yes, I would bet a little money that you will in fact collect your inheritance. Can you hold off Mrs. Joplin for a month?"

"No, that's the problem. Some other guy who wrote a book on ragtime wants to get his hands on Mr. Joplin's journal now, and publish it with a bunch of his own comments. He's working on a deal with a publisher, and I hear tell it's gonna go down next week. So, if I don't come up with the scratch…"

The frown on Pepper's face brought Brun to a halt. "Mr. Campbell, I do see your problem, and I really would like to help. But I can't go around proper procedure. I wouldn't want to lose my license to practice law."

"Well, sure, sure. I can understand that, but hold on a minute." Brun's face went crafty. "You said you'd bet a little money that it's all gonna go through, right?"

"Mr. Campbell—"

"No, wait. Listen to me. How about you give me five thousand now, and I sign all the sixty-four hundred over to you? Then inside of a month, you make a clear fourteen hundred profit. What about that?"

"You'd want to take a hit like that? Just to get the money a few weeks earlier?"

"Like I said. After this weekend, it ain't gonna do me much good."

Pepper went deep into thought. Looking at him, Brun drifted back sixty years in memory. Boy sitting on a riverbank in Oklahoma on a warm summer day. Little tug on his line, then a second, harder one. Set the hook, boy. "Mr. Pepper, you could draw up papers saying this whole thing, start to finish, was my idea, that I want to sign over the…what do you call it again?"

"Estate."

"Yeah, right. Put down on paper that I'm signing over Roscoe Spanner's whole estate to you for five thousand dollars on the spot."

Pepper bit so hard on his lower lip, Brun thought he might draw blood. "You're serious?"

"Never been more serious in my life. What do you say?"

Pepper's smile was like a field of reeds on a windy day. "Well, if that's what you really want…" He glanced at his wristwatch. "I'll need to take out a loan myself, but it's after four, the banks are all closed. Can you come by my office tomorrow, say about eleven?"

"That'll work just great." Brun looked at the business card, still in his hand. "This's your address, right?"

Pepper nodded. "Waiting overnight will give you more time to think this through. Talk it over with your wife. Make sure she doesn't have a problem with it."

Brun grinned. "Mr. Pepper, don't you worry about that. I'm sure my wife ain't gonna have the least little problem."

After Pepper left, Brun turned the sign in the door to CLOSED, locked up, then hustled down Venice Boulevard to the Rexall. He strode across the black and white tiles to the phone booth, pulled out the slip of paper with Bess' phone number, asked the operator to connect him.

"Forty cents."

Brun dug change from his pocket, dropped a quarter and three nickels into the slots. A couple of rings, then he heard, "Martin's Pharmacy, Ted Martin speaking."

"I'm calling for Miss Bess Vinson," Brun said. "She told me she lives upstairs."

"Right, right," said Martin. "But she doesn't usually get in till after five. You want to call back then, or give me a number?"

"I ain't got any phone where she can get to

me," Brun said. "Okay if I leave a real short message with you?"

"Go ahead."

"Thanks, I appreciate that. Just tell her Brun Campbell called and says she should come by tomorrow, in the afternoon, and I'll have the money for her."

The pharmacist laughed. "Bet that's one message she'll be glad to get. Does she know where to go?"

"Same place as always. My barber shop."

"Okay, Mr. Campbell. I'll tell her to meet the barber at the clip joint."

Brun chuckled. "Much obliged."

◇◇◇

All the way down Market Street to Selvin's Music House, Alan sneaked side glances at Miriam. Something going on with her today. At their lunch-hour concert, she'd been up and down on the piano bench, ants in her pants the whole hour. Once or twice, he'd been sure she was about to say something, but she never went through with it. When he'd asked if she was all right, she'd said, well, sure, of course, why shouldn't she be, why was he thinking that? And all the way downtown from Hobart High, seven blocks, she'd danced at his side, couldn't seem to walk three steps of a straight line.

As they drew up to Sweetie's Shoppe, a few doors before Selvin's, she tugged at his arm. "Let's go in and get a soda."

Here it comes, Alan thought. Bet she's been trying to get up the nerve to ask me to take her to the Senior Prom. The idea of renting a tuxedo and spending a whole evening in the damn thing didn't appeal to Alan, but he knew if she asked, he'd do it. He cut across the sidewalk, and opened the door for her.

Only one customer in the place, an old man sitting at the counter, sipping coffee, but she led Alan to the booth all the way in back, then slid onto the slick orange bench facing the wall. As he moved toward the bench opposite her, she grabbed his hand. "Sit here." She patted the seat. "Right next to me."

He smiled, if uneasily, then sat at her side.

The waitress' face said clearly what she thought of a couple of kids who'd made her walk all that way for no good reason. Alan ordered a chocolate soda with two straws. The corner of the waitress' mouth twitched.

Miriam watched the woman all the way back to the counter at the front, then turned back, rested a hand on Alan's arm, and murmured, "I've got something to tell you."

Finally, Alan thought. "Okay. I'm listening."

"Just one thing." Miriam shot a glance over her shoulder. "Whatever you do, don't shout or make a fuss. Don't say or do anything that'd make people look at us."

"What people? There's only one other—"

"Alan, *please*. And when the waitress comes back, make like we're just gabbing."

"Okay, fine, don't worry."

"Promise."

"I promise. Now, tell me, already."

Huge sigh. She opened her purse as if she were afraid a dangerous animal might spring out, then reached inside and grabbed a crumpled white envelope, which she pressed into Alan's hand. "Put this in your pocket."

"Huh? Miriam, what the hell's going on?"

"Just put it in your pocket. And keep your voice down."

Without taking his eyes off Miriam, Alan slid the envelope into his shirt pocket. Again, the girl looked over her shoulder. "That's your ticket," she said. "To Sedalia, Missouri."

"Ticket?" Alan grabbed for the envelope, but Miriam stayed his hand. "Alan, stop. I told you, don't…oh, Alan, you're such a tease. You stop that right now."

"Huh…oh." Alan looked around to see the waitress, holding a tray with a chocolate soda and two straws. "He's such a tease." Miriam mugged at the waitress. "He buys me a soda and thinks that means I owe him a kiss." She leaned over and planted a buss on Alan's cheek. "There. Paid in full. Okay?"

Alan grinned. "Yep. You want a receipt?"

Chocolate soda spilled onto the table as the waitress set the glass in front of them, then stalked away.

"I thought you didn't want to draw attention to us," Alan said.

"I don't. And if you'd just keep your hand out of your pocket, and your voice low, we won't. Now, listen. There's five thousand, two hundred dollars in that envelope. Five thousand for you to pay Mrs. Joplin for the journal, and the rest for train fare and food. I don't want you to starve."

The ball of ice cream slid off the edge of the glass, into the soda; more brown liquid splashed onto the table. Miriam sucked at one of the straws, then pulled a napkin from the holder and mopped at the table top.

Like nothing else is happening, Alan thought. It took all his will power to keep his hand from snatching the envelope out of his pocket. "Miriam—"

"Mmm, this is really good." She pointed at the other straw. "Have some."

"But—"

"Alan, it's going to look funny if you just sit there like a dummy. Go on, drink. Then, give me a nice smile."

He did as she said, though the smile fell considerably short of convincing. "Miriam, this is some kind of joke, right?"

"It's no joke. It's for real. You can get the journal, take it to Sedalia for the ceremony, and give it to Mr. Campbell. And then you can tell him he owes you a bunch of piano lessons."

"Where did you get fifty-two hundred dollars?"

"Ask me no questions and I'll tell you no lies."

"Oh no. I'm asking you, and you're going to tell me the truth."

"It'd be better if you just take it."

"'Just take it.' Miriam—"

"Alan, dear, lower your voice."

"Jesus!" A moan. "I can't 'just take' over five thousand dollars, say thank you and walk away."

"Why not?"

"Because. That's as much money as my father makes in a year, and you casually hand it to me in an envelope, and say go have a good time?" He shook his head. "Uh-uh."

She planted another kiss on his cheek, then motioned toward the soda: take a swallow. He opened his mouth to object, but as Miriam flashed him a death look, he rolled his eyes and sucked at the straw. The girl pulled a napkin from the holder, wiped at the lipstick on his face, all the while flashing a smile that said without doubt he was her sweet patootie. "I'd really rather not tell you."

Alan painted a matching grin over his own face. "You're going to anyway. Or else I'm giving it back." He reached toward his pocket.

She grabbed his hand. "You've got to promise not to tell anyone. Not for anything, ever."

He swung his hand up to cover his heart.

"All right, I'll trust you."

Alan felt a terrible tug at his throat.

"My father keeps a suitcase up in the attic, all full of money."

"What? Doesn't he believe in banks?"

Smug smile. "Listen, I'll tell you. Late one night, a couple of years ago, I got hungry, so I went down to the kitchen. I was just about to go in when I heard a noise, so I peeked around the corner. My father had a pile of money on the table, and it looked like he was sorting it or counting it up. When he finished, he went out the far door, up the stairs to the attic. I went up after him, just far enough so I could see over the landing. He lifted a couple of floorboards, and pulled out an old suitcase, you know, one of those big, heavy tan leather things. He set it on the floor, opened it up, and put the money inside. Then, he turned and looked all around. I don't know if he was just nervous, or if I'd made a little noise. Anyway, I ducked down and ran back to the kitchen, grabbed a few graham crackers, and got myself back in bed PDQ."

"But why does he keep money in the attic? That's weird."

"Maybe not so weird. I don't know for sure, but I've got a pretty good idea. You saw the way my father likes to quiz me about money and investments. Well, I'm not a dope. A lot of my father's patients pay him in cash, and I think he keeps that stash in the attic because then he doesn't have to declare it as income and pay tax on it."

"Whew!" Alan wiped the lipstick-smeared napkin across his forehead. "Do you make a habit of borrowing from the First National Bank of Dad's Suitcase?"

She giggled. "No, of course not. I never even touched the floorboard until yesterday, after dinner. My parents were in New York for a play, and Wednesday evenings, Slim always drives Sally down to the Baptist Church on Hamilton Avenue for some kind of ladies' meeting, and waits around till she's ready to leave… Alan, you're red as a beet. Are you okay?"

He'd been thinking that Slim probably didn't

just sit around and wait at the church. "I'm fine. Go on, tell me what you did."

"Easy. Soon as they were out the door, I ran up to the attic, lifted the floorboards, and pulled out the suitcase. Boy, was that thing ever heavy. Then, I set it on the floor and opened it."

"It wasn't locked?"

Miriam shook her head. "Those old things didn't have locks on them, at least this one didn't. I threw the catches on the left and the right and… oh, Alan, I couldn't believe my eyes. No wonder it was so heavy. It was loaded with money. Twenties, fifties, hundreds. I took out what I just gave you, closed the suitcase, and put it back exactly the way I found it. Then I waited for morning. I could hardly sleep, I was so excited."

"Isn't your father going to notice there's some missing?"

"I don't see how. There were thousands of bills in there, and it looked just the same after I took what I did. I can't imagine he counts what's already in the suitcase. That would take hours."

Alan felt as if his shirt pocket might have caught fire. He glanced down, then shook his head. "Miriam, I just don't think I can do this."

"Why not? My father'll never miss it or need it." Her voice shook, eyes shimmered. "Didn't you mean what you told me, about how much you wished you could get that journal and take it to Mr. Campbell in Missouri?"

"Well, yeah. Of course I did. But—"

"But nothing. You said you wanted to do it, so I got you the money. Now, all you've got to do is give it to Mrs. Joplin, get on a train, and there you are."

"Just like that. Bad enough what I got from my father last night. What's he going to say when I tell him and my mother I'm going to Missouri to attend a ceremony for a ragtime music composer, and meet a ragtime piano player who uses lousy grammar and punctuation?"

Miriam's face went wry. "I didn't think you'd bother to tell them you were going…oh, *damn*, Alan! If I'd known you were such a chicken, I wouldn't have bothered—"

He grabbed her by both wrists. "Keep *your* voice down. Listen, how the heck am I even supposed to find Mrs. Joplin, let alone give her the money and take the journal?"

"I thought of that. We'll go down to the library and get a phone book that has Harlem in it, and find her address. Do you know her first name?"

Alan squinched his eyes in thought. "It was in *They All Played Ragtime*. Lucy? No, wait. Lottie. Yeah, that's it, Lottie. But suppose she doesn't have a phone?"

"Suppose, suppose, suppose. Then we'll think of what to do next. Maybe there's a New York City Directory at the Library."

Alan sighed.

"Then, in the morning, you'll get up and get dressed just like you're going to school, but you'll go downtown instead, hop on a New York bus, take the subway up to Harlem, and get the journal. Then, you'll go down to Penn Station and catch the next train to Sedalia. Easy."

"You sure it's Penn Station? Maybe it leaves from Grand Central?"

"No. I guess I'm not really sure. But after the library, we can go over to the Lackawanna station and ask the ticket agent." The girl slid off the booth seat, extended both hands to Alan. "Come on. Pay for the soda and let's get moving."

Chapter Twelve

Friday, April 13
Morning

When Brun got an eyeful of Samuel J. Pepper's law office, he stopped mid-stride and gawked. The lawyer worked out of a shabby storefront, the white paint on the sign above the door weathered and chipped, black letters faded. It looked more like a bailbondsman's office than a lawyer's. On the other hand, how many poor colored clients in Venice were going to haul themselves downtown to see a lawyer with a posh office up in a skyscraper? Brun muttered a rebuke to himself, then pushed the door open and walked inside.

The small anteroom held three green vinyl and chrome chairs, and a receptionist's desk. An attractive young woman smiled at Brun. "I'll bet you're Mr. Campbell, right?"

"That's me," Brun said. "I must be a pretty important customer, you know me right off." He looked closely at the woman. "And I bet you're Mr. Pepper's girl."

She laughed. "You'd win. I'm working for my dad till I can get enough money together to go to law school myself. It's good training." The woman stood. "I'll show you in."

As the door to his office opened, Pepper looked up from behind his desk, dropped the document he was reading, slid off his black horn-rimmed glasses, and reached across to shake hands with Brun. "Mr. Campbell, glad to see you." He motioned toward a scratched wooden chair at Brun's side. "Make yourself comfortable."

Brun sat. Pepper watched his daughter out of the room, then turned to the barber. "So, Mr. Campbell. Are you still interested in that proposal, or have you picked yourself up some patience?"

Brun loosed a low whistle. "It ain't a matter of having patience, Mr. Pepper. Plain fact is, I need that money now. I told you why."

Pepper nodded. "All right, then." He slid the document he'd been reading across the desk to Brun. "Look it over. I want to make sure you understand all the details."

Brun adjusted his spectacles, and slowly mumbled his way down the page. Toward the bottom, he stopped, squinted, then looked up. "This says if I pay you the money back before the estate is settled, I get the whole ball of wax, less however many days-worth of interest got charged on the loan. And if I don't pay it back, I get what's left of the estate, except for the interest."

Pepper gestured with his glasses. "That's right."

"But there's no way you're going to make anything on the deal."

Pepper folded his hands on the desk in front of him, then blinked several times, a dark-skinned owl. "Roscoe thought very highly of you, Mr. Campbell. He told me you're one of the few people he met in his life who genuinely didn't care if a man was white or colored, and that you'd stood up for him several times when it really mattered."

A lopsided smile came over Brun's face. "We did have ourselves a nasty scrape or two over the years. You wouldn't know it to look at me now, but once upon a time, I could throw a pretty good punch when some yahoo started yelling nigger."

"So I heard." Pepper grinned. "And considering that, it doesn't seem right for me to profit from what you're trying to do."

Brun was shaking his head before Pepper stopped speaking. "What don't seem right is for me to take advantage of you being kind and helping me."

"We can argue all day," Pepper said. "But those are my terms. Take them or leave them. If it makes you feel any better, you can figure that doing it this way makes it much less likely I could be charged with an ethics violation."

Brun's mouth moved, but nothing came out. Finally, he managed, "How about we at least split the difference. You take half of—"

"Not a penny," Pepper said. "Roscoe told me you're up to your neck in projects to give Joplin his proper place in history, so you can use the rest of the money for those." A sly smile crossed his face. "Though I do have to say, Mr. Campbell, it's mighty white of you to offer."

◇◇◇

Alan knew his way around New York City. For the past five or six years, he'd been going in on his own to take in a movie and stage show at the Roxy, a Sunday matinee at Carnegie Hall, or a baseball game up at the Polo Grounds. This particular morning, he got off the B train at St. Nick's and 135th Street, two stops before the Polo Grounds. He took the stairs three at a time, and bounded up into bright sunlight. The April wind packed a chilly punch; the boy zipped his jacket, then started up Edgecombe Avenue.

His parents had often warned him not to go into Harlem, but he didn't think it looked danger-ous. Some of the pedestrians gave him a bit of a stare, but no one approached him or said anything. He passed grocery stores, confectionaries, clothing stores, small storefront restaurants that sent odors into the street he didn't recognize, but liked. At 138th, he turned right, walked to Eighth Avenue and across the street. Mrs. Joplin lived at 212 West 138th. Should be on this block.

He crossed to the north side of the street, and stepped up his pace. A man, sitting on a stoop, called, "Hey, boy, you lookin' for somebody?"

Alan slowed just a bit, tried to look casual, waved and shouted back, "I'm okay, thanks." Don't run, he told himself. His heart beat a Krupa riff.

The buildings on this street were different from the ones to the west: bigger, more gingerbread, better kept up. The boy tried not to hurry, but as the numbers fell, he couldn't keep from walking faster and faster.

Number 212 was a large brownstone. Alan climbed the worn stairs, and rang the doorbell. Then he stood, shuffling from one foot to the other. After a minute, he raised a hand to ring again, paused, then took a breath and pushed the button.

He heard a sound from inside, a slow, steady thump, coming closer. Then the door opened slowly, and he found himself staring at the homeliest woman he'd ever seen, hands down. She looked old beyond reckoning, hunched over, twisted fingers clutching a cane. A shapeless housedress, white with flower prints, hung loosely from her shoulders. Her white hair was scraggly, eyes rheumy, and she had the face of someone who'd just caught a strong whiff from a bottle of ammonia. The old woman craned her neck to look up at Alan. "Who you be?" she rasped. "What you be wantin' here?"

Her eyes bored holes through his skull. Alan gave serious thought to turning and running like hell. Go to a movie, then get back home in time to pretend he'd been at school all day. But the thought of meeting Scott Joplin's only white pupil, giving him Joplin's journal, and getting ragtime lessons from him kept the boy's feet in place. "I…I'm here f-f-"

"Spit it out," the old woman snapped. "I ain't got all day to stand here and listen at you stutter."

Alan closed his eyes. His throat was so dry, he couldn't swallow. When he opened his eyes, the woman was still there, but her gaze was softer. "Well, come on inside," she said, in a much more civil tone. "I shouldn't be talkin' at you like that. Just that it's hard for me to stay on my feet for any time."

Thoughts of Hansel and Gretel in his head, Alan walked into the vestibule. The walls were covered with photographs of colored people, mostly men. Alan paused in front of one he recognized; the woman chortled. "You know who that be, do you?"

"Well, sure," Alan said. "Who wouldn't know Duke Ellington? And he signed it."

The woman waved her free hand. "I always get 'em to sign for me, been doin' it more'n forty years now. Ain't one colored musician or composer in New York City hasn't been here one time or another. Lots of them as boarders."

She motioned Alan into a room to the left; he took three steps inside, then stopped and stared. A gleaming mahogany grand piano, draped with a faded blue and yellow scarf, held dominion over the room. Massive scarlet drapes framed two windows which looked out onto the street; an old oak record player, lid up, sat on an oak table under the near window. Not a square inch of wall showed between the framed photographs. The woman chuckled. "Ain't never seen a room like this, huh, boy? If you'da come here in 1920, it woulda looked just exactly the same. With a "Whoof!" she collapsed into a well-used tan wingback chair. "Now." She patted a matching chair beside hers. "Sit you down, and tell me what is it?" Her words floated on wheezes. "You can just take you' time, I sittin' now."

The woman gave off the same odor as Alan's grandmother, a mild, sweetish smell of decay. She was still incredibly ugly, but now, relaxed in her chair, she seemed far less scary. "You're Mrs. Joplin? Lottie Joplin?"

Her eyes lit. "That's who I be, all right. How about you?"

"My name is Alan Chandler, Mrs. Joplin, and I—"

She waved him silent. "You can stop with the 'Mrs. Joplin' stuff. 'Lottie' be just fine. Now, what on earth can I be doin' for you, huh?"

Alan patted the thick envelope in his pocket. "I'm here to get Mr. Joplin's journal, to give it to Mr.—"

"Oh, well, for heaven's sake. I shoulda knowed. That man was just bound and determined he was gonna get that book. He sent the money with you?"

Alan pulled the envelope from his pocket, gave it to Lottie. "Here it is. I'm going to take the journal to him—"

He intended to say, "In Sedalia, for the ceremony," but she cut him off. "Boy, what be goin' on here?" She jabbed a finger into the envelope. "This ain't no five hundred dollars."

"Well, no, it's five thousand. That's what he said I'm supposed to give you."

Lottie looked from Alan to the money, then back to the boy. "What you say is your name again?"

"Alan. Alan Chandler."

"And how old you be."

"Seventeen."

The boy thought he'd never seen a sadder smile. "Well, Alan, I got to tell you, gettin' old ain't no stroll through the park. Once upon a time, I could remember 'most anything. Forty years now, I been runnin' a boardin' house, and time was, I could tell you the name of every single one a my boarders, and how long he'd been there, and if his rent wasn't paid up, how much he owed. But now? Jeesh! I be lucky if I remember my own name sometimes. I got it in my head that I was supposed to get five *hundred* for that journal."

"No, ma'am…Lottie. I'm sure it was five thousand. I have it in writing."

The old woman started to cry silently. A drop fell onto the envelope. "Now, I'm gonna go and get all embarrassed." She wiped a sleeve against her face. "Well, God bless you, Alan, I just can't believe my good fortune. This'll probably keep me for as long as I get to stay on earth."

Alan wanted to cheer her. "It's really going to make people know who Scott Joplin was," he said. "It'll be a real splash in Sedalia, at the ceremony."

Lottie looked puzzled. "Hmmm, you don't say. I thought he was just gonna publish it."

"I think he will. But first, he's going to show it to people at that ceremony, and persuade them to build a statue for Mr. Joplin, and maybe a museum, too."

"A statue and a museum…" Alan could barely hear the old woman's murmur. Then, she seemed to recollect herself. "All right, now, listen here." She pointed out the open doorway. "Go on out there, down the hall, first doorway on the right-hand side. Watch your step goin' down the stairs. At the bottom, pull on the light-string, an' you'll see a li'l table just off to your right. The journal gonna be sittin' right there, waitin' for you. Go 'long, now."

Alan's hands shook as he gripped the handrail and started down the staircase to the cellar. As he came to the last step, a string brushed his cheek; he pulled it. A light bulb above the middle of the room came on.

Was there no end of wonders in this house? Beyond a little table holding a thick book covered in faded brown leather lay piles of paper, some on broken-down chairs, more on the floor. Alan walked slowly into the room, taking care not to step on anything. He plucked a handful of papers off the floor. Music manuscripts, most of them heavily syncopated. Some filled a page, some were just a few notes.

The boy wandered, sampling as he went. His head swam. There had to be thousands of pages here. He was too excited to think clearly, wondered whether he could sweep up an armful and take it away with the journal, but a shrill shout brought him back. "Boy...*Alan*! You find that journal okay?"

He cupped a hand around his mouth. "Yes. I'll be right there."

As he walked back into the sitting room, he held up the journal to Lottie. The old woman nodded. "Uh-huh. That be it, all right. Why'd you take so long?"

"I was looking at all the music down there. Is it Mr. Joplin's work?"

"Sure is. That man musta published only one piece outa every hundred he wrote. They had to be good enough, at least accordin' to him, else they just sat there."

Alan lowered himself into the chair. "What's going to happen to them?"

The old woman shrugged. "I don't rightly know. Sometimes I think I oughta give them to somebody, get 'em copyrighted and published, but I don't know who. What if they use their own name, an' just steal the music offa Scott? And then, if Scott didn't like 'em good enough to publish them hisself, would he be sore at me if I do it? Anyway, ain't nobody these days I can think of who'd want to publish music by Scott Joplin."

I can think of someone, Alan thought, but decided to keep the idea to himself, at least until he got to Sedalia and had a chance to talk to Brun

Campbell. Maybe he could put more than a journal into Mr. Campbell's hands. Come back from
Sedalia, pay Lottie another visit, get all that music
together and ship it to California. How many folios
could be made out of that mountain of paper? 'The
Music of Scott Joplin. Collected by Brun Campbell
and Alan Chandler.'"

"Boy, where be your mind? You look like you's
a thousand miles away."

Alan laughed. "I guess maybe I was. That's
how far it is from here to Sedalia."

"Mmm-mmm. Don't pay proper heed, you
can find you'self a mess of trouble."

"I'll be careful."

◇◇◇

Penn Station at mid-day was Pandemonium. Alan
pushed through the mob toward the Western
Union kiosk in the grand lobby. He had a little
more than half an hour; if there was no line, he'd
be okay.

The clerk, gray and bespectacled, sat behind
the little glass window, his face as blank as the
form Alan took from the holder on the counter.
"To Mr. Brun Campbell," he wrote. "711 Venice
Boulevard, Venice, California. I got Joplin journal STOP Bringing it to Sedalia STOP Be there
tomorrow STOP. Alan Chandler." He ticked off

the words with the pen, muttered "Damn, eleven," then crossed out the 'I'.

The clerk glanced at the form, then at the boy. "You want a night letter? That's the cheapest."

Alan shook his head. "I want to get it there soon as possible." He slid one of Dr. Broaca's twenty-dollar bills across the counter.

The clerk counted out his change. "Hope Mr. Campbell's got a good heart."

Alan gave him a blank look.

"It scares people, getting a telegram on Friday the thirteenth." The clerk loosed a phlegmy laugh, showing two lines of smooth, pink gums.

"Don't worry, he'll be glad to get this one." Alan hoisted his blue book bag, stuffed with the Joplin journal, fresh underwear, socks and shirts, and a toothbrush. He had eighteen minutes to get onto the *St. Louisan*. Change in St. Louis, and he'd be in Sedalia by nightfall tomorrow.

◇◇◇

Friday was always a big day for haircuts, the men and boys of Venice preparing to pass muster at weekend frolics. Brun started cutting the minute he returned from Samuel Pepper's office, and didn't stop all day, not even for lunch. A little after four, he was finishing up a butch-cut on a fourteen-year-old boy, while two men waited their turn, side-by-side on the piano bench. All of a sudden, the door to the shop slammed open. Bess Vinson blasted through the doorway, stomped up to the barber, hissed into his ear, "I've got to talk to you."

Brun snapped the striped cloth off the boy's neck, shook the cut hair onto the floor. One of the men on the piano bench stood, and started to walk toward the chair. "Didn't you get my message yesterday?" Brun asked Bess. "From the guy in the drug store?"

He thought she might swing her purse and clout him on the ear. "Oh yes. I got it all right."

The boy gave Brun two quarters and ran out. The man from the piano bench settled into the barber chair. Brun pushed the fifty cents into his pocket. "Well, okay, then. We're all set."

"What do you mean, 'we're all set?' You may think *you're* all set, Buster, but you've got another think coming."

Brun gestured toward the man still on the piano bench. "Look, Miss Vinson, I can't talk to you right now, I got customers waiting. I close at five, that's less'n an hour. I don't know what's eatin' you, but come back then and we'll get it square, okay?"

The woman shot a furious glance at each customer, then at Brun. "Okay! I'll be here at five. And you'd better be too, if you know what's good for you." She executed a military about-face, and stormed out the door.

A nervous laugh snaked through the room. The man in the barber chair craned his neck to look at Brun. "Hey, there, now what's going on? You got some secret you want to tell us, like how an old goat like you gets a woman half your age into a state?"

Brun fastened the cloth around the man's neck, just a little more tightly than usual. "I don't go tellin' people my trade secrets."

◇◇◇

He was nearly finished with the last customer when the door opened again. "Western Union. Mr. Brun Campbell?"

Brun looked over his shoulder. Skinny kid, six feet-plus, uniform trousers easily three inches too short. The barber nodded. "That's me."

"Got a telegram for you."

As Brun half-turned to reach a hand for the message, the man in the chair let out a howl of pain and grabbed at the side of his head. "Blast it Brun, pay your mind to your business. I'm gettin' to where I'd as soon go to the dentist as come here."

Brun mumbled, "Sorry," then jerked his head toward the counter. "Leave it there." He plucked a quarter from his pocket, flipped it to the delivery boy, who caught it neatly. "Thanks, Mr. Campbell." He laid the telegram next to the cash register, and ran out.

"Christ Almighty, Friday afternoons," Brun mumbled. He brandished his scissors and comb, and went back to work.

◇◇◇

Five o'clock, customers gone. Brun turned the CLOSED sign outward, limped to the sink, pulled a bottle of aspirin out of the cabinet. He shook two pills into his hand, threw them into his mouth, and swallowed them with a mouthful of water straight from the tap. Then he lowered himself into the barber chair, put up his feet, and waited.

She arrived five minutes later, by all appearances even hotter than she'd been an hour earlier. Brun started out of the chair, but thought the hell with it, he'd just stay where he was. Bess slammed the door behind her, and marched over to the barber. "You think you're pretty clever, don't you?"

Brun cocked his head. "Lady, I don't got the least idea what you're talking about. I called you yesterday, and told you I'd—"

"Yes, I know. That you'd have the money for me today. Very cute. How did you manage to get somebody back there to steal my father's journal?"

Brun sat straight up in the chair. "Steal?"

"Stop it," a screech. "God damn you, you lying, bunko-chiseler son of a bitch! Don't you just sit there and look innocent. If you know what's good for you, you're going to come across with the money. Now."

A woman gets sore at a man, Brun thought, she talks to him like he was her kid, just turned the outhouse over. Slowly, he worked himself out of the chair and to his feet. "Now, *you* listen," he said. "I'm telling you, and I'm telling you true. If that journal's missing, it ain't me that snagged it, and if you think you can feed me some cockamamie story and then I'm gonna hand over five grand, you're out of your mind. If I don't see that book in the flesh, you don't get a plugged nickel out of me."

"Cockamamie story? You old bastard! Some kid went to see Mrs. Joplin this morning, told her he was there to pick up the journal, and it was going to be a big deal at a ceremony in Sedalia. He told her the journal would make people want to put up a statue of my father, and build a museum in his honor. Does that sound just the least little bit familiar to you?"

Face to face now, both angry past reason. "Yeah, sure it does. First time you came here, I told you—"

"In a pig's eye, you did. You never said boo about any statues or museums."

"Well, if I didn't, how is it you know now? And for that matter, how do you even know some kid stole the journal in the first place?"

"That's none of your business."

"Oh yeah? I'd say if I'm putting up five thousand dollars, it sure as hell makes it my business." He pointed to the door. "Get yourself outa here before I call the cops."

"*You're* going to call the cops?" Hands on hips, mocking him fiercely. "What for?"

"Last I heard, selling stuff that don't exist is not exactly legal. Be interesting to see you try and explain about your little con game to the cops."

She aimed a finger at his chest. "If you think for one minute you're going to get away with this, you're a bigger damn fool than I thought you were. You're going to be sorry about this, Mister. Real sorry."

"Go on," Brun growled, and again pointed to the door. "Get outa my barber shop."

She turned a look on him that could have stopped a train, then marched out, slamming the door so hard, the bottles of tonics on the shelf in front of the mirror shivered.

Brun followed her, threw the lock, then trudged back to the barber chair and collapsed into it. Maybe May was right. Maybe he *was* a fool. There he'd been, ready and eager to hand over five

thousand dollars to some mush worker who'd probably read about him someplace or been to one of his
nightclub sessions, and seen a quick five thousand
in her purse. So she wrote a page from out of her
head, got a fake birth certificate, and played Brun
like a violin. He swiveled the chair so as not to be
able to see his reflection in the mirror.

Well, at least May didn't know about it, and
she wouldn't. And he hadn't lost his inheritance.
Monday, he'd go back to Samuel Pepper, thank him
for his kindness, and give him back the money.
Three days of five percent interest wouldn't break
the bank. But thinking about the Sedalia ceremony
now was painful. He'd play "Maple Leaf," big deal,
hello and goodbye. Hardly seemed worth making
the trip.

He blew out a deep sigh, then shuffled toward
the door, but as he passed the counter, he caught
sight of the yellow Western Union envelope. The
telegram, he'd forgotten all about it. Crap, what
now? He took a deep breath, picked up the envelope, ripped it open, unfolded the yellow page, and
focused on the block letters below the WESTERN
UNION logo. "Got Joplin journal STOP," he
read aloud. "Bringing it to Sedalia STOP Be there
tomorrow STOP. Alan Chandler."

He read it again, then a third time. Who in
hell was Alan Chand…wait a minute. That kid, the

one in New Jersey, who wrote to him and wanted tips on how to play ragtime? How did he know about the journal…"Oh, Lord!" Brun recalled the last part of his reply to the boy. Joplin's journal, five thousand dollars, Sedalia, statue, museum…

He snatched the pillholder from his pocket, quickly slid a nitro tablet under his tongue, slumped on the piano bench, lowered his head, took deep, slow breaths. Finally, as the pain wore off, he sat up, re-read the telegram. "How in thunder did that kid know how to find Lottie?" he asked the room, then thought, well, I guess it ain't hard, not these days. Phone book. City Directory.

Again, Brun read the telegram. The kid was going to get to Sedalia the next evening. Brun had figured to take a train early on Monday, which would get him to Sedalia Tuesday, but now he'd have to change his plan. Leave that kid walking around Sedalia with Scott Joplin's journal for a couple of days? Not on Brun's life.

The old man felt like a flat tire suddenly patched and pumped full of air. He crammed the telegram into his pocket, went out, locked the door, and started home.

◇◇◇

Two blocks from his destination, Brun felt a hand on his arm. He wheeled around.

Detective Magnus grinned into his face. "Sorry, I didn't mean to scare you. I just want to ask you a few questions."

"Okay with me. What about?"

"You had a visitor today, at the barber shop."

"I had a lot of visitors at the barber shop. Friday's the biggest days for haircuts."

Magnus' face tightened. "Mr. Campbell, please don't play games with me. I think you know I'm talking about that woman who came in right after you closed, and left with blood in her eye."

"You been staking out my shop?"

Magnus couldn't hold back a smile. "Not quite 'staking it out.' I was just coming by to see you, and she beat me to the door, so I decided to wait. Let's stop beating around the bush, Mr. Campbell. I'm having second thoughts about whether or not your friend Mr. Spanner's death was accidental. The toxicology reports showed there was no alcohol in his stomach or his blood stream, so it does seem a little odd he was holding a bottle of whiskey."

"Maybe he was gonna pour himself a drink when he got downstairs."

Magnus scratched at his ear. "Why would he have been going downstairs?"

"That's where he worked, fixing stuff. Kept his tools and all in the basement."

Magnus nodded. "Do you drink whiskey, Mr. Campbell?"

Brun went on full alert. No sense lying; his own wife would tell the cops her husband liked his booze at least as well as any man. "Yeah, well, sure. What about it? Plenty people have a drink now and again."

"But plenty of people aren't the sole beneficiary of a man who broke his neck falling down a flight of stairs, grabbing at the neck of a whiskey bottle like it was a life saver. And not every whiskey drinker favors Jack Daniels."

"How do you know I—"

"My job. It's not quite a state secret."

"What're you saying? You think I killed Roscoe?"

Magnus shook his head. "Relax, Mr. Campbell. Remember, I did say if we ended up suspecting foul play, you'd be the first person we'd have to look at. You reported the body. You drink the brand of whiskey Mr. Spanner was holding when he fell. And now it comes out that you've inherited Mr. Spanner's entire estate."

"Six thousand and some?" Brun spat. "You think I'd kill my best friend for six thousand dollars?"

"Mr. Campbell, I've been involved in cases where people were killed for a dollar and a quarter. Where money comes in, friendship can go out in a hurry." The detective held up a hand to stop the response he saw coming. "I'm not accusing you. I'm just telling you where we stand right now. And I have to admit, I'm curious about that woman who came into your shop and left in such a huff."

Brun coughed. If he lied, and then Magnus found her... "She says her name's Bess Vinson. First time I saw her was last Monday when she walked in my barber shop and told me she's Scott Joplin's daughter. You know who Scott Joplin is?"

Magnus nodded tolerantly. "I suspect thanks to you, everybody in Venice knows who Scott Joplin is. Or was."

"Okay then. Scott Joplin's wife had a baby in St. Lou, back in oh-two. It died, at least that's what everybody said. But this woman told me she was that baby, and Joplin's wife gave her away because she wanted out of the marriage and didn't feature being loaded down with a kid. Later on, the couple who adopted her told her the truth. She said she could get her hands on some kind of journal her father wrote, and she'd sell it to me, but I wasn't about to hand her over a bag of dough without even seeing the goods."

"How heavy a bag?"

Brun paused. "Five thousand."

Magnus' eyebrows went all the way up.

"Yeah, well, you see what I mean? How do I

know for sure she's Scott Joplin's daughter, never mind whether she really has got his personal journal? And where am I gonna get five thousand bucks?"

Magnus grinned. "From an inheritance?"

Brun shook his head. "My wife'd kill me."

"If she knew."

Brun told himself to stay cool. "Look, Detective. You asked me who the woman is, and I told you. She got sore because I said I didn't trust her enough that I was going to give her five grand for some book that might be the McCoy or it might not. Now, that's the way it is, and I can't say no more. If you want, why don't you go find the woman and ask *her* what's what. She says she lives in Santa Monica, runs a beauty shop there."

"I will. But first, let me ask you again why you were over there last Wednesday, trying to pump Mr. Randall for information."

"I already told you, over at your office. I wanted to find out if maybe he saw somebody…"

Brun's voice faded as he saw solemnity take over the detective's face. "Anyone in particular, Mr. Campbell? Someone you see in the mirror every morning?"

"Hey, wait. I didn't never—"

Magnus' hand went up. "That's it for now. But I don't want you to go anywhere I can't find you. Is that clear?"

Brun caught himself about to tell Magnus he had to get to Sedalia for the ceremony. Instead, he said softly, "I ain't deaf."

"Good." Magnus' lips drew tight. "Don't be dumb, either."

Magnus tipped his fedora; Brun returned the gesture, then watched the detective walk off. Did Magnus know about the telegram? He didn't say anything about Miss Vinson's first drop-by or seeing a Western Union boy, so probably not. Caught a break, Brun thought, but now what? That crazy kid's going to be in Sedalia tomorrow night, with Scott Joplin's journal.

Magnus vanished around a street corner. Brun set his jaw, and walked away, toward Amoroso Court.

◇◇◇

"Cal...*Cal*." Brun banged on the door. "Damn it all, Cal, come on, open up."

The door swung open. Brun looked into Cal's blinking eyes. "You were writin', right?" the old man said.

"Yeah, I *was*."

"Well, I beg pardon for interrupting you, but I got something really important going. Can I come in and tell you?"

"As if I could stop you." Cal stepped aside and

ushered Brun into the little living room. "Want a beer?"

"Sounds good right now."

◇◇◇

When Brun finished his story, Cal said quietly, "That it?"

"Well, yeah. Ain't that enough? Talk about stepping in dog shit. I get my hands on the dough to buy Joplin's book, then some kid back in Jersey goes and queers the whole thing."

Which he never would have done if you hadn't shot off your mouth and gone bragging to him in that letter, Cal thought.

"So now I've got to get there before he does something stupid."

"Like giving it to the mayor or the chairman of the ceremony committee, and getting the credit himself?"

"Aw, Cal, come on. How the hell could the cops be thinking I might've shoved Roscoe? You ever in your life hear anything so stupid?"

Give me a break, Cal thought. With more than six thousand dollars at stake? But he said, "No," and meant it. Brun was a windbag, and at times, a world-class pain in the ass, but Cal couldn't picture him killing anyone, let alone a friend of fifty years' standing. "Brun, tell me this. Where in hell did that kid get five thousand dollars?"

"You tell me. I don't know a damn thing about him, except he says he wants to learn how to play ragtime right. But I've got to figure he'll want to be paid back." Brun patted his chest; Cal noticed a slight bulge he'd missed till then. "So, what am I supposed to do now? What would you do with a guy in one of your books who's in my kind of a spot?"

Probably get another character to kill him, Cal thought. Or smuggle him onto a spaceship that goes off course and crash-lands on a planet where no one has ever heard of ragtime music or Scott Joplin.

The silence set Brun to squirming. "Hey, Cal, you gotta gimme some help. I can't just sit around Venice because some cop might want to talk to me, and I sure as hell can't let him pick me up and put me away. How would you go about getting a character like me out of town in one of your books?"

Cal took a swallow of beer, then pursed his lips, and thought about what he could say to an angry detective who accused him of aiding and abetting a felon in an escape. On the other hand, what would he tell his conscience if he walked into the barber shop next week and found Brun on the floor? The old son of a gun could make you tear out your hair, but you had to admire him. How many people are there who won't give up on a dream, won't budge an inch, when any normal person would be too discouraged to take another step?

Cal sighed. "Well…" Sly glance. "I guess that would depend on whether the character was a good liar."

Brun laughed out loud. "Well, say he is. Or he could be if he's got to."

"All right. Here's the story. After he gets an earful from the detective, my character goes home and tells his wife that one of the movie producers he's been chasing is suddenly very interested in putting out *The Scott Joplin Story*. The producer's in San Francisco, talking to some money people, and he wants my character to come right up. In fact, there's a meeting set for the next afternoon, so the character has to catch the first train north. His wife makes a big fuss, but he's used to that. After dinner, he goes upstairs, packs a suitcase—"

"I get it. Then, if the cops ask my…the guy's wife where he is, she says he's in Frisco. Hey, Cal, that's great. I knew you could help me. I'll—"

"Hold on a minute. I'm not done."

The barber narrowed his eyes, then eased back into the chair. "Okay, sorry. I'm listening."

"My character's not sure how interested the cops really are in him. No way to tell whether they've got his house under watch. Fortunately, it'll be dark by the time he leaves, so he goes out the back way, down the alley and past the garage to the street, then straight to the station. That's it. Now, I'm done."

To Cal's surprise, Brun didn't make a rush to his feet. The old barber frowned; the pain in his eyes startled Cal. "I keep thinking about Sedalia," Brun said softly. After I left, the town got itself all respectable, tryin' to play to business owners and get 'em to move in. They closed down all the joints and houses on West Main, and after that, the only music was in churches and concert halls. It's been fifty-two years, Cal, and truth, I'm afraid of what I'm gonna see there."

The young man laughed. "I didn't know you were scared of ghosts."

"Go laugh," Brun said. "But get to be my age, you'll have more friends in the cemetery than walking around, and then you can see what side of your mouth you're laughing outa. If it wasn't for this ceremony, I wouldn't set foot back there the rest of my life. I don't want to see—"

Cal knew what Brun didn't want to see, and quickly shifted the conversational direction. "I'll bet there're people still in town who were alive back then...when you *say* you were there.

"Oh. When I *say* I was there, huh?"

Cal smiled privately. "Go on home, Brun, get

ready. I guess I'll be listening to you go on about
this caper for the next ten years."

Brun's reply surprised him. Just a quiet, "Ten
years, huh? Yeah, I guess I'd settle for that."

◇◇◇

Alan Chandler, who'd never been west of Philadel-
phia, decided that riding a train across the country
was something else. He watched the scenery fly by,
cities gradually giving way to farms and towns, and
he met some interesting people. An encyclopedia
salesman. A pretty young woman going back home
from New York to St. Louis to marry her high-
school sweetheart. A middle-aged couple and their
son, Alan's age, on their way to California, for the
man to take a new job. Alan told them he'd been
to New York to visit his father, who'd moved there
from Missouri when he and Alan's mother had
divorced. The couple exchanged one of those looks
long-married couples use in place of speech, and
the upshot was, they stood Alan to dinner, which
helped make up for the fact he'd booked a sleeping
compartment.

About ten o'clock, the boy stretched across his
bunk, drew the curtain, opened his book bag, and
pulled out Scott Joplin's journal. He'd go through
some of it, then finish the next morning.

But it was after midnight when he turned

the last page, and closed the journal. He couldn't begin to imagine what Mr. Campbell was going to say when he read that stuff. It was nearly two o'clock before the boy's mind yielded to the regular clickety-clack of the train's wheels, and he dropped into sleep.

Chapter Thirteen

Saturday, April 14
Morning

Dr. Martin Broaca, spiffy in his yellow golf shirt and green-and-white plaid slacks, glared across the kitchen table at Slim. The huge colored man returned the look with interest. "Dr. Broaca, you' insultin' me. If you' gonna accuse me of stealin' your money, you oughta have *somethin'* to back it up. An' you ain't got nothin'. Nothin' at all."

The doctor sighed luxuriantly. Give them half a chance, and they'll rob you blind, but where do you find a white couple to do that kind of work for that kind of money? "Slim, please. I wasn't born yesterday. Somebody in this household thought they could take a few handfuls out of the suitcase, and I'd never be the wiser. A thief from outside would've run off with the whole kit and caboodle."

"So, how much money was gone?"

"Several thousand. There was clearly less in that suitcase than the last time I looked."

Slim turned a fish eye onto the doctor. "Let me understand this now. You sayin' you ain't even sure how much is gone, and that's enough for you to accuse me of stealin' from you? Could be you was just misrememberin' from the last time you done looked."

Broaca paused, then said, "I'm not 'misre-membering.' And I know the suitcase was opened because I always tie a thin thread between the two parts of the latch. With the light as bad as it is up there, no one would see it, and this morning, that thread was broken."

"And you know it was me. Dr. Broaca, how can you know that?"

"Because it wasn't me. And it wasn't Mrs. Broaca. She gets all the money she wants above board. Should I suspect Sally? Or Miriam?"

"How about that boy, was here for dinner the other night? I heard him and Miriam talkin' afterward. He said he could use money to pay somebody for a journal he wanted to take to some kinda ceremony in Missouri."

"How would the boy know about the suitcase?"

"Maybe Miriam tol' him."

"Bah." Scorn covered the doctor's face. "My poor little stick of a daughter would never have the brass to do something like that. I'm sorry, but there's only one person in this house I can suspect."

"So, how did *I* know about your goddamn suitcase. Tell me that."

Dr. Broaca shrugged. "You just told me you eavesdropped on Miriam and her friend. Maybe you sneaked up to the attic after me."

Slim leaned across the table. "If you think somebody went and stole your money, why don't you call the cops? In fact, why don't you go and tell them I done it and they should arrest me?"

The doctor's smile set a new standard for condescension. "I think you know full well why I'm not going to do that. And if you ever say anything to anyone about this matter, I will pursue legal action against you for slander. You're being fired for incompetence and insubordination, period. The rest of the money is now where no one will find it, not if they tear the house apart." He glanced at his watch. "It's getting late, and I have an appointment."

With a golf ball, Slim thought. Motherfucker, you.

"If you can prove to me that someone else took the money, I will apologize," said the doctor. "And you can keep your job. Otherwise, I want you out of here by the end of the day. Do you understand me?"

"Clear enough." Slim worked himself to his feet. "Plenty clear enough. Doctor."

◇◇◇

The valet watched from the living room window as Dr. Broaca's car rolled down the driveway, turned right onto Park Avenue, and vanished. "Bastard!" Slim stomped back and forth across the room, shaking both fists over his head. "Son of a bitch honky asshole! Sally's gonna throw a cat fit when she get back from her grocery shopping. An' I can't say a word to Mrs. Broaca. Nothin' she'd do except tell her husband, and then I got his pissant lawyers all over me, and I'm fucked both ways to China. If I find out who really took that money, I can keep my job, huh? Well, he can shove that job straight up…"

Midway across the room, Slim stopped pacing, slapped a hand against his thigh, laughed out loud. "Well, now, maybe that be just the thing. I can go find that li'l son of a bitch cabbage-picker, get me back the money, an' keep it for myself. Man want me to be a thief, he can just pay me for the honor."

He went by giant steps into the hall, up the stairs, to the open doorway of the first room on the left. Miriam lay on her stomach on the bed, reading a book, *The Economics of Something or Other*. The big man cleared his throat; the girl looked up. "Oh, hi, Slim. What's happening?"

He showed all the teeth he could squeeze into a smile. "I'm hopin' you and me could talk for a minute."

She set down the book, swung her legs over the side of the bed. "Sure. What about?"

Slim took care not to venture a step into the room, but if she tried to run, there was no way she'd get past him. "Well, it's like this, Miriam. You' daddy think I stole some of his money."

He saw it in her eyes, just for an instant. Her hand went to her mouth. "Why would he ever think that?"

Slim eyed the girl carefully. "He done kep' a suitcase up to the attic, all fulla money."

She didn't bite. Nothing after that one passing look in her eyes. "My father hid money up in the attic? Why?"

"Well, I only can tell you what I think. A man get paid with cash money, if he hide it away, he don't never pay no tax on it."

"And some of it was missing?"

Slim nodded gravely. "He always tie a tiny li'l string so if somebody open the suitcase, the string gonna break."

There it was again, in her eyes, a flash, then gone. Now, Slim was sure. "He found the string broke when he go up this morning, and he think I done it."

"But you didn't," Miriam said.

"'Course I didn't. But he think I did, and he fire me."

"But why did he blame you?"

Slim opened his eyes wide. "Well, he say *he* didn't do it, or your mama, or Sally, or you. So, it had to be me, there wasn't nobody else. He say if I can show him it was somebody else, I could keep my job. Otherwise, I gotta be outa here by tonight."

The girl started to cry, then jumped off the bed, ran over, and threw her arms around the big man. "He can't do that. You and Sally are part of our family. When he gets home after his dumb golf game, I'm going to talk to him. Someone's supposed to be innocent till proved guilty, not the other way around."

She ain't gonna 'fess, Slim thought. Not 'less I tell her what I heard the other night, but if I do, she just could know how to get hold of that boy and give him a tip-off. He patted the girl's head. "Now, don't you be sayin' nothing to him, Miriam. You ain't gonna change his mind, and anyway, even if he did listen, you think I'd come and work for him any more? But you been like my own li'l girl, and I didn't want to just walk outa the door without sayin' goodbye to you. I's gonna be just fine, don't you worry."

As Slim started down the stairs, Miriam threw herself face down on the bed, and bawled. I should have told him, she thought. Now I've got to tell my father...but if I do, there'll be police out in Sedalia, waiting for Alan to get off the train...oh, damn. Why do things have to get so complicated? She pounded her pillow with both fists, then flung the pillow across the room. It bounced off the wall, sending a photograph of her and her father at the New York Stock Exchange clattering to the floor.

◇◇◇

Slim drove up to a well-kept one-story brick house on East Twenty-ninth Street between Fourteenth Avenue and Roosevelt. He parked at the curb, then walked up to the door and rang the bell. Not half a minute passed before the door swung open. One glance at the woman who stood there told Slim he was too late. "Yes?" the woman said. "What can I do for you?"

Slim slumped his shoulders, and pasted on a big Stepin Fetchit smile. "I come here to pick up Alan, ma'am. I'm supposed to drive him and my boss' daughter into New York, to go to some kinda show."

A man walked up behind the woman; she turned to him, then pointed at Slim. "He says he's supposed to drive Alan into New York."

"With my boss' daughter," Slim said. "Ask me, I think they gettin' real friendly lately."

"Alan's not here. Who is your boss?" The man talked as if he kept a cigar cutter in his throat.

"Dr. Martin Broaca. But if Alan be someplace else, I can go get him."

The woman began to cry.

"Something the matter?" Slim asked.

"We haven't seen Alan since yesterday morning," the man snapped. We thought he was going to school, but he took off for New Orleans, to learn some of the 'music' they play there."

Slim feigned surprise. "My, my." He shook his head. "Kids these days."

"He left a note in the mailbox," the woman said. "I found it when I picked up the mail, late in the afternoon. Oh, that boy is going to be the death of me." She started to cry again.

Slim tipped his cap. "Well, I guess I better just go back, then. I sure hope it all work out okay."

The woman snuffled. "Thank you, I'm sure it will. The police say they'll be watching the bus and train stations down there, and they'll have him back home in no time."

"I'll kill him," said the man, through clenched teeth."

Back in the car, Slim allowed himself a long, low laugh. New Orleans, huh? He turned the ignition key. Sally'd be back by now. Take her down to her sister's in Newark, then go into New York and get himself on the first train to this Sedalia, Missoura place. He'd have his hands on that boy before the cops in New Orleans knew a thing. Grab the five thousand, then go an' spit square in Dr. Broaca's face. No, fuck Dr. Broaca. Just take the money, start up a li'l store with Sally, sell radios and TVs. Never have to say, "Yas'r" again to any shitface ofay doctor.

◇◇◇

A thousand miles down the line, the train slowed, coming into the station at Sedalia. Alan pulled his book bag from the vacant seat beside him, swung it into his lap, held the handle in a death grip. That bag had not been out of his reach for an instant since Scott Joplin's journal first went into it. It had spent the night in Alan's bed, under the sheet, and it would not be out of his sight until the journal was safely in Brun Campbell's hands. But then what? Go back to Hobart, back to school, take piano lessons from Mr. Bletter, practice classical music till it came out of his ears, finish the school year, graduate, go to Juilliard, get a job teaching music in some crappy high school, get married, have kids, die? Alan swallowed hard.

The train ground and wheezed to a halt; the

boy's mind lightened. Wednesday would be time enough to think about what to do after Tuesday. Meanwhile, he had plenty to keep him busy.

But where and how to start? He couldn't very well stand around in the train station and wait for a man he'd never set eyes on. For all he knew, Mr. Campbell could be here already. Should have set a place and a time to meet him, Alan told himself, but it had all happened so fast, he hadn't been able to think beyond getting his hands on the journal, then getting himself and it onto the train.

He ambled through the dingy station and out the door, then looked around. What he could see of Sedalia looked a lot like the fringe areas of downtown Hobart, small businesses elbow to elbow with little houses, and an occasional weed-grown empty lot. Which way should he go to get into town? Did he need to take a bus, or a cab? Did they *have* buses and taxicabs here?

He walked back into the station and up to the ticket window, then shifted from one foot to the other while a young man and woman paid their fares to Kansas City. As the couple moved away, the clerk adjusted his spectacles and acknowledged Alan with a nod. "Where you goin', Sonny."

"I just got in from St. Louis," Alan said. "Which way is it to downtown?"

The clerk made a odd sound in his throat,

somewhere between a cough and a chuckle. "Never been to Sedalia, huh?"

"No, sir. I'm supposed to meet my grandpa, he's coming in from Los Angeles, and taking me to the big ceremony on Tuesday for Scott Joplin."

The clerk screwed his face into a question mark. "Big ceremony, you say? For who?"

"Scott Joplin. You know, the ragtime composer. 'Maple Leaf Rag?' They're having a ceremony to honor him at the colored high school, Tuesday evening."

The clerk shrugged. "I don't keep up with the colored." He squinted at Alan, blinked. "Your grandpa's not colored, is he?"

"No, sir." Alan struggled to keep his voice even. "He was Scott Joplin's only white pupil. Took piano lessons from him here in Sedalia, back in 1899."

The clerk seemed to lose interest. "Okay. Where is it downtown you're supposed to meet your grandpa?"

"He said in front of City Hall."

"That's easy." The clerk pointed out the window. "Take Ohio Street there, across the tracks into downtown. Then turn right at Second and go one block more. Municipal Building's on the corner, Second and Osage. Think you can remember that?"

"Yes, sir." Alan waved. "Thank you."

In less than ten minutes, he stood on the corner of Ohio and Second. Wind whipped his pants legs into a flutter. The buildings looked old enough, most of them, to have been standing when Brun Campbell was taking lessons from Scott Joplin. Not many people around, especially considering it was Saturday afternoon. This Sedalia looked nothing like the bustling, exciting city Alan had read about in *They All Played Ragtime*. It put the boy in mind of an old man in faded clothes with frayed cuffs, shoes long past their retirement day.

Ohio looked like the main drag, so Alan strolled on, taking it all in. Really did look a lot like downtown Hobart. St. Louis Clothing Store. Heuer's Shoe Store. Andy's Tavern, a Firestone's, a B. F. Goodrich. In front of Bichsel's Jewelry, he stopped to gape at a monster clock atop a tall iron column, then moved on past C. W. Flower Dry Goods, disorderly piles of fabric filling its window. Uptown Theatre…well, look at that, *Sunset Boulevard*. He thought of Miriam, smiled.

The girl selling tickets in the glass-enclosed booth gave him the eye, then leaned forward to call through the round hole in front, "That's a real good movie. I saw it three times already."

Pretty girl, about his age. Lots of dark, curly hair, and big brown eyes. Lipstick perfectly applied, just a touch of eye shadow. Probably one of those popular girls, maybe a cheerleader, loves doing cartwheels to get the boys smirking and pointing at her legs. But those girls make a point of knowing everything that's going on. Alan walked over to the booth.

The girl's eyelashes fluttered. "Next full show's at seven," she said. "Saturday afternoon, they've got cartoons and serials for the kids, besides the two features and the newsreels."

Alan smiled politely. "Thanks. I've seen the movie."

The girl's eyes widened. "Oh, wasn't Gloria Swanson marvy? I just cried and cried." She flicked the tip of her tongue against her upper lip. "Bet you didn't cry."

Miriam had sopped through a dozen tissues. Alan smiled again.

The girl smiled back. "Strong, silent type, huh? Hey, you don't live in Sedalia, do you? I haven't ever seen you around."

"No, I'm in from New Jersey."

"Wow. That's a long way."

"More than twenty-four hours on two trains."

"Why're you here?"

I came for the ceremony to honor Scott Joplin Tuesday night."

She cocked her head and shrugged. "I haven't heard about any ceremony…to honor who?"

Doubt surged in the pit of Alan's stomach. He'd thought the whole town would be gaga, but it seemed no one here had even heard of Scott Joplin, never mind the ceremony. "He wrote ragtime music, played piano. The ceremony's at the colored high school."

"Hubbard?"

Now it was his turn to shrug. "I guess."

"But you're not colored."

"Not the last time I looked."

The girl's laugh fell short of wholehearted amusement. "What's your name, wise guy?"

"Alan. Alan Chandler."

Big smile. "That's a nice name."

It's a name, Alan thought. What's she getting at?

"My name's Eileen."

"Glad to meet you, Eileen."

"I get off at six, and I don't have a date tonight." Her mother would have a cow, Eileen thought, but her mother wasn't here, and this boy was really cute.

"Well…" Alan scratched at his head. "I just got here, and I'm not sure I'm going to be free." He saw disappointment cover the girl's face, and told himself not to cut off any possibilities. "But in case

I am, why don't you give me your phone number."

She brightened. "Sure." She scribbled on a pad, then passed the paper through the hole in the glass. "I hope you can make it."

"Me too…oh, hold on a minute. Can you tell me how to get to the Maple Leaf Club?"

"The Maple Leaf Club? Is that in Sedalia?"

"On Main Street. I think East Main, actually."

Eileen looked like a student being asked a question on the math homework she hadn't done the night before. "Main's just a block and a half down, the way you came from. Didn't you see it?"

Alan shook his head. "I didn't notice any sign. I thought it was probably First, since the next street was Second."

"No, what ought to be First is Main." The girl hesitated. "But I don't think you really want to go there."

"Why not?"

"The wrong kind of people hang around on East Main. It's not a safe place."

"I'll be careful," Alan said. "Thanks. I'll try to make it later."

"Neat-o. We could go out to the Wheel-Inn and have a Guber-burger. Bet you never had a Guber-burger."

Alan couldn't help laughing. "I've never heard of a Guber-burger."

"And they've got all the good songs on their jukebox. You can dance, right?"

"A little."

"I'll show you all the new steps. Oh, we'd have just a great time. All the kids go there Saturday night."

And all the kids would see her walking in on the arm of the mysterious stranger from New Jersey, Alan thought. He waved, then walked away.

◇◇◇

He'd no sooner turned onto East Main Street than he realized what Eileen had been trying to tell him. All along Ohio, almost everyone was white, but the faces on East Main were entirely black. Well, so what? Alan's friend Tony Moseley lived on Hamilton Avenue, right in the heart of the Negro section of Hobart, and Alan never gave a thought to walking down to Tony's, any time of day or night.

Two old Negro men sat, smoking corncob pipes and talking, on a bench in front of the Archias Seed Store, a large brick building that Alan thought could have been standing at the time of the Revolutionary War. He remembered Huck and Jim had smoked corncob pipes on their raft as they drifted down the Mississippi, but he'd never seen a real live person puffing away at a hollowed-out cob. One of the men, a wrinkled ancient with an impressive top-mop of white wool, caught Alan staring. He pulled his pipe from his mouth, jabbed it in the boy's direction. "Help you with somethin', young mister?"

He looked old as Sedalia, but in considerably better repair. Blue suit clean and pressed, high button shoes polished to a fare-thee-well. He was clean-shaved, and his eyes shone bright and clear. "Where's the Maple Leaf Club? I've read about it, and now I'd like to see it," Alan said.

The man glanced at his friend on the bench, then turned back to Alan, and pointed at a two-story building across the street. A large sign covered the space between its two floors: CARL ABBOTT'S REC-REATION CENTER. "Well, there be the building it was in, but the club's gone fifty years and more. See them long windows with the curvy tops, up to the second floor? That was where it was. I spent many a good hour there, and oh, how them boys could play piana."

Alan's heart raced. "So you must have seen Scott Joplin, and heard him play."

"Oh, yes, sure 'nough. Not that he was the fanciest player, mind you. I don't think he ever did win a single cuttin' contest. But when Scott Joplin was in the right frame of mind, he could play ragtime fit to tear out your heart. I used to think how the angels was puttin' down their harps to listen."

The second old man nodded emphatic

agreement. "Never heard nothin' like that before or since."

"Did you know Brun Campbell, too?" Alan could barely speak the words.

The wool-haired man stared into the distance, then slowly shook his head. "Name does ring a li'l bell, but I can't say I do recall him. He play ragtime too?"

"Oh, yes. He was Scott Joplin's only white pupil. Took lessons from him here in Sedalia, back in 1899."

Again, the old man shook his head. "No, afraid that don't help. Scott Joplin, I sure do recall, and many others too. But not no white pupils, sorry."

Alan felt disappointed, but told himself it didn't really matter. "Have you heard about the ceremony at the Negro high school Tuesday in honor of Scott Joplin?"

"I surely have," the old man said. "I figure to go and see it."

"Well, Mr. Campbell's going to be there," said Alan. "He's going to play piano. And make a speech—"

He stopped abruptly as the old man's body stiffened. Alan bent to touch his shoulder. "Are you all right?"

"Oh, yes, sure, I be fine. Get to be a hundred years old, sometimes your body plays you tricks."

"That's how old you are?" Alan asked. A hundred?"

"Be a hundred and one later this year. And I expect it's been close to half them years since anybody done walked up and asked me about Scott Joplin or the Maple Leaf Club. I'm thinkin' maybe you oughta go and see Mr. Tom Ireland, he live up the road a bit. Got a mem'ry like nobody's business about the ol' ragtime folk, and he'll talk your ear off all night, you give him half a chance." The old man pushed himself up off the bench, stretched, rubbed at his lower back. "Matter of fact, as you can see, I ain't got no pressin' business to hand, so I will take you to Tom's myself, if you like. That is, if you got no objection to goin' slow. I do walk a li'l lame these days." He waved at his friend on the bench.

The man returned the gesture. "See you later."

Tom Ireland! Alan's heart leaped. He remembered that name from *They All Played Ragtime*. And Brun Campbell, in his letter, had called Tom Ireland an old friend. "That sounds great." The boy extended a hand. "My name's Alan Chandler, and I came out from New Jersey for the ceremony. I love Scott Joplin's music, and I'm determined to get Mr. Campbell to give me some tips on how to play it right."

Again, the old man's muscles tightened, but

only for a moment. He gripped Alan's hand. "Isaac Stark. Most pleased to make your acquaintance."

Another familiar name.

But before Alan could say anything, the old man took him by the elbow. "Let's be on our way, then."

◇◇◇

Isaac led Alan back to Ohio and across the railroad tracks. At the first intersection, they turned left, walked a block to Osage, then turned right and continued on, past small houses, most with little gardens in front and to the sides. Isaac smiled at the boy. "Look a li'l different here, hey? This place, they call it Lincolnville."

Pretty clear why, Alan thought. Everyone they passed was Negro. And not a single person who caught sight of them failed to wave at Isaac, or call a greeting. "Looks like you know everybody," Alan said.

"Live in a place some sixty-seven years, that happens. It was 1884, I come here. Mr. Arthur was president, after they shot Mr. Garfield. Long time ago."

Alan tried to get his mind around the idea that this old man at his side was actually around and could recall what to him were no more than lines in a history book. "Then you must be able to remember when Lincoln was shot," the boy said.

Isaac's face went grave. "Saddest day in the life of a colored man," he said. "We was all 'fraid they was gonna put us back on the plantations… Well, there, yonder, that's Tom Ireland's house."

Alan's eyes followed the bony, knobbed finger. A man sat on the porch of what Alan would have called a small cabin, rocking slowly. As he saw his visitors come up the concrete walk to the porch, he stood, then shaded his eyes.

"'Afternoon, Tom," Isaac called. "I brung you a caller." He stepped onto the porch, Alan a half-step behind.

"I see that," said Ireland.

"He want to talk about Scott Joplin."

Ireland's bony face relaxed into a smile. "Well, I guess you knew where to bring him." He put out a hand to Alan. "Tom Ireland."

"Alan Chandler. I read about you in *They All Played Ragtime*. I'm really glad to meet you."

Ireland was slim, a light-skinned Negro with a prominent forehead and scooped-out cheeks. Alan figured him to be about seventy.

"Except for Mr. Rudi Blesh a couple of years ago, it's been a good while since anyone's come to talk to me about Scott Joplin," Ireland said.

"Well, this boy come all the way from New Jersey," Isaac said. "He's going to the ceremony

Tuesday night, and get a man called Brun Campbell to teach him how to play piana like Joplin."

Ireland's eyebrows rose. "I didn't know Brun was coming out. I hear from him now and again. He was a wild kid, rode a train to Sedalia from Oklahoma, the summer of 'ninety-nine, just about the time Joplin and John Stark signed their contract to publish 'Maple Leaf Rag.' As I recall, there was a good deal of commotion, and Brun was square in the middle of it somehow. He left town right after, pretty sudden."

Alan patted his book bag. "Mr. Joplin wrote all about that commotion in his journal. I read it on my way out here."

Ireland chewed his upper lip, just below the thin, gray mustache. "You're telling me you've got a journal of Scott Joplin's with you? How did you—"

"It's a long story, Mr. Ireland."

"I've got plenty of time."

Ireland and Isaac exchanged glances, then Ireland stepped toward the front door. "Come on in," he said. I'll start a pot of coffee, and you can tell me all about it. That is, if you don't mind."

"Oh, I don't mind at all. I'll tell you whatever you want to know. And you can tell me what you know about Scott Joplin."

Isaac laughed. "Boy, I don't think any one of us got enough time on earth for that."

◇◇◇

Alan thought the whole of Ireland's house would fit into his parents' living room. The boy sat on a scarred, straight-backed pine chair, balancing a coffee cup on a knee. Ireland and Isaac, side by side on similar chairs, listened as Alan told them how he happened to have Scott Joplin's journal, and why he'd brought it to Sedalia. He didn't tell the exact truth about where the five thousand dollars had come from; it seemed better to say Brun had wired it to him. But all the rest was the straight scoop.

When the boy finished, Ireland smiled genially. "Well, Alan that is some story. Hard to believe you beat out Rudi Blesh. That man's a demon, chasing down material he can write about. I'd say you did Brun Campbell proud."

Alan beamed. "Thank you."

"Where are you supposed to meet Mr. Campbell and give him the book?"

Alan shook his head. "He never did set a time and a place with me. Just told me he'd be out here for the ceremony."

Ireland laughed. "Well, that does sound like Brun. He never was what you'd call a planner. But you've got me curious. Would you let me have a look at the journal?"

"Sure, if you're interested." The boy picked

up the book bag from the floor between his feet, opened it, pulled out the journal. "Here."

Ireland took the book, then looked back to Alan. "I'd be most interested in seeing what he said about the commotion in Sedalia."

"I can find that part for you, if you'd like." Alan reached for the journal.

"I would," Ireland said. "I'd like that very much."

◇◇◇

The two Negroes worked their way slowly through three and a half handwritten pages, then looked at Alan.

"I was really surprised when I read that," the boy said. "There was nothing at all about it in *They All Played Ragtime.* And Mr. Stark, when you introduced yourself, back on Main Street, I recognized your name from in the journal. You worked for John Stark, Scott Joplin's publisher. Funny, you and he have the same last name."

"Nothing funny about it," Isaac said. "I took Mr. John Stark's name because of he did me a great kindness back in 'sixty-five."

Ireland held up the journal. "Okay if we look through this a little more?"

"You bet. Take your time. Then, will you tell me some of what you know about Scott Joplin?"

"I'll be glad to. Though I'm not sure I have anything as interesting as what you're showing me."

◇◇◇

The sun was low in the west when Ireland, Isaac, and Alan came out onto the little porch. Alan pulled his jacket closed, set the book bag between his legs, zipped the jacket. "I just can't thank you enough," he said to the two older men. "I feel almost like I know Scott Joplin personally. Maybe it'll help me play his music better."

Ireland raised a finger. "Just remember, 'Do not play this piece fast. It is never right to play ragtime fast.' If I heard him say that once, I heard it a hundred times."

"I'll remember. And I guess I'll see you at the ceremony Tuesday."

"Oh, yes. You can be sure of that."

The Negroes watched the white boy trot down the path, turn onto Osage, and march off in the direction of downtown. Then they walked back into the house. Ireland reloaded the coffee pot, put it onto the stovetop, and reached into the belly to stir up the fire.

Finally, Isaac said, "A man ain't never safe in this world, is he?"

Ireland shook his head sadly. "I never knew… was that really what happened?"

"Every word. We all swore never to talk about it to anybody. Poor Scott musta been bad-sick in his head that he'd even think about writin' down that stuff. But the business with Brun and the girl is news to me. No wonder he got himself outa town in such a hurry."

Ireland's brow wrinkled. "That girl still lives here. And Brun's coming to town for the ceremony? Oh, my."

"Tom, what on earth we gonna do?"

"I don't know. When the boy went out to the privy, I thought about ripping out those pages, but then he'd have known, and we'd be even worse off. We've got to get the journal away from him, the sooner, the better. Let him show that stuff around Sedalia, and they'll have those bodies dug up in nothing flat. And then what?"

"'Fraid I can imagine. Only thing worse'd be if Rudi Blesh got it, and put it in a book for the whole world to see."

Ireland poured coffee. He and Isaac sat across the kitchen table from each other, sipping, thinking.

They were on their second cups when Isaac said, "Best thing I can come up with, we keep a good eye on the boy, and just as soon as ever we can, we grab the book."

Ireland frowned. "Couple of problems there. For one thing, I'm eighty-five, and you're over a hundred. We're not going to outrun a teen-age boy. And for another thing, now that he knows us, it'd be tough to sneak up on him."

"Well, of course." Isaac was indignant. "You didn't let me finish up. How about we get Alonzo Green? All the stuff he used to do on the Q.T. all them years for the cops in Kans' City, he oughta be able to snatch a li'l book off a green kid. And I don't expect he'd mind makin' a few dollars for himself."

Ireland set down his cup, deliberated a moment. "I can't think of anything better." He pulled his watch from his pocket. "Six-thirty, Lonzo'll be home by now. Let's go have a word with him."

Chapter Fourteen

Saturday, April 14
Evening

This kind of job was why Alonzo Green gave up working for the police in Kay Cee. If an operation was a pebble in a cop's shoe or likely to turn messy, all he had to do to keep his nose clean and his ass warm was slip the colored guy a few bills under the table. Alonzo had wiggled himself into a gang setting up to knock off a bank. He'd stood out-of-doors for hours in twenty-degree weather, watching for some stud who'd been too handy with a knife. Corraled a girl who'd run off from a farm to have a little fun in the big city. Tailed a newspaperman who was working on a story of police corruption, took pictures of the bozo in a cathouse. No wonder he got to deciding he'd do better to run a little farm, raise a few chickens, grow vegetables. But there were no better men on earth than Tom Ireland and Isaac Stark, and if they said it was important to get their hands on a journal some white kid was carrying around, then Alonzo would find them that journal. He'd made off with a whole lot more in his time than some dead musician's diary.

The kid was brand-new in town, so likely he was either laying low, waiting for that old guy to come in from The Coast, or walking around, trying to find some other people connected with the ceremony. Green figured to start with the streets. A man with coal-black skin and hair like steel wool couldn't exactly walk through white hotel lobbies and ask clerks if they had a white boy staying there, name of Alan Chandler, he was carrying a dark blue book bag you couldn't get off him with pliers.

Green strolled up Ohio, looking both ways, seeing no one who fit the kid's description. At Fifth, he turned right, walked the half-block to the Liberty Theatre, went inside and scanned the square-dance crowd. No luck. Back out to Ohio, across the street, and into the doorway of Beverly's Snack Shop. He shaded his eyes. Fair bunch of kids in the booths, but no one he hadn't seen before. A pretty young waitress came up to him, little white hat perched to the right side of her head. "I'm sorry, sir," she said. "We aren't allowed to serve colored here."

Green bit on his tongue, nodded, turned away. Outside, he took a moment to cool down and get his mind back onto his work. Saturday nights, a lot of kids went to the Wheel Inn, over on Broadway, to dance to the jukebox. The detective walked back through the thinning crowds along Ohio to the corner of Main, where he got into his 'thirty-six Ford, drove to Broadway and into the Wheel Inn lot.

The instant he was out of the car, music enveloped him. Glenn Miller, "In the Mood." Vanilla ice cream crap. He strolled up to the round building, topped by an oversized wagon wheel, then peered through the plate glass. All the tables were filled; kids covered every inch of the dance floor. Green saw the Klein girl, jitterbugging with the Gardiner boy, big-shot high-school football player. The dark man shook his head. When a man's wife cheats on him, or his daughter goes whoring around, he's the last person to ever find out. God's mercy, Green thought. If Otto Klein ever found out what his daughter did nights, he'd beat her to jelly.

But there was no sign of the person he'd come for. Green checked his watch, near eleven. Time to pack it in. Get some sleep, start fresh in the morning.

◇◇◇

After Alan left Tom Ireland's house, he walked back across the railroad tracks into downtown. Coming up on Main Street, he got a heavy whiff of good cooking, so he followed his nose to the red-brick Pacific Café, went inside, sat at an empty table. He slid his book bag across the table top, then looked around. Every wall was covered with framed photographs of major-league baseball players. Some, Alan had no trouble recognizing from his seat, Joe DiMaggio, Babe Ruth, Pee Wee Reese. Stan Musial, bat cocked, seemed to have a place of honor, occupying an entire wall panel at eye level. Well, sure, this was St. Louis territory.

The waitress, a thin, gray-haired woman in a flowered apron, flashed him a motherly smile as she handed him the menu. "You from out of town, young man?"

Alan nodded. "Yes, ma'am, I just got in from New Jersey." The boy's gut punctuated his sentence with a gurgle.

The woman laughed. "Sounds like you could use some of our chicken-fried steak and mashed potatoes. We make our own white gravy from scratch, and it's the best in Missoura. Tastes even better than it smells."

When Alan finished the heap of food, the waitress told him he wouldn't be sorry if he topped off his meal with a piece of their own apple pie, a la mode, the only way to have it, and no, he wasn't sorry. As he paid the bill, he asked the cashier if there was a good hotel nearby, nothing fancy, just clean.

"Sure is," she told him. "The Milner'll do you. Outside the door, you go left, cross Ohio, then go another block to Lamine, and you're right there."

Alan thanked her, followed her directions, and was up in his room a quarter-hour before Alonzo Green began to look for him. He considered going back down to the lobby to watch the western movie they had on the TV, but once in the room, all the excitement of the past two days hit him. The boy took off his clothes, stood under a warm shower, then hit the bed and didn't see the world again until almost nine o'clock next morning.

◇◇◇

As the boy left his room to hunt up breakfast, it occurred to him to stash his book bag in the dresser drawer, but he shook his head, no. He'd heard about maids going through peoples' stuff in hotel rooms.

The Pacific Café's pancakes and eggs sounded really good, but so did the biscuits and gravy; he resolved the dilemma by ordering the first with a side of the second. Smart choice. They sure did know how to cook in Sedalia, and they weren't skimpy with their servings. He paid his bill, then walked out. and up West Main, past the entrance to the Main Street Cigar Store, where a dark man in a bashed tan fedora idly thumbed through magazines in a wire rack.

Now what? The streets and sidewalks were deserted, and from every direction came the sound of church bells. Alan wished he had at least some idea of when Mr. Campbell was due in. Maybe there'd be a reception for him, a bunch of people at the railroad station, rolling out a long red carpet and cheering as he stepped off the train.

The boy retraced his steps along Main, then turned the corner. The colored man at the magazine rack stepped out of the doorway and smiled as he watched Alan cross the street and go into the MoPac Station.

Inside the station, the boy walked up to the ticket window. Different clerk from yesterday, good. "What time does the train from Los Angeles come in?"

The clerk smiled. "Expecting somebody, sonny?"

"My grandpa."

"Didn't he tell you what train he'd be on?"

Alan shook his head. "He just said he'd be here today."

The clerk's face went sour. "I swan, people today! Well, from Los Angeles, your grandpa's gonna have to change in Kans' City, and there'll be more'n one train come in there from L. A. So I really don't know what to tell you. Sorry."

"That's okay," Alan said. "Thanks anyway."

He walked out into what was developing into a sunny day. pulled his jacket tighter around himself, zipped it. He wanted to do something, felt as if he had to do *something*.

His eyes fell on a sign at the street corner: Liberty Park, with an arrow below the words. On Sundays back home, sometimes he'd go up to Eastside Park, play some tennis, go to the carousel with the big organ, have some ice cream or popcorn. Some Sundays, there were concerts on the bandstand. He hurried back inside. "How do I get to Liberty Park, please?" he asked the ticket clerk.

The man eyed him. "Bit of a walk."

"I don't mind."

The clerk pointed outside. "Go down to Third, then turn right and keep on walking. Liberty Park starts at the corner of Third and Park. You miss it, you need to get yourself some glasses."

Alan thanked him, and went out. All the way down Third, the boy and the dark man moved in tandem, two blocks between them.

◇◇◇

Liberty Park was pretty, but not much was happening, just a couple of families enjoying picnics on the grass. Maybe after church was out, it'd get livelier. Alan walked toward the lake, where ducks and geese fed at water's edge, found a comfortable spot under a maple tree just coming into leaf. He sat against the tree, opened the book bag and took out the journal. Might as well have another read, see if he'd missed anything important.

Alonzo Green hunkered down behind a giant maple next to the bandstand. Damn, if those picnickers were just a little farther away, he could amble over and make like a snake, grab the book out of the kid's hands, and take off. But if the kid gave him any trouble, or started yelling, the picnickers could decide to have themselves a little Sunday coon-chase. Alonzo told himself to cool off. He'd been on stakeouts a lot longer than this one.

An hour and a half later, the kid closed the book, slipped it into the bag. Green started to stand, but then the kid put the bag under his head and stretched out on the grass. Green couldn't see whether his eyes were open or shut. Didn't matter. He had to wait this one out.

◇◇◇

While Alan lay under Green's surveillance, daydreaming about how grateful Brun Campbell was going to be and how he might show that gratitude, a mountain of a Negro man, neatly dressed in a dark suit, white shirt, Navy-blue tie, and black derby got off the train from St. Louis. He wasn't about to admit it to anybody, but it did make him nervous, coming out to this little burg in the middle of Noplace, Missouri to scratch around and find a white boy with five thousand dollars. No question, people were going to notice him, and he wondered whether he should've dressed down a bit. Nah, probably not. Any way he dressed, the Reubens weren't going to miss a six-foot, six-inch, three hundred-pound colored man who shows up out of nowhere. If he was lucky, he'd get his business done in a hurry, and if he was really lucky, the kid would still have the money on him. But if he'd already bought the book from this Mrs. Joplin, wherever the hell she lived, he'd take the little bastard there by the ear, and get back the dough.

Slim followed the crowd out of the terminal. He felt one small step away from starving. That stuff on trains they call food looks and smells like somebody already ate it and it came outa one end or the other. First move, he'd get a good meal inside of him, and then he'd find a place to stay. He scanned the crowd, saw a young colored man in a slick yellow suit, derby to match. Slim hustled up, tugged at his arm. The dude spun, hand inside his suit jacket in nothing flat. Man's got a problem, Slim thought. Best it don't get to be mine. He smiled. "Sorry, didn't mean to make you nervous. You know where a man can get some decent food here on a Sunday?"

The young man relaxed. His pencil-thin mustache spread even thinner. "If'n you was white, I could tell you a lotta places. But since you ain't, I'll take you by Davis' Café, over on East Main, I gotta go that way anyhow. Maybe it ain't the Ritz, but 'least you won't get poisoned."

Slim tipped his hat. "Much obliged."

◇◇◇

The big man leaned back in his chair and burped louder than he'd intended. The pork chops and gravy had gone down real easy, and the custard pie hadn't been any trouble, either. He waved at the waitress, a chubby young woman with ebony hair halfway down her back. Girl must spend half her tips on Mrs. C. W. Walker's hair straightener.

She smiled at Slim. "Bring you something more?"

He shook his head. "Just the tab. And if you can tell me which hotel I oughta be goin' to, I'd be obliged."

The waitress gave him a long, hard look. "You ain't from 'round here, are you?"

"No, I'm just in from N' Jersey. Why you askin'?"

"'Cause if you was from these parts, you'd know you ain't gonna be stayin' at no hotel."

"That's how it is here? I thought I was comin' to Missoura, not Miss'ippi."

The waitress jutted a hip. "Listen, Mister, I been to Miss'ippi, and it ain't nothin' here like it is there. Colored and white gets along pretty good in Sedalia, we don't have no trouble. Long as you knows your place and stays there, you be fine. But a wise-mouth nigger's gonna go back to Jersey without the teeth he came here with. Now…" She pointed toward the street. "You just take you'self down Main to Kentucky, 'bout three blocks. Right past the feed store, you go up the li'l stairway, and that be Olive Simmons' place. She gonna give you a good, clean room, seventy-five cents a night. An' that be ninety cents for your dinner."

Slim pulled a small roll of bills from his pocket, put one in the woman's hand, then replaced the bills and brought out a handful of change. "Keep the dime, and here's another quarter for your kindness."

The waitress' face brightened. "Wish we had more like you here, Mister."

"Ain't no more like me any place." The big man threw back his head and laughed.

◇◇◇

He trudged along Main Street, glancing right and left. Sad-lookin' burg, no wonder that girl got so happy over a quarter. A man could live here a whole lot cheaper'n in New Jersey, that is if you could call it livin'. Slim's legs felt weighted, his suitcase heavy. After that long damn train ride, and with a belly-full of food, he had himself a good case of the Sunday afternoon drowsies. Before he did anything else, he'd go get that room at Miz Simmons' and grab a nap.

He crossed Ohio, not a moving car in sight, and walked slowly along West Main. But at the corner of Osage, his fatigue suddenly vanished. Halfway down the block, coming right at him, there was that boy. Alan. Carrying some kind of blue knapsack…hold on. He's setting down the sack. Tying his shoelace.

Slim's eyes bulged. His nostrils flared, then he dropped his suitcase, took off across Osage, and as he approached the boy, went into overdrive. Alan looked up, saw the huge man bearing down on him, grabbed his book bag and started to run, but Slim caught him from behind, spun him around, then steadied him on his feet and turned on a grin the size of Texas. "Well, now, Mr. Alan Chandler, what a surprise we got here. Fancy us just chancin' to meet like this in Sedalia, Missouri."

Alan tried to wrench away, but Slim had a firm hold on both his arms. If that lad was white before, the big man thought, now he be bleached. Slim shoved him against the wall next to the window of the Main Street Cigar Store. "Boy, you just hold you'self real still now, or you gonna be sorry you ever was born." Slim pulled back the lapel of his jacket, just enough to show a pistol in a holster. "Make one bad move, and it be the last move you ever make. Now. I do b'lieve you got something in that bag there for me."

Alan clutched the book bag to his chest. "You wouldn't shoot me right here on the street."

Slim's jaw fell. Kid had moxie, give him that. "Look here, boy," a growl. "You take just one step to run off, you ain't never again gonna walk on them legs. Anybody sees, I gonna tell 'em I be a detective from Jersey, Dr. Broaca hired me to get back the five thousand dollars you stole offa him. Then you can go back home and spend the resta your life in a wheelchair." Slim extended a hand. "Now, gimme here, real nice and easy." He grabbed for the book bag.

Alan swung the bag to the side. "Get away from me, or I'll yell for help. I don't have the money."

"You got that book then." Slim wiggled fingers. "That'll do. Gimme."

"Hell I will. *Help! Help!*"

The boy dodged to the left, but ran squarely into Slim's fist. He reeled back against the brick wall, then sank by degrees to the sidewalk. Slim yanked out the pistol, pointed it at Alan's face. "I swear, boy, you have got me real close on my limit. You try shoutin' or runnin' again, you be full of lead."

Alan shook his head, tried to focus his eyes.

Slim squatted, tore the book bag from the boy's hand. But as he got to his feet, he heard, "Hands up, Nigger. Quick."

Slim turned, pistol in one hand, book bag in the other. A rangy man with blue eyes and blond hair spilling down from under the bill of a blue baseball cap stood ten feet away, pointing a large gray pistol squarely at the black man's chest. "Drop 'em both," the intruder growled. "And put up your hands. I ain't known much for my patience, and I ain't gonna miss a fat piece of shit like you."

Slim opened his fingers. The book bag thumped to the sidewalk, the gun beside it.

The white man gestured with his pistol. "Okay, now. Get your hands up on that wall and keep 'em there. Turn your head and I'll blow it off." He swept up Slim's gun, stuffed it into his pocket.

Slim glanced sidewise at Alan, spat on the boy, then slowly moved into position.

Alan pushed himself to a crouch, grabbed the book bag, pulled it toward him. The white man bent over him, put fingers to his face. Alan winced.

"Just a cut lip," the white man said. "Lucky for you
I come outa the restaurant right then. What the
hell's that buck want with you, anyway?"

Alan pointed at the book bag. "I think he's
crazy, sir. He says there's five thousand dollars in
here, and he wants it."

"Listen here," Slim shouted, being careful not
to turn his head. "I come out from New Jersey to
get back—"

The white man's eyes narrowed to slits. "Shut
it. When somebody's pointin' a gun at you, you
speak only when spoken to. Now, get your black
lard-ass the hell outa here. If you got a brain in
that thick head, you'll be on the next train to New
Jersey."

Slim lowered his hands, flashed Alan a look
that sent the boy edging backward, then started to
walk away. As he crossed Osage and snatched up
his suitcase, the white man waggled his gun, and
called, "Keep going. Train station's a block down
and across the tracks."

Alan got to his feet. He and his rescuer watched
Slim vanish around the corner. The white man put
away his gun, then cleared his throat. "That true,
what he said? You come out from Jersey with five
thousand dollars in that bag?"

Alan paused just long enough to bring a tight
smile to the man's face. "No, 'course not. I'm out

here for the Scott Joplin ceremony Tuesday night, and I've got a journal that Mr. Joplin wrote. I'm going to—"

The man laughed in his throat. "Tell you what. You had dinner yet?"

"That's why I was coming along here. I had supper last night at the Pacific Café, and I was starting to get hungry, so I decided to go back there."

The man draped an arm around Alan's shoulders. "Come on, I'll stand you to dinner."

"Oh, you don't have to do that," Alan said. "You did plenty for me already. Besides, you already ate."

The man waved him off. "We got pride in our city, and we don't feel right when a stranger who comes out to visit gets slugged by a nigger. So, figure dinner on the house is Sedalia's way of sayin' we're sorry. I'll have another cup of coffee, and while you're eatin', you can tell me the rest of why you're here and what-all you got there in the bag." He put out a hand. "I'm Jerry Barton."

The boy gave Barton's hand a quick shake. "Alan Chandler. I'm glad to meet you, Mr. Barton."

"Jerry'll do. Pleasure's mine, Alan."

◇◇◇

Slim marched far enough up Osage to be sure he was out of sight. Then he set down his suitcase, took a pack of cigarettes from his shirt pocket, tapped out a smoke, absently slipped it between his lips. Before he could get to his matches, a very dark Negro in a well-worn tan fedora walked up to him, flicked a lighter, and reached up to light Slim's smoke. Slim nodded. "Thanks."

The Negro nodded, replaced the lighter into his pocket. "You don't mind me sayin' so, Mister, that was not real clever of you. Tryin' to do that boy right there on West Main Street, an' in broad daylight."

Slim's eyes flared, but the fire receded quickly. "I come all the way out from Jersey to find the kid, and not an hour after I get to town, I walk right into him on the street. So, yeah, I got hasty. Sheet! Shoulda drug him in an alley, sapped him, and just took...just left him there."

"What's that boy matter to you, huh?"

Slim took a moment to study the man's face, but got no enlightenment. "He stole a bunch of money from my boss, and my boss think I done it. He say 'less I get it back, I don't have a job no more."

The dark man shrugged. "I think if a man tell me I stole his money and I didn't, I'd just tell him where to put his job."

Slim wondered whether he ought to come clean, but decided he'd already been dumb once that afternoon, which was one time too many. "I thought about doing that," he said. "But there's more to the story."

The dark man adjusted his hat. "Seems like there always be more to a story. Like that boy gave your boss' five grand to Scott Joplin's widow, and now he's got Joplin's personal journal in his book bag."

Slim's cigarette dropped to the ground. "How you know that? Who you be, anyway?"

"Alonzo Green." The man stuck out a hand. "And you."

"Slim Sanders. But you still ain't told me how you know—"

"I'm working for a man here, he wants that journal bad." Green pointed down the block to where wooden soda bottle cases stood in piles in front of a brick storefront. "Come on, take a load off, an' let's do a li'l talkin'. We can see from over there when the boy comes out, and whether his friend's stayin' with him. Oh, and by the by, it's a good thing you didn't mess with that man. There ain't a better shot in all Pettis County than Jerry Barton, and he wouldn't give a first thought, never mind a second one, to air-conditioning a nigger."

"So you do got white trash," Slim said. "I'd been thinking, people here're really nice."

"Most of 'em are," said Green. "But I ain't sure you can rightly call Barton white trash. He runs one of the biggest wheat farms in the county. Got him some livestock too."

"Sometimes trash come wrapped in a pretty package," Slim growled.

Green laughed. "Ain't gonna argue that."

◇◇◇

While Alan wolfed down a heap of meat loaf and potatoes, he told his rescuer something close to the real story. "Mr. Brun Campbell was Scott Joplin's only white pupil," the boy said. "And he'll be here for the ceremony Tuesday night, to honor Scott Joplin. Do you know about it?"

Barton smiled. "Well, sure. You already said that's the reason you came out."

Alan swallowed a mouthful. "Yes, sir. And Mr. Campbell wants to do better for Mr. Joplin than just hanging a plaque in the high school. He says he could use Mr. Joplin's journal to get people talking about putting up a statue of Mr. Joplin, and maybe even starting up a ragtime museum. So he asked me to get the journal from Mr. Joplin's widow in New York, and bring it out to him."

Both pairs of eyes went to the book bag in Alan's lap. "And you got that journal in there," said Barton.

Alan nodded, and without thinking, pulled the bag in closer to his body.

The motion was not lost on Barton. "Well, that's really interesting. But why did that colored man think you had five thousand dollars in there?"

Alan laughed. "Well, I did, back in New York. I gave it to Mrs. Joplin, to pay for the journal."

"You did? Five thousand dollars?" Barton loosed a low whistle. "You don't mind me asking, where'd a kid like you…I mean, how old are you?"

"Seventeen."

Barton half-closed one eye. "Hmmm. Not many folks ever get to have five thousand bucks to spare their whole lives long. Not to be nosy, but how'd you ever come up with that kind of scratch?"

"I guess Mr. Campbell's got money to burn. He said he didn't want to send it straight to Mrs. Joplin, 'cause she's pretty old and sick. Besides, he didn't want to take a chance that the journal might get lost in the mail. So he told me if I would go get it and bring out here, he'd wire me the five thousand, and also pay my train fare."

"When are you supposed to meet him?"

"I'm not sure. He just said to get the journal, and he'd meet me here."

Barton kept his response to a bland smile. Was he supposed to believe a man would wire a boy five thousand dollars to bring a book out from New Jersey to Missouri, and not set up a time and place to meet him? But what kind of idiot would spend anything like that kind of money on a diary from some spade who played piano in cat houses fifty years ago? "What about the big colored guy, the one who said you stole the money off his boss?" Barton asked. "Why was he hasslin' you?"

"He's a detective," Alan said. "From back in New Jersey…well, all right. My parents weren't going to let me come out here all by myself, so I ran off without their permission. My father hired that guy to come here and drag me back home."

Barton grinned. "You didn't just happen to run off with five thousand of your old man's dollars, did you?"

"No! I told you, Mr. Campbell sent it. But that was another thing. My parents were afraid I'd get robbed or maybe even killed, carrying all that money around." Alan scooped the last bit of potato onto his fork, licked it off, pushed his plate aside.

Barton signaled the waitress. Alan and he were now the only customers in the restaurant. As the girl came up to the table, Barton said, "I think this young man could do with a piece of your world-famous apple pie. Fact, I suspect he could also put away a scoop of ice cream to go with it." He shifted his gaze to Alan, winked.

"I'll give it my best," Alan said.

The waitress fluttered her eyelashes at him, blushed, then walked off. Barton watched her all the way back to the counter. "You've got a way with the ladies," he said.

Now, Alan blushed. "I don't know."

Barton reached across the table to punch his arm lightly. "Coming out half-way across the country all by yourself, to bring that journal out here? I'd say you are a most determined young man."

"I am that, sir, though I guess my mother would say I'm just stubborn. Whatever, when I set my mind to do something, it's pretty hard to stop me."

"I'll warrant that. But why are you so bound to do this?"

"It's the music, Mr…Jerry. The first time I heard ragtime, I was hooked. Mr. Campbell's been writing to me, telling me how to play it, and when he asked if I'd help him out with this ceremony, I jumped at the chance. It's something I'll remember all my life."

Barton grinned again. "Must be great to be young, and have that kind of enthusiasm. I can't say I care much for any kind of music myself, but on the other hand, I know if a man's community don't prosper, neither will he. So, I do what I can to make my community prosper. If a museum's going to bring in bunches of tourists, then I'm all for that museum. That's why I'm on the committee for the ceremony you've been talking about."

"You are? Really?"

Barton grinned again. "Cross my heart."

Alan shifted forward in his seat, leaned across the table. "I've been hoping I'd find somebody like you while I'm waiting for Mr. Campbell. Maybe *I* could play a piece in the ceremony, you know, show the people that it's not just old men who like ragtime. If a white kid from New Jersey goes up on the stage and plays 'Maple Leaf Rag,' I bet the newspapers would notice that, and so would the radio station Mr. Campbell said was going to broadcast the whole thing."

Barton's eyes widened; he nodded in time with Alan's speech. "You know, you just might have something there. Tell you what. The committee's having a meeting tonight, and I'll talk to them. Bet they'll be interested."

"You'd do that for me? You haven't even heard me play piano."

Barton noticed that the boy's growing passion did nothing to loosen his hold on the bag in his lap. The waitress smiled as she set a piece of pie in front of him, twice the usual size, with a monster scoop of vanilla ice cream on top, but he barely thanked the girl. His eyes locked with Barton's.

"Put it this way, Alan," Barton said. "A boy as determined as you ain't likely to be blowing smoke about how he can play piana. 'Cause he knows if he can't deliver the goods, there's no way he's gonna be able to fake it. So, I figure I'm looking at good odds. Where're you staying?"

Alan took a moment to swallow a mouthful of pie. "Milner Hotel, over on East Second Street. Why?"

"'Cause you don't have to spend your money on a hotel. You can stay at my place."

"Oh, no, I couldn't put you out like that."

"Won't be any trouble at all. I've got a farm off toward Smithton, a little way down the road, and there's plenty of room. It's just me living there. You don't think that colored detective actually did run off and get on a train, do you? Bunk at my house, and you won't have to worry about him sneaking up on you again. Next time he tries, I might not be around to help."

Alan nodded. "It sure was good luck you were here this time."

"It sure was. My old man always used to say, better lucky than good."

Alan put away another chunk of pie. "I guess it makes sense, if it really wouldn't be any trouble."

Barton laughed out loud. "This ain't the east coast, Alan. Out here, folks go outa their way to make a stranger welcome." He brushed hair back from in front of his eyes, then pushed back from the table. "Okay, then, it's settled. I'll take you by

the Milner, and you can check out. Then we'll go
back to my place."

◇◇◇

From behind stacks of soda-bottle cases, two col-
ored men, one small, one large, watched Barton and
Alan get into a red Chevy pickup, drive off down
Osage, then turn left on Second. Green nodded to
Slim, then motioned: come on.

◇◇◇

Barton walked to a tan vinyl armchair next to a
fan, opposite the desk in the Milner Hotel lobby.
"Go on up, get your things," he said to Alan. "I'll
wait here for you."

The boy nodded. "I might be a few minutes.
I'm going to call my parents and tell them I'm all
right, and I'll be staying with you. Maybe that'll get
them to take Slim off my back."

Barton broke into laughter. "Slim, huh? That's
what you call him?"

Alan turned away quickly, before the panic on
his face could give him away. Lucky that Barton
thought Alan had just made up the nickname as a
joke. He'd have to watch his step.

Barton watched the boy climb the stairs. This
was one nervy kid, pretty damn good at playing
fast and loose with truth. But if he thought for one
minute that Barton believed he was going to call

his parents, he was mistaken, sorely so. Clever little move to put Barton on notice that someone would know where he was staying, but the last people in the world a runaway kid would call were the mother and father who'd put a detective on his tail.

◇◇◇

Up in Room 214, Alan locked the door, sat on the bed, closed his eyes, thought hard. Then he picked up the phone receiver, and asked the desk clerk for the long distance operator. When he heard "Long distance, number, please," he said, "Hobart, New Jersey. Lambert 8-4144."

The phone rang once, twice, three times. "Be there, the boy murmured. Please be—"

"Broaca residence. This is Mir—"

"Miriam, oh boy. Am I glad you're home."

"Alan? Are you in Sedalia? Did you get the journal okay? What's going on? Listen, I've got to tell you something."

"Miriam, Miriam, hold on. Let me talk, okay?"

"I'm so glad to hear your voice, Alan. I wish I could see you."

"Could anyone there be listening in?"

"On Sunday afternoon? You've got to be kidding. My parents are off playing golf. But my father found out the money was gone. He had a little string tied so if anyone opened the suitcase, it'd break. He accused Slim of stealing the money, and fired him, and then Slim went off with Sally, I don't know where."

"Well, *I* know where Slim is. He's here."

"In Sedalia? How did he know to go to Sedalia?"

"Beats me. But he found me, told me he wanted the five thousand dollars back that I stole from your father, and if I didn't have it, then he wanted Scott Joplin's journal. And he had a gun."

"Oh, God. What happened? Did you give him the journal?"

"No. We were out on the street, and a man came along, saw what was happening, and got the drop on Slim. The man took away Slim's gun, and told him to get lost."

"Oh, no. Slim will be furious. I've got to talk to him."

"Slim *is* furious, and there's no way you can talk to him. But the man who got me away is on the committee for the ceremony. He's offered to let me stay at his house. I just wanted to tell you what's happening, and see if you know how Slim managed to find me."

"I don't have any idea. But he's not somebody you want to fool around with."

"No kidding. But I should be okay as long

as I'm with Mr. Barton. He's the man who helped me, Jerry Barton. He's got a farm out of town, near some place called Smithton, so I won't even be in the city. Slim won't know where to look for me."

"Alan, you don't know Slim."

"Listen, this is going to cost a fortune. I better go. I'll try to call you again when I get the chance."

"Alan—"

"I'll call you again. 'Bye."

As Miriam heard the line click dead, she slammed down the receiver, jumped out of the chair, pounded a fist on the wall. "Oh, Slim will kill him." She launched a shriek, no one in the house to hear it other than the shrieker, which inflamed her all the more. She wiped a sleeve savagely across her eyes. The minute her parents got home, she'd talk to her father, and then, when Alan called again, she'd tell him to tell Slim she'd confessed. That would take care of the immediate problem. As for what might come later, she'd figure it out then.

◇◇◇

Behind the registration counter of the Milner Hotel, the desk clerk pulled the headphones from his ears, set them onto the counter, and leaned across. "Hey, Jerry," he called in a stage whisper. "Better come over here a minute."

Barton trotted over, listened to the clerk's

throaty narrative, then muttered, "God damn that little bastard," and reached for the telephone at the end of the counter."

◇◇◇

Alan replaced the receiver, flopped back onto the pillow, stared at the ceiling. How the hell did Slim know he was going to Sedalia? The boy shook his head. Things were getting complicated. But he was where he wanted to be, he still had the journal, and now he had someone to help him until he could find Brun Campbell. He'd even wangled a shot at getting himself onto the program. He jumped to the floor, ran into the bathroom, picked up his toothbrush and toothpaste, threw them into the book bag along with his extra shirt and underwear, and ran out of the room and back down the stairs.

◇◇◇

Out on the sidewalk in front of the hotel, Barton suddenly stopped walking and slapped the side of his head. "Doggone, I just remembered. I ain't gonna have room for you, darn it. My aunt and her husband and three kids are coming in for a visit later today." He turned a sheepish grin on Alan, then gave the boy a conspiratorial nudge to the arm. "Guess that's something I didn't really want to remember, huh?"

Alan shrugged. "That's okay. I'll just go back

to the hotel. I can keep my eyes open for Slim."

Barton reached for the boy's arm. "I've got a better idea. I'll take you to Otto Klein's. His wife and him'll be glad to put you up."

Alan shook his head. "I don't want to trouble them. I mean, I don't even know them."

"It won't be any trouble. Otto Klein's on the ceremony committee too, and I know he'll want to hear about that journal of yours." Barton gave Alan a gentle push toward the truck at the curb." Come on. I'll drive you over to Kleins'."

◇◇◇

Green and Slim watched the man and the boy drive off down Lamine. "They's turnin' left on Fifth," Green said. "That ain't the way to Barton's place. God knows where he's taking the kid."

Slim made a face, muttered something Green couldn't make out. He tugged at the big man's arm. "Let's see if we can't catch up to them."

As they turned off Lamine onto East Fifth, Green tapped Slim's arm. "Look there."

Slim shaded his eyes. "Truck's parked just a few blocks down, an' they's gettin' out…goin' up to a house." The men quickened their pace.

Green motioned Slim to stop at the corner of Fifth and Washington, a half-block up from the red Chevy truck. "Don't want to take a chance either of them might see you," Green said. "You wait here. Be right back."

◇◇◇

As Barton rang the doorbell of the little white frame house on East Fifth Street, he said to Alan, "You'll like staying here. Otto and Rowena are the best sort of people. And they got a daughter, nice girl, just about your age."

The door opened. Alan looked at a fireplug of a man with a bullet head, short-cropped hair in full retreat over a sloping forehead. He wore a blue denim shirt and a pair of old dungarees, torn at one knee. "Hi, there, Otto," Barton said. "This boy here's come all the way from New Jersey for that ceremony Tuesday night, and he needs a place to stay. Alan… dang, I'm sorry. What'd you say your last name is?"

"Chandler." Alan hitched the blue carrying bag up onto his left shoulder.

"Right. Alan Chandler, this's Otto Klein. Like I said, he's also on the committee. Otto, I'll bet my farm you're gonna be interested in hearing what this young man has to say."

Klein showed yellowed teeth. "Well, now, if you say so, Jerry, I'm sure I will. And no trouble puttin' him up while he's here." He clapped a ham of a hand onto Alan's shoulder. "Come on in, boy, and let's hear it."

◇◇◇

Slim watched Green saunter along Fifth, pause briefly between the truck and the house it was parked in front of, then disappear around the next corner. A few minutes later, he reappeared on Washington, and walked quickly up to Slim. The big man hunched his shoulders. "So?"

"So the name on the mailbox there is Klein. That'd be Otto Klein. Him an' Barton, they's ham an' eggs, if you figure there's worms in the ham and the eggs is spoilt. Wonder what the hell they're up to."

"What do we do now?"

Green pulled a package of cigarettes from his pocket, tapped out two smokes, gave one to Slim, struck a match on his shoe. "Guess we gonna wait an' see what develops."

◇◇◇

In Otto Klein's living room, Barton sat next to Alan on a sofa with a spectacularly-garish cover of green, yellow, and white swirls. Alan could almost hear his mother sniff. "Peasants!" Klein sat on a matching armchair opposite his visitors. The boy took care to tell his host the same story he'd told Barton earlier, but all the while he talked, he had trouble keeping his eyes off the framed color print of Christ on the wall behind Klein, the Savior's eyes turned toward heaven, his hands clasped in apparent fervent prayer.

When Alan finished, Klein said "My, my, my," then shifted his attention to Barton. "So, Jerry, what do you think about that diary?"

Barton shrugged. "Can't really think anything about something I ain't seen."

Klein raised an eyebrow, then grinned and extended a hand in Alan's direction. "Well, come on, then, boy. Let's have us a look-see."

Alan glanced toward the door.

"Mr. Klein's right." Barton's words flowed like melted butter. "Sounds like that book could be the biggest thing at the ceremony, but how are we supposed to get it in the program without us ever seein' it? We ain't got a whole lot of time. Got a meeting tonight, and then tomorrow we do the final preparations."

Alan tightened his grip on the book bag. The day before, he'd felt certain he could get the journal back from two ancient colored men, but here, in Klein's living room, with a couple of very able-bodied Joes, the boy's confidence was far from complete. "I don't know…just seems like I should show it to Mr. Campbell first."

"Do that, and it'll be too late," said Klein. "Programs're set to be printed up tomorrow morning, and Mr. Campbell ain't comin' in till late tomorrow."

"Did he tell you that?" Alan asked.

Klein nodded. "He called me up a couple weeks ago. Said he'd be in the night before the ceremony."

Mr. Campbell doesn't have a phone, at least not a listed one, Alan thought. But I guess he could've called from a phone booth.

Barton leaned toward the boy. "Think a little bit about what Mr. Campbell's gonna say when he finds out he coulda had that book mentioned in the program." Barton motioned toward the bag. "You need to give Mr. Klein and me a look."

Alan hesitated, then opened the bag and pulled out the journal as if careless handling might cause it to explode. Klein reached to take it, but Alan shifted to the right, toward Barton, and motioned Klein to sit at his left.

Klein looked like an urchin in a candy store who'd just been told to keep his hands behind his back. "You don't trust us or something?"

"It's not that," Alan said. "I'm sorry, but I promised Mr. Campbell I wouldn't let this journal out of my sight or my hands, not for anything. I'll turn the pages for you." He opened the diary to the first page.

He'd turned five pages when Barton said, "I

guess that's enough. Gives us something to talk about at the meeting tonight."

Klein grinned. "How about we take Alan along, and he tells them about the book?"

Barton seemed to be chewing a cud. "He wants to play piana at the ceremony, too. Ain't that right, Alan?"

"If I could, sure."

"So maybe it'd be better if just you and me talk to the committee tonight, Otto. Couple of those guys can be pretty touchy if they think somebody's tryin' to squeeze them. If they're interested, there'll still be time in the morning to get him on the program."

Klein looked dubious. "Well, okay, if you think." He hauled himself off the sofa. "Let me go get my wife and daughter. They can show you your room."

"You sure it's not a problem, Mr. Klein? I wouldn't want to put you out."

Klein waved off the concern. "No trouble at all."

He walked through a swinging door on the far side of the living room, then came back with two women in tow. The older one was thin, pale-faced, with mousy hair drawn severely back, and lips drawn as tight as the hair. The daughter, on the other hand…well, Alan had seen her before, hadn't he, and she was just as pretty now as then. Big brown eyes, creamy skin, dark curls down over her shoulders. "Alan," Klein said. "I'd like to have you meet my wife and my daughter, Eileen. This here's Mr. Alan Chandler, darlings. He's in from New Jersey for that big ceremony, you know, and he's gonna stay with us for a few days. Maybe you could show him the guest room."

Alan thought Mrs. Klein's wan smile took every ounce of effort she could muster. Eileen gave the boy's hand a polite squeeze. "Sure, Daddy, I'll be glad to." She motioned Alan along. "Mama, you don't need to come. I can show him the room."

"All right, dear, thank you. Don't forget to give him towels."

"I won't, Mama."

She led Alan up a straight staircase, and down a hall into a room with a bed, a plain pine desk and chair, and a couple of bookcases. The bed was covered with an orange, blue, and yellow spread, different from the color scheme that ruled the living room, but no less awful. On the headboard lay a Bible, and directly above where the head of a sleeper would be, another polychrome Jesus offered up prayer.

The girl watched him, smirking for all she was worth. "Guess you didn't want to take me to the Wheel-Inn last night."

"No, no. It wasn't that." Alan shifted his book bag. "I'd have been glad to, but I'd been on the train for more than a day and a night. I got some dinner, found a hotel room, and just lay down on the bed for a few minutes. But then I didn't wake up till this morning."

Eileen twirled hair between thumb and forefinger. "Well, maybe you can make up for it. Tonight, I've got to go…" Her face turned disgusted. "…to a Bible Class supper. It might be at least a little fun if you'd take me."

"Well, sure. Sure I will."

The girl's face lit. "Hey, groovy. I'm really glad Mr. Barton brought you over, but I'm curious why. I mean, what with you already having a room at a hotel."

Alan hoisted the book bag. "I've got a journal here that I brought out for the ceremony. It's pretty valuable, and just a couple of hours ago, somebody tried to steal it off me on the street. Lucky for me, Mr. Barton came by and ran the guy off. We got to talking, and he said I could stay at his house, but then he remembered he had family coming from out of town. So he brought me here. He said your father'd be glad to put me up."

The longer Alan talked, the brighter became Eileen's smile. "Neat-o," she said. "And I'd sure love to hear more about that journal. But let me get you some towels, and then we better go back on down." She rolled her eyes. "My parents are *so* square, and Mama's a real prude. You can tell me about it afterwards."

◇◇◇

Eight cigarettes and nearly half an hour later, Green had heard Slim's whole story, and had told the big man a good deal about Tom Ireland. "I don't got any idea why he be so fired up over that book," Green said, then jumped as he felt a hand on his shoulder. By reflex, he ducked away and whirled around. A young white cop looked the men up and down, then grinned. "Little nervous, boy?"

Green put on an aw-shucks face. "You did take me by surprise."

"What're you boys up to? Standin' around on the corner for all this time."

Green saw Slim's body tighten, and prayed the hothead would leave the talking to Green. "We ain't up to nothin', officer," Green said. "Just havin' a smoke an' catchin' up a bit."

Behind the patrolman, Green saw Jerry Barton come down the stairs from Klein's porch, get into his truck, and drive off. No sign of the kid.

"I think maybe you ought go do your catching-up in Liberty Park or Lincolnville," said the cop. "'Stead of loitering in this part of town."

Green grabbed Slim's elbow. "We'll be right on our way, officer." He moved the big man in the direction from which they'd come. "I'll take you to meet Mr. Ireland," Green said. "The man I been tellin' you about."

Chapter Fifteen

Sunday, April 15
Mid-afternoon

Slim frowned as he followed Green up the concrete walkway to the little house. Sufferin' Jesus, the big man thought, what a dump. If a colored man can't hope for nothing better in his life than a tiny old cottage like this, there ain't a whole lot of point in tryin'.

Green led the way onto the porch, knocked at the door. He peered through the glass pane, then knocked again, more loudly. A couple of minutes later, Tom Ireland opened the door, and blinked at his visitors.

"Okay if we come in?" Green asked.

"Well, sure. Sorry, Alonzo, I guess I must have nodded off in my chair." Ireland chuckled. "My daughter-in-law knows how to make Sunday dinner."

Slim studied the old man. Probably comin' up on eighty, but he keeps himself good. Stands up straight, clear eyes. A man you'd be a fool to sell short.

"Tom Ireland, Slim Sanders," Alonzo said. "Slim's from New Jersey."

Ireland's eyes opened full. "You've come a long way."

He extended a hand, which Slim gripped, then released. "I got me a good reason," the fat man said.

"Slim's got a story I think you oughta hear." Green looked around. "I thought maybe Isaac, too."

"Isaac's at his daughter's." Ireland laughed. "You want to find an old colored man on Sunday afternoon, go to his daughter's house, or his daughter-in-law's." He motioned Slim and Green into his living room. "I was a newsman all my life, and one thing I can't resist is a good story. I can catch Isaac up later."

◇◇◇

When Slim finished, Ireland was perched on the very edge of his chair. "That boy took five thousand dollars from your employer to buy the journal from Mrs. Joplin?" He glanced toward Green. "He told us Brun Campbell had wired him the money."

Slim showed teeth. "Guess that ain't the first time somebody told a story about how he just happened to put his hands on a little lettuce that wasn't his."

"A little lettuce? Five thousand dollars isn't exactly pocket change? How did he—"

"By gettin' himself real friendly with my boss' daughter. Sweet li'l thing, I been with the family since she was born. She ain't much to look at, and I'd swear on a Bible she don't put out for the boys. Must be some reason that kid was spendin' all his time with her. After my boss fire' me, I went and talked to her, and I thought sure she was gonna wet her pants. She musta found her daddy's suitcase in the attic, and saw a way she could buy herself a boyfriend. By the time I run over to his house, he was long gone. So I figured the onliest way left to me was to come out here myself, find him, get my hands on that stupid book, and go sell it back to the lady he got it from."

Ireland and Green exchanged a quick glance. "Maybe we ought to work together," Ireland said quietly.

Slim bit on his upper lip. Ireland waited. Finally, Slim asked, "Why is it *you* wants that book?"

"Some of what's written in there would be a very severe embarrassment for certain people."

Slim straightened in his chair. "Mr. Ireland, look here a minute. If we gonna even think about helpin' each other, we both gotta talk straight. I already tol' you, I'm aimin' to get the book from that kid, then see if the ol' woman'll give me back the five thousand for it. That'd at least make gettin' fired off my job worthwhile. And even if she won't give back the money, I gotta figure if the kid and that Campbell guy paid five thousand for it, so will somebody else. Maybe somebody'd pay more than five thousand, who knows? That book just might be my first-class ticket outa bein' a nigger. But it sound to me like you just want to hide it away till hell freezes. So how we supposed to work together, huh?"

"Fair enough." Ireland's face was like chiseled tan marble. "For one thing, if we work separately, one of us is definitely going to be unhappy. And if we get in each other's way, we both might come up empty-handed. But if we can cooperate, then once we have the journal, we can sit down and decide what to do. Maybe we could sell it to a museum or some other institution with the stipulation that it be kept sealed for fifty years. Any money we'd get would go to you."

Slim just stared at the older man.

Which didn't seem to bother Ireland. "If you don't want to work along with Lonzo and me, then so be it," he said. "But we know this town. We know the people. And you're not just a stranger, you're a colored stranger."

A grimace twisted across Slim's lips, then worked itself into a feeble grin. "You got a way of putting things, Mr. Ireland."

"It's called straight," Ireland said. "People always know where they stand with me." He held out a hand.

Slim breathed a huge sigh, then grasped the hand. "Okay, then. Figure I'm in."

Green coughed. "Where you stayin', Slim?"

The big man held out both hands, palms up. "Waitress at Davis' said I should go by Miz Simmons' on West Main. That's where I was headin' when I spotted the kid."

"You can sleep on my couch if you want," said Green. "My rates are even better'n Miz Simmons'."

Slim's smile spread over his face. "Well, I've slept on worse, an' I thank you. But for right now, could one of you please aim me in the direction of the privy?"

Ireland pointed. "Out the door from the kitchen back there, then straight on back."

Slim nodded thanks, took a few steps toward the kitchen. Ireland called after him. "One more thing, Mr. Sanders."

Slim turned.

"If all you want from that five thousand dollars is to buy your way out of being a nigger, you might as well go home right now, and save yourself a lot of trouble and a heap of disappointment. You could have five *million*, and you'd still be a nigger. A rich nigger, but a nigger all the same."

Slim seemed on the verge of saying something, but turned away and continued on out the door. Ireland and Green sat silent until they heard the outhouse door slam. Then, Green gestured with his head toward the back of the house. "Tom, who the hell you know gonna pay five grand to hide that journal away for fifty years?"

"Nobody in particular. But just because I don't know doesn't mean there's not somebody out there. Lonzo, in eighty-five years, you learn to attend to one problem at a time. Till we've got that journal, there's no point scratching around for somebody to buy it."

Green nodded. "But if that Campbell guy gets together with the kid before we can snatch the journal, we're done. And I don't even know what Campbell looks like."

"I'll recognize him," Ireland said. "And so will Isaac. He's down at the station right now, checking every train that comes in from Kay Cee. We'll know when our boy is here."

Green laughed. "I thought he was at his daughter's, Mr. Straight-shooter." Then, seeing the look that came over Ireland's face, the dark man quickly added, "Well, I guess you got it all covered, Tom. I shoulda known."

"Yes, Lonzo. You should have."

◇◇◇

As the rail car rolled out of Knob Noster, next stop, Sedalia, Brun Campbell's heart pounded a rapid, irregular rhythm. The old man slipped a nitroglycerin tablet out of the little pocket container and slid it under his tongue, then closed his eyes and waited for the squeezing in his chest to let up. He'd once promised never to set foot in Sedalia again, another vow about to be broken. By the time the train pulled into the station, the pain in his chest had eased, but his heartbeat was as heavily syncopated as any of the tunes he'd been banging out of pianos for the past half-century.

He stepped off the train into a blast of wind, welcome to Sedalia. The old barber shivered. Damn, he thought, it ain't under fifty degrees, and look at me. When he was growing up back in Kansas, his old man used to say it wasn't cold until your snot froze before it could drip down your face. All those years in California must've thinned out his blood.

A colored man, real old-timer, slowly made his way toward Brun. The barber absently reached into his pocket for a coin, but the man never put out a hand. Instead, he looked Brun straight in the eye, and said, "Now if I ain't makin' a mistake, you be Mr. Brun Campbell, ain't I right?"

Brun, doubly glad he'd taken the nitro, blinked at the apparition. His jaw moved, but nothing came from his mouth.

"You the one they call The Ragtime Kid, rode a rail to Sedalia back in eighteen and ninety-nine to get Mr. Scott Joplin to give him piana lessons." The Negro's entire face creased in a smile; his eyes beamed mischief. "Talked himself into a job at Mr. John Stark's music store. Worked with Mr. Light Stark and Mr. Dark Stark."

Brun cocked his head. "Isaac? Can't be."

"None other."

"But how old—"

"Next birthday, I be a hundred and one."

"Isaac!" Brun grabbed the Negro by the shoulders, then loosened his grip as if he were afraid the human antique might crumble in his hands. "You moved to St. Louis with Mr. John Stark, didn't you? Back in oh-one?"

"And then we both went up to New York City, but we came back in nineteen-ten. Mrs. Stark, she got real sick, wanted to die at home. Then, in 'twenty-seven, when Mr. Stark passed, I come back here to live out my days." He laughed, an old man's cackle. "Just didn't figure I had so many of them."

"But what are you doing here? In the train station?"

"Waitin' on you. I hear tell you's gonna meet

a boy, brung you out a diary writ in Scott Joplin's own hand."

Brun scanned the station. "The boy's here? Where is he?"

"That, I can't tell you, 'cause I don't know. But yesterday, he was out by Tom Ireland's, and—"

"Did he have the journal?"

"Oh, yes. Yes, he surely did. Tom and me, we got a good look at it, and it's got some stuff in it you're gonna remember."

Brun's face asked questions.

Isaac gestured with his cane. "Best you comes with me up to Tom's place, Brun. I think we got us some talkin' to do."

◇◇◇

Ireland pushed two wooden chairs up closer to the wood stove in the kitchen, and motioned Brun and Isaac to sit. Then, he settled into a chair at the side of the scarred table. Across from him, Slim's ample hindquarters spread beyond the edges of his seat; Green, at his side, perched on a step-stool. Nobody spoke. Finally, Ireland said, "It's a joy to see you again, Brun. I didn't think that ever was going to happen."

"Life takes some funny turns, don't it?" Brun said. "I just wish I had my friend, Cal, back in Venice, out here with me. He don't believe I really did take lessons from Scott Joplin fifty years ago. He thinks I made it all up."

Ireland laughed. "I'd tell him it's not likely I'd forget the freshest, nerviest kid I ever did see. But you always came through." Ireland's face went solemn. "And if I needed proof, one look at that diary is all it would take."

Throats cleared, chairs squeaked as rumps shifted, the sounds you hear when a group knows the preliminaries are over, and the real business is about to begin. Ireland acknowledged the fact by looking around, then saying, "Brun, I'm glad Isaac happened to see you. We hoped we could get hold of you as soon as possible."

"Something about the ceremony?"

"You might say that. Actually it's…well, hell's fires, Brun, let's get right down to it. There's a boy running around Sedalia with a journal of Scott Joplin's. He says he got hold of it to give to you."

Brun was instantly on his feet. "That's what Isaac told me. Where is he?"

Slim barked a derisive laugh. "That be the sixty-four dollar question. Every last one of us in this room want to know that."

Ireland, traffic cop at a conversational crossroads, held up a hand to Brun, another to Slim. "We don't know where he is. He got in yesterday and found his way here. He said you wrote to him about wanting to have that journal at the ceremony Tuesday, so he went into New York, got it from Mrs. Joplin, then hopped on a train and brought it here. He let Isaac and me look it over. And Brun, that journal simply can not come to light."

Brun was back on his feet. "Now, wait a minute, Mr.—"

"No, Brun. You wait a minute. Sit down and listen."

Brun lowered himself slowly, not taking his eyes off Ireland.

"When it came to writing music, Scott Joplin was in a class by himself." Ireland's voice was gentle. "But he was also a man, same as any one of us, and sometimes he didn't use the best judgement. There are things he wrote in that journal that never should have been put on paper."

"Like what?" Brun's tone made it clear he'd require some convincing.

Ireland fixed his hardest stare on the barber. "If you'll remember, there were some nasty goings-on during that summer when you were in town. Stuff that you and a few other people agreed to keep under wraps."

"That's what Mr. Joplin wrote down? No. I can't believe it."

"Every word. Every detail."

"I'll be…" Brun coughed, reached toward the

little pillbox in his pocket. "We all took an oath to keep it secret. I never told a soul, not my wife, not anybody. But still, I don't see where we got any problem. That was so long ago."

"Some of those people are still around," Ireland shot back. "You, for one. Isaac, for another. And for good measure, Miss Luella Sheldon, who got so jealous of you fooling around with another girl, she cut herself up in some embarrassing places, and warned you if you didn't leave town right then and promise never to come back, she was going to tell her uncle you'd done it to her."

Brun felt color drain from his face. "Oh, Lordy. She's still around, huh?"

"Her name's Mrs. Rohrbaugh now, but yes, she's right here in Sedalia, a pillar of her church, or maybe better, the whole darn foundation. Brun, listen to me. We've still got people who'd take any excuse to stir up the worst kind of trouble for the colored. Not all that long ago, the Klan was holding their meetings right out in the open, in Liberty Park. Just think what they'd do to the families of the mayor, the police chief, the state senator, and the attorney who helped cover up the fact that a bunch of white people ended up dead that night. And then there's Isaac, who helped bury those white people. You think he'd get to see a hundred and one?"

Brun tapped a nitro tablet out of the pillbox, slipped it under his tongue. "We had to do it. Didn't have any choice." The words came out all mushy.

"Sure you had to. But there was a good reason you all swore to keep it in the dark. And just for good measure, there's also a couple of pages about how Irving Berlin stole a piece of Scott's music to write *Alexander's Ragtime Band,* and then a few years later, swindled Scott out of a musical play Scott wrote, and tried to frame him for murder. From all I hear, Berlin is one very tough nut. He'll probably have lawyers all over everybody who has anything to do with letting that stuff out."

Brun's wind was returning. He took in a long breath. "Mr. Ireland, I can't believe Berlin could do us harm for something Scott Joplin wrote."

"Maybe yes, maybe no. But in any case, Scott was terribly sick his last few years. His mind was in pieces. Do you want to see his name dragged through the mud, what with all you're doing to get people to respect him and his music?"

During the last few exchanges, Slim had wiggled harder and harder on his chair. Now, he got to his feet. "Listen, you all," he growled. "I done had all I can sit through. I don't give a rat's ass about what's in that book. What *I* cares about is the five thousand dollars that boy went and stole to buy it. You think maybe we can talk about that a li'l?"

Brun looked to Ireland.

"Your young man, Chandler. He stole five thousand dollars from Slim's employer to pay Lottie Joplin for the journal. The employer blamed Slim, and fired him. Slim wants to get that money back."

Unconsciously, Brun patted at the money pouch under his shirt.

"You never did know about that, huh?" asked Slim.

Brun shook his head. "How the hell do *you* know?"

Slim lit a cigarette, took a long draw, blew two streams of smoke from his nostrils. "My boss' daughter is that kid's girlfriend, and I heard the kid tellin' her how much he wished he had five thousand bucks to get some book for you so you could show it to everybody out here this Tuesday. And next I know, my boss say he be missin' a pile of money, and it musta been me stole it. So you tell me, huh? Where's a seventeen-year-old kid gonna get his hands on five thousand dollars, less'n maybe *you* give it to him? Did you?"

Brun shook his head. "No."

"All right, then. He say you wired that money to him, so if you ain't a liar, he gotta be. I ever get my hands on him, he for sure ain't gonna be tellin' no more lies. He won't be tellin' nobody nothing."

Ireland scrambled to his feet, waving his hands

in all directions. "All right, hold on. Everybody. We're not getting anywhere like this. Brun, the four of us are working together to find that boy and the journal. Why don't you come aboard? Maybe we can figure a way to satisfy everyone."

Brun chewed his lower lip. "Mr. Ireland, I've got the greatest regard for you, and I'm proud to count you as a friend. But I think we gotta go our own ways on this thing. I've come too far to quit now. The boy brought the journal for me, and I'm bound to have my own look in it. But I will ask him where he got the money."

"Damn your eyes, you don't *have* to." Slim was beside himself. "I already done tol' you that."

Brun started toward the door. "I'll check in with you from time to time, Mr. Ireland. I hope we ain't gonna have any hard feelings."

The room stayed quiet until the colored men heard the front door open and close. Then, Slim said, "I already got myself some pretty goddamn hard feelings."

Ireland's eyes looked far away. "People don't change," a murmur. "He was a headstrong, stubborn boy, and now he's a headstrong, stubborn man." Ireland smiled sadly. "Of course, if he weren't headstrong and stubborn, he never would have hopped that train and talked Joplin into giving him piana lessons."

◇◇◇

A few minutes after five, Eileen and Alan waved good-bye to her parents. "I don't mind driving you over there, if you want," Klein said.

"No, thanks, Daddy, we can walk," Eileen called back. "That way, we can get acquainted a little before we get to the church."

Klein nodded. "Okay, then. Alan, you're sure you don't want to leave your book so's the whole committee can look it over?"

The boy shook his head. Klein closed the door.

Eileen gave her escort the fish eye. "Do you really need to carry that thing along? You could leave it in your room. My dad's not going to steal it."

"It goes where I go," Alan said.

The girl tapped the toe of her shoe. "Well, at least tell me why it's so important." She took his hand, then pulled him along, down the porch stairs to the sidewalk.

By the time Alan finished his story, they were around the corner and two blocks down. Eileen stared at him, spellbound. "You mean your parents let you come all the way out here with something as valuable as that?"

"Not exactly. I didn't ask them. I just did it."

"Whoa. You mean they don't even know where you are?"

"No."

"Oh boy. I don't think I'd want to be in your shoes when you get back. So, you haven't even met that Mr. Campbell?"

Alan shook his head.

"And he trusted you with five thousand dollars?"

"Well…yeah. Like I said, we've been writing back and forth, he's been helping me learn to play ragtime. I guess he figured I was okay."

She fluttered her eyelids. "You must be good with words."

"Yeah, I am. Do you know your name is a complete sentence?"

She gave him a playful slap on the arm. "I better watch myself around you."

He smiled. "What's this thing we're going to that meets in a church basement?"

She stuck out her tongue and made a gagging sound. "Mrs. Rohrbaugh's Sunday Night Supper. She has it once in the fall and once in the spring. The old bat looks about ninety, but she's actually sixty-something. She teaches a Bible class. The kids call it Mrs. Pruneface's School For Good Little Christian Boys and Spotless Virgins. Every Sunday morning, we sit in that damp, smelly basement and listen to her tell us what's right and what's wrong. Mostly, what's wrong." Eileen's face went sly. "Mama used to call me a little pitcher with big ears, and I've heard some stories about Holy Mrs. Rohrbaugh. Like when she was younger than us, she had a big crush on a boy, and he had to up and leave town in a hurry, quiet-like. What do you think of that?"

Alan shrugged. "From what you say, I think he was lucky to get away."

She slapped his arm again. "You're terrible, Alan."

The boy grinned.

◇◇◇

Alonzo Green looked over to his sofa, where Slim lay snoring. The big man had gone down for the count right after supper, and now looked set for the night. Good. Green smiled, walked toward his bedroom, quietly pulled the door closed. Then he went back through the living room and outside, climbed into his old Ford, and drove off.

Not five minutes later, he pulled up in front of a late-model Pontiac at the corner of Fifth and Washington, set the brake, and killed the motor. "Black man's one thing," he muttered. "But ain't nobody gonna care about a black car loitering on a Honkytown street corner." He sank low in the seat, and fastened his eyes on Otto Klein's porch.

◇◇◇

As they approached the basement entrance at the

side of the Calvary Baptist Church, Eileen suddenly pulled her hand from Alan's, then led him down the stone stairs, and inside. Old single-bulb ceiling fixtures gave off patches of light, but did little to dispel the sense of cheerlessness in the large room. Boys and girls sat around large round tables, eating and talking quietly. Smells like an old bookstore on a rainy day, Alan thought.

Eileen led her escort up to a thin woman in a plain black dress, dark hair piled up on her head like a beehive. The corners of her mouth seemed set in the down position, and her cheeks were twin mazes of wrinkles. Mrs. Pruneface, Alan thought, and struggled to keep his own face straight.

"Mrs. Rohrbaugh," Eileen said, "I'd like you to meet Alan Chandler. He's from New Jersey, and he's staying with my family for a few days."

Mrs. Rohrbaugh took a moment to scrutinize Alan. The boy wasn't sure she approved. "Welcome to our social evening," she said through her nose. "I didn't see you at worship this morning."

"I wasn't here," Alan said.

The woman ignored Eileen's stifled giggle. "Do you attend a different denomination?"

"I'm not religious, ma'am. I think what some people call the Word of God was actually said and written down by people just like you and me."

He felt Eileen hold her breath. But Mrs. Rohrbaugh smiled, if faintly. "I'll say a prayer for you," she said, then looked at Eileen. "I'm glad to have your friend spend the evening with us." She glanced toward Alan. "Or is he family?"

"No, ma'am," said Eileen. "Just a friend. He brought out an important historical book for a man who used to live here back in 1899, and took piano lessons from Scott Joplin. The man's going to give a speech at that ceremony Tuesday at the Hubbard School, and show off the book. He thinks it'll make people appreciate Mr. Joplin more."

Mrs. Rohrbaugh's face contorted into a sickly simper. "Really. Who is this man from California? What's his name?"

Eileen looked at Alan.

"Campbell," Alan said. "Brun Campbell. Except for Scott Joplin himself, he's the greatest ragtime piano player who ever lived…are you all right, Mrs. Rohrbaugh? You look a little pale."

"I'm fine, just fine, thank you. It must be that awful light down here." She clapped loudly, twice. "Girls, boys. We have a visitor this evening from New Jersey, a friend of Eileen Klein's family. I trust you'll make him welcome."

Behind Mrs. Rohrbaugh's back, Eileen gave Alan's hand a quick squeeze.

◇◇◇

The talk in Jerry Barton's basement was heated. Barton called for quiet. "Listen here. Nobody'd like to see Charlie Bancroft's grocery or Herb Studer's real estate go up in smoke more'n I would, but compared to blowin' up that school, it's like pissin' in the ocean. Besides, we stretch ourselves too thin, we're more liable to get nailed. Bancroft's place and Studer's will still be there next year, or even in six months. We ain't none of us gonna forget."

Mumbled comments, then Rafe Anderson said, "Okay, Jerry, makes sense to me. Better to save part of a big dinner for tomorrow, 'stead of eatin' the whole thing and pukin' your guts all night."

Barton smiled. "Christ, Rafe, I never knew you were a goddamn poet."

"But I still ain't sure we wouldn't do better all goin' down to set the charge," Anderson said. "You know. Give Johnny a hand."

Johnny Farnsworth was instantly on his feet. "What the hell's your problem, Rafe? You think I don't know how to do it?"

"Cool off, Johnny…Rafe." Barton said. "Listen, the less people down in that school basement, the less chance somebody's gonna leave a fingerprint or a footprint, or snag their pants on a nail and give the feds a piece of cloth to check out.

Johnny's the expert here, so let's stay outa his way and keep the job clean."

Clay Clayton snickered. "Good enough for me that we're all gonna get to see the school go up."

"No trouble there," Barton said. "On our way out here, Otto and me checked that empty house on Moniteau, right back of the school. It's wide open, we can just walk right in, watch the fun, and then by the time the black rain stops falling, we'll all of us be back here, playin' a li'l poker, been playin' all evening. Yeah, we did hear a noise…"

Raucous laughter. Anderson slapped his thigh.

Cartwright waved a hand. "But what if they figure the charge *did* get set ahead of time?"

Farnsworth motioned Barton silent. "Ain't no worries there. I don't think there's gonna be anything but powder left of the timers, but even if I'm wrong, so what? None of you guys knows shit about dynamite, so they ain't gonna bother you. And if they come after me, just figure I'll be ready. Ain't no way they'll be able to pin it on me. I'll make good and goddamn sure I don't leave any threads loose."

Barton looked around the room, saw heads nodding agreement. "Okay, then. Tomorrow night, eleven o'clock, we get back together here, and go on down by the school. Johnny does his thing, we all take us a look at the empty house, then we do up the alibi, tight as a drum. That oughta do it for now."

As the men got to their feet, and filed out the door, Barton touched Klein's arm. Their eyes met. "Gotta use the crapper," Barton said, loud enough for everyone to hear.

"Good thing," Clayton called back. "Maybe then you won't be so full of it."

Everyone laughed.

A few minutes later, Barton returned, buttoning his pants. He looked around the room. "They're all gone?"

"Well, yeah. But why—"

"We gotta talk a little about that kid and his book."

"How come you didn't say nothing at the meeting?"

"'Cause it sounds like that book of his is worth big money. Five thousand dollars? How'd you like to lay your hands on half of five thousand bucks."

A smile crept across Klein's face.

"If it was worth five K to that coot in California, it's got to be worth that to somebody else. Maybe the California guy'd pay us another five to get hold of it, who knows? But if everyone's in, the dough gets split six ways. You want eight big, or two and half grand?"

Now, Klein's smile covered his face. "Twenty-five hundred sounds better to me."

"All right. There you are."

"So what're we gonna do?"

Barton shrugged. "What do you think? We'll get that damn bag away from him, then kill him."

Klein looked disgusted. "But my wife and daughter have seen him now. What the hell am I supposed to tell them about where he went."

"Easy. He's a kid, rolled into town, said he was from New Jersey, but how do we know he was telling the truth about that? Maybe he's running away from his parents, or the law. Maybe he's crazy. You tell your wife and daughter he must have taken it into his head to go off, that's all. Now, here's the plan. Before you leave for work in the morning, tell the kid he'd better not go outside till he hears from us, else Big Black Sambo might catch him. Your daughter'll go off to school…when does your wife do her grocery shopping?"

"Right about eleven."

"Fine. I'll watch for her to leave, then I'll ring the bell, tell the kid the committee's all excited about his book, and I'm gonna take him to talk to the chairman. I'll drive him out in the woods back of Melvin Armstrong's, kill him, take the journal, and bury him there."

"But what if somebody sees you going off with him?"

"What if?" Barton laughed. "Who's gonna know who he is? Who's gonna report him missing?"

Klein laughed, but it sounded uneasy.

"What's the matter, Otto? Your little feetsies gettin' cold?"

"Nah." Klein shook his head slowly. "Just that you got such brass balls, it sometimes takes a little getting used to."

Now, Barton laughed, not at all uneasily. "My ex-wife used to tell me she didn't know if I was a cross to bear or a bear to cross."

Chapter Sixteen

Monday, April 16
Very early morning

All of a sudden, Alan was fully awake. Had he been sleeping? Maybe he'd dreamed that noise. The radium-dipped hands on the little alarm clock on the bedside table told him it was ten minutes after one. He closed his eyes, listened hard. Nothing. Maybe it *was* a dream.

No, it wasn't. There came the sound again, a soft rustle. Slowly, carefully, Alan raised his head. Dark, but his eyes were starting to adjust. Someone was bent over the desk where he'd piled his clothes and the book bag. The intruder held the bag up, worked it open.

Now what? Jump out of bed, run over and grab the guy? What if he had a knife or a gun?

The intruder set the bag down, and in the same motion, turned and started toward the door. Was that the journal in his right hand? Alan thought so.

If he was going to do anything, it had to be now. The boy slid out from under the covers, lowered himself to the floor, and as the thief reached for the doorknob, Alan padded up from behind, dropped a shoulder, and in one quick motion, threw his left arm around his adversary's neck, and struck sharply with his right arm behind the knee. The intruder let out a little shriek, and went down in a heap. Alan rolled over on top of him, pinning his neck.

"Alan, *Alan*," a hissed whisper. "Get *offa* me."

"Eileen?" The boy sprang to his feet, snapped the light switch on.

Eileen sprawled near the door, her legs and most of her thighs visible below the hem of a baby-blue nightgown. She tugged the gown downward. "Quit staring!" The girl rubbed her throat. "You dope, you could've killed me. Broken my neck."

He snatched the journal from the floor near her hand. "Would've served you right. What were you doing, sneaking in here and trying to steal this?"

"Keep your voice down. And turn off the light. If my father comes in and finds me in my nightgown and you in your underwear, he'll probably kill us both."

"You should have thought about that before you snuck in. Now, what the hell's going on?"

The girl stood, smoothed her nightgown, then walked slowly across the room, rubbing at her leg, and plopped onto the edge of the bed.

Alan stood over her, waited.

She brushed a handful of curls away from her left eye. "I'm really…well, it's embarrassing, Alan. You're the most interesting thing that's happened in this stupid town since I can remember, coming half-way across the country like you did, all by yourself, with an important book that might make history. I just wanted to see what was in that book."

"You could've asked me."

"Would you have shown it to me?"

Silence.

"Well, see?" Her eyelids moved like butterfly wings. "I didn't think you would, and I was so jazzed up, thinking about it, I couldn't sleep. So finally, I thought why don't I just come in here on my tiptoes, take the book back to my room, read it, and then bring it back. I didn't think that'd do any harm. Oh, Alan, I'm sorry, I really am. I like you. You're fun. I hope I didn't mess everything up."

"Just my night's sleep," Alan muttered. "Look, I'm sorry I hurt you, all right? You've been nice to me, and I appreciate it. After I get the journal to Mr. Campbell, I'll ask him if it's okay to show it to you." He got off the bed, walked to the door, opened it a crack. "See you tomorrow."

As she sailed past him, she whispered, "Meanie!"

He closed the door behind her, then trudged back to bed, but his eyes wouldn't stay shut. It seemed like everybody in Sedalia wanted to get their hands on Scott Joplin's journal, and if Mr. Barton was right, Brun Campbell wouldn't be coming in for another whole day. How could he keep the journal safe in the meanwhile?

He looked around the room. The desk where he'd left his stuff? It had a solid back; the journal would fit behind it. He threw back the covers, but stopped before his feet hit the floor. Probably not the best idea to hide the journal in his own room. Where, then?

A thought came to him, but he'd have to wait a little while. He slid back under the covers.

His mother had a saying about how watched pots never boil, and it seemed to take the little clock four hours to get to half-past two. When it finally did, the boy got up, walked out into the hall, and crept down to Eileen's room at the far end of the corridor. He turned the knob, opened the door slowly, slipped in, shut the door.

From the bed came the sound of regular deep breathing. He smiled. Across the room was a dresser, the tall, wide kind that girls need to hold all their clothes. Even better, it sat directly on the floor. Perfect. Alan started toward it, but enthusiasm outstripped caution, and he caught his toe on an old steamer trunk at the foot of the bed. He fell heavily against the bedpost, muttering a curse as he saw the figure in the bed sit up. "Eileen," a groan. "Don't scream. It's me, Alan."

"Alan? What—?"

"I couldn't sleep. I felt bad about the way I talked to you, and I thought you might be awake. I want to say I'm sorry."

"Well, you might at least come up here where I can see you when you say it."

"Wait a minute, I'll be right there."

"What do you mean, 'you'll be right there?'"

"Eileen, jeez. Wait just a minute. I banged my big toe and it hurts like hell."

"You want me to kiss it for you? Make it all better? Bring it over here."

"Hold on a second."

"Alan!"

He limped alongside the bed. "All right, I'm here, see? I'm sorry I was rude to you, Eileen, I apologize. Okay?"

Her teeth gleamed. "That's a start." She threw back the covers. Come on in and tell me how sorry you are."

"Eileen…"

"Hey, it's cold with the covers off." She patted the bed. "Bet you could warm me up."

◇◇◇

Brun Campbell sat in the Milner Hotel's restaurant, alternating forkfuls of bacon and eggs with mouth-fuls of coffee and pulls at a cigarette. Yesterday had been a waste. Nothing open except churches and a few restaurants. He'd pounded the streets, but none of the teen-aged boys he'd talked to was the one he was looking for. He'd been glad to see Tom Ireland, of course, though finding out they were on opposite sides of the fence troubled him. He had to get his hands on that boy and the journal before Ireland did, or it'd probably be gone forever, and the Scott Joplin Ragtime Museum right along with it.

Sedalia was giving him the creeps. Everywhere he went, he saw ghosts. Was that John Stark down the street? Mrs. Stark? Mr. Higdon, Mr. Hastain? Was that Otis Saunders at the table across the room?

He drew deeply at the cigarette, set it onto the corner of the ashtray, and shoveled in a mound of eggs. But before he could swallow, he saw a woman with a beehive of gray hair, standing on the oppo-site side of the table, studying him from behind rimless glasses. He hadn't heard her walk up. She looked familiar, another ghost? Then, recognition hit. Brun coughed, choked, reached for his glass of water. He took two giant swallows, wiped at his eyes, and looked up.

"I beg your pardon, Mr. Campbell," the woman said. "I didn't mean to startle you." She paused, seemed to be weighing alternatives, then added, "Fifty-two years is a long time. Do you remember me?"

Brun scrambled out of his chair, stood awkwardly, shifting from one foot to the other. "If I ain't mistaken, you're Miss Luella…" What the hell did Tom Ireland say her name was now?

"Rohrbaugh," the woman said. "But you knew me as Luella Sheldon."

Brun scanned the fingers of her left hand; she caught him. "I've been a widow for twenty-five years. I stopped wearing the ring a long time ago."

"Oh. Well, I'm sorry to hear that."

"Thank you."

Her face gave nothing away. Neither did her tone of voice. Brun thought a moment, then said, "I'm only gonna be in town a couple days, for the Scott Joplin ceremony at the high school. Then you won't never see me again. I hope you're not gonna make me any trouble."

She raised a hand. "I'm not here to trouble you in any way, Brun. What happened in 1899 was a long time ago."

"But I am sorry, Miss Luella." Brun caught himself at the antiquated way he'd addressed her. The woman couldn't stop a wan smile. "I really am sorry for what happened, Mrs. Rohrbaugh. Always have been."

"I'll wager there have been other incidents which left you feeling sorry," the woman said. "You were an impulsive boy. You acted without forethought, or considering consequences, but I've long since forgiven your rash behavior. In any case, please feel free to call me Luella." She smiled, a formality.

Brun motioned to the chair she stood beside. "Would you like to sit down? Have some breakfast?"

"I've had breakfast, hours ago," Luella said. She pulled out the chair. "But I will sit. I have some information I believe will interest you."

Brun hustled around the table to pull the chair out for the old woman, then went back to reseat himself.

"I heard you were coming to town," Luella said. "You're going to play piano at that ceremony, and you're going to show the crowd a certain diary that Scott Joplin kept, in the hope of persuading them to build a museum downtown for him and his music."

Brun studied the woman. Fifty-some years had carved channels like river beds into her cheeks. "How do you ever know that?"

"This is a small town, just as it was in 1899. I happened to meet a young man last evening, an

Alan Chandler. He has that journal in a shoulder bag, which he won't let out of his hand for an instant. He's looking for you, but has no idea where you are, or how to find you."

Brun's food was forgotten. "Do you know where he is?"

"I'm quite sure I do, and I'm equally sure I don't like it. I teach a Bible class, which I imagine doesn't surprise you. One of my students, Eileen Klein, brought your young man to our Sunday evening supper last night. She said he was a family friend from New Jersey, and that he was staying with the Kleins. But Otto Klein is not a man I'd expect to have anything to do with a ceremony in honor of a colored man. In fact, Mr. Klein has long been active in the Ku Klux Klan. Alan seemed like a nice boy, and I wouldn't want to see him get into a bad situation. So I decided I'd try to find you."

"How'd you know where I'm staying? I only got in last night."

"A simple process of elimination. I asked at hotel registration desks. The Milner was my third stop."

Brun was half-out of his chair. "You know where that kid is, then? I was gonna try and find Abe Rosenthal, the guy who's in charge of the program, and get a few things straight about my part, but I can sure wait on that till after I see the kid."

"I know where Otto Klein's machine shop is, and I'll be glad to take you there," Mrs. Rohrbaugh said. "Just as soon as you're finished eating, if you'd like."

Brun took a swallow from his water glass, then pushed away from the table. "I'm done." He threw a dollar on the table, then trotted around to help Luella out of her seat. "Let's get a move on."

◇◇◇

"Mrs. Campbell?"

May looked up into the face of the man who'd just rung her doorbell. She nodded. "Yes?"

He held a billfold out toward her. "Detective Robert Magnus, Los Angeles Police. Your husband's not in his barber shop today. Is he at home?"

May shook her head, then stuffed all her exasperation into an extravagant sigh. "He went to San Francisco Friday night. He's been trying to get a movie produced about Scott Joplin, you know, the ragtime piano player. Friday afternoon, Brun got word that someone in San Francisco was interested in making the movie and needed to see him right away, so off he went. Hardly took time to pack his suitcase."

The detective called on every second of his professional training and experience to keep from screaming. "Have you heard from him since then?"

Another headshake. "We don't have a phone."

"Right. Mrs. Campbell, do you know a woman named Bess Vinson? A colored woman, she lives in Santa Monica?"

May shook her head. "I don't know many colored at all. My husband does…oh, wait. That's the woman who came looking for him, just a few days ago, and I sent her over to the barber shop. Brun told me later that she claimed to be Scott Joplin's daughter, and wanted to sell him Joplin's diary for five thousand dollars, can you imagine?"

"Did he buy it?"

"I don't think so. I have no idea where he'd get anything like five thousand dollars."

Now, Magnus sighed. Bess Vinson hadn't said anything to him because he hadn't found her. The druggist downstairs from her apartment had told Magnus he hadn't seen her for a day or so, and had no idea where she might be.

"All right, Mrs. Campbell." The detective gave May a business card. "If you do hear from your husband, please let him know I need to talk to him. And then *you* call me."

May looked from the card to the detective. "Is Brun in some sort of trouble?"

When I get my hands on him, he'll be in trouble like he's never seen, Magnus thought. But he smiled and said, "I just need to ask him some

questions. Thank you." Then he hotfooted back
to the station, and got a sergeant on the phone to
check into movie producers in San Francisco.

◇◇◇

Slouched low in the cab of his pickup, Jerry Barton
watched Rowena Klein, shopping bag in hand,
leave her house and walk briskly along East Fifth
toward downtown. He waited till she'd covered a
good three blocks, then jumped out of the truck,
trotted down the street to Klein's, pushed the
button next to the front door. No answer. He
leaned on the button a second time, and pounded
on the door. "Come on, you little bastard," he
muttered. "Open up."

◇◇◇

Before Mrs. Klein left, she pressed a book into
Alan's hand. *"The House of Fear,"* she said. "It's a
mystery story by a man named Robert W. Service.
Do you know him?"

Alan shook his head.

"Oh, he was so popular when I was a girl. He
was a great poet who wrote the most interesting verses
about all those places up north. This book should be
just right for a boy your age. It's a grand story."

It took less than five pages for Alan to decide
it stank on ice. When the doorbell rang, he set the
book down gratefully, started toward the door, but

stopped after just a couple of steps. All he could do was tell whoever it was that Mrs. Klein would be back in an hour.

The bell rang again, long, loud, followed immediately by a series of heavy knocks. "All right," Alan called, then hurried across the room and pulled the door open.

Jerry Barton grinned at him. "Ready to wow the committee chairman, kid? When I told them about your journal last night, they got all worked up. Mr. Rosenthal wants to talk to you before the program gets printed." Barton pointed at the blue bag next to Alan on the couch. "Come on, grab your book there, and I'll drive you over to his office."

◇◇◇

Otto Klein, working at a huge lathe, pulled back his hands and swiveled his head as he heard the little bell that sounded when someone opened the door to his shop. Christ, that old bitch, Luella Rohrbaugh. What the hell was she doing here? And who was that coot with her? Klein snickered. Maybe Luella had stuff going that nobody knew about. A guy would have to be pretty desperate. "Be right with you," Klein shouted.

He set down the chunk of metal he'd been shaping, and flipped the switch to turn off the lathe. Then he wiped a shirt sleeve over his fore-head as he walked to the counter. "'Morning, Mrs. Rohrbaugh," he said. "Mister…?"

"Brun Campbell."

Klein looked like a person trying to put his finger on a missing piece of a jigsaw puzzle.

Luella's face turned severe. "Mr. Campbell is here from California to meet a young man from New Jersey who has a book Mr. Campbell needs."

Klein shrugged. "Okay."

"Mr. Klein! I'm talking about the young man who's staying at your house, the one who escorted Eileen to the supper last night. She introduced him to me as a family friend. Alan Chandler."

Light came into Klein's eyes. "Oh, yeah, sure. Alan. Sorry, I don't know what I was thinking." He pointed toward the lathe. "I got a real rush on that piece, and I guess I was concentrating." He glanced at the big clock on the wall to his right, quarter past eleven, good. Jerry'd have the kid away by now. "Well, I'm glad you're here, Mr. Campbell. Alan's probably sittin' over in my house, being bored, so whyn't the two of you just go on over. I'd take you myself, but…" He pointed again toward the lathe. "This guy'll have my ears if I don't get that work to him by noontime. Hear him tell it, his whole farm's sittin' and waitin' on it."

Luella glanced at Brun. "Very well," she

snapped. "Thank you for your time, Mr. Klein."

Klein shrugged. "Glad to be of help, Mrs. Rohrbaugh. Mr. Campbell." He went back to the lathe, turned it on, picked up the workpiece.

After the bell rang and the door slammed shut, the machinist counted to fifty, then shut off the lathe, took the piece of steel from the chuck, and stashed it under a cloth beneath the lathe. It'd take those mossbacks at least ten minutes to get to his house, and that long to come back. Klein turned the sign in the door to CLOSED, hurried out, locked the door, ran to his car, and drove off, leaving a cloud of gray smoke in front of his shop.

◇◇◇

Alan cracked the window of Barton's truck. The weather was turning nicer, sunny and warming a bit. Barton smiled. "Air out here smells different from back where you live, huh?"

The boy nodded. He clutched the bag in his lap, wondered what to say to Mr. Rosenthal to explain why he didn't have the journal with him. He'd think of something. He always did.

The grassy smell from outside the truck struck Alan odd. They'd driven out of Sedalia, up through the colored section where Mr. Ireland lived, across Highway 65, and now they were cruising along the Georgetown Highway, which was actually just a

two-lane country road like the ones in western New
Jersey, farms all along both sides. "Mr. Rosenthal's
office is out here?" Alan asked.

Barton shrugged. "Why not?"

"I don't know. Just seems like an office'd be
in town."

"That's the trouble with you east coast yokels."
Barton snickered. "You think if something ain't in
the city, it ain't worth thinkin' about. Mr. Rosenthal
sells oil to farmers, so he has an office out close to
his clients. Lot of us farmers do all we can to not
have to go into the city."

Barton turned onto a dirt road; Alan bounced
in the seat. This wasn't right. The boy started to ask
what was going on, but decided to hold his tongue.
He looked all around, trying to fix the route in his
mind.

They drove through a meadow and into a
stand of trees. A hundred yards in, just like that,
the road ended, dense forest on three sides. Barton
stopped the truck, shut off the motor, set the brake.

◇◇◇

Some twenty-five yards into the woods, Richard
Curd, Jr. stopped digging, and listened. Nothing.
He was sure he'd heard a car, but who'd be coming
out here this time of day? Not that it mattered.
Mr. Armstrong used to let his daddy dig here every

spring, and when Daddy died, Mr. Armstrong told Richard, Jr. he could dig in the woods. "Don't want to be responsible for half the people in Sedalia to die without their spring tonic," Mr. Armstrong had said. Curd shrugged, and went back to work.

◇◇◇

Barton gestured toward Alan's book bag. "Give here."

Alan pulled the bag away, grabbed at the door handle.

"Uh-uh," Barton snarled. "Get both of your hands on the bag. Now." He reached inside his jacket, and Alan found himself staring into the barrel of a pistol that looked as big as a cannon. "Open up that bag," Barton said. "Gimme the book." He snickered. "And I tell you what, you piss on my seat there, you're gonna lick it up before I blow out your brains. Now, do like I tell you."

Slowly, Alan undid the catch, slid his hand inside, then put on the best look of amazement he could manage. "It's not here."

Barton grabbed the bag with one hand, shook it upside down, peered inside. Then he flung it to the floor. "God damn, boy, I'm startin' to lose my temper with you. Where the hell is that book?"

"I don't know," Alan said. "It was in here. Maybe it dropped out somewhere."

Barton half-closed one eye. "'Maybe it dropped out?' How thick d'you think I am?"

"No, really. I slung the bag down on Mr. Klein's couch when I sat there this morning. The book could've slid out and gotten under a cushion."

"And you didn't notice how light the bag was when you picked it up?" Barton waved the pistol. "Get out of the truck."

Long hike back to town, Alan thought, but that would be a bargain. He'd go straight to the police station, ask the cops to go with him to Kleins', get back the journal, and then hole up in a hotel room with a chair wedged under the doorknob until the ceremony. Mr. Campbell would just have to wait till then.

But as Alan pushed the door open and stepped down to the ground, Barton jumped out from his side, ran around the truck and up to the boy. "Okay, now." The man's face was blotchy, lips twisted into a snarl. "One more time. Where's that book?"

"I told you, I don't—"

Barton delivered an open-handed crack to Alan's cheek, then brought the handle of his pistol down hard against the side of the boy's head. Alan staggered, fell.

Barton nudged him with a boot. "Get up."

Alan tried to stand, couldn't get past hands and knees. Barton grabbed him by the shoulder and hauled him to his feet. "I got all day, boy. Keep messing with me, an' you're gonna be hamburg steak. Now, where the hell is—"

Barton froze. Car coming down the dirt road, and from the sound, it was not somebody out for a nice drive in the country. Damn, couldn't be the cops, could it? How would they know? He loosened his grip on Alan, who crumpled to the ground.

A brown Hudson roared up and screeched to a stop, practically on the rear bumper of Barton's truck. Before the engine had completely quieted, Otto Klein was out and running up to Barton.

◇◇◇

Richard Curd, Jr. stopped digging again. Another car? Something ain't right. He cocked his head toward the clearing, listened.

◇◇◇

Klein looked wildly from the man to the boy on the ground. "You didn't kill him," Klein shouted.

"Not yet. I'm just getting started. Little son of a bitch's got that book hid away somewhere. Otto, what the hell you doing out here?"

"We can't kill him," Klein bawled. "He took my daughter to the Bible school supper last night, and met Old Lady Rohrbaugh there. So now she knows he's been staying with us. She just came around my shop with a geezer from California,

he looks like death warmed over. He's the one the
kid picked up the book for."

Barton's expression said if they made stupider
people than Otto Klein, he didn't want to see them.
"Christ Almighty, Otto. Why in holy hell did you
let him out of the house in the first place, never
mind to go and talk to a room full of people?"

◇◇◇

Curd frowned. He couldn't quite make out words,
but no problem picking up on the fact he was
hearing two angry men shouting at each other. He
started walking toward the edge of the forest.

◇◇◇

"What was I supposed to do, huh?" Klein howled.
"What was I supposed to say when Eileen wanted
to take him to the supper? I don't got any idea how
Rohrbaugh and the California guy got together,
but it don't matter. Question is, what the hell we
gonna do now?"

Barton blew out a chestful of vexation. "God
damn, Otto, you are a lily-liver. Lettin' some old
bag get your bowels in an uproar, then hightailin'
it out here. What did you tell her about where the
kid was?"

"I said I left him at the house when I drove
Eileen to school and went to work. Told 'em to go
ring the doorbell."

Barton wiped the back of his hand across his mouth. "Fine. No problem. The kid ain't got the book here, but you better believe I'm gonna get him to tell me where he stashed it. Then I'll do just what we planned with him. If Rohrbaugh or anybody else comes around asking, you say you don't know where he is, he was there when you left the house. Rowena'll say the same, because he was. Maybe he ran off, he was a weird kind of kid. Maybe he just ain't right in his head."

Now it was Klein's turn to look disgusted. "Sure, Jerry, great. That Rohrbaugh bitch was loaded for bear, God knows why, and you gotta figure the old goat from California's gonna be plenty pissed off if he's out the five K he paid for the stinkin' book. Between the two of them, I'm gonna have the cops on me, and what then?"

◇◇◇

As he approached the clearing, Curd walked slowly, carefully, balancing himself at each step with the handle of his shovel. He slid up behind an old-growth maple tree at the edge of the woods, then peered around the edge. Jerry Barton and Otto Klein, Lord! For damn sure, they couldn't be up to anything good. Let them see him, and he'd have problems he didn't even want to think about.

He squinched behind the tree, and edged his

head forward, just far enough to see they had a man down on the ground. Curd's palms went cold and slippery. He wiped them on his pants. Better get himself far away, fast. He took a half-step toward retreating, but Klein was facing his way, so he slid back behind the tree.

◇◇◇

Barton glanced at Alan, who'd just pushed himself to his knees, then pointed the gun at the boy. "Stay down there, kid, or you'll be dead before you're all the way up." Then he turned a face full of contempt onto Klein. "'What then?' Damn it to hell, Otto. You tell the cops exactly the same thing. No one's gonna come out here lookin' for him, and even if they did, I'll fix the hole so nobody'll ever notice."

◇◇◇

Curd's stomach knotted. *That ain't no man they got there, it's jus' a boy. An' they means to kill him.*

◇◇◇

Barton rested his free hand on Klein's shoulder, spoke softly. "Listen here. Cool off, or you're gonna have a goddamn stroke. Get yourself back in your shop before Rohrbaugh and her friend see you're missing, and wonder about that."

"I told them I had to make a delivery over lunch hour."

"Good." Barton felt as if he were talking to a little kid who was sure he'd just seen the bogeyman. "That's great. Now, haul your ass outa here, and let me do my work. I'll get back to you soon's I'm done and we'll take it from there."

Klein trudged back to his car. Behind his back, Barton shook his head. As the Hudson chugged out of sight down the dirt road, the man turned to face Alan. "You heard all that, huh?"

"Just the last part."

"So you got a good idea what you're in for. You can make it tough for yourself or easy. Tell me where that book is, and you're not going to have any more pain. Otherwise…" Nasty grin. "You play piana, huh? Guess I'll start with your fingers."

Barton reached for Alan's right hand; the boy scuttled away. Barton cursed him, stepped forward, grabbed. A sense of motion toward his right side pulled him up short, then a blinding red light filled his vision. He fell to his knees, agony bouncing back and forth inside his skull. Another blow sent brilliant white stars shooting through his head, and he fell forward into blackness.

◇◇◇

Alan watched the twitching man go still, then goggled at his rescuer, a well-built colored man in a blue work shirt and dungarees, and wearing an old broad-brimmed leather hat stained with years of sweat and dirt. The man held a long-handled shovel by the business end. He bent to touch the side of Alan's head; the boy winced. "Dirty dog gave you a good li'l shot there," the man said. "Well, I give him one better, an' one for good measure." He bent to pick up Barton's gun, jammed it into his pocket. "Can you get up?" he asked.

The boy nodded. "I think so, yeah." He struggled to his feet.

The colored man had started moving off toward the woods. "Be right back. Go on over by his truck, get inside."

By the time Alan had slid into the passenger seat, the man was back, carrying a large gunnysack over his shoulder. In one motion, he slung the sack and his shovel into the truck bed, and hopped in behind the steering wheel. "Glad he left us the keys." The man turned on the motor, began backing out. "Gotta get us a good head start."

For once in his life, Alan said nothing.

When they got to the Georgetown Highway, the colored man turned southward, drove half a mile, then pulled the truck to the side of the road, killed the motor, slipped the key into his pocket, and got out. Alan followed suit, pausing just long enough to grab the empty book bag from the floor. The man picked up a twig, bent over the right rear tire, unscrewed the cap from the stem, and pushed the twig into the recess, sending air hissing out. A couple of minutes, the tire was flat. The Negro nodded approval, then grinned up at Alan. "Mr. Barton see this, he think we was headin' to town and had a flat." The man motioned toward the woods at the other side of the road. "We goin' that way, though. I knows my way through these woods like nobody else, an' he ain't never gonna find us." He grabbed his sack from the truck, slung it over a shoulder, then snatched up his shovel. "Come on, boy. Best we get us movin'."

Alan trotted across the road after him. Every step made the side of his head pound, but he was not about to complain. Once they'd entered the woods and the road had disappeared from view, he said, "I didn't even have a chance to thank you. Who are you, anyway?"

"Lotta people call me Samson, but my right name's Richard Curd," the man called over his shoulder. "Richard Curd, Junior. But let's just keep walkin' for now. We get ourselves clear, there'll be plenty time for the formalities. Anyways, it was my pleasure to give that motherfucker Barton a couple good cracks upside his head."

◇◇◇

Brun looked around the tidy living room, and

thought he might have taken a trip in one of Cal's time machines. Sedalia, 1899. Tufted chairs and a sofa, antimacassars set just so on their arms. A small music box rested on an oak table under the window; a Bible sat on the little mahogany table inside the door from the hall. Only a telephone on the wall above the Bible seemed out of place.

That the woman would be in any way kindly disposed toward him surprised Brun no end. Damn her eyes, if it hadn't been for her, he'd have stayed in Sedalia, kept taking lessons from Mr. Joplin, then gone along to St. Louis with Mr. Stark and his new music publishing business. And when Mr. Joplin and Mr. Stark both went to New York, how different Brun's life would've turned out. He'd be a big shot in the music business now, not a dinky-town barber in a shop too small to swing a cat in.

Luella showed no sign of finishing up her phone conversation, so Brun walked across the room, opened the lid of the music box, peered at the shiny brass cylinder and steel comb. He bent stiffly to read the colorful card with its list of eight tunes, pinned to the inside of the lid. Six opera songs, all Italian names, then "Home Sweet Home," and last, "Alexander's Ragtime Band."

Damn! All those years he'd pissed into the wind, talking up Scott Joplin and ragtime music, and people still thought Irving Berlin had sat down one morning on Tin Pan Alley and invented ragtime. Well, maybe this ceremony and Joplin's journal were going to turn things around. He had to get that journal, whatever it took.

As he heard Luella hang up the phone, he quickly closed the lid to the music box.

"Would you like to hear it?" Luella asked.

He waved off her offer. "Thanks. Did you get hold of Mr. Rosenthal?"

"Not yet. His wife said he had to go to St. Louis today, but he'll be at the Hubbard High School all day tomorrow, getting ready for the ceremony. She said you should go see him then. She'll tell him to expect you."

Brun swallowed disappointment. "Took a long time for her to say that."

She smiled. "No phone conversation with Fannye Rosenthal is short."

Again, Brun wondered why she was going miles out of her way to help him. He coughed politely, then said, "Well, I sure do appreciate all your kindnesses."

Gray eyes flashed behind rimless glasses. "I don't know that I'd call it kindness. As far as I'm concerned, it's Christian charity, a proper concern for others, and I'm not talking about you. You've somehow bamboozled a boy into coming out from back east to bring you an important book, and I'm concerned he's fallen into some very bad company. I think it's time for you to tell me the whole story. Then, I might be better able to help him, and yes, perhaps you, in the process."

Brun drew a breath, but before he could speak, Luella said, "The real story, Brun. All of it, and straight."

He smiled. She didn't.

He began to talk.

When he finished, she sat for a moment, studying him. "Is that the whole story?"

"Yes. God's truth."

She almost told him not to take the Lord's name in vain, but settled to make a wry face. "You're as impetuous as ever, Brun. You have no regard for the harm your reckless behavior might cause others. I don't believe in gambling, but if I did, I would bet everything I own that all you have on your mind right now is how to get your hands on that journal and wave it around in front of people tomorrow night. Just where did that boy get his hands on five thousand dollars?"

The way Brun banged a fist against his chest, Luella thought he was doing a *mea culpa*. But then he said, "I got the money in a pouch here. I'm gonna make that right."

Just a bit of wind left her sails. "Well, good. I'm glad. But that's not nearly my greatest concern.

Otto Klein is a despicable man. He hates the colored. I don't know how or why he got your young man to stay at their house, but it makes me fear for the boy's safety. Brun, aren't you at all concerned? Just a little?"

He lowered his eyes, didn't speak.

"Well, at least you do have some capacity to feel shame. Now, why didn't the boy answer the door when we rang the bell?"

"I don't know. Maybe he was in the toilet? Maybe he was asleep."

"At nearly twelve noon? And when we came back here and called, he didn't answer the phone either. Brun, that boy is not there, or if he is—"

"Does Klein got a wife? Maybe we could talk to her."

"Hah! Rowena Klein is afraid of her own shadow, probably because when she sees it, she thinks it might be her husband's. We'd get nothing out of her."

The venom in her voice took Brun aback. He worked his glasses off the bridge of his nose, pulled out a handkerchief, slowly wiped at the lenses. "You think we oughta go talk to the cops?"

A sour look came over Luella's face. "I've thought of that, but it's probably not a good idea. The first thing they'd do would be to talk to Klein, and he'd tell them exactly what he told us. And then

Klein might get scared enough to do something he hadn't originally intended. I think it would be safer to keep our counsel, and try to find the boy and the journal ourselves."

Brun reached absently into his shirt pocket, pulled out the little container, took a pill between his fingers, and slid it into his mouth.

"Would you like a glass of water?" Luella asked.

Brun shook his head. "Unda mah toeng."

"That's the medicine they use for heart pain?" Luella struggled to keep her voice even.

Brun nodded. "Nitroglycerin."

She remembered the beautiful fifteen-year-old boy, full of energy, radiating desire and ambition. "Just imagine," her Uncle Bob had said to her. "Fifteen years old, he runs away from home because he wants to learn to play this ragtime music, and only Scott Joplin's good enough to teach him. I've never seen a boy with so much get up and go. He could be president of the United States if he doesn't get hung first."

"Whew." Brun took a deep breath. "That stuff really works fast."

Luella looked at the old man, slumped in his chair, dewlap under his chin, bags under his eyes, and willed tears not to pour down her cheeks. Fortunately, just then, Brun pulled out a pack of cigarettes. "No!" Luella barked. "Not in my house, you don't smoke."

He wondered why her voice was so quavery. "Beg your pardon." He slid the pack back into his pocket.

"Thank you," she said primly. "All right, now. Thinking about Rowena Klein gives me an idea. We wouldn't get any information from her, but Eileen is another story."

Brun cocked his head. "Eileen?"

"Otto and Rowena's daughter, the one who brought Alan to the supper last night. How a girl can be so different from her mother, I'll never know. But I'll bet…I believe if she knows anything, I can get her to tell us."

Brun started out of his chair; Luella motioned him back. "School doesn't let out till three-twenty. Just sit back and rest a bit. I'll make us some lunch."

Brun's smile could have broken her heart. "Like I said, Luella. I appreciate your kindness."

Smile at Eileen Klein like that, Luella thought, she'll spill every bean in the pot. "As *I* said, Brun, just consider it Christian charity. For the boy."

◇◇◇

Alan couldn't imagine how this was going to end. He'd followed Richard or Samson or whatever the man's name was for miles through the woods, getting smacked in the face by low-hanging branches, tripping over roots. His feet and legs ached all the way to his armpits, and his head pounded something fierce. Samson didn't seem the least bothered, never mind the big gunnysack, filled with God knew what, slung over his shoulder.

As they drew up to a half-rotted tree trunk, Samson signaled for Alan to sit, which he did gladly. The colored man pulled a canteen from his belt, handed it to the boy, who drank deeply, then passed the water back to Samson. "Thank you," Alan said softly.

Samson grinned, took off his wide-brimmed hat, mopped his face with a raggedy sleeve. "Sorry to make you move so fast, young mister, but I figured before Mr. Barton woke up, we better get as much space as we could between us and him. Nobody knows these woods good as I do, so I believes we's safe. Just in case, though, I got me a trusty shotgun in my house."

Alan looked all around.

"You gonna see it soon enough. But first, I thought we oughta talk a bit just between us. I got me a wife an' a daughter back at the house, an' no point them hearin' what they don't got to. Now, if I'm not bein' too nosy, I would sure love to know how you got to be out in the woods there with Mr. Barton."

Alan laughed. "I don't mind telling you," he said. "But it's a pretty long story."

Samson clapped his hat back onto his head, and settled onto the log next to the boy. "One thing I got plenty of is time, young mister. But say, I don't believe you ever did tell me your name. Or if you did, it went right on past my ears."

The boy reached a hand. "Alan Chandler. And I sure am glad to meet you."

◇◇◇

When Alan stopped talking, Samson said, "Well, that's sure a-plenty. We got to get you away from here before Mr. Barton can go back out lookin' for you. They's trains to St. Lou pretty much all through the day. I can get you to the station…"

Samson's speech ground to a halt as he saw how hard Alan was shaking his head. "No, I can't do that. I've got to get the journal back and give it to Mr. Campbell."

"You was lucky once, boy. You can't count on me bein' there the next time."

Alan chewed at his lip. "What *were* you doing out there, anyway?"

The colored man laughed, showing wide gaps between yellowed teeth. He picked up his sack, reached inside, came out with a dirt-crusted, gnarled piece of wood; a dense, earthy odor rose up. "Sassafras," the man said. "For to make sas-safras tea, which is the best tonic you can take in the springtime. Keep you healthy all year. That no-good stuff in the drugstores they calls sassafras ain't nothin' but the old, dried-out bark. Only the roots can do the job right, and they gotta be dug up soon's the sap starts runnin'. My daddy used to dig roots an' sell 'em to the people in town. His name was Richard, like me, but ever'body called him Sassafras Sam, which is why I got to be called Samson. Daddy allus took me along an' learned me how to tell which plants was good that year and which wasn't. Then when Daddy got hit by a car and kilt, the people was all upset, didn't know where they was gonna get their sassafras, so I fig-ured I'd carry on. Lucky for you I was diggin' out there. I heard Mr. Barton and Mr. Klein yellin', so I come up real quiet to see what they was up to." Samson cackled. "Don't ever let nobody tell you sassafras ain't good for your health. But I tell you, boy, even sassafras ain't gonna be no help to you if Mr. Barton get anywheres near you again."

"Mmmm." Alan sighed. He stood, plucked a blade of grass, chewed at it. "I think I've got an idea."

"What you thinkin'?"

"When I came into town…" Alan paused. "It was just Saturday, but it seems like a month ago. I met Mr. Tom Ireland and another man, a hundred years old."

"Had to be Isaac Stark."

"Right. They said they remembered Mr. Campbell from when he was here in 1899, and they were really interested in the journal. If you can tell me how to get from here to Mr. Ireland's house, I'll go there tonight and fill him in on what happened. I'll bet he'd let me stay there till morning, then tomorrow, he could help me find Mr. Campbell. And after we do, I could go to the police about Mr. Barton."

"Think the police gonna believe you when Mr. Barton tell them that what you say never happened? He a big shot here, and it be your word against his."

"No it wouldn't. You're my witness. You can—"

"Hold on right there, boy." Samson shook his head slowly, emphatically. "Colored who don't know when to keep they mouth shut don't get to be near as old as me. Mr. Barton be mean as they come, an' he got himself a bunch of friends every bit as mean, so even if he do get put away, that still gonna be the end of me and probably my family too."

"Sure." Alan made a face. "I wouldn't ever want you or anyone in your family to get hurt because you saved my life."

Samson grinned. "Sometimes a man got no choice, he got to take a chance. Else, he don't belong on this earth."

"I won't say anything to anybody," Alan said. "Not even Mr. Ireland. I'll tell him I got away from Mr. Barton on my own. Just show me the way from here to his house."

"No sirree!" Samson stood, stretched his back. "I ain't sending you off on your lonesome, not through these woods, and not along the big road either. And for sure, not while it be light out. Tonight, real late, I'll walk you down to Mr. Ireland's, an' we both tell him what happened. I know he gonna help you."

"You could just take me as far as his house. Then I'll go in alone, and he won't have to hear anything about you being involved."

Samson smiled. "Not to give you offense, but Tom Ireland's no man's fool. You go in there and tell him you got yourself away from Mr. Barton, then found your way back all on your own, he ain't gonna believe a single word outa your mouth. But don't worry none. If I can't trust Tom Ireland, there ain't nobody nowhere I *can* trust." Samson gestured: get up. "Gonna take you to my house now." He smiled. "Bet my daughter Susie's gonna love hearin' a white boy, talks funny the way you do, tell her all about New York City. An' I 'spects a nice cup of sassafras tea gonna do you a world of good."

Chapter Seventeen

Monday, April 16
Late afternoon

Elliot Radcliffe thought there must be a better way to make a living than as an editor in a major publishing company. Across his desk, Rudi Blesh barely sat in his chair, broadcasting fury. Blesh was the consummate gentleman, civil and civilized, but right then he appeared on the verge of flying from his chair, sailing over the desk and taking Radcliffe by the throat. The editor focused a pair of blood-shot eyes on the author. "Rudi, please. Calm down. I've never seen you in a state like this."

Blesh's fist pounded the desk. Papers shook; a small ashtray bounced off the edge and clattered to the floor. Blesh didn't seem to notice. "I've never *been* in a situation like this," he roared. "Finally, after almost two years of pleading, begging, cajoling…groveling, for heaven's sake! *Finally*, I get Lottie Joplin to understand how important that journal might be. And then what happens? An entire publishing house sits on its collective rear end while the Big Boss has a nice little European vacation. And while the boss suns himself in Italy, that halfwit barber Campbell makes off with the journal. What I can't understand is how in hell he even knew about it."

"Maybe he's not such a halfwit," Radcliffe said, and immediately regretted it. Now, Blesh was on his feet, his face the color of marinara sauce, pumping his fists like a six-year-old who'd just been told he'd clean his room or else. "Rudi, all right, now, stop," Radcliffe pleaded. "Maybe we can figure out what's happened, and do something constructive. How do you know it was Campbell?"

Blesh took two exaggerated deep breaths. "Who else could it have been? Look, Ellie. You called me this morning, and told me Mr. Knopf gave his okay, so I went right over to Lottie's and what did I find?" He began to tick off points on his fingers. One. Some Negro man came by two or three times last week, told Lottie he was a musician, working with me, and tried to get her to give him the journal. Two. Friday morning, a teen-aged kid came in, she thought his name might have been Alan. He said he was there for Mr. Blesh, paid her five thousand dollars, and went off with the journal."

"Five thou—"

"Yes, Ellie. Five thousand dollars. Where did a teen-aged boy get that kind of money, and where did that particular number come from?"

The editor drummed fingers on the desk top, wondered whether he ought to say what he was thinking, decided he had to. "You *are* sure Mrs. Joplin said the boy told her he was there to pick up the journal for you?"

"Yes. And then the boy said he was going to take it to Sedalia for a ceremony honoring Joplin. There actually *is* going to be a ceremony there, tomorrow night, in fact. And who's been trying to work with the locals on that ceremony for more than half a year now? Campbell, that blasted fool. But that's not all. Lottie told me another interesting story."

Radcliffe willed calm. "Go ahead, I'm listening."

"She said a little while after the boy left with the journal, that same Negro man came in and asked her again to give it to him. She said he got angry when she told him the boy had already picked it up. She has no idea who he is, and couldn't say any more than he was a nice-looking young colored man. The poor woman was terribly upset. I told her not to worry, that I'd get it all straightened out, and damn it, Ellie, I will." Blesh pushed up his sleeve, checked his watch. "If I leave right now, I can get to my travel agent before she closes, and have her book me on the first morning flight to Kansas City. I'll have two hours in my favor, so I ought to be able to catch a train out of Kay Cee, to Sedalia and get there in time for that ceremony. If Campbell's there and he has that book, there's going to be hell to pay."

"Okay, Rudi." To his own ear, Radcliffe's words sounded weary to the point of being patronizing. "Just don't forget, what's happened might be underhanded, but it may not be illegal. You've got no claim on that journal. Mrs. Joplin was free to sell it to whomever she wanted. Don't do anything stupid. Please."

Blesh was halfway to the door. "I'm not a stupid man, Ellie."

"No, you're not," Radcliffe said. "You're one of the brightest men I know. But bright men can do some pretty goddamn stupid things when they get as worked up as you are."

◇◇◇

Brun helped Luella clear the lunch dishes off the table, then picked up a towel, and as she washed, he dried. He partially stifled a burp, excused himself. Luella half-smiled. "I'm pleased that you enjoyed the meal."

"That I did. I guess I got a lot of reasons to be glad you found me. If you hadn't, I'd be walking the streets in circles right now, getting noplace in a hurry."

She turned a prim look his way, nose tilted upward. "The Lord works in mysterious ways."

Brun set down the dish he was drying, picked up another. "Guess I can't argue with that," he said, and thought, I ain't that dumb.

"We should be able to leave for the school in about half an hour," Luella said. "It's a fair little walk, down Ohio to Broadway, then a couple of blocks east. I hope that won't be too much for you."

"No, it oughta be fine," Brun said. Her solicitousness both moved and irritated him.

She hung the dishrag on the edge of the sink. "Well, you'll let me know if you're having a problem. I think the farther from her home we can catch the girl, the more likely she'll be to talk to us."

"You're the doctor."

◇◇◇

They were on Ohio, approaching East Fourth, when Brun felt a tug at his arm. He turned, and found himself staring into the well-appointed but very angry face of a middle-aged, light-skinned colored woman. She smacked a hand onto each hip. "You look like you don't even recognize me,

Mr. Campbell. Bet you thought you were never going to see me again."

A tall, muscular dark man beside her took in Brun and Luella from under the peak of a woolen tweed cap. He looked no more cordial than the woman.

"Well, sure I remember you," Brun said. "You're Miss Vinson. Scott Joplin's daughter."

"Yes," a hiss. "And this is my brother-in-law, Mickey Thurman. From New York. The one who works at Knopf."

Two colored men, one large, one smaller, who'd been walking down Ohio a half-block behind Brun and Luella, hustled to make up most of the distance, then turned into the sheltered doorway at Jack's Clothing. Each lit a cigarette, then stood, ears bent toward the animated foursome.

Without changing expression, Thurman tipped his cap toward Luella. Brun picked up. "This here's Mrs. Luella Rohrbaugh," he said. "Friend from way back. She and I got to know each other back in 'ninety-nine, when I was here taking lessons from Mr. Joplin."

"I'm pleased to make your acquaintance, Miss Vinson, Mr. Thurman," Luella said.

Bess nodded. Her face said she wasn't pleased about anything right then. "I'm giving you fair warning;" a snarl. "You figured you were pretty smart, didn't you, getting that kid to steal my father's journal from Mrs. Joplin."

Mickey Thurman began shuffling his feet. Brun thought he looked nervous. "What're you talking about? I told you back in California, I didn't get any kid—"

"How stupid do you think I am?" Bess' anger seemed to grow with every exchange. She was shouting now. "Let me tell you something. Mr. Thurman and I are going to get that journal back, and then he's going to take it to New York, and call Rudi Blesh. I didn't want him to have it, but I'm not about to let a scumbag like you diddle me. If Mr. Blesh wants it, *he* can pay me five thousand dollars. And if not, someone else will."

In the doorway, Green's eyes bulged. Slim grinned.

Bess extended a hand toward Brun. "If you're smart, you'll give me that journal now, and save yourself a lot of trouble."

"Can't give you what I don't have," Brun said. "But even if I did have it, I wouldn't give it to you. Beat it. Get outa here."

Thurman took a heavy step toward the old man. Luella moved quickly to come between them. "Mr. Thurman, Miss Vinson!" The words could have cut through a steel plate. "You've said quite enough. Now, either you move along, or I will call a policeman and complain that you're making a public nuisance and threatening us. And I will do the same if I see you following us around."

Bess glanced toward Thurman, then locked eyes with Brun. "You're going to be sorrier than you've ever been in your whole damn life," she snapped. "We'll be around, all right, and we'll be watching. And for sure, we'll be at the ceremony. Just try and show anybody that journal, and it's going to be me who calls a cop. Then you can explain how you happened to get your greasy hands on a journal that belonged to my father."

She glared at Luella, but she might as well have tried to intimidate a stone statue. "Get away from here," Luella ordered, then wheeled around and started walking down the sidewalk. Brun stepped along to keep up with her pace.

Thurman grabbed Bess by the arm. "Woman, you better quit that stuff before you get us time in the workhouse. Hell's bells, we ain't just colored. We're colored from New York."

Bess pounded one fist into the other palm, spat on the sidewalk, and stomped away, Thurman trailing in her wake.

In the doorway, Slim whistled softly. "Whoo-whee. Something new every minute. Looks like we got us even more competition."

Green nudged him toward Brun and Luella.

"Go see what they be up to. Maybe they'll take you to the kid." He inclined his head ever so slightly toward Bess and Mickey. "I'll try an' find out more about them."

Slim strolled out of the shelter and along the sidewalk, taking care to stay a block behind Brun and Luella.

◇◇◇

Brun felt like he'd wandered back into Cal's time machine. So many buildings on Ohio looked just the same as they had in 1899. That damn Vinson woman had stopped them right outside what used to be Doc Overstreet's office. The barber craned his neck to look down West Fifth, to where he'd worked in Mr. Stark's music shop. The Starks had been so very good to him. Back in 1910, in Tulsa, Brun heard that Mr. Stark had brought his wife back from New York, to die in St. Louis. He could have gone and visited, but never did. Why the hell not?"

Luella nearly asked whether he was having heart pain again, but caught herself. They walked the rest of the way to Broadway in silence.

◇◇◇

Teen-agers poured out of the Smith-Cotton Junior-Senior High School. Luella led Brun to the corner of Broadway and Lamine. "We'll wait here," she said. "Whether the girl's going directly home or is going to stop with friends for ice cream or soda pop, she'll pass this way."

The kids scrambled by, a sea of youth, their chatter white noise to Brun's ears. Luella scanned the crowd. Every now and then, one of the girls said hello or good afternoon, and Luella answered each one by name. Knows everyone in town, and probably all of their business, too, Brun thought. But if it takes a busybody to find the kid and the journal, okay.

A girl with lots of dark, curly hair, brown eyes, and a look about her that Brun thought oughtn't to be on any girl under eighteen said, "Hello, Mrs. Rohrbaugh. What're you doing here?"

"We're waiting for you, Eileen." Luella reached bony fingers to take the girl by the arm, then worked her off the sidewalk, out of the crowd, and said, "This is Mr. Brun Campbell. He's come all the way from California to find the young man who escorted you to the supper last night."

The girl flushed.

She got to know him pretty well, Brun thought.

Luella stepped closer to Eileen. "Do you know where we can find him?"

The girl looked puzzled. "He's at our house. He told me he was supposed to wait there and see if the ceremony committee wanted to put him on the program for tomorrow night."

Brun started to say something, but stopped when Luella kicked his shin. "We've already been to your home, and there's no one there. Do you have any idea where we might find him? It's very important."

The girl moved her head slowly, side to side. "I don't know where he could have gone."

"Eileen, just how long have you known Alan? Have you ever visited his family back east?"

"No. I just yesterday met him for the first time. I think there's a big misunderstanding. I didn't say last night that he's a friend of our family, I just said he's a friend and he was staying at our house. Actually, Mr. Barton brought him over to stay with us. Mr. Barton's one of Daddy's friends."

"Yes, dear. I know Mr. Barton."

And you don't like him one bit, Brun thought.

Tears started down Eileen's cheeks. She tried to cough them away.

Luella edged the girl farther off the sidewalk, away from the flow of teen-aged traffic. "You don't have to cry," the old woman said. "Mr. Campbell and I are concerned about Alan, the way he's apparently disappeared. You seemed quite a little fond of him last night. Wouldn't you like to help us?"

She nodded vigorously, then blurted, "Yes,

'course I would. He's peachy…I mean, he's really nice. He was so excited about having the journal and showing it to Mr. Campbell. On the way out to the supper last night, I asked him why Mr. Barton had brought him to our house, and he told me about how a big colored man had pulled a gun on him and tried to take away the journal, but Mr. Barton rescued him, and got him to check out of the hotel he was in. Then he brought him to our house so he'd be safe, away from the colored man."

Luella felt weary. Was the girl lying? Was the boy lying to her? Was Brun lying about the way the boy had taken it upon himself to get the journal and bring it out?

Eileen went on. "I tried to sneak a look at the journal while Alan…" Her face went scarlet. "…while Alan wasn't there. But he came in and caught me, and he seemed really upset. I told him I was just curious, and…and, oh, Mrs. Rohrbaugh, I don't have any idea why my father and Mr. Barton would be having anything to do with that ceremony for the colored piano player. They don't like colored people. I don't understand this whole thing."

"Neither do I," Luella said, her voice softer now. "But I'm going to find out. And you know, Eileen, when I say I'm going to do something, I do it."

The girl nodded vigorously. "I don't want Alan to get hurt."

Luella put an arm around her. "Neither do we. Now, I'm going to ask you to help by not saying anything to anyone about our little talk."

Eileen looked relieved. "Thank you, Mrs. Rohrbaugh. I won't say a word, I promise."

Brun looked across the street, at the large colored man lounging against a lamp-post, smoking a cigarette. Gave him the willies. He was starting to imagine things.

◇◇◇

As Luella and Brun watched Eileen walk off down Broadway, Brun asked, "You think she was telling the truth?"

Luella gave him the fish eye. "I suppose I should be asking you that. Set a thief to catch a thief."

"Okay, you want it that way, yeah, I think I do believe her. I just hope she ain't gonna go home and start blabbing to her parents. Girls that age… you know."

"Yes, I'm afraid I do. But I think her concern for the boy will keep her quiet. Considering what we know now, perhaps we ought to go back to the machine shop, and have another talk with Otto Klein."

He fell into step beside her.

"Br…Brun?" she stammered.

"What's that?"

"I need to apologize to you. For that nasty remark about setting a thief. It was uncalled for."

His laugh came through just a little hollow. "Naw, don't worry about it. If a shoe fits, you gotta put it on and pay the piper."

◇◇◇

As the door to his shop opened, sounding the bell, Otto Klein glanced up, then set down his calipers and gawked. Barton looked like he'd been through a war. Blood all down the right side of his shirt, a mouse just below his hairline on the right, face scratched and bruised. "Jesus, Jerry. What in hell happened to you?"

"I got on the wrong end of a nigger's stick," Barton growled.

Klein hustled to the other side of the counter, pulled Barton into a chair. "Sit down, sit down. You're tellin' me some nigger did this to you? He ain't gonna see the light tomorrow, the black bastard."

Barton looked up at Klein, then winced as he absent-mindedly rubbed the knot on his head. "Otto, shut the fuck up for just a minute, would you? I don't know who it was. Remember when you came tear-assin' out back of Armstrong's? Well, right after you left, I was getting set to persuade the kid to spill where he hid the book, but then all of a sudden, the lights went out. I got just this quick look, a great big nigger. I think the son of a bitch hit me twice."

"And the kid got away?"

Barton sneered. "No, Otto. He hung around till I woke up, then he brought me a drink and helped me get up so I could start working him over again."

Klein backed off a step. "Hey, Jerry, no call to be snotty."

Barton sighed. "When I came to, I was face-down in sticker-bushes. My truck was gone, so I started hikin' out. About half a mile down the Georgetown road, there's my truck, off on the side with a flat. And no key." Barton patted his right pants pocket. "Good thing I always carry an extry. I jacked up the truck, fixed the flat, and here I am. Oh yeah. I stopped home just long enough to pick up another gun."

Klein opened his mouth, but before he could say anything, Barton shouted, "Yeah, Otto. The nigger took my gun, too."

Klein pounded the counter-top. "Hey, now, it ain't my fault you screwed up an' let the kid get away and all." He pointed toward the back of the shop. "You want to yell at somebody, I got a mirror back in the crapper there."

Both men froze as the door bell tinkled, and Brun and Luella marched up to the counter. For a moment, everyone just stared. Then, Luella said, "Mr. Barton, you look as if you've had an accident."

Barton grimaced, swallowed hard, then did a half-way job on a smile. "You should see the other guy."

Klein leaned forward, across the counter. "Can I do something for the both of you? You find that kid all right?"

"No, we didn't, Mr. Klein, and that's why we're here. No one answered the door at your house. I'm quite concerned for the boy."

Klein shrugged. "Maybe he was sleepin'. Or he didn't feel like answerin' the bell. Could be he just took it in his head to run off, who knows? He was a funny kind of kid."

"He wouldn't do that," Luella said. "He couldn't wait to find Mr. Campbell and give him that journal."

Ice water spread across Klein's palms. He tried to keep his face calm, his voice level. "Maybe he was just sayin' he had it. We don't really know anything about that kid."

"I can't help wondering how he happened to be staying at your house, Mr. Klein."

Barton reacted to the silence. "How he

'happened to be stayin' there' is I took him there. Yesterday. When I came out from havin' Sunday dinner at the Pacific Café, there was this great big colored guy, got hold of the kid and yellin' how he better hand over all of his money. So I pulled my gun and ran the coon off. The kid told me he was in town for some kind of celebration or other, and now he was afraid the colored guy might catch him again. If I lived in town, I'd'a taken him home myself, but since I don't, I stopped by Otto's, and Otto said sure, the kid could stay there for a couple of days. Okay?"

Klein jabbed a finger toward Luella. "Mrs. Rohrbaugh, that boy ran off from his own home. Jerry and me tried our best to look out for him, but if he took it in his head to run off from here too, we couldn't help that. It ain't right, you should talk to us like you're doin'."

Butter would melt in his mouth, Luella thought. "Very well, Mr. Klein. If you happen to see the boy, please tell him Mr. Campbell is staying at the Milner. Or, he can come see me."

"I'll do that, Mrs. Rohrbaugh. I surely will."

◇◇◇

The door had barely closed behind Brun and Luella when Barton said, "Okay, Otto. The room the kid was staying in? That's where he must've hidden the book. When you get home, tear that room apart. We find the book, it's still gonna be money in our pocket."

"But how about the kid? If he opens his mouth—"

"We're dead, that's what. So we've got to make sure he's dead first. I'll go on back to where I had him, an' check in the woods all around. I'll look all along the Georgetown Road. We gotta get our hands on him before he shows up at the ceremony, that's for damn sure."

◇◇◇

Barton had barely stepped outside when he stopped in his tracks. Old Lady Rohrbaugh and the geezer from California were most of the way to the corner, and there behind them, walking close-in to the buildings, was that giant coon he'd chased off the kid the day before. Barton took off like a flash, ran up behind the big man, spun him around. "You the gutless nigger, snuck up behind me with a stick?" he shouted.

Brun and Luella turned, watched.

Slim gave Barton a steady up-and-down. "Mister, I don't know what you talkin' about," he said. "But if somebody done laid into you with a stick, I sure wouldn't mind shakin' his hand."

Barton's hand drifted toward his pocket. Slim tensed, clenched a fist.

"Fight! Fight!"

Six schoolboys charged across the street, then stood at the curb, laughing as they waited for the show. Barton glared at them, then lowered his hands. Slim uncocked his fist. "Next time you see me, you better pray there's people around then, too," Barton snarled.

Slim did an abrupt about-face. All the way down the street, he felt the white man's eyes on his back. Casual as he could manage, he nodded at Brun, tipped his hat to Luella. Guess that's the end of me following after them, he thought. I'll get me a drink, then go back to Mr. Ireland's and wait for Alonzo.

Brun squinched his eyes. "I swear I saw that guy out by the school, while we were talking to the girl. He was across the street, smoking a cigarette."

Luella shook her head. "There's some very funny business going on here, and I am going to get to the bottom of it." She set her jaw. "That boy will not get hurt, not if I can help it."

Brun wondered why she was so concerned about some kid she hardly knew, but he was not about to ask questions.

◇◇◇

Alan followed Samson Curd out of the little kitchen, into the living room. Almost six o'clock, early-spring sunlight fading. Curd struck a match, lit the coal-oil lamp, settled into a chair, then motioned Alan to sit beside him. Mrs. Curd and Susie, the daughter, stayed in the kitchen to clean up. Alan suspected they knew when the head of the family required privacy, and behaved accordingly.

Curd patted his belly. "Hope you got your fill. I don't like nobody leavin' my table hungry."

"I'm stuffed, thank you," Alan said. "I couldn't eat another bite." Or drink another mouthful of sassafras tea, he thought.

"You ever have possum before?"

Alan shook his head. "No. But I like trying new things. It was good."

Curd rolled a cigarette, offered it to Alan, who declined politely. Curd smiled, lit up, blew out smoke. "You a clean-living boy, ain't gonna get no Tee-Bee in you' lungs. You smarter'n me."

"I wasn't so smart I could've gotten away from Mr. Barton. On my own, I'd have been dead a long time before you."

Curd laughed. "You got a pretty good mouth on you."

"People tell me that."

"So you come all the way out here 'cause of Scott Joplin? How you know about Scott Joplin?

Not many in Sedalia even do. But a white boy from New York? How you come to be playin' nigger music?"

"I heard Mr. Campbell play it on a radio program, but that's not what he called it. I never heard anyone call it that."

Curd laughed, a real ho-ho-ho. "Must be real different back there. Out here, we got nigger crapper-cans, nigger drinking fountains, nigger movie seats, nigger restaurants, nigger music, nigger everything. You sayin' that ain't the way in New York?"

Alan shook his head. "I thought it was only like that in the South."

"Better have yourself another think. There ain't worse crackers in Mis'sippi an' Alabam' put together than Mr. Barton and Mr. Klein an' their pals. They'd shoot down a colored man in the woods, then tell the cops they thought he was a deer. Like colored men got these big horns on toppa they heads." Curd tapped ash into a metal tray. "So, tell me now. That book you carried out here? It's in Mr. Joplin's own hand?"

"I guess. It came straight from his widow. It's got a lot of stuff in it that's not in *They All Played Ragtime*, which is supposed to be the last word."

Curd grinned. "There ain't never no last word, boy, not about anything. Your Mr. Campbell must think that book's pretty important."

"He said if he had it, he might be able to get a statue put up in the middle of downtown for Mr. Joplin."

Curd took a long draw at his cigarette. "Well, maybe he know something I don't. Put a plaque up in Hubbard High School, nobody gonna complain. But I can't see no statue for any colored man goin' up south of Main Street." Curd paused as he saw the puzzled expression on Alan's face. "Main Street, that be the dividin' line in Sedalia. North of Main, they calls Lincolnville. But south of Main, that be for the white. See what I be sayin'?"

Alan felt his face go red. "Yes."

Curd looked off into the distance. "Not sayin' Scott Joplin don't deserve a statue. My daddy used to hear him play, down by the Maple Leaf Club, an' he told us no matter how much was goin' on in a room, when Scott Joplin sat down on the piana bench, you could hear a pin drop. Everybody used to say, he one day gonna be King of Ragtime."

"Did you ever hear him play?"

Curd stubbed his cigarette in the metal tray. "No, to my eternal regret. I was born in oh-one, and by then, Mr. Joplin had moved off to St. Louie. But we all played his music." Curd nodded in the direction of a battered mahogany upright piano in the far corner of the room. "Daddy never did learn how to play, but he made sure us kids did, not that any one of us was ever any good. We didn't have much money, but Daddy bought all of Scott Joplin's tunes, and Arthur Marshall's and Scott Hayden's, too, they was Mr. Joplin's students here." A sly smile came across Curd's face; he waggled a finger toward the piano. "It's all there, in that piana bench. Every piece of ragtime music Scott Joplin ever wrote."

Alan was halfway to the bench before he remembered his manners. "Could I look?"

"Sure, go right ahead. Why you think I tol' you? You can even play it if you wants, that is if you can stand for the piana bein' bad outa tune. We just gotta leave us some time to get a li'l shuteye before we goes out to Mr. Ireland's. Won't do to start off tuckered."

The boy threw back the piano bench lid, and began to leaf, open-mouthed, through the four-inch-thick pile of sheet music. Curd laughed out loud. "Careful, now. Play too much of that nigger music, you just might find you own skin turnin' black."

"I wouldn't care," Alan shot back.

Curd's face went grim. "Better watch, boy. Boots that don't fit right ain't gonna pinch when you first puts 'em on, but walk a couple miles in 'em and you're gonna have you some serious pain."

Chapter Eighteen

Monday, April 16
Early evening

Eileen couldn't concentrate on her homework. Across the living room, her mother knitted away at a sweater, but not in her usual calm way. Tonight, she jabbed the needles as if the wool had said something to rile her. Her face was a mask, deep grooves between her nose and the corners of her mouth. Eileen had learned long ago to step softly when those tight furrows appeared.

The girl heard a noise on the stairs, turned to see her father coming down. He'd been up there for almost an hour. When Eileen had asked her mother why he was making the guest room a shambles, Mrs. Klein had snapped, "Don't go looking into other peoples' business. Nosy Parkers get into trouble." Eileen was sure it had something to do with Alan and that book of his.

As Klein stomped across the living room,

Eileen saw her mother shoot him a silent question. He answered it with a barely-perceptible shake of his head, then walked on, into the kitchen.

As Eileen started to speak, and her mother raised a warning finger, the front door flew open, and Jerry Barton burst into the room, firing wild glances in every direction. "Otto?" Barton bellowed, then even louder, "Otto!"

Eileen screamed. Mrs. Klein dropped her knitting, and jumped from the couch.

Klein tore back in from the kitchen with a bottle of Moerschel's beer in a death grip. Four people stared at each other. Eileen thought Mr. Barton looked fit to bust. Finally, her father cleared his throat. "Jerry? What the hell's goin' on?"

Barton seemed to draw himself together. He nodded toward Mrs. Klein. "Sorry to run in like this, Rowena, but I need to talk to Otto."

The woman picked up her knitting, then, without a word, started to the kitchen. Partway there, she looked over her shoulder. "Eileen!"

The girl gathered up her book and papers, and followed her mother out. They'd barely gotten into the kitchen when Eileen hissed, "I'm surprised they don't just snap their fingers and expect we'll go out like whipped dogs."

Mrs. Klein set her knitting onto the table. "Hush up, Eileen." Drawstrings seemed to pull her mouth tight. "Some goings-on, it's better not to know about."

◇◇◇

Klein watched his women disappear into the kitchen, then turned to Barton. "Something go wrong about tomorrow night?"

Barton waved off Klein's guess. "I was down by Andy's Tavern, having myself a beer, and who comes in and walks right past me but Alton Whitaker."

Klein wondered if his friend had gone over the edge. "Yeah? So?"

"Alton Whitaker," Barton repeated. "With that big, floppy hat he's always wearing. And then I remembered. I only got a real quick look before I went down, but that nigger who nailed me out by Melvin Armstrong's had on the exact same kinda hat. All them sassafras trees out there? Hell, Otto, that was Samson Curd, hit me."

Klein slowly, carefully, set his bottle onto the top of the television set, next to the rabbit ears. "Well, okay, then. So maybe after tomorrow night we could—"

"After tomorrow night, horseshit!" Barton brought a fist down on the TV, setting Klein's beer into a little dance. "I'm bettin' you didn't find that book in the room where the kid was sleepin', am I right?"

"Well, no, but—"

"I'm also bettin' Curd's got the kid out by his place, and probably the journal, too. Maybe the kid has it hid under his shirt. I'm going over there and get it, and while I'm there, I'll teach both of them a lesson about what happens to a nigger that cold-cocks a white man."

Klein grabbed at Barton's sleeve. "Jerry, hold on a minute, huh? I don't blame you for bein' sore, but we're meetin' the boys in just a few hours. We gotta make damn sure Johnny gets the charge set okay, and we're square on the alibis. You don't want to screw up the plans."

Barton pulled roughly away. "Christ, Otto, you're such a goddamn old woman. We're talking about a five-thousand-dollar book, and all you can do is snivel about 'the plans.' I'll be back by eleven, easy, and I'll have me a pair of nigger ears in my pocket. And if I don't have that book in my other pocket, I'll have two ears from offa a white kid instead. Shoot! I was gonna ask if you wanted to come along, but I don't need you crappin' your pants and stinkin' up my truck. I can handle it myself."

As the door slammed behind Barton, Eileen started to her feet, but her mother reached across the table to restrain the girl. "Just wait a bit," Mrs. Klein said. "Give him a chance to cool off before we go out there."

"Mo-ther," Eileen whispered. "Do you know what they're up to."

"No," said Mrs. Klein. "And furthermore I don't want to." She picked up her knitting, then added, "And if I did know, I wouldn't tell you."

"Oh!" Eileen balled both hands into fists, brought them down hard against her thighs. Then she threw the kitchen door open and rushed past her father, up the stairs, into her room.

Mrs. Klein heard the bedroom door slam. She braced herself.

Klein stormed into the kitchen. "What's going on with that girl? She gives me a look like I just hit her, then runs on up to her room and bangs the door shut so hard they could hear it all the way to Lone Jack. I got a good mind to give her what-for."

"Don't, Otto." Mrs. Klein's voice was like a violin string. "Teenage girls are flighty sometimes. They can't help it."

Klein's face worked itself into a statement of disgust. "Women. Huh!"

Mrs. Klein tightened her grip on her knitting needles.

◇◇◇

Eileen threw herself onto her bed and launched a two-fisted attack on her pillow. Eventually, she ran out of steam, then rolled over onto her back, which put her in mind of that boy, Alan. He was so sweet last night, so embarrassed. She smiled. He stood there by the side of the bed for the longest time, just talking, till she finally sat up, took him by the hand, and pulled him into the bed. He said he'd never done anything like that before, and she practically had to tell him how to do it. He wasn't like any of the other boys. When she was making out with Tim Baker in the back of his car, all he did was take off her brassiere, and then he made a big mess on her skirt, lucky she was wearing dark blue. And that night last summer in the corn-rows with Mark Nelson, she had to keep telling him to be careful, if he ripped her clothes, she was going to have a hell of a time explaining to her parents what happened. Then there was the night she'd left her window open so Lew Gardiner could shinny up the drainpipe to the roof to come into her bedroom. She giggled, remembering how he was in such a hurry, he almost fell, but then he was so rough with her, and he got done almost as soon as he'd started, then laid there like a big lump till she couldn't breathe and had to push him off. But Alan just fooled around for the longest time, and when she finally told him to go all the way, he said, "You're sure? You're sure you want to?" "Yes," she said. "Please." But she had to help him get ready, and even when he was inside of her, he took almost forever. She'd never felt anything like that in her life, thought she might go crazy. If he were in the room right now, she'd make him do it again… whoa. Make him?

She sat up. What boy sneaks into a girl's bedroom in the middle of the night just to say he's sorry for being rude? She thought it was obvious what he'd really come for, so why did he just stand by her bed, apologizing, till she pulled him in? Oh, she was as stupid as her father, her stupid, stupid father, tearing the guest room apart. But he didn't find what he was looking for, did he?

The girl jumped to the floor, peered underneath the bed, but aside from a few dust bunnies, nothing. She took a moment to gauge just where Alan had stood, then lifted the edge of the mattress, reached beneath it, came out with a leather-bound book. "Oh, damn you, Alan Chandler," she muttered, and slammed the journal down onto the bed. "All you came in here for was to hide this stupid journal. Well, all right for you, then."

The girl took a deep breath, climbed back onto the bed, picked up the book, and started to read.

◇◇◇

By the unsteady light of the coal-oil lamp in the living room, Alan told Samson and Irma Curd and their daughter Susie about New York City. "Ain't none of us ever been outa Pettis County in our lives," Curd said. "I seen pictures of New York, and I can't believe there really do be places like that on this earth. Them skyscraper buildings…" He shook his head.

"And all them people," Irma said. "I'd be scared outa my wits."

"Well, I wouldn't be scared." More than a trace of mockery for the old folks in Susie's voice. "I want to go and see it all for myself. See if I don't one day."

Curd laughed gently. "When you be fifteen, you got all kinds of big plans for yourself."

"Sure, I got big plans. You think I want to live out my days, never settin' foot outside of Pettis County, Missoura? Times is changed from when you and Mama was young. Now, Mr. Alan, I want to hear about the Empire State Building. Ain't that supposed to be the biggest building in the world?"

Before Alan could launch into his story about taking an elevator to the observation deck of the Empire State Building, a hundred and two stories up in the air, and looking out over the whole city, Curd put a finger to his lips. "Shh. Listen."

The room went still. A faint sound caught Alan's ear. "A motor."

Curd nodded.

"How did you ever hear that?"

"Be black as me, you keeps your eyes and ears wide open, even when you be sleepin'." Curd motioned Alan out of the chair. "Come on."

"Where're we going?"

"Out to the woodshed. You gonna sit in there for a bit, till we sees what's what. We don't usually hear no motorcars out this way, this time of night."

Alan followed his host out the front door, off the porch, and around the corner. By the light of the lamp, he saw a ramshackle little building next to the house. Curd pulled the door open, then motioned Alan toward a six-foot woodpile to the left. "Get yourself down back there, nobody gonna see you, not 'less they lookin' awful hard. Don't move till I comes for you, hear?"

"Yeah." Alan started back, tripped over an ax, stumbled behind the woodpile. Curd chuckled, then closed the door.

The boy worked himself into a sitting position, then stared into the darkness. He thought about the music he'd played earlier, out of Curd's piano bench. "The Cascades," it was called, and it said on the cover that it had been composed for the 1904 St. Louis World's Fair. Alan imagined a piano keyboard before him, and began to move his fingers.

In the back of his mind, he heard the motor draw closer and closer. Then, a car door slammed.

A moment later, he heard a shout. "Hey, Curd." A banging noise. "Open up the door or I'm comin' in shooting."

Alan stopped playing, listened hard. No sound. He tried to go back to his keyboard, but it had vanished. He worked saliva around his dry mouth.

◇◇◇

In the living room, Curd, his wife, and his daughter stood respectfully. Barton ignored the women, zeroed in on Curd. "You was out diggin' sassafras today, huh?"

"No, sir," Curd said. "It ain't quite the right time yet."

"Oh." Barton's face twisted into a sneer. "So I guess you been workin' somebody's farm, then. Whose farm you work today? You tell me that, then you and me is gonna go talk to whoever it is."

Curd shook his head slowly. "Mr. Barton, sir, I wasn't workin' on no farm today." He pointed to the door, still open from Barton's entry. "I been fixin' things around the house. Like the door, it done broke itself offa the hinge las' week. And the roof, lot of the shingles came off in the big storm back in January. You can see, they's new ones on the back, to the wind side."

Barton sneered again. "Smart nigger. I bet

there's new shingles back there, but you didn't just put them on today. 'Cause today, you was out diggin' in the woods behind Mr. Armstrong's, and you found me with a boy there and gave me a good knock on my head. That boy had him a book, and I want it, and I want the boy with it. And I don't got a lot of time to be foolin' with you."

Curd shook his head again. "Mister Barton, please. I ain't got the littlest idea about no boy and no book. I be sorry for what happened to you, but I don't know nothin' about it."

"You don't? You're real sure about that, huh?"

"Yes, sir."

"Oh. Well, okay, then." Barton's tone denied the casual nature of the words. "Maybe I can help you remember."

He glanced across the room, to where Curd's hat hung on a nail, just inside the door, then turned a smile on the colored man that congealed the blood in his heart. "Yeah," Barton said. "That's the hat you were wearin'." He grabbed Susie's arm, pulled her half-off her feet. "Get your dress off, pickaninny. Quick."

Susie screamed, tried to pull away, but got nowhere. Curd stepped toward Barton, but stopped when the white man pointed a large handgun at him. "Come one step closer, you're gonna be a nigger with no knees," Barton growled. He pulled at Susie's dress once, twice. The third time, the fabric came away in his hand. Susie screamed again, then bent low and crossed her arms in front of her body. Barton turned the gun onto her. "Outa that filthy underwear," he said. "I don't want to touch my hands to it, but I will if you make me. Now, Samson, any time you want, you can give me that book and tell me where the kid is. Otherwise, I'm gonna go right on with what I'm doin'."

◇◇◇

Susie's first scream sent Alan scrambling to his feet; the second one mobilized him to the doorway of the shed. Carefully, he worked the door open, then made his way toward the house as if he were crossing a freshly-waxed floor. A small branch cracked under his foot; he stopped, listened. Nothing.

The boy drew a deep breath, then edged around the corner of the house and up to the porch. Crouching low at the foot of the rough wooden stairs, he peered through the open doorway, saw Susie pull a long undergarment up over her head as Barton waved a gun in her direction.

Alan turned away, fury and embarrassment raging through his mind. Back he ran to the shed, grabbed the ax from the floor, hefted it. Bigger than the ones he'd used on camping trips, heavier, a longer handle. Probably a good thing. He hurried back to the porch stairs. Susie was on her knees now, in front of Barton, who held his gun to the side of her head. Barton's back was to the door. Alan felt dizzy, took a moment to slow his breathing. Then he tiptoed up the three stairs, to the doorway, and into the room.

Mrs. Curd was crying. As she caught sight of Alan, she clapped a hand to her mouth. The look on Samson's face was one Alan hoped never to see again. The boy prayed no one could hear the thumping of his heart. One step, another, a third, and he was within a pace of Barton. He thought Mrs. Curd's eyes might pop out of her head.

The boy raised the ax, which threw him just a bit off balance. As he struggled not to fall sidewise, he came down hard on his left foot. The flooring groaned.

Barton pulled away from Susie, raising his gun as he turned. Alan stepped up, swung the ax. Too late, Barton saw the part he was playing in the ballet, moved directly into the blade, took it full in the face. He loosed a terrible noise, part moan, part howl, clutched at his ruined nose and mouth, then collapsed, slow-motion, into a half-crouch. The gun clattered to the floor. Alan raised the ax again, brought it down full force onto the crown of Barton's head. Without another sound, the man sank to the ground.

Susie whisked her dress and underwear off the floor, and ran into the kitchen. Alan dropped the ax, retched mightily, but managed to hold onto his dinner. Curd felt at Barton's neck, shook his head. His wife kicked at the body. "Pig!" she cried. "Filthy pig!"

Curd squeezed her shoulder, then wrapped both arms around Alan, who had begun to sob. "Boots startin' to pinch a little?" Curd said softly. "Your skin look six shades darker than when I first laid eyes on you. You done put your life on the line for the colored, same as Mr. John Brown. Not many do that."

"After what you did for me?" Alan wiped at his eyes. "What else was I going to do?"

"You coulda run off. Saved your own skin. But you didn't." Curd's lips formed a grim smile. "Our Mr. Barton didn't figure on findin' a nigger in the woodpile."

◇◇◇

Inside an hour, the Curds and Alan had Barton's body rolled up in an old blanket, and all the blood scrubbed off the living room floor and walls. They rinsed the buckets and the brushes, then flopped onto chairs around the kitchen table. It was Alan who finally spoke. "This doesn't seem real. It's like

I'm having a bad dream and can't wake up. Samson, did you ever kill a man?"

Curd shook his head. "That way, I been lucky."

"What are we going to tell the police?"

Curd hauled himself to his feet, stood over the boy, rested a hand on his shoulder. "We ain't gonna tell the police nothing. A boy just in from New York, sittin' around in a house with a bunch of colored people, and a white man, a real important man in these parts, gets his head bashed with a ax? We're all four of us lookin' at a rope with a big knot in it. We never did set eyes on Mr. Barton, understand? Not for a minute, not the whole night through."

Alan pointed into the living room, where the rolled-up blanket was easily visible. "But—"

"I gonna take care of that."

"How? You going to bury him some place?"

"Just you trust me, okay?"

Alan nodded. "Sure."

"Good. Now, then, we better get a move on. Nice of Mr. Barton to leave us his truck. Irma an' Susie an' me, we gonna take that truck out by Jeff'son City, where her sister live, and far's anybody else knows, we been there since yesterday, came in on the train for a visit. B'fore we leave, I gonna draw you a map. You'll go down this dirt road out front, through the woods to the Georgetown Road, into

Lincolnville an' right straight to Mr. Ireland's. You tell him what happen' here, but not a single soul other, understand?"

Alan had never known his hands to shake, but right then, he couldn't hold them still. Curd noticed. "You be all right," he said. "You can count on Mr. Ireland to help you. If'n I could, I'd take you there myself, but best nobody see me around here tonight, and for sure, not with you."

"Can't you take me along to Jefferson City?" Alan paused, then added, "I've never been so scared in my life."

Curd shook his head. "Wouldn't be smart. We tryin' to make nobody notice us, and nothin' personal, but in the colored part of Jeff City, you gonna stand out like a cow in a field fulla sheep. An' if Mr. Law see us on the road, we don't want to be givin' him no reason to go an' look in the back of that truck."

Four pairs of eyes glanced at the bundle on the living-room floor.

"But what if someone stops me on the road into town?" Alan asked.

"You's comin' in from Kans' City, got you a ride along the big highway, but the man was goin' on to St. Lou, so you got out and started walkin'. Happens all the time. Nobody gonna think a thing about it." Curd grinned. "And I warrant that wouldn't be the biggest story you ever told a person, now would it?"

Alan silently promised that if he got out of this alive, he'd never tell another lie. "No."

"Good." Curd pounded the boy's back. "Come on, then. Help me get that piece of human dirt in the truck, and then we all be on our way."

Irma Curd pushed back her chair, hesitated, then rushed over to Alan. "I ain't never gonna forget you and what you did," she said. "I never did imagine, not even in my wildest dream, I'd be sayin' anything like this to a white boy, but you be a son to me now." She threw her arms around him. He choked back a sob, and embraced her.

◇◇◇

By the time Irma and Susie came outside with a small, battered suitcase, Curd and Alan had stashed Barton and the blanket on the floor in the rear of the truck cab, under gunnysacks of sassafras root. The Curds got into the truck, Susie in the back seat, her parents up front. Curd started the motor. "We be seein' you again," he called, and waved at Alan. "In the meantime, good luck to all of us."

The boy watched the truck all the way down the dirt road until it made a turn. When the tail lights vanished, he pulled Curd's map from his pocket. His shoulders sagged. Every muscle in his body ached; his legs felt rubbery. What was it, five miles to Sedalia? Maybe more. He shuffled back to the house, walked inside, and flopped onto the sofa. Grab a few minutes' rest before the hike.

◇◇◇

Eileen turned the last page of Scott Joplin's journal, closed the cover, stared off into space. Boy, there was some interesting stuff in there. She hadn't had the least idea what a wild place Sedalia was in the 1890s, thought it would've been fun living there then. But she didn't think Mr. Campbell was going to be very pleased with the book, not when he saw what Scott Joplin had written about him. And that girl, Luella Sheldon, what a fruitcake. Funny, she had the same first name as Mrs. Rohrbaugh, the same unusual way of spelling it. They couldn't be the same person, though. Mrs. Rohrbaugh couldn't in a million years ever have done what Luella Sheldon did.

Why on earth was her father so interested in that book? No members of their family were mentioned; if she'd read anything about Kleins or Bergschaffers, it would have jumped right off the page at her. And why had slimy Mr. Barton decided to bring Alan to their house in the first place? It didn't make sense. None of it did.

The girl jumped as she heard the front door

slam. She ran to the window, watched her father get into the car and drive away. Where was he going at almost eleven o'clock?

She walked back to the bed, sat, stared out her side window at the little expanse of roof over the parlor, saw the drainpipe. If Lew Gardiner could shinny up that pipe, why couldn't she shinny down it.

Halfway to the window, she stopped and laughed. Who did she think she was, Nancy Drew? Her father was gone, her mother would be sound asleep down at the end of the hall. She grabbed a jacket from her closet, threw it on, then tiptoed down the stairs and out the front door.

◇◇◇

The men outside Jerry Barton's farm house were in a foul mood. Rafe Anderson peered through the dark at his wristwatch. "Christ Almighty, it's near-on eleven-thirty," he said. "Where the hell's Jerry?"

Heads shook. There was a murmur like a cloud of bees, driven from their hive.

Klein, quiet till now, spoke. "He went out by Samson Curd's place a few hours ago. He had a score he wanted to settle."

"A score? With that foolish coon?" Luther Cartwright slapped his thigh. "What kind of score's so important that we gotta stand out here like cigar-store Indians?"

Klein tried to sound casual. "He said Curd sassed him in town this afternoon. Got real uppity."

"And that's why he ain't here?" Clay Clayton was furious. "Shit, Jerry must be dumber than Curd, runnin' out tonight of all times to teach a lesson to a smart-mouth nigger. An' now, we're supposed to just stand around with our finger up our ass, waitin' for him to get done? Fuck that and fuck Jerry. I say let's just bust in the cellar door, get the stuff, and go ahead without him."

Klein held up both hands. "Hold on, now. We break up Jerry's cellar door and leave his house wide open, I don't want to be the one to try and tell him why."

"No, you wouldn't," Clayton shouted. "Jerry says, 'Shit,' and you say, 'How much and what color.'" He walked toward the cellar door. "Just a little turn-bolt inside. Couple good kicks, we're inside easy."

"Hey, shut the hell up a minute. Alla you."

Everyone turned to Johnny Farnsworth.

"Listen, we got to work together, else we're gonna screw this thing up past fixin'. We ain't against the wall yet. Maybe Barton run into some trouble out there, or maybe he's havin' too good of a time and lost track of the hour. I say let's get in somebody's car and go on out by Curd's. If Jerry's there, we can straighten him out, and if he ain't, well, then we can come back here and do what we gotta do. At least we can tell him we tried."

A pause, then Clayton said, "Okay. I'm for that." A momentary mumbled agreement, then the five men piled into Clayton's black Oldsmobile, and took off down the county road toward Georgetown.

◇◇◇

Curd left Irma and Susie at his sister-in-law's house on the outskirts of Jefferson City, then drove into town, through the business district, and up to Williams' Funeral Home. No one around, not at this time of night. Curd walked around the side of the building, and up a gravel driveway to the back door. He pushed the button next to the door. No answer. He rang again.

A minute later, the door opened. An elderly colored man with a shiny dome and a fringe of cotton above his ears, blinked sleepy eyes at Curd.

"Mr. Williams, I be Richard Curd, from Georgetown. I got me a problem."

All of a sudden, Williams looked fully awake. "Problem, huh? With Mr. Charlie, I bet."

"He come by my place with a gun, was bound

to shame my daughter. Had all her clothes off when I sneaked 'round behind him with a ax."

"Son of a bitch," Williams murmured. "There ain't no end to them hellhounds, is there?"

"I reckon not."

Williams sighed. "Okay, then. Where you got him?"

"Truck out front."

"Drive up to here, so we can bring him in easy. I can manage the feet-end."

Curd started to walk away, then turned. "One other thing. That be his truck I got him in."

"Sweet Jesus." Williams shook his head. "You don't make things easy, do you?"

"Sorry, Mr. Williams. But some things just ain't easy, no matter how you cuts 'em."

"How I knows that. Okay, when we done gettin' him in here, I'll back out the hearse into the driveway, and you put the truck inside. We'll get off the license plates, then first thing in the morning, I'll call Little Harry, and he'll take it away. Time he be done with it, no one gonna be able to tell."

"How much that gonna cost me?"

Williams shook his head. "Harry'll sell the truck, a piece in St. Lou, a piece in Kay Cee. Everybody'll come out okay. 'cept maybe your friend out there. An' I guess he won't care none."

◇◇◇

In the crematory, Curd and Williams unrolled the blanket from around Barton's body. "Leave it underneath him," Williams said. "That way, we can just lift him inside, blanket and all. Won't be nothin' left but a li'l ashes." The old man looked into what remained of the corpse's face. "You did some number on him," the mortician said. "Thought you tol' me you come up from behind."

"That I did do," said Curd. "But he heard me, and started to come around."

"Well, fine and dandy. Good he got to see what was comin' his way." Williams turned to address the body. "Guess it's time to say a last prayer for you, Mr. Charlie. I'm prayin' that every white devil ends up in the fire, both on this earth and below. Like you gonna do now."

Curd saw a young white boy, a bloody ax at his feet, shaking like he had the St. Vitus Dance. "Ain't all white folks bad," he said softly.

"No, I guess not," said Williams. "Problem is, you go tryin' to sort 'em out, you like to end up dead yourself." He swung the crematory door open. "Let's get this done."

◇◇◇

The sound of a car door slamming sent Alan up off the couch and onto his feet. Voices outside, coming closer. The boy took a step toward the front door, then reversed course and ran back, fast as he dared in the darkness, through the kitchen, and out onto the little porch. He left the door part-way open, crouched low, listened.

At first, just voices, but then someone shouted, "Jerry. Hey, Jerry. You here?"

The boy heard bangs and thuds, saw shafts of light darting this way and that. Flashlights. Were they moving furniture, looking under chairs?

"This…shithouse," someone said. "Way these people live. Don't want…touch anything."

"Too bad…didn't…sawdust," a tenor whine, hard to follow. "Do…like…school."

Alan rubbed his ears, tried to listen harder, but all he could make out was the shifting and banging of furniture, and occasionally the sound of glass or china breaking. Then, a familiar voice said, "Jerry musta come and gone, else his truck…out front."

Klein's voice. Alan almost shouted it.

Another man said, "I'll check…back."

Alan glanced left, then right. He'd never make it to the woodshed or the privy. And if he tried to run off into the woods, they'd hear him crashing through underbrush. But the house was up on cinder blocks, and the crawl space looked high enough for him to squeeze into. He dove off the porch, got his head under cover, swung his legs around and inside. Something furry brushed his cheek, then skittered away. A possum? Rat? The boy covered his mouth with a hand.

A flashlight beam scanned the yard. The back door slammed. Alan tried to will away both the men in the house and the wildlife sharing his hide-out. Finally, he heard a car engine turn over, but he lay still. No idea how many cars they came in.

Once the sound of the motor faded, Alan moved an arm. It was stiff to the point of being painful. He stretched, then began to crawl toward the edge of the house. His hand touched something cold and slimy; he shrieked disgust, then scuttled the rest of the way out, and without looking, wiped his hand on the seat of his trousers. He tiptoed to the back door, edged it open, listened. Silence. He went inside.

The bastards had done some job. The kitchen table lay on its side, one leg broken. Four chairs were strewn among shards of glass and pottery. The living room was worse. Overturned furniture created an obstacle course. The piano bench, resting against a wall, sent Alan sprawling into a mess of shredded paper, every piece of music Scott Joplin ever wrote.

Moonlight through the window reflected off something white near the boy's hand. He picked it up, turned it over. A photograph, the one picture in the house, two generations of Sassafras Sams and their families. It had been pulled from the wall, ripped out of its wooden frame, torn, and tossed onto the floor.

'Way these goddamn people live.'

Alan sank onto the sofa, wept quietly. This can of worms, every bit of it, was on his account. A week ago, he'd been a high school student in New Jersey, playing ragtime over his lunch hour, and now look at him. Out in the middle of nowhere, hiding in a Negro family's shack, hands covered with filth, slime, and blood. Half of Sedalia hot on his tail, and five thousand dollars worth of journal under Eileen Klein's mattress. He wiped a sleeve across his eyes. Maybe he ought to follow Samson's map into Lincolnville, but instead of going to Mr. Ireland's house, go to the railway station and catch the first train to St. Louis, then on to New York.

And leave the journal where he'd hidden it? After he'd caused all this trouble for the Curds, after he'd spent the five thousand dollars Miriam had stolen for him, after he'd killed a man, did he really think he could just forget about the journal and go back home. Pretend nothing ever happened? The boy shook his head. He had to see it through. It might not come out well, but that couldn't be as bad as spending the rest of his life wondering what if. He pushed himself up off the floor, stretched, took the pencil-drawn map from his pocket, then started walking, out the door, onto the dirt road.

◇◇◇

A few minutes past three, Johnny Farnsworth walked through the back door of the little frame house on Moniteau Avenue. Klein took his cigar from the corner of his mouth, flicked ash on the floor. "Y' done already?"

Farnsworth laughed. "Piece of cake. When that stuff goes off, it'll take out every bit of support under the auditorium, and down she'll go. Good bet the whole stinkin' place'll come down right on top of it."

Clay Clayton pointed out the window. "Damn, it's dark out there, Johnny. I never even saw you comin' back."

"Dark as a nigger's asshole," Farnsworth said.

All the men laughed.

"But that's just fine," Farnsworth added. "It's gonna look like the biggest Fourth of July fireworks anyone ever saw. Nice of Lincolnville to put up a grandstand for us. Right straight across open land from the school, empty lots on both sides."

"Huh." Rafe Anderson didn't sound amused. "What all them empty lots and vacant houses means is that the niggers're movin' into town. Livin' on the same streets as you and me."

"Maybe this'll make 'em think twice. Might even get 'em movin' back with their own kind." Luther Cartwright sounded like a schoolmarm, warning what was going to happen to the bad boys who'd been throwing spitballs. "But I think we got a problem. We've been figuring to go out to Jerry's after the school blows, but it looks like Jerry bailed out on us."

"Something's wrong," said Klein. "Jerry wouldn't just go off like that."

"Oh, sure." Anderson sounded even more aggrieved than he had after Farnsworth's comment. "If I saw Jerry Barton pissing on a hydrant, you'd tell me I was wrong, it musta been a dog. Maybe you don't remember we took a blood oath, but I do, and if Jerry ever shows his face to me again, I'll spit right in it. And if you don't spit with me, I'll give you a dose, too."

"Rafe, we can't be worryin' about Jerry right now," said Klein. "Luther's right, we got a problem. But I think I know what we can do. If Jerry don't show up tomorrow and have a good reason for tonight, we'll go over to my place instead of his. I'll set up a card table in the cellar, put some half-smoked cigars and drinks around, and leave the outside cellar door unlatched. Then, after the school blows, we'll go on down there, real quiet, and far as anyone's concerned, we been there all evening, minding our business."

Cartwright raised a hand. "We were gonna go over to Jerry's 'cause he's the only one of us doesn't have a wife and kids. What about Rowena? And your daughter?"

Klein made a thick disparaging sound in his throat. "I'll tell Rowena to stay upstairs from suppertime on. What I tell her to do, she does."

"And Eileen?"

"Christ, Luther. She's a sixteen-year-old girl. She ain't gonna notice a thing, and even if she did, who the hell's gonna listen to her?"

◇◇◇

Alan couldn't have said how far he'd walked, but every step now was an effort. He tripped over roots; low-hanging branches stung and scratched his face. Mr. Barton's head seemed to float in the air before him, eyes bulging, mouth agape, wildly trying to escape from the ax blade a split-second from splintering his skull. Alan knew what he'd done was justified, he'd had no choice, but still, he'd killed a man. He was a murderer. His father, always so goddamn certain about what was right and what was wrong—what would The Professor say right now? A wave of contempt burned the boy's cheeks and squeezed his throat, but then he was surprised by the realization that he had to feel sorry for a man who'd condemned himself to plod through life like a blindered horse, struggling at every step to keep the least bit of color from invading his tight little black-and-white world.

◇◇◇

He came into a clearing at the Georgetown Road, trudged a short distance south, then followed Curd's map along a footpath to Clay Street. Two short blocks along Clay took him to the corner of Osage, just across from Tom Ireland's cottage. The boy checked his watch, nearly four o'clock. He quickened his step, trotted up the walk to the door, knocked.

No answer. He knocked harder, still no response.

He turned the knob and pushed the door open. "Mr. Ireland," he called. "Mr. Ireland. It's Alan Chandler. I need…"

His voice trailed off as Ireland shuffled into the room, a coal-oil lamp in his hand. Under other conditions, Alan would have laughed. In his long, white nightshirt and white cap, the old man looked exactly like an illustration of Mr. Barkis that Alan had once seen in a copy of *David Copperfield*. Ireland walked up to the boy, cocked his head, scrutinized him.

"Mr. Ireland, I need your help," Alan said, as evenly as he could manage.

"From the looks of you, I'd say you need somebody's help." Ireland waved the boy into the kitchen. "Come on, sit down. I'll make up some coffee, and you can tell me about it."

◇◇◇

Ireland listened without saying a word. When Alan finished, the old man drummed fingernails on the table, and sighed. "Got ourselves a real mess, don't we? But there's nothing we can do right now. I'll draw you some water, you can clean up, then get yourself some sleep."

"What are we going to do, though? We can't go to the police."

"I know what we can't do, boy. What I don't know yet is what we can do. I hope by the time you get up, I'll have some idea of that."

Chapter Nineteen

Tuesday, April 17
Morning

The sun was just coming up when Ireland padded past Alan, sound asleep on the living-room couch. The old man paused long enough to drop a note on the boy's shoes: HAD TO GO OUT, BACK SOON. DON'T YOU DARE SET A FOOT OUT OF THIS HOUSE.

Once outside, Ireland walked the few blocks to Lamine, strolled up to Alonzo Green's house, eased the door open, slipped inside. The sound of wood being sawed came from Slim, on Green's couch, a mountain of flesh under a light blanket. Ireland walked past the sleeper, into the back bedroom, and immediately found himself on the business end of a pistol. "Lonzo, put that damn gun away," Ireland whispered, and closed the bedroom door. "Got to talk to you."

Green lowered the pistol, set it back onto the little nightstand next to the bed.

Ireland walked up to the bedside. "You're a hell of a light sleeper."

"In my business, I better be. Damn, Tom, why you come sneakin' in like that?"

Ireland pointed toward the living room. "I wanted a private audience."

Green's eyes opened wide. "Something happening?"

Ireland nodded. "The boy's had himself quite a little time with Klein and Barton. He managed to get away, but he doesn't have the journal now. Says he hid it in Klein's house. Once I'm sure Klein's off to work, the boy and I will go get it back, but I don't want to take any chance that our friend out there might see him and upset our apple cart. Here's what I need you to do. Tell Slim you're going to have a talk with Barton about the journal, and you want him along in case things get nasty. Be careful no one sees you going up to the house, and if the door's locked, break it in. Then go through the place, room by room. Take all morning. By then, the boy and I should have had enough time to get the journal back."

Green looked toward the living room. The sound of Slim's snoring went on without pause.

"But what if Barton's there? Or if he comes back and catches us going through the house?"

"He won't be there, Lonzo."

"But what if he—"

"He won't be there."

Green nodded slowly. "Okay, Tom. You say I ain't gotta worry, I won't."

"That's right, Lonzo. Don't worry. Just keep that hothead out of my way." Ireland started toward the door. "People with more temper than brains can be a real pain in the ass."

◇◇◇

Detective Magnus looked across the desk at Samuel J. Pepper. "I appreciate your coming in early for me, Mr. Pepper."

The attorney waved off the thanks. "Only way I could talk to you today. I've got to be in court from nine o'clock on. What can I do for you?"

Right to the point. Magnus liked that. "It's about your client, Roscoe Spanner, and his inheritance. I understand Mr. Brun Campbell is the sole beneficiary."

"That's correct. They've been friends since forever. Mr. Spanner had no heirs, and he left everything to Mr. Campbell."

"Can you tell me when the will was written? Was it recent?"

"No, we did it at least ten years ago. If you want, I can check the date."

"That's all right. Do you know whether Mr. Campbell had any prior knowledge of the inheritance?"

Pepper pursed his lips, then shook his head slowly. "Not that I could say. I guess Mr. Spanner might've clued him in, but from the way he looked the first time I talked to him, I'd say if he did know, he ought to be on the stage." Pepper frowned. "One thing, though. As soon as I told him about his inheritance, he couldn't wait to get his hands on it. He said he'd been trying to buy a diary of some sort that Scott Joplin wrote. He wanted to take it to Sedalia to present it at a ceremony they're having there, I think tonight, actually, to honor Joplin. So I arranged an advance for him…Detective, are you feeling all right?"

"Yeah, sure. Just haven't had my morning coffee yet. Where is it again you said Mr. Campbell was going?"

"Sedalia. In Missouri." Pepper chuckled. "I don't think wild horses or the National Guard could've stopped him."

Magnus thanked Pepper as politely as he could manage, then tore back to the station, ran inside, thrust his head into the switchboard operator's cubicle, and bellowed, "Get me the chief of police in Sedalia, Missouri." He slammed the door, and stormed down the hall to his office. He'd have that goddamn barber back and in front of a grand jury in record time, and he wasn't going to be satisfied till he saw the son of a bitch swaying on the end of a rope.

◇◇◇

Brun sat in an armchair in the corner of the Hotel Milner lobby, his nose buried in a newspaper. He never noticed Luella walk in, and up to his chair.

"Brun?"

He lowered the paper. "Oh, Luella. Say, did you see the papers today?" He held up the one he'd been reading. "This here ceremony's getting big-time attention. Look, on the first page of the *Democrat*. 'Today's leading authority on Joplin and his music is Brunson Campbell, of Kenice, California.' They spelled Venice wrong, but still. And then they go on and say that except for Mr. Joplin, I'm the greatest ragtime player ever. How about that?"

"I'm impressed. I trust they didn't misspell your name."

The irony in Luella's voice went right past Brun's ears. He folded the newspaper, slipped it under his arm, then got to his feet. "Guess we better get movin', huh? I can't wait to hear what Mr. Rosenthal's got to say."

◇◇◇

Ireland couldn't remember feeling more nervous. An eighty-five-year-old man, and a colored man at that, being the only protection for the boy? Dicey. If Klein happened to be at home, things could get ugly in a hurry. I ought to have a white man along, Ireland thought, but the only possibility that came to his mind was Brun Campbell. He shook his head. Do better to pray for good luck.

"Mr. Ireland?"

Ireland snapped out of his thoughts. The boy looked pale, skin taut over his cheekbones. "What is it, Alan?"

"I'm thinking about Mr. Klein and those other guys who were out at Curds' last night. After I've got the journal, how am I going to get it to Mr. Campbell without having them come after me again?"

Ireland draped an arm around the boy's shoulders. "Just as soon as you have that book in your hands, we're going back to my house, and we're going to stay there. I've got someone I can send out to find Mr. Campbell and bring him by, and then we'll all sit down and decide what to do with the journal. And if those idiots try anything funny, I'll call the police. Chief Neighbors and I have known each other a long time, and if I tell him a gang of yahoos is bothering me, he'll have officers out there before I've hung up the phone. We won't have to say anything about what happened last night. Don't worry. Let's just get hold of that journal."

Alan smiled. "You're okay, Mr. Ireland. If it wasn't for you and Mr. Curd, I'd probably be dead three times over."

"Best not to talk about Mr. You-know-who," Ireland said. "Sometimes there's ears where you never see them or suspect they're there."

"Mr. Who?"

"Mr. Cu—" The look of mischief on Alan's face stopped Ireland midway through the word. He laughed, tousled Alan's hair. "All right, wise guy. Let's get done what we came here to do."

They walked up the steps to Kleins' porch. Ireland rang the bell, got no response, rang a second time. The old man peered through the glass panel in the door. "Looks clear. How long will you need to get the journal?"

"Just as long as it takes to run up the stairs, into the room where I left it, and back down. I bet less than a minute."

Ireland squeezed the door handle and pushed. "Go." His voice was hoarse. "Before you come out, look through the glass here. If I'm scratching my nose, turn around and go out the back door, and through the yard to Fourth Street. Wait for me there."

Alan shot into the house. Ireland closed the door, then walked as slowly as a man could walk to the edge of the porch. Then he seemed to recall something, trudged back, pretended to ring the bell again, and shaded his eyes to peer through the little glass panel in the door. There was Alan, bouncing down the stairs two at a time. Lordy, Ireland thought. Don't fall.

The boy's eyes met his through the glass. Ireland opened the door just enough for Alan to squeeze through. "Good job," the old man said. "Now, let's get out of here."

"Mr. Ireland." Alan looked to be on the point of flying out of control.

"What?"

"The journal. It's not there."

Ireland edged the boy toward the street. "You're sure?"

"Absolutely. I looked all around where I left it. It's just not there."

Ireland tried to keep his exasperation to himself. "All right. If it isn't there, Klein must have found it, and he's not going to be an easy nut to crack. Let's go back to my house, and do some thinking." He gave Alan a quick once-over. "We'll stop by Jack's Mens Wear on the way. You're going to attract way too much attention in those dirty rags."

◇◇◇

Luella led Brun through the halls of Hubbard High School, past small groups of Negro children who turned curious looks on the old white couple. They went past the Administration Room and the principal's office, then turned a corner and walked down a long hallway, classrooms on either side. Brun heard piano music. "'Maple Leaf Rag,'" he said. "And I'll warrant that's a white man playing it. I'll show him how it oughta be done."

The double doors at the end of the hall sported gold capital letters: AUDITORIUM. Luella pushed past the door on the right; Brun followed her inside. From the back of the room, he saw a woman at the piano up on the stage. Another woman and a man stood behind her.

Luella and Brun walked up the aisle, climbed the stairs at the side of the stage, then made their way to the piano. The pianist and her companions turned to face the newcomers, then the man stepped forward. "Mrs. Rohrbaugh, how do you do? What brings you here this morning?"

Brun thought he looked and sounded like some kind of college professor. He was well-groomed, with a high forehead, black hair graying at the temples, dark-complexioned, with a prominent beak of a nose. He wore a sharply-cut dark suit, with a dark tie straight up and down over a white shirt.

Luella nodded in Brun's direction. "Mr. Rosenthal, this is Mr. Brun Campbell, from California. He wants to speak with you about the program for tonight."

Recognition lit Rosenthal's eyes, but Brun saw his body stiffen. "Well, Mr. Campbell, I'm very pleased to make your acquaintance." He extended a hand, which Brun gripped firmly. "I've heard a great deal about you, and I'm delighted you were able to come out for the ceremony." Rosenthal half-turned toward the small woman at his side. "This is Miss Lillian Fox, our marvelous accompanist for the Choral Club. And that's Mrs. Blanche Ross, a fine pianist. Ladies, Mr. Brun Campbell. He was a student of Scott Joplin's."

The ladies smiled. "Not just a student," Brun said. "I was Scott Joplin's only white pupil. And I was also the first white pianist to ever play 'Maple Leaf Rag.'"

Which seemed to impress the women. Rosenthal, however, looked as if his trousers had begun to itch. "Well, Mr. Campbell, as I said, I'm very glad to meet you, and I hope you'll be favorably impressed with our ceremony." He pointed toward the front row of seats in the auditorium. "Miss Fox, Mrs. Ross and I are going through our final preparations.

If you'd like, you and Mrs. Rohrbaugh would be welcome to listen."

The message came through to Brun, loud and very clear. "Actually, Mr. Rosenthal, I came over to talk to you about my part, like I wrote in my letter. You did get my letter, right? About a month ago?"

Rosenthal went into a stance of deep thought, lids slitted, one hand on his chin. "Yes. Yes, I did."

"Okay, then. What did you think about what I said I wanted to do?"

By now, the women looked at least as itchy as Rosenthal. Mrs. Ross stood, and mumbled something to the effect of taking this opportunity to visit the powder room. Miss Fox said she'd go along. Brun watched them walk backstage, thought they'd better get there in a hurry or they'll piss their pants.

Rosenthal forced a smile. "Well, Mr. Campbell, you see, this is going to be a Sedalia effort, all local talent. We decided it would be better not to involve, uh, outsiders."

"Outsiders? What the…Mr. Rosenthal, what're you talking about? Scott Joplin taught me piano right here in Sedalia, and I can play 'Maple Leaf Rag' just exactly the way he showed me. You sayin' people wouldn't want to hear that?"

"I'm sure they would, Mr. Campbell. But Mrs. Ross is perhaps the best pianist in Sedalia, and I'm sure she'll do credit to the piece. And in any case, the arrangements have been finalized, and the program is printed."

"So I guess you're telling me you also don't have space for me to say a few words about Scott Joplin, huh?"

"Mr. Studer, our mayor, is going to give a fine talk about Joplin and Sedalia and the birth of ragtime music." Rosenthal's growing irritation showed in his clipped, staccato speech. "And Mr. Brown, the president of the Choral Club, will say a few words, as will Dr. Hylick, the school principal. I'm sorry, Mr. Campbell, but our program is set, and it's too late to make any changes."

Brun felt the world slipping away from him. "There's something else." He tried to keep from sounding frantic. "I'm gonna have a journal, Scott Joplin's own diary, and after Mrs. Joplin says her piece over the radio, I can show that book to the audience. Then, people in Sedalia just might start thinkin' Scott Joplin oughta have more than just a plaque on a high-school wall. Like, say, there should be a ragtime museum, right in the middle of downtown."

Luella Rohrbaugh had never cried in public before, and was detemined not to start now. She worked a full package of starch into her face.

"Mr. Campbell…" Rosenthal spoke softly, but his tone was ominous. "We've had to cancel the simultaneous broadcast with New York."

"You *what?* What in hell's going on here?"

Rosenthal glanced toward stone-faced Luella Rohrbaugh, then said, "We had to cancel the broadcast because Mrs. Joplin isn't well. Apparently, there was some sort of commotion over that diary, and she got quite upset and had to be hospitalized."

Brun's sails sagged. "She's not…"

"I'm sorry. All I know is that she became ill and had to cancel."

"But I got Louis Armstrong to present her that plaque."

Luella turned away. The memory of that fifteen-year-old boy, so full of energy and plans, next to the sight of this stoop-shouldered old man, pleading his hopeless case, was more than the starch could handle. She pulled a handkerchief from her sleeve, dabbed at her eyes."

"Please, Mr. Campbell," Rosenthal said. "We really do have to get back to work. I'll tell you what. Perhaps Mayor Studer could introduce you from the platform, and you can stand and be recognized."

Brun pursed his lips, nodded a few times. He straightened, then spoke. "No need of that, Mr. Rosenthal. Thanks for your consideration, but I don't gotta stand up and be recognized. I'll get outa your way now." He motioned with his head to Luella.

"Thank you for your time, Mr. Rosenthal." Luella's tone could have turned Tahiti into Iceland. She fell into step beside Brun.

◇◇◇

They walked in silence down Osage Street. Brun thought he'd never felt so bad in his life. Roscoe would've been glad to know he'd made it possible for Scott Joplin to get the recognition he deserved, but now that wasn't going to happen. The barber wondered if the cops were ever going to find out who'd killed his friend, or if it was just going to be another old colored man dead, big deal.

A block from the high school, Brun suddenly felt as if a hundred-pound weight had dropped onto his chest. He signaled for Luella to stop, then grabbed a nitro pill from his pocket, slid it under his tongue. Within a minute, the pressure eased off, whew. That stuff was a miracle. But one of these days, the miracles were going to run out. Here he was, out of the program, didn't have the journal, and to top it all off, Lottie had gotten sick, and they'd canceled the radio broadcast. How many more chances was he going to get? He saw the gravestone May would put up for him. *Sanford Brunson Campbell. Husband, Father, Fool.*

"Brun, are you all right?"

"Yeah. That nitro's great stuff. Let's go."

◇◇◇

At the corner of Ohio and Second, Luella nudged Brun. "Look there."

Brun stared. "Tom Ireland. And some kid."

The couples came face-to-face. Brun and Ireland nodded to each other. Luella said, "Good morning, Alan. Mr. Ireland."

Ireland acknowledged the greeting with a smile. "Good morning, Mrs. Rohrbaugh. I didn't know you were acquainted with my young friend."

"Eileen Klein brought him to our supper Sunday night at the church." Luella glanced toward Brun, then at Alan. "You don't have your blue book bag today, Alan."

Brun's eyes widened. "Alan, huh? You're the kid—"

Ireland gave silent thanks that they'd stopped at Jack's. With his new duds, the boy didn't look like someone who'd spent the night tramping through the woods from Georgetown with the hounds of hell at his back. "Brun, yes, this is Alan Chandler. The boy who came from New York to give you Scott Joplin's journal."

Brun's heart skipped a beat, then another. Damn, he thought, Ireland got to him first.

"Unfortunately, he hasn't got the journal now."

Ireland looked all around. "Let's go someplace a little more private, and talk about it."

Luella pointed down the street. "My house is just a few blocks from here."

◇◇◇

They sat in the living room, Luella in the chair beside the music box, Brun next to her. Alan and Ireland occupied the sofa. "That's really the truth?" Brun asked. "You got no idea where Mr. Joplin's journal is?"

"Mr. Campbell," Luella said, and by the tone and the 'Mr. Campbell,' Brun knew he had trouble. "If you lived in Sedalia the past fifty years, you'd know Mr. Ireland's word is not to be doubted."

Lord help me, Ireland thought. After what's come out of my mouth the last couple of days.

"Sorry," Brun said. "I didn't mean any offense. Just…you know."

"No offense taken," Ireland said. "Let's get down to business. Alan here—"

The doorbell rang.

Luella sprang to her feet. "Hold on." She marched out of the room, into the vestibule. Alan, Brun and Ireland heard the door open. "Yes, offi-cer?" they heard Luella say. "What can I do for you?"

A man's voice came through, but not clearly enough that they could make out his words. Then,

Luella spoke. "No, I'm sorry. I have no idea where he is…yes, I know he's been seen with me, but he's not here now. He's staying at the Milner. You might want to check there…yes, I'll be sure to do that."

Luella was back in the living room practically as soon as the the front door had closed. She shot Brun a look he hadn't seen since the day he returned from his 1899 runaway to Sedalia, and his mother met him at the door. "Brun, perhaps you'd like to tell me why the police in Los Angeles want to talk to you."

Brun clapped a hand to his brow, shook his head, muttered something no one could hear, then looked up. "All right, here it is. My best friend back home, he fell or got pushed down the stairs and left me everything he had. The cops were looking into it and told me they didn't want me to leave town, but I wasn't gonna miss this ceremony. Maybe I shouldn'ta done it, but I did. That's the story, it's God's truth, and you can believe it or not."

Luella clasped her hands behind her back, lest she haul off and smack him into next week. "Brun…" She groped for the right words. "Brun, have you ever in your life owned one ounce of common sense?" She held up a hand to make certain the question remained rhetorical. "Yes, for what it's worth, I do believe you. It's no trouble at all to imagine you doing just what you did. But didn't it even occur to you to tell the police you had this engagement, and you'd be here in case they wanted to find you?"

Again, Brun shook his head. "I went and talked about it with one of my friends, a guy who writes fiction stories. We came up with a way for me to get out of town real quiet. I guess maybe that wasn't the smartest thing to do."

Luella slapped her hands against her thighs. "'A guy who writes fiction stories.' The two of you together must have been something to hear. Oh, Brun, I lied to that policeman for you! Told him you weren't here."

Ireland cleared his throat. "What's done is done. Brun, do you want to go to the police and turn yourself in?"

And let you get the journal? Brun thought. "No, I come this far and I ain't gonna miss the ceremony."

"All right, then. Let's try to figure a way out of this mess. The five thousand dollars Alan paid Lottie Joplin for the journal was, uh, stolen from the father of a friend of his in New Jersey, and it cost one of the servants in the house his job. The man followed Alan here, and tried to get the journal away from him, so he could give it back to Mrs. Joplin in return for the money. I've managed to keep him out of the way for the time being, but we're having problems with some other people who also want to get their hands on the journal."

"Otto Klein and Jerry Barton," Luella said. "I can't for the life of me understand why they'd be interested."

"They found out what Alan paid," said Ireland. "Five thousand dollars must have looked mighty good to them. They put him up at Kleins' overnight, then Barton drove him out into the woods yesterday, and got rough with him. It was good luck that all the interest in the journal had made him uneasy, and during the night, he hid it in Klein's house. He managed to get away from Barton, and came to my place, but when we went to Klein's, the journal wasn't where he'd left it. I've got to think Klein found it."

Luella made a face. "We won't get far talking to Klein, but I wonder whether Eileen could tell us anything at this point." She glanced at her wrist. "It's just past eleven-thirty. Why don't I go down to the school and catch Eileen during lunch hour. We don't need to take a committee, and get people staring at us, wondering what we're up to. You can wait for me here."

"I don't know," said Ireland. "I'm thinking when the police don't find Brun at the Milner, they could decide to come back and talk to you some more, and this time, they might come inside.

Maybe when you leave, we should too. We can go to my house, and you could come up there after you're through. If you wouldn't mind."

"Why should I mind?"

Ireland covered his mouth, coughed, then turned to Brun. "Best you wait a little after the rest of us leave, then go out the back door. Just in case that cop's waiting around out front."

"Sure. Least I can do."

◇◇◇

Miss Judith Allison, receptionist at the Milton Oil Company, studied the man who'd swept through the door and demanded to see Mr. Rosenthal. He was not local, not with that expensive suit and tie, and that accent to his voice. With his bushy eyebrows nearly meeting in the middle, the funny little island of hair front and center, and neatly-trimmed Van Dyke beard, Miss Allison thought if his ears were just a little pointy, he'd be the perfect image of a New York devil. But she was not about to let him intimidate her. "I'm sorry, sir," she said. "Mr. Rosenthal is not in the office today. He's busy all day, elsewhere. Perhaps you'd like to make an appointment for tomorrow." She gave him her most accommodating smile.

"Miss…" He glanced down to the name plate on the front edge of the desk. "Allison! This time yesterday, I was in New York City. I've taken a flight and a train to get here today, and it's today, not tomorrow, I need to see Mr. Rosenthal."

"I am sorry, sir. Mr. Rosenthal is preparing for a ceremony this evening. He's in charge of the whole program."

Miss Allison fought to hold her ground as Blesh leaned across the desk, but in the end, she pulled back into her chair. "I know about the program." Blesh's voice sounded as if he had it on a leash, and was struggling to hold onto his end. "And that is why I'm out here. Now, kindly tell me where Mr. Rosenthal is, and I will take matters from there."

Miss Allison wondered whether Mr. Rosenthal would be annoyed with her for giving out the information, but decided to take her chances. "He's at the Hubbard High School," she said. "That's where they're having the ceremony. You go over the railroad tracks on Ohio Street, then turn left onto Jefferson, and right at Osage. The high school's just a block and a half up from there."

Blesh smiled. "Thank you, Miss Allison."

◇◇◇

Abe Rosenthal wondered whether he was ever going to be left in peace to put the final touches on the evening's program. "I'm glad to meet you,

Mr. Blesh," he said. "I've heard so much about your book."

But you haven't read it, Blesh thought.

"One of these days, I will have to take some time and read it."

Blesh's smile required a major effort. "I hope you'll enjoy it. I also hope you can give me some information. There's a man from California, Mr. Sanford Brunson Campbell, an old piano player. I need to know what part he's going to play in this evening's program."

Rosenthal shook his head. "None. He was here a while ago, asking to play piano and give a talk, but I told him this is a local affair, and that the program is already printed. I told him the mayor could introduce him to the crowd, and he could stand and receive acknowledgement. If you'd like, we can do the same for you."

Blesh took a moment to compose himself. "That won't be necessary. Why I'm here…" He glanced toward Miss Fox and Mrs. Ross, then returned his attention to Rosenthal. "Well, it's a long story, and I don't imagine you want to take the time to hear it. An important document was stolen from Scott Joplin's widow a few days ago. I have reason to believe it's here in Sedalia, and further, that Mr. Campbell might have it. The thief told Mrs. Joplin that Mr. Campbell was going to present it at the ceremony."

Rosenthal raised a finger. "I think you're on the right track. Campbell did mention that he wanted to show off some journal of Joplin's."

"That's it!" Blesh pounded a fist into his open palm. "Lord, that man is a loose cannon."

"But I told him we simply could not accommodate him."

"He must be going to try something else, then." Blesh looked wildly around the room. "Mr. Rosenthal, can you tell me where I might find him? I need to get this matter sorted out as quickly as possible."

Rosenthal whistled softly. "He was here with Mrs. Luella Rohrbaugh. She seemed to be serving as his guide. But I don't know—"

"I can give you directions to Mrs. Rohrbaugh's home."

The men turned to Miss Fox. Blesh broke into a broad, open smile. "I'd appreciate that."

◇◇◇

By mid-afternoon, dishes from lunch still covered the scarred wooden table in Tom Ireland's kitchen. In the living room beyond, Ireland, Brun, and old Isaac slouched on the sofa. Luella sat primly in a faded horsehide armchair. Alan

pulled a straight-backed chair as far from Slim as
space permitted; the big man couldn't seem to stop
shooting eye-daggers at the boy. Green sat in front
of the window, between Slim and Alan, whittling
at a stick.

"We're getting nowhere fast," Ireland said.
"Eileen Klein couldn't tell Mrs. Rohrbaugh
anything. And the two of you found nothing interesting at Barton's? Are you sure? Nothing at all?"

Slim and Green shook their heads. "We went
through the place, room by room," Green said.
"Not a sign of the journal or anything else. Just that
the cellar door was stove in. Almost like somebody
wanted to make it easy for us."

Ireland shrugged. "Who knows? I guess all we
can do is watch for Klein at the ceremony tonight.
See if he's got the journal on him."

Green hit the spittoon dead-on. "I just hate
sittin' here doin' nothing in the meanwhile."

Alan eyed the piano in the far corner of the
living room, a lovely polished-mahogany Kimball
upright. "Mr. Campbell…?"

Brun sat up. "What say?"

"While we're just sitting here doing nothing,
you could give me a piano lesson."

Ireland laughed out loud. The kid had made
away with Scott Joplin's journal, come out to Missouri on a train, had the journal stolen off him,

damn near got himself killed, and all he could think of was getting a piano lesson.

Brun almost leaped to his feet. "Sure, kid, why not?" He set his fedora at a rakish angle, then motioned Alan to the piano bench. The boy was there instantly. Brun sat beside him, raised his hands. "Now. This's the way Scott Joplin taught *me* to play." He lowered his hands, struck the keys.

My God, Ireland thought. Man just dropped thirty years.

◇◇◇

Rudi Blesh pushed the doorbell at the little house on East Third, but no one answered. A second and a third try were no more productive. He pounded at the door. "Mrs. Rohrbaugh," he called. "Mrs. Rohrbaugh!"

A window came up in the house to the right, then a woman stuck out a head bristling with pink curlers. "She ain't home, Mister," a shrill shout. "Went off just a little while ago."

"Damn," Blesh muttered, and gave the porch railing a token jab of resigned disgust. He called a thank-you to the woman, then marched off the porch and down to the street. Go get a sandwich and a drink, he thought. Just have to keep my eyes open at that ceremony and hope I get lucky.

◇◇◇

One by one, the Klansmen ducked through the smashed cellar door into Barton's basement. Johnny Farnsworth came in last. He strolled directly to the bar, but before he could pick up a bottle, Klein called, "Hey, Johnny, no booze, remember?"

Farnsworth sagged, then turned and looked around the room. "Yeah, okay. Jerry still ain't here, huh?"

"No." One short word from Clay Clayton, pure irritation. "We was startin' to get worried maybe you was gonna crap out on us too."

"Well, you don't have to worry about me. You wasn't bothered last night when I set up the charge, slick as snot. Wasn't for me, there wouldn't be none of us havin' fun tonight."

Klein stepped forward. "Come on, boys, let's cool it off, okay? We're gonna make us some history tonight. Our kids and grandkids're gonna read about us in newspapers and history books. Course, they won't know it's us, but still."

"I just can't figure it with Jerry," Rafe Anderson said. "It ain't like him at all."

"He was pretty sore about Curd," said Klein. "Probably took him and his whole family off someplace real quiet."

Anderson shook his head. "Nah, it's been way

too long. You think maybe Curd got him on the wrong end of a razor?"

"Who the hell knows?" Klein growled. "Tomorrow, we can go out lookin', an' if it's Curd we find, we know how to get him to tell us what happened. But let's first take care of tonight. It's workin' out even better'n I was thinkin' yesterday. Tuesday nights, Rowena's got her Ladies Auxiliary meetings, so she'll be there from before suppertime till about eight-thirty. I'll tell Eileen I'm gonna be havin' an important meeting myself, in the basement, then go down there and out the cellar door, and meet you guys at the shack behind the school. Eileen won't even think about me or the basement, 'cause tonight's Milton Berle, and you couldn't get her off the TV with a prybar. By the time Berle's over, we'll all of us be back, and when Rowena gets home, she'll come down an' find us playin' poker. Women oughta be good for something, huh?"

Luther Cartwright laughed. "They are good for something, but it don't hurt if they're good for something else now and then."

Everybody laughed. The disagreeable mood from the beginning of the meeting vanished in a cloud of good fellowship.

◇◇◇

A little past six, twilight of a cloudy day. Brun

stood up from the piano bench and stretched. He patted Alan on the back. "That oughta hold you for a while."

Alan nodded vigorously. "I hope I can remember it all."

"You will," Isaac piped from across the room. "Boys your age is sponges."

Luella walked over to Brun, hesitated, then rested a hand on his arm. "I don't think he'll forget that lesson the rest of his life. Did you see his face while you were teaching him those tricks?"

He almost said, Damn, they weren't *tricks*, but swallowed the words.

Alan filled the breach. "Did I look funny?"

Luella smiled. "Not at all."

"Well, I felt sort of funny," Brun said. "Like I was standin' on the wrong side of a fence."

"No," Luella said. "You weren't." She looked at her watch. "When I talked to Eileen earlier, she said that after all she's heard about the ceremony, she wants to go to it. I told her I'd pick her up before her father gets home from work, and we'd stop for a bite of supper first. Suppose we meet you at the school at a quarter past seven?"

Mixed chorus of "Right" and "Yeah."

As Luella walked out and closed the door, Ireland jiggled a finger toward the floor at Green's feet. "Lonzo, look at what a mess you're making.

You figure to just leave all that sawdust sitting on my floor?"

Green laughed an apology. "Don't worry, Tom. I clean up my own messes."

Alan grinned. "One of those guys at…one of those guys I was hiding from said he wished they'd brought some sawdust so they could do, something about a school."

Ireland, Green, Isaac, and Brun all stiffened. "Something like what about sawdust and a school?" Ireland asked.

The heat in Ireland's words made Alan's voice shake. "I don't know. I couldn't hear real well, and that was all I could make out."

"What you goin' on about?" Slim had dozed through the piano lesson, but now he looked fully awake. "Sawdust? Boy just didn't hear right, that's all."

"Yes, he did," Ireland said. "Out here, sawdust is another word for dynamite."

"Sweet Jesus." Green whistled low. "They're gonna blow up the high school. We better call the cops." He shot a cuff, checked his watch. "Fast."

Ireland raised a finger. "Hold on. We'd have to tell them how we know about it, and take my word, if what Alan has been through the past two days ever comes out, we'll be in the middle of a stew we don't want any part of. Lonzo, you've worked with dynamite."

"Well, yeah. I did a fair bit with the cops in Kay Cee." Green clearly didn't like what he saw coming.

Ireland pulled himself to his feet. "Best if we can take care of things ourselves, but if we can't, I guess we'll have to make an anonymous call. Tell the police to close the high school, that it's going to be blown up during the ceremony."

"Then who they gonna come after?" Slim asked. "After they trace that call."

"There are phones in the offices at Hubbard," Ireland said. "If we don't have everything under control before the ceremony's due to start, I'll sneak in and get hold of the police."

Slim was halfway to the door before Ireland finished talking. The big man extended a hand like a football player trying to fend off a tackle. "So *we's* supposed to go an' clear out that dynamite? That's what you sayin'?"

Ireland looked puzzled. "Well, yes. What else—"

Slim shook his head violently. "You can just count me outa that." He flung the door open. "I ain't havin' no truck with no dynamite. The book's gone, the money's gone, an' now I'm supposed to get my balls blown all the way back to Jersey?

Uh-uh, forget 'bout that. I'm gonna take 'em there myself, first train outa this place. I wishes you all good fortune." He frowned, glared at Alan. "Ceptin' for you, mammy-jammer.'" He stomped outside, slammed the door.

Ireland hustled into the kitchen, returned in an instant, stuffing a flashlight into a pants pocket. "We've got five less minutes now than we did when we tumbled." He looked at Isaac, reaching for his cane. "Maybe you ought to stay here and wait. We're going to have to move fast as we can."

"Nosir." Isaac started toward the door. "You all go on ahead. But I ain't missin' that ceremony."

"But they might blow up—"

"Tom, now, get you'self movin' so maybe they don't." Isaac motioned with the back of his hand. "Go on, now, quit wastin' time. Shoo."

◇◇◇

Eileen had the door open practically the instant Luella rang the bell. The girl threw a jacket over her shoulders as she rushed outside. "Your father's not home yet?" Luella asked.

Eileen shook her head. "Not for about another fifteen minutes."

Good, Luella thought. "Aren't you going to say good-bye to your mother?"

Eileen closed the door. "Mom's off at her

Ladies Auxiliary meeting at the hospital. I left her a note. Where are we going for supper?"

Luella smiled. "I thought we could try Puckett's. They just opened last month."

"I heard. Sally Arthur was there with her family. She said the fried chicken was super, and the apple pie was just divine."

Luella held herself to a tolerant smile. God's very own apple pie. "Well, that settles it, then. Let's be on our way."

Ireland, Green, Brun, and Alan crouched at the back wall of Hubbard High School. "Ain't gonna be outside here, where anybody could spot it," Green whispered. "Odds are they snuck in the basement at night and set it someplace down there. Let's see if'n we can't spot anything what tells us where they got in from. Tom, you an' the boy go around to the right there. Me an' Brun'll check the left. Meet here, soon's we can."

Within just a few minutes, they were back. Ireland shook his head. "Just windows down into the furnace room on that side, and they're all locked from inside, and none of them are broken. What about over there?"

"Door down to the cellar," Green said. "Padlock on it, but it don't look like it's been fooled with. Only one other thing." He made a circular motion with a hand.

The four walked to the left rear corner of the building. Green pointed. "Coal chute." He bent, pulled at the wooden cover; it came away in his hand. He waved it at the group. "Looks like somebody was in too much of a hurry to fix it back right."

Alan stared through the opening in the wall, at the metal slide running down and into a nearly-full coal bin.

"Big enough for a man to get through. An' look." Green wiped his hand over the chute, then held up the palm. Ireland pointed the flashlight, shaded the beam with his free hand.

"No coal dust," Brun said.

Green laughed. "Shiny as a nigger's heel."

"How'd they get out, though?"

"No trouble there," said Ireland. "You can't get into the school after hours, but you can always get out. The doors lock from the outside, but there's a bar on the inside, you push it and the door'll open. When those guys were done, they could've gone up the basement stairs, into the hallway, and right out the back door."

Green made an exaggerated bow to Alan. "There you go, young mister. Show us the way. Take you'self a li'l ride."

Alan swung himself onto the upper edge of the chute.

"Don't bang your feet," Green hissed. "Quiet."

Alan balanced himself from behind, wiggled his legs and body straight, then let go of the edge. He hit the coal standing, staggered to the side of the bin, and vaulted over it to the floor. A moment later, Green came down the slide, and jumped out of the bin. Alan looked back and up the chute.

"It's just you and me, boy," Green said. "Your friend with his heart pills better not be takin' no joy rides, an' Mr. Ireland's gonna go make sure he can get to the phone if he has to." Green pulled Ireland's flashlight out of his pocket. "Now, let's start lookin'."

"I don't even know what I'm looking for," Alan said.

Green began to shine the flashlight around the room. "Something that just don't look like it belongs where it is."

Alan walked back to the coal bin. Could they have put it under the coal? Not likely. Would've been a hard, dirty job, and then the coal would take out a lot of the blast, wouldn't it? The boy walked to the furnace, saw it was not lit, and carefully opened the door. Green suddenly appeared behind him, shone the light into the furnace. Nothing but ashes.

Alan got down on his knees to peer under the

boiler. He swung his hand back and forth beneath it, but felt nothing. As he wondered where to look next, Green pulled at his shoulder. "Over here."

He followed Green halfway across the room, to the foot of a wooden column more than two feet thick, one of a row supporting a huge horizontal beam that ran the width of the basement. Green directed his flashlight to the base of the column. "See there?"

Alan squatted, squinched his eyes. "I don't see anything."

"Shee-it, boy. Lord wasted his almighty time givin' you eyes." Green grabbed Alan's hand, stubbed the index finger into the floor at the base of the beam. "Now, you gonna tell me you don't see nothin' there but dirt?"

Alan looked closely. "Just a little sawdust."

"An' where you think that sawdust come from, huh?" Green played the light around the lowest part of the beam. "That sawdust be tellin' you where be the sawdust. See the li'l saw-line on the post? Here, hold me the light on it."

Alan watched Green pull a knife from his pocket, flip open a nasty-looking blade, then carefully apply the length of the cutting edge to the side of the column. A twist of Green's wrist, and Alan heard the creak of a nail being pulled. The colored man reached across the column, twisted the knife again, then came away with a small wooden object in his left hand. "Look at what we got here, boy. Thin li'l piece of fir, same wood as the post, there. A cover."

Green dropped the wood, pulled the flashlight from Alan's hand, knelt to shine light into the recess. "Um-hm! Okay, quick now. See that red stick, wires goin' to a li'l alarm clock?"

Alan squatted to peer into the cavity. "Twenty minutes after nineteen? What kind of clock is that?"

"Twenty-four-hour clock, prob'ly army surplus. These guys knows what they's doin'. An' see? The li'l alarm hand's set to go off right at a quarter till twenty. That's a quarter till eight."

"So we've got less than half an hour."

Green played the flashlight over the device. "We be okay. It ain't sweatin'."

"Huh? The *dynamite* isn't sweating?"

Green laughed. "Yeah, you is, and me too, but not it. Dynamite gets old, the nitro breaks down and sweats through to the outside. That happens, you don't dare fool with it, it can go off in your hand. But this stuff's okay." He scrambled to his feet, pulled at the boy's wrist. "Come on. Let's check the other posts."

◇◇◇

In less than five minutes, Green and Alan had pried

covers from two more support columns. Then, Green led the boy to the steps going up to the school, sat, wiped at his face with a handkerchief. "Auditorium's right above here, and that big beam's what's holdin' it. The three of them charges're gonna go off right at the same time, and when that happen, there goes forty feet of support, and the whole room come down."

"But they're all still set," Alan said. "Aren't you going to disconnect the wires?"

By the flashlight's beam, Alan saw a tight smile bend Green's lips. "Boy, you better learn, sometimes it ain't the smartest idea to try an' do somethin' in a big hurry. Won't take me but a minute to disarm them Dinah sticks, but it can be just a li'l tricky. So I'm gonna sit down here an' have me a smoke, make my fingers nice and calm. An' you's gonna go up there, find Mr. Ireland, an' tell him it's all under control."

"But don't you need help? I can hold the flashlight for you."

While Alan talked, Green lit a cigarette, drew deeply, blew smoke toward the boy. "I be fine now," the colored man said. "I can put the light on the floor an' see all I got to."

"But—"

Green jumped to his feet. "Damn you, boy! Here I am, tryin' to get myself cool in the head, and you just go on and on at me like an ol' woman. What I got to do to get you to shut up your mouth an' go tell Mr. Ireland he ain't got no worries no more? Go on, now. Git!"

Alan was off, up the stairs like a shot. Green, a grin all over his face, watched him the whole way. As the boy reached for the bar to open the basement door, the colored man called, "*Move*, kid." Alan stumbled, fell forward into the hall, then scrambled to his feet, and took off running. The door slammed shut.

Green chuckled, sat back on the step, took a couple of puffs at his cigarette, then dropped the butt to the ground near his foot, and carefully ground it out. "Okay," he told himself. "Time to get this job done."

He was on the floor in front of the first column, flashlight perfectly adjusted, when he heard, "Go down flat on your face, quick, else I gonna crease your head with this tire iron I got in my hand."

Green followed the order. "There be dynamite down here," he called out of the corner of his mouth."

"Well, I ain't got no trouble seein' that. Good thing I heared the door to down here slam and figured I better take me a look."

"You the janitor?"

"Uh-huh. Bad luck for you."

"Listen, it's gonna be bad luck for a lot of people, you and me included, if you don't let me get the wires off this stuff. It's gonna go off—"

"Mister, stop flappin' your lip. Just keep your hands out front of you, an' get up on your knees. Slow-like."

Green did as he was told. "Listen, janitor. You gotta listen at me—"

"Long as I be holdin' this tire iron, you gotta listen at me." Now. Put your hands up toppa your head, then stand on up. We goin' to take a walk upstairs, you can tell your story to the coppers in the lobby there. I bet they be real interested."

"But—"

"Mister, one more word outa you, and you won't be talkin' no more, maybe not ever. Hear?"

Shit, Green thought. He glanced at the explosive in the column, then started to work his way to his feet. The man behind him scooped up the flashlight, and directed its beam toward the stairs.

Chapter Twenty

Tuesday, April 17
Evening

They opened the doors to the Hubbard High auditorium just before seven. Abe Rosenthal watched people file in and start taking seats. Whites came through the left door, blacks through the right, and seats filled progressively from both sides inward. A Sedalia police officer stood at each door, and every person who entered the room got a careful up-and-down. "Looks as if we could have a full house," Rosenthal said to Lillian Fox, who was making a final tuning check on the piano. "And there are as many whites as colored."

Miss Fox considered that since whites in Sedalia outnumbered colored ten to one, Mr. Rosenthal's observation didn't mean very much. But she just nodded and smiled.

Rosenthal's eye caught a mixed group, four whites and two colored, walking in together and seating themselves as a virtual island near the center of the room. Old Isaac Stark and Tom Ireland entered the pew first, followed by Luella Rohrbaugh and that Campbell character from California. Rosenthal again wondered what their connection could possibly be. At Campbell's left, the Klein girl pushed her body against a boy Rosenthal had never seen. The conductor shook his head. "I'm going back to make sure the chorus is all set," he said to Miss Fox.

She smiled again. No amount of preparation was ever too much for Mr. Rosenthal.

Bess Vinson strolled in on Mickey Thurman's arm. They started toward the *de facto* colored section, but as she swept the room with her eyes, she caught side of Brun in the tiny patch of integrated seats, and changed direction on a dime. Thurman muttered a useless protest, then followed after her.

Bess leaned into the pew to jab a finger into Brun's shoulder. "Just so you know," a snarl. "I'll be watching you, every minute. And if you so much as show that journal or even mention it, I'll be up there right next to you. I'll tell them who I am, and how you clipped that journal out of my stepmother's hand. And then I'll call in those cops from out in the hall."

Brun turned his head away from her. Bess put her hands on her hips. "Think I'm kidding, don'tcha?" When that brought only silence, she added, "Mess with me, you gonna be mighty sorry." Without taking her eyes off Brun, she wheeled around, led Thurman across the aisle and settled into a seat.

◇◇◇

Otto Klein heard the front door open, peered over the top of his newspaper. Rowena? What the hell was she doing here this early? The paper fluttered to the floor.

Mrs. Klein gave him a quick up-and-down. "Otto, what's the matter? You look like you've seen a ghost."

"Bah. Just wasn't expecting you so soon, that's all."

She heard his voice quaver, wondered why.

"So many of the Ladies Auxiliary are going to that ceremony at Hubbard, we finished up our meeting early…Otto, you've gone so pale. *Are* you all right."

"He grabbed at the newspaper. "Damn, woman, yes. I'm fine. Stop looking at me like that."

"Well, I'm sorry. I was just concerned for you. Where's Eileen?"

"I haven't seen her. I thought…"

You didn't think anything, Mrs. Klein said to herself. It didn't even occur to you to wonder where your daughter was. She walked to the closet, hung up her jacket, then started toward the kitchen.

"Rowena…"

He sounded like he was choking on the word. She turned. "What? Otto, what *is* it?"

"Listen, if anybody asks you, I been down in the basement since six o'clock. Playing poker."

Her hands went to her hips. "Playing poker since six o'clock? What ever are you talking about? Who's going to ask where you—"

"Shut up, and do like I say. I been down there since six o'clock, playing poker with Rafe Anderson, Luther Cartwright, Johnny Farnsworth, and Clay. You got that?"

She started to ask another question, but the look on his face stopped her. She wheeled around, then took off into the kitchen, heels clicking on the linoleum.

A moment later, she was back, waving a slip of paper. "Eileen left us a note. I guess you didn't see it."

"Nah." A grunt.

"She says Mrs. Rohrbaugh offered to stand her to dinner, then they're going to the ceremony at Hubbard. Isn't that nice of Mrs. Rohrbaugh to take such an interest—"

"She's going *where*?" Eyes bulging, body poised like a snake ready to spring.

Mrs. Klein took a step backward.

"Eileen's at that ceremony? Is that what you said?"

"Well, yes. But really, Otto. I know you don't care for the colored, but a lot of very fine people are going to be there."

All color drained from his face. His mouth twisted, lips quivered.

"Otto!" She ran to him, grabbed his shirt-front. "You've done something, haven't you, you and those friends of yours? What's going to happen at that ceremony?"

Klein tried to pull away, but she held fast. "Otto, what have you done?"

"That school is going up in pieces," he howled, then shot a glance toward his wrist. "In just about twenty minutes."

They stared into each other's eyes, two white masks with gaping mouths. Klein gave his wife a savage shove; she fell, half her husband's shirt clutched in her fist. Klein flew to the front door, threw it open, tore outside. The door banged against the wall, knocking the picture of Christ to the floor.

Mrs. Klein flung the rag to the floor as if it were contaminated. Then she scrambled to her feet, trying not to scream. She'd need all her breath to get to Hubbard High School in time. And if she didn't make it, she'd kill Otto, stab him with a kitchen knife, again and again and again, wouldn't stop until they came and carried her off.

◇◇◇

By seven twenty-five, only scattered empty seats remained in the Hubbard auditorium. Brun glanced at the program, forced himself not to curse aloud. "Stout-Hearted Men." "Drink To Me Only With Thine Eyes." "The Lost Chord." "The Green Cathedral." Scott Joplin would have puked. How the hell do these jays figure they're honoring the greatest colored composer in American history by having a chorus of white businessmen sing a bunch of the sappiest snow-white tunes ever written? And how about a middle-aged lady pianist playing "Maple Leaf Rag," when they could have had Scott Joplin's only white pupil?

A hum through the audience brought him back. A big man in a police uniform, built like a tree trunk, with a no-nonsense look on his round face, walked down the middle aisle to the stage. He took the microphone from its stand, scanned the crowd through horn-rimmed spectacles. Luella leaned toward Brun. "Ed Neighbors," she said. "The chief of police. I wonder what's going on."

Neighbors cleared his throat. "Good evening, ladies and gentlemen. I'll only take a moment of

your time. Is there a Mr. Sanford Brunson Campbell in the audience?"

"He must have known you'd be here," Luella
whispered.

Brun got to his feet, waved a hand. "Over
here."

Neighbors caught his eye. "Okay. Mr. Campbell, would you be so good as to step outside for a
moment. I need a word with you."

Brun shrugged at Luella. She stood to let him
pass. Ireland scrambled after him. "I'll go with you."

"I'm coming, too." Luella gripped her purse in
both hands. "I've seen this matter through so far,
and I'm not going to stop now."

As the three started up the aisle, Bess Vinson
glared at Brun. "Bastard!" she hissed at Thurman.
"He probably called in the cops on me. If they try
and make me leave, they're gonna have themselves
one holy fuss, I promise you that."

A blood vessel on Thurman's temple began to
pulsate. "You know what, Bess? I'm gettin' a little
sorry I went in on this business with you."

Like pouring gasoline on a fire. "Oh, you are,
huh? Well then, I'll tell you what. I'll take care of
the rest by myself, and when I get my hands on
that money, I'll just keep it all. How do you like
that, Chicken Liver?"

Without waiting for a reply, she was on her

feet, stalking up the aisle toward the door. Thurman sighed long and hard. She just *would* walk
away with that five grand, wouldn't she? But the
idea had been his, and he wasn't about to turn his
back on twenty-five hundred dollars. He jumped
up, followed after her.

From his aisle seat in the back row, Rudi Blesh
watched Campbell, Ireland, and an old woman go
through the doorway, with a colored woman and
man on their heels…wait a minute. One reason
Blesh did so well at interviews was his knack for
remembering names and faces. He couldn't put a
name to that man, but he'd seen him, all right, vacu-
uming the floor in Ellie Radcliffe's reception room.
What was he doing here at this ceremony, with a
woman who looked like she was going to blow fire
through her nostrils? Something was very rotten
in Denmark. Blesh got up and walked to the door.

◇◇◇

Klein burst into the dilapidated shack on Moniteau, arms flailing, eyes wild. "Listen, we gotta call
this off."

Clayton looked at him as if he'd said they all
had flap their arms and go flying out the window.
"Call it off? Otto, what the hell you talking about?
We can't call it off now, it's too late."

"My daughter," Klein screamed. "Eileen. She's

in there. Johnny, you gotta disconnect the timer, quick."

Farnsworth shook his head. "I ain't got long enough now to even get in there, let alone shut off the charge. Christ Almighty, Otto, wasn't your daughter supposed to be watchin' Milton Berle? Ain't that what you said? You're nuts if you think I'm gonna get myself blown into pieces because you were too fuckin' dumb to keep your eye on your daughter."

He staggered back as Klein punched his face. "Damn you, Johnny. I'll go do it myself."

Klein took a step toward the door, but Anderson, standing to his left, put everything he had into a sockdolager to the side of Klein's jaw. Klein went down in a heap.

Anderson shook his head. "I hate to see his kid get blown up, but what we gonna do, huh?"

"I got another question," said Cartwright. "What happens when he wakes up? Think we oughta shoot him?"

"No," Anderson said. "Let the cops find him here with a bullet in his head, and they'll start askin' questions we ain't got answers for. I mean, what's he gonna do, turn us all in? He screwed it up, he'll have to live with it. It ain't our fault he let that girl run around like the goddamn whore of Babylon.

Least now, she ain't gonna shame him by gettin' herself pregnant."

The hall outside the auditorium was a circus. Brun stood with Chief Neighbors, another policeman, Ireland, and Luella, while just a few feet away, Bess Vinson pretended to chat amiably with Thurman as she tried to keep up with the conversation to their left. Brun leaned toward Neighbors as if the chief had spoken indistinctly. "You're gonna hold me for *what?*"

"Suspicion of murder. Flight to avoid prosecution. I'm acting on the request of Detective Robert Magnus in Los Angeles. He warned you to stay in the city, but you ignored that order. We'll have to return you to him under guard."

Before Brun could reply, a smallish man with blazing eyes and a Van Dyke beard rushed up to Bess and Thurman. He paused just long enough to nod toward Ireland, then pointed a finger at Thurman, and announced, "Is Knopf using janitors now to pursue acquisitions?"

Brun forgot what he was going to say. He and his companions turned, and became an audience for the little drama going on next to them. Clear from the look on Thurman's face, he was checking exit routes. "I…I don't know what you're…who the hell are you, anyway, Mister?"

"Yes," Bess snapped. "Just who do you think you are, busting in like that? My friend and I are having a private conversation."

Blesh drew himself to full-height. "My name is Rudi Blesh, and not that long ago, I was having what was supposed to be a private conversation with Mr. Elliot Radcliffe, at Knopf. And your friend here was in the outer office, with the door open between us. Next thing I knew, the manuscript I had interest in was stolen from its owner, who'd promised it to me, and according to the owner, the thief was going to bring it here to give it to him." Blesh directed a finger toward Brun.

Neighbors scratched at an ear. "You do get around, Mr. Campbell."

"That woman's been after me for damn near two weeks, now," Brun shouted. "She said she was Scott Joplin's daughter, the one who was supposed to have died in St. Lou in oh-two. She told me she had the journal, and wanted to sell it to me for five thousand dollars."

"Scott Joplin's daughter? Hah!" Blesh was furious. "She's no more Scott Joplin's daughter than I am. I interviewed a man, Roscoe Spanner, who was a bartender in Tom Turpin's saloon. He was a good friend of Joplin's, and made all the funeral arrangements for the baby." Blesh turned toward Bess. "Whoever you are, you're not only unpleasant, you're an unmitigated liar."

Brun walked the few steps to come face to face with Blesh. "You interviewed Roscoe Spanner?" Brun said. "In L. A.?"

"Yes." You could have cut Blesh's sarcasm into slices and put it on bread. "Don't you remember, he was in your barber shop when I came to interview you, so I talked to him as well. I didn't put his information into the book, because frankly, it didn't seem that important." Blesh paused. Creases deepened across his forehead; his eyebrows drew together. "Actually, the interview *was* in the manuscript, but I took it out in the first galleys." He glared at Thurman. "And those galleys are still in the book's working folder, in Mr. Radcliffe's office."

'He had his booze and his skirts.' The comment from Roscoe's neighbor echoed in Brun's mind. He sidestepped, so as to push Bess against the wall. "Now, I get it," he barked. "Your pal there went in the files and found out about Roscoe and the baby in St. Louie, and how him and me were friends. Was it your idea or his to shove the old man down the stairs so he couldn't queer your con?" Brun paused just long enough to decide he'd maneuvered the game onto his own turf, and he ought to go on. "But the guy lives next door saw you. He told me a woman went in Roscoe's house, then came out just a little later and ran off in one big hurry. I bet he can give the cops a pretty good description of you."

Any further argument was forestalled by Thurman, making a break for the door down the corridor. The policeman with Neighbors grabbed him, wrestled him to the wall, spun him around, cuffed him. "You told me not to worry, the old man wasn't going to talk," Thurman howled at Bess. "But you didn't say why." He looked at the chief. "I didn't have anything to do with that."

By now, the two policemen who'd been at the entry doors to the auditorium had walked over to see what was going on. Neighbors nodded toward Bess. One of the officers put handcuffs on her; the other took possession of Thurman.

Blesh looked like a man at a tennis match, eyes going back and forth between Brun and Bess. Neighbors turned to him. "What did you say your name was, sir?"

"Rudi Blesh. I'm from New York."

Neighbors smiled. "So I gather. I'll want a statement from you. Would you please stop by my office after the ceremony?"

Brun said, "They already started. Is it okay if my friends and me go back inside too?"

"Your friends can," said Neighbors. "But I'll

have to talk to Detective Magnus before I can release you. Please go along with the officers."

Ireland touched the chief's arm. "Ed, I'll warrant Mr. Campbell won't go off. I'd put up my house as bond, and everything in it. Scott Joplin was his piano teacher here, fifty years ago, and he came all the way out from California for the ceremony. It'd be a terrible shame for him to miss it."

Neighbors' eyes softened. "You hear that, Mr. Campbell?"

Brun nodded. "Yeah."

The chief sighed. "All right, Tom. You are, as of this moment, a special deputy in charge of Mr. Campbell. Take the prisoner back inside, and do not let him out of your sight, not for anything. If he goes to the bathroom, *you* go to the bathroom."

"Thank you." Brun's voice was barely audible.

Neighbors and Ireland exchanged looks worth ten minutes of conversation. The chief smiled. "After I talk to Magnus, I'll get back to you. Then—"

◇◇◇

The heel of one of Rowena Klein's shoes caught a stone; she stumbled, almost fell. Tears streaked her cheeks. With every breath, fire flared in her chest. If she didn't get to the high school in time, she'd go back home and wait for Otto just inside the door, lights out, biggest knife in the kitchen in her hand. She had to make it, *had* to. Only two more blocks. If only her damn skirt wasn't slowing her down. She reached back, released the hook, and as she pulled at the zipper, she felt, more than heard, a blast, followed closely by a second detonation. She stood, paralyzed, watching a fireball rise into the night sky, then shrieked till her wind ran out, and crumpled to the pavement. She never did hear the third explosion.

◇◇◇

Slim was walking toward the St. Louis train when he heard it. The platform shivered. "Damn stupid morons," the big man muttered. "Least I'm gettin' outa here in one piece." He hurried onto the train.

◇◇◇

Whatever Chief Neighbors intended to say to Ireland vaporized in the triple blast. The school building shook, then trembled. Glass panels in the entry doors down the hall shattered.

"Jesus, Mary, and Joseph!" Neighbors' eyes blazed behind his thick spectacles. He pointed at the officers holding Bess and Thurman. "Take them down to the station, then get right back here." He pointed to the third cop. "Call in all available officers."

Blesh and Luella stood, transfixed. Ireland and

Brun took a step toward the entry doors. Neighbors grabbed Ireland's arm. "Tom, all of you. Back inside."

Ireland turned to Blesh. "Come sit with us. I'll tell you what's been going on with that journal during intermission."

Blesh managed a tentative smile. "I'd appreciate that."

The chief followed his charges into the auditorium. Up on the stage, the Mens' Chorus stood silent. A hum of low-pitched chatter filled the room. Some of the audience had left their seats and were moving up the aisles toward exits.

Neighbors raised both hands, and bellowed, "Everybody, please stay where you are. We don't know yet what that noise was, but while we're looking into it, you'll be safer in here, and you'll also be out of our way. Mr. Rosenthal, please go on with the program."

"Right, Ed." Rosenthal turned back to the chorus. "'The Green Cathedral.'" He bent toward Lillian Fox, at the piano. "From the top."

She nodded, set her jaw, and hit the opening chord. "I know a green cathedral," the chorus sang. "A leafy forest shrine. Where leaves in love join hands above and arch your prayer and mine."

Sorry, Mr. Joplin, Brun thought. I wish I coulda done better for you.

Alan watched Chief Neighbors charge out into the hall, then as he turned back, he caught sight of Alonzo Green in a last-row seat, looking for all the world like the Sphinx in the Egyptian desert.

◇◇◇

At intermission, Alan excused himself and started up the aisle, toward the hall. An usher glided past him and up to Eileen, then delivered a short message. The girl grabbed at Luella's arm.

"I'll go with you, dear," Luella said.

When Alan returned, he was shaking his head. He scanned the little group. "Where's Eileen? And Mrs. Rohrbaugh?"

Ireland rolled his eyes. "One thing on top of the last. The police found Mrs. Klein on the sidewalk a couple of blocks away, and took her to the Bothwell Hospital. It sounds as if she just fainted, but Eileen was quite upset, so Mrs. Rohrbaugh thought she ought to go along. If all really is well, she should be back by the end of the program."

"I went to look for Mr. Green," Alan said. "But he's gone. I went all up and down the hall, and into the men's room, but there was no sign of him."

Ireland shrugged. "If Lonzo doesn't want anyone to find him right now, I'd say he's doing something that needs doing. After the show, we'll go back to my place and sort things out."

◇◇◇

After the ceremony, three coloreds and four whites walked in a tight group up Osage, toward Ireland's house. Ireland, Alan, and Green led the procession, with Brun and Luella behind them. Blesh and Isaac brought up the rear. Alan wanted to detour a block to go past the mob of police, firemen, and onlookers at the smoking remains of a little house on Moniteau, but Ireland and Green put a quick kibosh on the idea. "Maybe okay in New York," Green said. "But here, when there's trouble, a colored man best make himself invisible."

Alan looked over his shoulder at Luella. "Eileen and her mother really are okay?"

Luella sighed. "Yes, they're both fine. Mrs. Klein may not stop talking for days. She said when Mr. Klein found out Eileen was at the ceremony, he got very upset, told his wife the school was going to be blown up, and ran off. She was trying to get to the school in time to warn everyone, and when the blast went off, she thought she'd been too late, and fainted. No one can find Mr. Klein."

Alan glanced at Green, who raised his eyebrows, then started to whistle "Dixie."

Brun walked in silence. By rights, he ought to be standing back at the school, people crowding around him, asking did he really take piano lessons from Scott Joplin, and telling him a Scott Joplin Museum downtown would be just the thing to pump a little life into this burg. Shoot, Brun thought, I'm tired.

Luella leaned toward him, whispered, "Are you all right?"

He made a face. "Yeah."

She slid her hand into the crook of his arm, the way she'd done on those warm summer evenings so long ago, when she'd contrived to get him to take her walking through the city to buy ice-cream sodas.

Rudi Blesh wished he could have just thanked Ireland for his invitation to come back for a cup of coffee, and gone to the bar in the hotel to drink himself silly. But Ireland had gone so far out of his way to help Blesh find people to interview for *They All Played Ragtime* that the author couldn't find it in his heart to decline. Well, it probably wouldn't be the worst impromptu soiree he'd been jockeyed into. He wouldn't have to stay long.

Alan glanced back at the smoldering ruins, then tapped Green's arm. "I've got to ask you something."

"You do, huh?" Green smiled. "Way you been lookin' at me all this while, I expect I knows what. Mr. Ireland was not about to tell me just what you done yesterday, but he did say you crossed yourself over a very important line, so I gonna let you in on some details." Green lowered his voice to a conspiratorial level. "After we found that stuff in the basement, I sent you off so I could get rid of it without havin' you bother me with a bunch of questions. But the janitor heard the door shut behind you, and snuck up on me with a tire iron. He wouldn't listen to reason, so I had to get a little rough with him. While he was standin' me up, I got to where I could hook his leg, duck around, and give him a straight-up shot so he gonna be singin' soprano in the choir for a good long while. Then when he bended over, I put him to sleep with my sap an' took the sticks outa the posts. But I didn't unconnect the wires."

Green paused to chuckle as Alan's eyes widened. "I ran up the stairs, out the back door, across the field, an' planted the stuff underneath that shack. Then I humped it back even faster'n I went over there. I was just comin' up the stairs to the school when it went off, so I hid in the bushes, an' when there wasn't no more cops runnin' past me, I came on in and sat in the back row. Intermission, I went to the upstairs men's, figured nobody was gonna see me there, an' got myself cleaned up. Gonna be six less white sheets around Sedalia now."

"White sheets?"

"Ku Klux, boy."

"Mr. Klein's gang? They were in there?"

"You got it."

So if I hadn't brained Mr. Barton with the ax, Alan thought, he'd be just as dead now anyway. Which didn't lighten the boy's mind. "How did you know?"

"Remember Sunday, when Barton left you off at Klein's? Me and Slim were on you. Then later, I ditched Slim an' sat in my car where I could watch the house. I saw Barton come back and go off with Klein, so I followed them. They went right to that old shanty yonder, and inside, so I snuck up and listened. They was plannin' how they was gonna make something happen, an' sit in the shack to watch it. Then, they went out to Barton's and had a meeting in the basement with four other yahoos, but I couldn't hear a thing there. I thought they was gonna burn a cross on the lawn like they usually does, but when you started in talkin' about sawdust, I had to change my ideas."

Alan shook his head. "What about the janitor? Won't he be able to identify you?"

"Don't think we gotta worry about that, dark as it was down there. An' I had my back to him the whole time till I gave him that shot in the jewels. Prob'ly he can say it was a colored man, but not any more'n that. B'sides, it couldn't have been me, could it? Didn't you see me sittin' there in the back row the whole time?" Green poked an elbow into Alan's ribs, cackled.

"Whew." Alan stared at Green for a moment, then whispered, "You blew up fi…six men. Just like that."

Green's face tightened. "Listen at me, boy. A colored man can't spare his enemy, not ever. Don't blow him up into tiny li'l pieces when you got the chance, next morning you gonna find you'self hangin' in a tree. I do regret it, but that just be the way."

Tom Ireland wiped at his eyes. When he was much younger, he'd thought he might see the day when these accounts would be squared and settled for all time. "How long, oh, Lord?" he murmured.

◇◇◇

They sat on chairs and stools around the open wood stove in Ireland's kitchen, sipping at cups of coffee. Luella broke a long silence. "We need to talk about Scott Joplin's journal."

"Mr. Klein must have found it." Alan's voice was dull, colorless. "I guess that's the last we'll ever see of it."

Heads nodded. There were a few dispirited yeahs.

"No," Luella announced. "Mr. Klein did not find it."

She had everyone's full attention.

"Mr. Klein did *not* get it," Luella repeated. She opened her handbag, pulled out a thick leather-covered book, held it up.

Brun sprang from his chair and grabbed; she pushed him sharply. "Sit down." She looked around the circle. "It so happens that Eileen found this object of shame and greed." She lowered her head to fix a stare on Alan. "Exactly where you hid it."

The boy felt his cheeks flame.

"She knew her father was interested in it, and after he tore apart the room you stayed in, his behavior made it clear he hadn't found it. She thought about how long you'd stood where you did late Sunday night, and sure enough, there it was. She read it, and—"

"Oh, dear God." Ireland lowered his head into his hands.

"Don't be concerned, Mr. Ireland," Luella said. "Eileen and I had a long talk about how the journal happened to be where she found it, and what her mother might think of that, and I can assure you, she will never speak to anyone about anything she read. In any case, when she saw her father leave the house and drive away late last night, she felt she needed to talk to someone." Little smile. "I suppose she thought I was the best of a bad lot."

Blesh was on his feet. "Mrs. Rohrbaugh, I

hope you appreciate the historical importance of what you're holding. We need to be certain it is handled properly."

"I have every idea of this book's importance," Luella snapped. "And I intend that it will be handled properly." She gave Brun a doozy of a hot eye. "Do you remember the details of our agreement, fifty-two years ago? That you were going to leave this city instantly, and not speak to another person?"

"But I—"

"But you didn't. You obviously spoke to Mr. Joplin, because every detail of that affair is down on paper here. Who else did you speak to?"

"Mrs. Stark, that's the only other one. I couldn't just run out of town without letting her and Mr. Joplin know."

"Your promise to me to the contrary. Now, would you like to know Mr. Joplin's evaluation of you as a pianist."

Across the circle, Tom Ireland held his breath. All that woman needed were nails, a hammer, and a couple of sticks of wood.

Luella opened the journal to a page with a paper marker, and began to read. "I'm sorry to see the boy leave town. I can't help admiring his enthusiasm and hard work. But he'll never be a great, or even a good, classical ragtime pianist or composer.

He plays the right notes, but not in the right way, and it isn't as I first thought, that he lacks a proper ear. It's deeper than that, a matter of soul. His is an unfettered nature, and the same impulses that led to his forced and immediate departure cause him to play my music the way he does. But how many whites are eager or even willing to play my music at all? I'm grateful to the boy, and I wish him well."

Luella closed the journal with a smack, then looked at Brun, shoulders slumped, tears coursing down both cheeks. "I'm sorry," she said softly. "But do you want that material available for anyone and everyone to read?"

Ireland ground his teeth. "You didn't need to do that, Mrs. Rohrbaugh. There's more in there that's a whole lot worse."

"Whatever it is, it's history." Blesh struggled to keep his voice even. "A personal view of ragtime through Scott Joplin's eyes would be invaluable for scholars and musicians. It must be published."

Luella gave him a cold stare, then turned back to Brun. "That boy over there paid a good deal of money for this book. Alan, where did you get all that money?"

Alan started to speak, but paused as he saw the looks coming his way from Ireland, Green, and Isaac. Green smiled. "Good thing the fat man took off."

Alan coughed. "I got it from a friend's father."

Luella pulled herself to full height, tightened her lips. "He gave it to you?"

Alan shook his head.

"You stole it, then."

"Well…not exactly."

"But close enough." Luella waggled the journal in Brun's direction. "You told me you brought money to pay for this. Give that money to Alan. And Alan, you will take it back home, confess your crime to your friend's father, and return his money. You have a long life ahead of you, and take my word, you do not want to live it under a cloud."

Brun unbuttoned his shirt, pulled the purse free, placed it into Alan's shaky hand. "Hang it 'round your neck and under your shirt," a monotone. "Don't let anybody see it, understand?"

Alan nodded, then ducked his head into the loop of the strap and pushed the little purse down, out of sight.

Brun turned to Luella. "Okay? Now, I've paid for it." He held out a hand.

Blesh bounded up to Luella. "You can't give that book to a man who makes a habit of playing fast and loose with historical truth. He'd have people believe there was a great procession of carriages at Scott Joplin's funeral, with the titles of Joplin's rags on banners hung from the sides of the carriages. He made that up out of whole cloth. Joplin had a very humble funeral, and was buried in an unmarked grave."

"Well, the way I told it, that's what Mr. Joplin deserved," Brun howled. "That's how it *should've* been."

Luella gave the combatants equal doses of visual scorn. "Brun, you've just given your money to someone who had no right to offer you the journal in the first place. I'd say that invalidates your claim. As for you, Mr. Blesh, what Mr. Ireland said is right. So much in this book would bring shame to so many people. My Uncle Bob Higdon's whole family, and mine, would be horrified. So would Mr. and Mrs. Stark's children and grandchildren. And for heaven's sake, both Brun and Isaac were involved in the blood bath here that August. What might happen to them if this information gets out?"

Blesh couldn't contain himself. "It's *history*, for heaven's sake."

"Well, I say it's dirty laundry," Luella snapped. "People do not have the right to stick their noses into the private business of others, and wallow in it like pigs in mud."

"Something else," said Ireland. "All that talk toward the end of the journal about Irving Berlin swindling Scott out of a musical drama, and trying to frame him for murder? Joplin was a very sick man by then, and I'm sorry to say it, but I can't believe it really did happen. What do you think Berlin will say and do when he sees *that* in the papers?"

Blesh ran fingers through his hair. "Documents can be sealed for as long as anyone they might affect is still alive."

Luella gave him a long look down her nose. "Mr. Blesh, would you really agree to have this journal kept sealed for years and years?"

Blesh came right back. "We could publish excerpts. Some of the things people told me for *They All Played Ragtime*, I marked 'Do not publish this.' And I didn't."

Luella looked as if she'd suddenly picked up on an unpleasant odor. "After what happened very recently in your publisher's office, can you really be so sure no one else will get hold of those notes, and betray the trust your interviewees had in you?"

"Oh, nonsense. Mrs. Rohrbaugh, if everyone had your exquisite sense of social squeamishness, historical research would be in dire straits."

"Humph!" Luella turned to Alan. "I'm not going to ask what happened to you between yesterday and today, but I wonder how you'd feel if you were to pick up a book one day, and there your story would be, for everyone to read. Would you be willing to relinquish your privacy to satisfy the

curiosity of people who aren't satisfied to attend to
their own business?"

Alan studied his shoes.

The corner of Blesh's mouth started to twitch.
"Let me try to talk some reason to you people. How
many of you have read this book?"

"I have," said Ireland.

Isaac nodded. "Yup."

Alan raised a hand.

"And I," said Luella. "And the girl, Eileen."

"Well, then." Blesh held out both hands,
palms up, and slapped the most reasonable smile
he could manage onto his face. "When more than
one person knows a secret, it's no longer a secret."

"Well, I'm not going to say anything to
anyone," said Luella. And neither is Eileen, I've
made certain of that. Are you going to tattle, Alan?"

He shook his head. "About what?"

Ireland laughed out loud. "Nobody'll get
anything from me, either. How about you, Isaac?"

"My lips is sealed."

Brun cleared his throat, looked sidewise at
Luella. "Guess I ain't the only liar in this bunch."

Luella scanned the room. "Good. It's settled,
then." She tucked the journal under her arm, and
reached for her pocketbook.

Blesh lunged toward the journal, but in one
motion, Luella grabbed it with both hands and

twisted away. Blesh barreled past her, slammed into the table. The historian rubbed his hip, glared at Luella.

She pressed the journal to her chest, and set her jaw. "Thank you, Mr. Blesh. I admit to having had some doubt, but now you've resolved it." She stepped directly in front of the wood stove and launched an underhand pitch.

Brun saw it coming. Off-balance, he grabbed at the journal, but flames roared up, engulfing the dry paper. Brun loosed a bellow of pain, then pulled away, clutching his wrist and shaking his hand fiercely.

Ireland ran to his side. "Lonzo," he shouted. "Go get some ice outa the icebox. I'll get the liniment."

Luella took Brun's arm. "That's a nasty burn. I'm going to get him to a doctor."

"Let's first put on ice and liniment," Ireland called over his shoulder. "Then we can both take him by Dr. Stauffacher's." He rolled his eyes. "Where he goes, I go, remember?"

"That'll also give us some time to think what we gonna tell the doc, why a man stuck his hand inside a wood stove," said Green.

Blesh stared into the fire. "You've burned a major historical document."

"Nah." Green favored him with a sneer. "From

what I hear, it wasn't nothing more'n a li'l gossip. And you never did see it with your own eyes, so you can't say different."

Luella passed Brun's hand to Ireland, who began to apply liniment. Brun winced.

"If that music is as good as you all seem to think," Luella said. "It will survive with or without the revelation of embarrassing personal secrets." Her eyes challenged Blesh to argue the point.

The historian sagged onto a chair. He rubbed his eyes, then looked up at Luella. "All right. The game's over, and I've lost." Spoken so softly, everyone leaned in his direction. Isaac cupped a hand to his ear. "I still believe my goals were reasonable and honest, but if my zeal offended you, Mrs. Rohrbaugh, I apologize."

Alan walked slowly across the room to the piano, sat on the bench, began to play "Maple Leaf Rag." He thought of his benefactors, Samson Curd and Tom Ireland. He thought of Brun Campbell, braggart, liar, prophet, slipping nitro pills under his tongue to keep himself alive to spread the gospel of Scott Joplin. He thought of Mrs. Rohrbaugh, forgiving a sick old man, but still needing to punish a fifteen-year-old boy. He thought of pretty Eileen Klein, her silly mother, and her vile father. He thought of horse-faced Miriam Broaca, eyes beaming pride and adoration as she pushed five

thousand red-hot dollars into his hand. He thought
of Jerry Barton, savior, betrayer, murder victim. He
thought of Alan Chandler, murderer, hero, pianist,
and caught a glimpse of his life to come, a Gordian
tangle of joy and sorrow.

He lifted his hands from the keyboard to
silence. Every face in the room was turned his way.
Finally, Green loosed a low whistle. "Boy's a piana-
playin' fool."

Ireland let go of Brun's hand, then, without
taking his eyes off Alan, screwed the cap back onto
the tube of liniment. "Mother of God. How did
you ever learn to play like that?"

Alan couldn't speak.

"If I closed my eyes, I could've been listening
to Scott Joplin, back in his good days," Ireland
said. "There were plenty of players more showy
than him, but Scott had a way, it made you stop
whatever you might be up to, and think, how on
earth did he do that? It wasn't something you heard
with your ears. You *felt* it, in your heart.

Luella took Brun by the elbow. "We ought
to get him to the doctor." She pulled, but his feet
seemed glued to the floor, his eyes fixed on Alan.
That hand must hurt like the very deuce, she
thought, but the old man's face looked serene as
any angel's.

Epilogue

Alan sat next to Miriam in a booth all the way in
the back of Sweetie's, a chocolate soda on the table
between them. "You really did tell your father?" the
boy asked. "What happened then?"

Miriam snorted. "I told him straight-out it
was me who stole the money so you could buy the
journal and go to Sedalia, and that he needed to
apologize to Slim and give him back his job. He just
looked at me for a minute, and then he laughed.
Laughed. He said he knew I was just trying to get
the blame off Slim, and hell would freeze before
he'd tell 'that colored thief' he was sorry, *or* hire him
back. He just laughed me off, me and five thousand
dollars. Can you imagine that?"

Alan drew at the straw. Her indignation made
her look comical, but he didn't dare crack up. Her
old man must have made her feel like some kind

of unfortunate accident that had developed out of a pinhole in a rubber.

Miriam narrowed her eyes. "You look different from last week."

"Different? How?"

"I'm not sure. Kind of...*older*. More serious."

Alan saw the ax descend, rise, fall again. He shrugged. "Maybe I'm just a little tired."

He's faking me, Miriam thought, but decided not to go any further along that conversational road, at least not right then. "I feel bad for Mr. Campbell," she said. "He must've been so upset, going all the way out there, and seeing that old woman throw the journal in the fire. And getting his hand burned..." She made a face. "Ow!"

"No kidding, ow. And it was awful how he had to sit in front of everyone and listen to what Mr. Joplin wrote about him in the journal. While we were waiting for our trains the next day, I made sure to tell him how much I learned from the piano lesson he gave me, and that made him look a lot happier. He put his arm around me, and said, 'Kid, any time you want to come out to California, I'll give you all the lessons you want, free.' And then he gave me this."

The boy pulled a silver coin from his pocket, put it into Miriam's hand. She flipped it over. "Wow. 1897."

"Yeah. Mr. Campbell said Scott Joplin gave it to him for a good-luck piece."

She returned the coin as if it were a sacred object, then rested her hand on his. "I'm glad, Alan. I'm glad you got that lesson, I'm glad it made Mr. Campbell feel better, I'm glad I took my stupid father's money so it all could happen."

"Speaking of which…" Alan tapped at his chest. "I'm going to give the money back to your father. I'll tell him it was actually me who took it."

The girl pounded a fist on the table top; the soda glass did a little dance. "No, you won't. You won't say a word to him about it. You'll give it to me." The girl extended a hand.

"But—"

"Give it here, Alan. Now. I'm not kidding."

He paused just a moment, then pulled the strap clear of his neck, worked the little purse up from under his shirt, slid it across the table to Miriam. She opened it, glanced inside, then shoved it into her pocketbook and locked the clasp.

"What are you going to do?"

Crafty smile. "You told your parents you wouldn't run away again, right?"

He shrugged. "Fastest way to get them off my back. But what's that got to do with—"

"Bet you didn't promise, though."

He laughed. "No. I didn't promise."

"So you might…you *are* going to go off again. To California, to take more lessons from Mr. Campbell. Aren't you?"

He took her hand between his. "Mr. Blesh gave me Joe Lamb's address in Brooklyn, and said I should go in and see what I can learn from him. I *will* do that, and then, yes, maybe I'll go out to California. Maybe I'll stop in Sedalia on the way, and get Mr. Ireland and Mr. Stark to tell me more stories about what it was like there when Scott Joplin was just getting started." And see how Mr. Curd and his family are doing, he thought. "Then I'll go play ragtime every place I can. I'm going to write it, too. I'll make records." He lowered his voice. "Maybe some day, *I* can get a museum built for Scott Joplin."

"Well, next time you go away, I want to go with you." Miriam held up her free hand, silence. "Oh, Alan, I love you so much, maybe as much as you love ragtime music. I know you're not going to be my boyfriend, but—"

"But I *am* your friend," Alan said. "And I *am* a boy."

That started a flood which she didn't even try to hold back. "Alan, don't talk like that, it hurts. When I think about you being off God knows where, and I'm stuck here with my rat of a father and idiot mother, I just want to die." Her face brightened, sunlight bursting from behind gray clouds. "I'm not just going to tag along, either. I'll be your manager."

"You'll be what?"

"Your manager. That's why I wanted you to give me my father's money. I'm going to take it to New York, to a stock broker."

He laughed, just couldn't hold it back. "I don't think you can do that. Won't you have to get your father's signature, and then he really will find out…"

His voice faded as he saw her smile turn sly. "I've already got my father's signature. The day after he laughed me off, I went in and picked up all the forms for a minor to set up an account. I told my father I wanted to invest the money I've made working summers. He didn't even look at the papers, just scrawled out his name, and told me to tell the broker to buy IBM." She patted the purse. "Now I'm going to put the five thousand dollars into the account. My father'll never know a thing, and by the time we're ready to use the money, we'll have even more than five thousand. How much more depends on how much time you're going to give me."

"But there's a lot more to being a manager than buying and selling stocks. Do you really think—"

"I managed you all the way out to Sedalia to meet Mr. Campbell, didn't I? And I negotiated a minor's stock market agreement with my father. We'd be a great team, Alan. You won't have to think about anything but the music, and I'll take care of everything else. I'll make sure you don't have to wash dishes for a meal, or sleep under railroad overpasses. I'll find you good places to play your music and record it, and I'll make sure nobody takes advantage of you on a contract." Her face hardened. "But if you ever run off without me, I'll find you, I swear, and when I do, you won't like what happens. That's a promise. And I keep my promises."

Alan nodded. "All right."

"We've got a deal?"

"Guess so."

"That's not good enough. Promise."

"Promise."

◇◇◇

As quickly as he opened his front door, Cal's eyes went to the white bandage. "Brun, what happened to you?"

"I got burned."

Impishness covered the young man's face. "Maybe some day you'll learn not to stick your hand where it doesn't belong. How bad is it?"

"Doc said I'll be playing again in about a month. That'll give me a chance to finish up those articles I've been working on, and maybe my book too. You want to hear all about it?"

Cal motioned him in. "I'll get a couple of beers."

◇◇◇

By the time Brun finished, there were eight bottles on the table between them. Cal loosed a low whistle. "Sounds like a lot more went on than you even know about. Damn, I should've gone along. Writers give eye teeth to get in first-hand on stories like that."

"Well, nobody stopped you. You could've come."

Cal drained his glass. "I wouldn't have bet a nickel on that kid from New Jersey showing up."

"Yeah, some kid. Moxie to burn. All the time I was there, he wouldn't stop buggin' me for a piano lesson, so I finally gave him one, almost the whole afternoon. He was pretty good, but after I was done with him, he was a whole lot better."

"God help that boy." Cal made a face. "I suspect Mrs. Campbell isn't too pleased with you right now."

Brun shook his head. "Madder'n a hen in a hailstorm. Mostly about why I told her I was going to San Fran, and made her look like a moron in front of the detective. I had to explain that one before both of my feet were in the house."

"What'd you tell her?"

Brun cracked a one-sided grin. "The truth."

Cal started to laugh, couldn't stop. "I'll bet not the whole truth."

"Well, no."

"And not nothing but the truth."

"Course not."

Cal wiped at his eyes. His face turned serious. "Did your heart give you any trouble while you were out there?"

Brun shook his head. "My heart's good, Cal. Thanks."

The Last Word

May 29, 2009

By all accounts, Brun Campbell led a bang-up ragtime life. The catch is that most of the accounts were Brun's, and a good deal of later research has shown that The Kid was, to put it mildly, an embellisher. The story about Scott Joplin's funeral, with its long procession of carriages bearing the names of Joplin's rags, seems to have been a complete fabrication, probably based on Brun's desire to see his old mentor receive proper recognition and honor.

Brun claimed in his autobiography that after he left Sedalia in 1899, he worked as an itinerant pianist throughout the midwest, playing for all manner of celebrities from Buffalo Bill to Billy the Kid, until 1908, "when I married and retired from music." Then, in the late 1920s, he moved his family to Venice, California, and opened the barber shop at 711 Venice Boulevard, where he worked for the rest of his life. But as his friend and interviewer,

Paul Affeldt, pointed out after Brun's death, this information was inconsistent: it would have made Brun's wife eight or nine years old at the time of their marriage. Brun told Affeldt privately that he had in fact retired from music performance in 1908, but had then spent some time as the piano-playing pet of a famous madam, until he married in 1921. Affeldt thought this account more plausibly explained Brun's reluctance to talk publicly about a period in his life he did not want to come to his wife's attention.

In doing research for the three books in this trilogy, I uncovered some new information regarding Brun's early years. The 1895 and 1905 Kansas mid-decade censuses show Brun and his brother Harold residing in Arkansas City, Kansas, with their parents, L. E. and Lulu Campbell. A little arithmetic shows that Brun's parents were seventeen and fifteen at the time of his birth, so Brun would seem to have come honestly by his impulsiveness. Mr. Campbell was listed as a salesman, but he was also an inventor, holding a number of patents for farm-related devices.

By 1910, Brun was in Tulsa; there are two U. S. Census listings for him. One has him living with a woman named G. Ethel Campbell; another places him in a rooming house several blocks distant from the first address, and states he is single.

In both listings, he is said to be a barber. I could find no other information on G. Ethel.

In 1914, Brun, now 27 and still in Tulsa, married 18-year-old Lena Louise Burrough of Ft. Smith, Arkansas. G. Ethel and/or Lena Louise might explain Brun's statement to Affeldt that he married in 1908. I could find no record of children born to Brun by either woman.

Brun's World War I draft registration card shows he was still living in Tulsa in 1918, married to "Mrs. Sandford (sic) B. Campbell, and working as a barber. Under conditions that might have prevented him from serving in the armed forces was written, "Shot through joint of big toe on right foot." Probably that was neither the first time nor the last that Brun was shot in the foot.

Brun claimed that after he returned home from his 1899 jaunt to Sedalia, his father went to drink, and his parents separated. But according to the 1905 Kansas census, the family was intact, and in the 1920 U. S. census, Brun's name appears with those of his parents and brother, but in Los Angeles. Brun is listed as married and a barber, but no wife's name is specified. This entry was made during the first week of the year, so it's possible Brun was not actually living there, but might have been visiting his family over the holidays.

The 1930 U. S. census places Brun, still a

barber, in Venice, Los Angeles District, with his wife May, and three daughters, Dorothy, Louise, and Patricia, aged eleven, nine, and five. The Campbells had been married for twelve years, and according to the census, May and all three daughters had been born in Oklahoma. If that information is correct, Brun did not move to Venice before 1925. Reportedly, the reason for the move was to provide a better climate for one of the daughters who suffered from severe asthma. Aside from the census form, the earliest record I have so far been able to find which places the Campbells in Venice is the 1930 Voter Census. Brun registered as a Republican, his wife as a Democrat.

Mrs. Campbell reportedly disapproved of ragtime, so Brun was forced to play piano either in the garage behind his house or in his barber shop. Affeldt wrote, "...I was met at the door by his wife, and informed that his family didn't wish to be bothered by the trashy crowd interested in his ragtime past." Neither Mrs. Campbell nor Brun's offspring would talk to historians, so details of his life in California are almost as sketchy as those of his earlier existence.

As the ragtime revival of the 1940s took off, Brun began to play during intermissions at clubs in and around Venice and Santa Monica. Before long, musicologists and historians took note of him, and like Joe Lamb on the opposite coast, Brun became better known than he'd ever been during the heyday of ragtime. Since he hadn't played professionally for twenty-five or thirty years, musicologists came to regard him as a living time capsule, someone who had not needed to adjust his playing style to suit changing times and tastes, and so was playing ragtime the way it had sounded in the rough bars and barrelhouses of the early twentieth century. Fortunately, an extensive body of remastered acetate-disc recordings of Brun playing and speaking is available in CD form as *Brun Campbell, Joplin's Disciple*, Delmark DE-753.

Brun was never one to overlook an opportunity, and as he realized he had developed an audience, he began to write newsletter and magazine articles about ragtime, Scott Joplin, and Brun Campbell. He cut some 78rpm ragtime records, one of them "Maple Leaf Rag," and donated the proceeds to Lottie Joplin, who was ill and in need of money. He tried to promote interest in a movie, possibly featuring Ethel Waters, on Scott Joplin's life. Wherever there might have been a chance to further ragtime, Brun was the man on the spot.

He began work on a book to be called *When Ragtime Was Young*, and when Rudi Blesh and Harriet Janis interviewed him for *They All Played Ragtime*, he turned his material over to them.

Later, he came to regret that, and in his letters to the ragtime pianist, Jerry Heermans, warned the young man to be very careful about giving anything to Blesh and Janis. He claimed that Blesh had appropriated the material in *When Ragtime Was Young*, such that Brun would no longer be able to get his own book published; he also told Heermans that Blesh would not respond to Brun's *post-facto* requests for "25 books for the use of my manuscript and fifteen percent of the motion picture rights." I doubt that Blesh was guilty of any skulduggery. More likely, Brun had acted in his characteristic haste, then regretted at leisure.

Despite Brun's personal shortcomings, historians appear unified in their overall assessment of him, concluding that he was a real character, at times crotchety, not always accurate in his storytelling, but possessed of honorable intentions and genuine dedication.

Brun died of arteriosclerosis and congestive heart failure, on November 23, 1952. I can only wonder about his state of mind in his last days. Was he depressed, both at his own clearly-imminent mortality and his perceived failure to return Scott Joplin to the exalted position he'd held fifty years earlier? I'd rather think that, like Joplin, Brun had faith his efforts would in time bear fruit. The picture I painted of him at the end of my trilogy may or may not be true to fact, but the way I told it, that's what Mr. Campbell deserved. That's how it *should've* been.

Brun is buried in Valhalla Cemetery in Los Angeles. His gravestone reads: *In loving memory, Sanford Brunson Campbell, 1884-1952.* Rest easy, Brun. A man who's never been a fool is one of God's sorriest creations.

◇◇◇

Tom Ireland was born December 8, 1865, and so, missed by eight days being born a slave. His father, a member of a prominent white family, named him George Thomas, after his own brother, who became governor of Texas in 1872. The family provided support to the governor's nephew and the boy's mother for some years.

Mother and son came to Sedalia in 1867, and young Tom attended school there. In the 1880s, he went to Central Tennessee College in Nashville, finished his high school education, and took college courses. His major occupation was as a newspaperman, but he also was part-owner of a saloon, a storekeeper, custodian of the Pettis County Courthouse, an employee of the Missouri Pacific Railroad, and Chairman of the Queen City Republican Club. He built his own house at 1001 North Osage Street, reportedly in 1882, and lived there until just a few years before his death at 97, in 1963.

For nearly all his life, Ireland enjoyed excellent health and vitality. He was a cyclist of note, regularly riding the bicycle he bought in 1903 on trips as long as sixty or seventy miles. Each year on his birthday, he took a bike excursion. On December 8, 1949, he rode to Georgetown and back, a distance of about seven miles. "The wind was against me today, and I had trouble getting up the Georgetown hill," he told the staff in the *Sedalia Democrat* newsroom. "But I made it."

Ireland moved comfortably among both Blacks and Whites. An indication of the regard in which he was held throughout Sedalia is that while city directories still printed (col) after the names of Blacks, this opprobrious designation did not appear after Tom Ireland's name.

Ireland was a musician, primarily a clarinetist. He did in fact own the Kimball upright piano that Alan Chandler played in *The Ragtime Fool*. He was a member of the famous Queen City Band, where he met and became friends with Scott Joplin. After his death, his daughter-in-law said of him, "He knew Joplin and he knew ragtime and he knew Sedalia. Yes, I guess he knew as much first-hand about Joplin and the old times as anybody."

◇◇◇

Rudi Blesh was both scholar and gentleman. Born in Oklahoma, he came to San Francisco as a young man, worked in Interior Design, then moved to New York in the 1940s. After he'd become a jazz critic and interpreter, his friend, Harriet Janis, persuaded him to turn his attention to ragtime. The result was the collaboratively-researched and written book, *They All Played Ragtime*, a history more social than musical. It took Blesh and Janis only about a year to find and interview large numbers of surviving ragtime pioneers and their close relatives. Since its publication in 1950, *They All Played Ragtime* has been reprinted several times. Though subsequent research has uncovered factual errors, the book is still regarded as the most influential work on ragtime history, and is often referred to as "The Bible of Ragtime."

Blesh went out of his way to make certain that people knew of his associate's key roles in undertaking the project, conducting the interviews, taking photographs, and keeping notes. Mrs. Janis' absence as a character in *The Ragtime Fool* should in no way be taken to imply that she was unimportant in the real-life story. Simply put, she did not step forward with something to contribute to my tale. Let's assume she was out of town during mid-April of 1951, so Blesh had to proceed on his own.

Blesh's communication skills and his store of knowledge were legendary; in addition, countless numbers of ragtimers have praised his personal qualities, particularly his generosity and kindness. Max Morath, the dean of ragtime composers, performers, and historians considers him "one of the most civil and civilized people I have ever had the pleasure of knowing." But the man could be difficult. Morath wrote that *Shining Trumpets*, Blesh's earlier (1946) book on jazz, "bristled with denigration," and the work excited considerable controversy. Many of the vituperative comments that came the author's way can be easily found on the Internet. In addition, Blesh was stubborn and unshakable in support of his principles. His 1947 radio show, *This Is Jazz*, was a huge hit, but was canceled after less than a year because Blesh featured music by racially-integrated bands. According to Morath, who had talked with Blesh's grandson, "…the network 'suits' would come to the broadcasts, begging him to change his open-race stance. 'We have *sponsors*! Please reconsider.' The usually courtly Rudi gave them…a rude gesture from the control room. The show was canceled."

In 1946, with Harriet Janis, Blesh founded and operated the independent firm, Circle Records, to record and preserve jazz performances that commercial companies would not touch. Circle's most prominent product was a twelve-volume Jelly Roll Morton set, featuring selections from Jelly's Library of Congress recordings. The company also recorded many other significant performances, none of which otherwise would ever have been heard beyond the moment.

After Harriet Janis died in 1963, Blesh seemed to lose a great deal of his energy and drive. He continued to work, turning out several significant pieces on ragtime, as well as the first biography of Buster Keaton. In the mid-seventies, when *The Sting* was at its height of popularity, Blesh was offered the opportunity to write a biography of Scott Joplin, but couldn't summon the energy for the task. As time passed, his mental state progressed to frank depression. He needed constant medication, and from time to time had to be hospitalized. He died on August 25, 1985.

◇◇◇

Lottie Joplin hung on until March 14, 1953, when she died of "natural causes" at 79. What became of the huge store of Scott Joplin music in her basement is uncertain. As described in Chapter 13 of *King of Ragtime*, by Edward A. Berlin, much of it passed through the hands of executors, trustees and lawyers, some scrupulous, others careless, still others possibly dishonest. A jazz historian and writer recalled seeing "a duffle bag full of Joplin manuscripts, including a piano concerto." But in the end, it all vanished, and ragtime enthusiasts still dream that one day, they'll be going through an old trunk in an attic or an antiques store, and...

◇◇◇

Richard Curd, Sr., aka Sassafras Sam, known for his wide-brimmed hat and friendly smile, pursued his trade in and around Sedalia until one day in 1933, when he walked onto a highway from between two parked cars, into the side of a Ford V-8 coupe, and was killed. He was 62 or 63 years old.

Curd's eldest son was Richard, Jr., who was born in "about 1902" and died in 1984. His wife's name was Irma or Erma, and the 1930 census shows he had an infant daughter, whose name was not Susie. I found nothing to indicate that Richard, Jr. was ever called Samson, or followed his father into the sassafras business, though Hazel Lang wrote in her book, *Life in Pettis County, 1815-1973*, "In the later years of [Richard Curd, Sr.'s] life, he left the digging of the sassafras roots to members of his family but he always would go along to see that they went to the right spots."

◇◇◇

Abe Rosenthal, conductor of the Sedalia Symphony and founder of the Sedalia Mens Choral Club, was a Canadian who emigrated to Sedalia in 1930 from Canada, where he'd been concertmaster and conductor of the Hamilton (Ontario) Symphony. His future wife, then Fannye Hanlon, was a booking agent for Columbia Broadcasting, and on one of her trips to Canada, booked Mr. Rosenthal for a lifelong tour in her home town. Rosenthal's day job was as Division Manager of the Milton Oil Company. The Rosenthals' daughter, Willis Ann, a talented flutist, was awarded a scholarship to study at the Eastman School of Music in Rochester, New York.

Miss Lillian Fox, "Sedalia's Daughter of Music," was a versatile and accomplished musician from early childhood, a music teacher, and a prominent figure in the arts world of her town. She was particularly known for her work as accompanist for the Sedalia Mens Choral Club.

Mrs. Blanche Ross was a respected Sedalia pianist who played at innumerable local concerts and other events.

Herb Studer, Republican, served as mayor of Sedalia between 1950 and 1953, when he resigned to accept President Eisenhower's appointment to serve as Federal Housing Adminstrator for Western Missouri; his predecessor in that office was the brother of former president Truman. Studer died of a heart attack in 1960, at the age of forty-two.

In the same April 1950 election that sent Mr.

Studer to the mayor's office, Edgar (Ed) Neighbors, a Democrat, was re-elected Chief of Police.

◇◇◇

Jerry Barton, Rafe Anderson, Clay Clayton, Luther Cartwright, Johnny Farnsworth, Luella Sheldon Rohrbaugh, Isaac Stark, Alonzo Green, Slim and Sally Sanders, Bess Vinson, Mickey Thurman, Susie Curd, Roscoe Spanner, Elliot Radcliffe, Cal (whose last name I never did learn), and the Chandler, Broaca, and Klein families were products of my imagination. They bear no resemblance to any person in my real world.

◇◇◇

A ceremony did in fact take place at Hubbard High School in Sedalia, on Tuesday, April 17, 1951, to honor the city's most prominent musical son, Scott Joplin. There was music and there were speeches, and a plaque was presented, to be placed on a wall in the school. Brun Campbell, the old Ragtime Kid, did not come out for the festivities, but from his home in California, he tried to persuade pianist Dink Johnson to play at the ceremony, and lobbied to have the proceedings carried by radio to New York, where he hoped to arrange for Louis Armstrong to present a scroll to Lottie Joplin. Brun wangled interviews with newspaper reporters; on the day of the ceremony, the *Sedalia Democrat* reported that "Today's leading authority on Joplin and his music is Brunson Campbell, of Kenice (sic), California…Campbell is regarded as the number one 'rag-time' pianist still living, and second only to Joplin among the many who have played this music." Unfortunately, the broadcast Brun tried to promote to New York never took place, and the event proceeded with exclusively local performers.

◇◇◇

More than fifty years have passed since that dedication ceremony. By the 1950s, the Ku Klux Klan no longer held open meetings in Liberty Park, and thereafter faded into memory as an organization openly dedicated to the intimidation of Blacks and other allegedly-inferior ethnic groups. Today in Sedalia, Whites sit with Blacks in restaurants and theaters, and people of all races live side-by-side throughout the city. Lincolnville has become increasingly a ghost neighborhood of abandoned small houses and vacant lots, one of which, at 1001 Osage Avenue, was the site of Tom Ireland's home. And as Luella Rohrbaugh predicted, the destruction of Scott Joplin's journal did not impede the growth of regard and respect for his music. Every year during the first week in June, Sedalia swings to a syncopated beat, thanks to the lively, well-attended Scott Joplin Ragtime Festival.

I sympathized with Mrs. Rohrbaugh, Tom Ireland, and Isaac Stark, but couldn't help hoping that Rudi Blesh might succeed in convincing the trio to preserve the journal and have it sealed until all those who would have been harmed or embarrassed by revelation of its contents had passed beyond those concerns. Clearly, there was interesting material in that book. Just why did Miss Luella Sheldon resort to such bizarre and dramatic measures to coerce young Brun Campbell to leave Sedalia in 1899? Even more intriguing, what went on among Brun, Scott Joplin, the Starks, and lawyer Robert Higdon that ended with multiple deaths and a cover-up, and was so potentially explosive as to cause Tom Ireland to fear for the safety of Brun, Isaac, and others if the episode were to become public, a half-century after the fact? What transpired late in Joplin's life between him and Irving Berlin? Or, as Ireland put it, what did Joplin *think* transpired?

Thanks to Luella Sheldon Rohrbaugh, you won't find this information in any work of history. But it is available to interested parties in two books, *The Ragtime Kid* and *The King of Ragtime*, both by Larry Karp, who, being a novelist and therefore destitute of conscience, scruples or principles, has laid out the sordid affairs in full detail.

◇◇◇

When I visited Sedalia last June for the 2008 Joplin Festival, I found that during the previous year, Hubbard High School had been demolished. I wondered what had become of the plaque that had been put up fifty-seven years earlier, to honor Joplin. No one I talked to had any idea of its whereabouts.

◇◇◇

The Uptown Theatre on Ohio Avenue, where Eileen Klein sold tickets on Saturdays, has been dark for many years. But there's talk now among Sedalians about renovating the old building and converting it into a ragtime museum.

Selected Ragtime Resources

Radio Shows

"The Ragtime Machine," David Reffkin, Host. KUSF-FM, San Francisco, Monday, 9-10 pm Pacific Time.

Streaming at http://www.live365.com/ stations/kusf

"Ragtime America," Jack Rummel, Host. KGNU-FM, Boulder, Thursday (except 2nd of month), 8-9pm Mountain Time

Streaming at www.kgnu.org

Websites

Edward A. Berlin's Website of Ragtime and Scholarship.

www.edwardaberlin.com/index.htm/

Jack Rummel's Ragtime Music Reviews.
   www.ragtimers.org/reviews/

"Perfessor" Bill Edwards' Ragtime MIDI, Sheet
   Music, Nostalgia and Ragtime Resource.
   http://www.perfessorbill.com/

Scott Joplin International Ragtime Foundation
   http://www.scottjoplin.org/

West Coast Ragtime Society
   http://www.westcoastragtime.com/

Indiana Historical Society
   http://www.indianahistory.org/

John William (Blind) Boone Society
   http://www.blindboone,missouri.org/

Library of Congress Home Page
   http://www.loc.gov/index.html/

Mississippi State University Libraries
   http://library.msstate.edu/

A Ragtime Compendium
   http://users.chariot.net.au/~mathewm/

Parlor Songs MIDI Collection.
   http://www.parlorsongs.com/

John Roache's Ragtime MIDI Library
   http://www.johnroachemusic.com/

Colin D. MacDonald's Ragtime-March-Waltz
Web Site

http://www.ragtimemusic.com/

Cylinder Preservation and Digitization Project.

http://www.cylinders.library.ucsb.edu/

The Ragtime Ephemeralist.

http://home.earthlink.net/~ephemeralist/
index.html

The Lester S. Levy Sheet Music Collection

http://levysheetmusic.mse.jhu.edu/

Historic American Sheet Music

http://library.duke.edu/digitalcollections/
hasm/

Selected Bibliography

Brun Campbell, The Ragtime Kid

Affeldt, Paul A. The Last of the Professors. *Jazz Report*, Vol 3, No 1, Oct 1961.

Affeldt, Paul A. The Saga of S. Brun Campbell. *The Mississippi Rag*, Jan 1988.

Anonymous. Looking Backwards. Round the "Houses" with Brun Campbell. *Jazz Journal*, Jun 1949.

Campbell, Brun. Early Great White Ragtime Composers and Pianists. *Jazz Journal*, Vol 2, May 1949.

Campbell, Brun. From Rags To Ragtime and Riches. *Jazz Journal*, Vol 2, No 7, July 1949.

Campbell, Brun. More on Ragtime. *Jazz Journal*, May 1951.

Campbell, Brun. Ragtime (Silk Stockings, Short Skirts, Silk Blouses, and Velvet Jackets). *Jazz Journal*, Vol 2, Apr 1949.

Campbell, Brunson. The Amazing Story of the Silver Half Dollar and the Ragtime Kid. *Venice Independent*, Oct 24, 1947.

Campbell, S. Brun. From Rags to Ragtime, A Eulogy. *Jazz Report*, Vol 6, 1967.

Campbell, S. Brun (as told to R. J. Carew). How I Became a Pioneer Rag Man of the 1890s. *The Record Changer*, 1947.

Campbell, S. Brunson. Letters to Jerry Heermans, unpublished.

Campbell, S. Brunson. Preserve Genuine Early Ragtime. *The Jazz Record*, c 1946.

Campbell, S. Brunson. Ragtime Begins. *The Record Changer*, Vol 7, Mar 1948.

Campbell, S. Brunson and Carew, R. J. Sedalia, Cradle of Ragtime. *The Record Changer*, Jun 1945.

Campbell, S. Brunson. The Ragtime Kid (An Autobiography). *Jazz Report*, Vol 6, 1967-68.

Campbell, S. Brunson. They All Had It. *The Jazz Record*, c 1946.

Claghorn, Charles Eugene. *Biographical Dictionary of American Music*, Parker Publishing Company, West Nyack NY, 1973.

Egan, Richard. *Brun Campbell, The Rag-Time Warp*. Electronic publication, undated.

Egan, Richard A., Jr. *Brun Campbell, The Music of "The Ragtime Kid"*. Morgan Publishing, St. Louis, 1993.

Lasswell, Paul. Some Thoughts About Brun Campbell And Ragtime.

Rag Times, May 1980.

Levin, Floyd. Brun Campbell, the Original Ragtime Kid of the 1890s. *Jazz Journal*, Vol 23, Dec 1970.

Thompson, Kay C. Reminiscing in Ragtime, an Interview with Brun Campbell. *Jazz Journal*, Vol 3, No 4, Apr 1950.

Carew, Roy and Fowler, Don E. Scott Joplin: Overlooked Genius. *The Record Changer*, Sept, Oct, Dec 1944.

Willick, George C. Brun's Boys. *Jazz Report*, Vol 10, No 2, May 1981.

Rudi Blesh

Hasse, John Edward. Rudi Blesh and the Ragtime Revivalists. In *Ragtime, Its History, Composers, and Music*. Schirmer Books, New York, 1985.

Morath, Max. Rudi Blesh: A Profile. *Mississippi Rag*, Nov 1998.

Morath, Max. Personal communications.

Curd, Richard Sr. (Sassafras Sam)

Lang, Hazel. Springtime and Sassafras. In *Life in Pettis County, 1815-1973*. Privately published, 1975.

Singer, Betty. Personal communications.

Tom Ireland

Anonymous. Tom Ireland, Nephew of Texas Governor, Born Just 8 Days After Slavery Abolished. *Sedalia Democrat*, May 18, 1952.

Anonymous. Another Year Rolls Around Thursday for Tom Ireland. *Sedalia Democrat*, Dec 8, 1955.

Anonymous. Tom Ireland Dies Friday; Known for Varied Talents. *Sedalia Democrat*, Nov 1, 1963.

Anonymous. Tom Ireland, Link to Joplin Years. *Sedalia Democrat*, Jul 21, 1974.

Ireland, G. Tom. Letter To Brun Campbell, unpublished, Jul 19, 1947.

Lang, Hazel. Tom Ireland, A Gentleman Of Color And Character. In *Life in Pettis County, 1815-1973*. Privately published, 1975.

Singer, Betty. Personal communications.

Lottie Joplin

Berlin, Edward A. In *King of Ragtime*. Oxford University Press, New York, 1994.

Berlin, Edward A. Personal communications.

Thompson, Kay C. Lottie Joplin. *The Record Changer*, Vol 9, Oct 1949.

Histories of Ragtime

Berlin, Edward A. *King of Ragtime.* Oxford University Press, New York, 1994.

Blesh, Rudi and Janis, Harriet. *They All Played Ragtime*. Grove Press, New York, 1959.

Gammond, Peter. *Scott Joplin and the Ragtime Era.* St. Martin's Press, New York, 1976.

Haskins, James. *Scott Joplin.* Doubleday, New York, 1978.

Hasse, John Edward, ed. *Ragtime, Its History, Composers and Music.* Schirmer Books, New York, 1985.

Jasen, David A. and Gene Jones. *That American Rag.* Schirmer Books, New York, 2000.

Jasen, David A. and Tichenor, Trebor Jay. *Rags and Ragtime.* Dover Publications Inc, New York, 1978.

Waldo, Terry. *This Is Ragtime.* Da Capo Press, New York, 1991.

Waldo, Terry. *This Is Ragtime.* The Complete 1972 NPR Radio Series. Waldo-Lee Music Productions, New York, 2008.

Social, Political, & Historical Aspects of Life in Sedalia in 1951

Anonymous. McCoy's City Directory For Sedalia MO, 1899.

Anonymous. Choral Club Sings Tonight. *Sedalia Democrat*, Apr 17, 1951.

Anonymous. Concert as a Tribute to Scott Joplin. *Sedalia Democrat*t, Apr 15, 1951.

Anonymous. Plaque to the Memory of Scott Joplin. *Sedalia Democrat*, April 8, 1951.

Anonymous. Scott Joplin Memorial Plaque Presented by the Choral Club. *Sedalia Democrat*, April 18, 1951.

Claycomb, William B. *Pettis County Missouri, A Pictorial History.* The Donning Company Publishers, Virginia Beach, VA, 1998.

Imhauser, Becky Carr. *All Along Ohio Street.* Walsworth Publishing Company, Marceline, MO, 2006.

Imhauser, Rebecca Carr. *Images of America: Sedalia.* Arcadia Publishing, Charleston, SC, 2007.

Lang, Hazel N. *Life In Pettis County, 1815-1973.* Privately published, 1975.

McVey, W.A. *History of Pettis County, and Sedalia, MO.* Privately published, 1985.

Neibarger, Clyde B. Ragtime Pioneers In Sedalia, Mo. Gave That Music a Big Boost Toward Fame. *The Kansas City Star*, April 16, 1951.

Singer, Betty. Personal communications, including many photographs of the city, and newspaper articles on a variety of topics, including descriptions of Ku Klux Klan activities in the Sedalia area.

Venice, California In 1951.

Alexander, Carolyn Elayne. *Images of America: Venice*. Arcadia Publishing, Charleston, SC, 2004.

Hanney, Dolores. Venice, California. A Centennial Commemorative In Postcards. Center for American Places, Santa Fe, NM, 2005.

To receive a free catalog of Poisoned Pen Press titles, please contact us in one of the following ways:

Phone: 1-800-421-3976
Facsimile: 1-480-949-1707
Email: info@poisonedpenpress.com
Website: www.poisonedpenpress.com

Poisoned Pen Press
6962 E. First Ave. Ste. 103
Scottsdale, AZ 85251